DATE DUE

ALSO BY DAVID RITZ

Brother Ray (with Ray Charles)
Search for Happiness

The Man
Who Brough

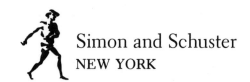

Simon and Schuster
NEW YORK

the **Dodgers**

Back to Brooklyn

David Ritz

Acknowledgments

Thanks to my wife Roberta, my daughters Jessica and Alison, Ann Patty, Ron Busch, Alan Eisenstock, Molly Friedrich, Barry Jagoda, Peter Schwed, Aunt Clara, Barney, and Secret, who in his own quiet way led me to Squat.

Copyright © 1981 by David Ritz
All rights reserved
including the right of reproduction
in whole or in part in any form
Published by Simon and Schuster
A Division of Gulf & Western Corporation
Simon & Schuster Building
Rockefeller Center
1230 Avenue of the Americas
New York, New York 10020

SIMON AND SCHUSTER and colophon are trademarks of Simon & Schuster
Designed by Irving Perkins Associates

Manufactured in the United States of America
1 2 3 4 5 6 7 8 9 10

Library of Congress Cataloging in Publication Data
Ritz, David.
The man who brought the Dodgers back to Brooklyn.
I. Title.
PS3568.I828M3   813'.54   80-39796
ISBN 0-671-25356-5

Grateful acknowledgment is hereby made to the Famous Music Publishing Companies for permission to quote lyrics from the song, "Let's Keep the Dodgers in Brooklyn" by Roy Ross, Sam Denoff and Bill Persky, copyright © 1957 by Famous Music Corporation.

For Aaron Priest

. . . *Conditioned mind, or prejudice,*
Grappling with instinct
For the soul.
And instinct bound to win,
Because we ran for passes when we were nine
And cheered the Dodgers in Ebbets Field.
　　　　　—from "Kip's" by Richard L. Cohen

Prologue

Me and Bobby are hurrying down Empire Boulevard, hurrying 'cause we don't want to miss the first pitch, when suddenly I see it off in the distance. It sweeps around four corners of Brooklyn, the four corners of the world—Montgomery, McKeever, Sullivan and Bedford, smack in the middle of Flatbush. It's got this odd shape and it's made of dirty brown bricks. It looks like a fort, or a factory, or a warehouse, or a palace. It's just squeezed in there, cozy as the corner movie theater. Oh man, does the place have character—with all those weird windows and arches, with the flags flying on top. We get closer and just down the street I can make out the green lawns of Prospect Park, and there, right across from the ballpark, is the Stahl-Meyer frankfurter stand, and now we're shoulder to shoulder with thousands of people rushing through those main doors just below the awning, with the letters high above, all in white, wrapped around the curved front entrance: EBBETS FIELD. And as me and my pal go through the turnstile we're hit with the steamy smells of sauerkraut and beer. But I'm not hungry 'cause I'm too excited. I don't care about nothing 'cause today's Sunday, today's the last game of the season, today's October 1, 1950, and the Phillies are falling apart and the Bums are about to catch them. Eleven days before, they were nine games ahead of us; now they're just a single game in front. Which means if we win today, we'll tie 'em. And the Philadelphia Whiz Kids will be the Philadelphia Fizz Kids and we'll kill 'em in a playoff game. I know we will.

The guy tears our tickets, which are cut-rate, 'cause we been saving our Elsie the Borden Cow Dixie Cup lids. Now we're inside, hurrying through the marble rotunda with all the vendors hawking scorecards and pencils and little toy baseball bats with tiny pictures of Pee Wee Reese and Preacher Roe and all our other heroes. "Dodja souvenirs," they're shouting, "get ya' gen-you-wine Dodja souvenirs here," while everyone is hunched over walking up those huge ramps, scurrying to find their seats. But me and Bobby, we don't gotta worry about finding where we're going 'cause we know every inch of this place, every catwalk and broom closet. We were even in the press box once. We poked our heads in where Red Barber does the broadcasts and he winked at us. Sometimes, when the games are sold out, we watch from outside the ballpark—through the knotholes and the cracks and under the fences—and sometimes, when it isn't crowded, we sneak into the box seats behind the plate, or, best of all, in back of the Dodger dugout, where we stand and yell out, "Hey Campy! Hey Carl! How 'bout an autograph?" Actually Bobby always does the yelling, 'cause I'm too shy.

Today we follow the ramps till we get way out in the left-field bleachers, and when we walk up the stairs and leave that dingy mess of dirty steel girders and finally see daylight, finally see the field, the thrill comes back to me, strikes my heart like it's the first time all over again: the clean open field, the diamond, green and sparkling and perfect, the infield dirt all smoothed over. And I'm not listening on the radio, I'm not imagining it, I'm really looking at the Schaefer beer sign in right field, which is without doubt the most beautiful scoreboard in the world. It don't do the fancy stuff that scoreboards do now—it doesn't have cartoons or instant replays or exploding cannons—but if Jackie beats out a bunt, the H in Schaefer, which is outlined in neon, lights up for HIT, and if Cox bobbles the ball at third (which ain't very likely) the first E lights up for ERROR. And beneath the scoreboard there's this thing that says HIT SIGN WIN SUIT, ABE STARK, who's some guy peddling clothes over on Pitkin Avenue. All this is on the crazy curved wall with the big ads for Bulova watches and Gem razors and Esquire boot polish and Old Gold cigarettes, the wall that's bent in the middle and runs along Bedford Avenue, the wall that Carl Furillo, our sensational right fielder, knows better than his own mother.

We get to our seats high up in the bleachers and Bobby starts screaming, "Hilda! We're here, Hilda!" And sure as I'm sitting there, right down the aisle from us is Hilda Chester, wearing a long brown coat and a button which says GO TELL THE WORLD I'M FROM BROOKLYN, waving this ridiculous cowbell over her head which I'm sure they can hear back in Philly. Bobby goes over and kisses her on the cheek and calls her the real Borough President. Everyone in the bleachers knows Bobby 'cause he and me are here all the time and he goes around asking questions and striking up conversations with perfect strangers.

Now here comes the Dodger Sym-phony traveling through the stands—boy, are they bad!—and the crowd starts booing and cheering them while they're playing their trombones and tambourines and wearing their sloppy tuxes and crooked top hats. The leader, who's called Shorty Laurice, has a half-smoked stogie in his mouth, and he waves and smiles and calls out, "Hey Bobby! How's tricks, kid?" Out in the bullpen Happy Felton's Knothole Gang, the TV show that goes on before the game, is just about over, and then suddenly—like rockets blasting into space—the Dodgers burst out of the dugout and land at their positions. My eyes are eating up the colors—the pure white and blue of their uniforms—and I can feel how they're ready to play, ready to leap at the ball.

"Ladies and gentlemen," the loudspeaker booms, "please rise for the national anthem as played by our organist, Miss Gladys Gooding." Now I'm too nervous to sing, I just want the song to hurry up and be over with, 'cause today's the day, and I thank the Lord I'm here to see it all. Big Don Newcombe is out there on the mound, waiting to fire the ball down to Campy.

I know this game is gonna be tense. Has to be. Newk is 19–11 this year and so is Robin Roberts, the Phillies' starter. Identical records. Maybe the two best pitchers in baseball. What a battle! Win this game and we'll pull off one of the great comebacks in baseball history. So everyone's on edge, except for some guys sitting next to us playing pinochle or gin rummy, talking out of the side of their mouths and watching out of the corner of their eyes.

Me and Bobby, we ain't missing nothing; we're looking straight ahead. We're keeping a scorecard. And just as I thought, it's a pitchers' duel. No score for the first five innings. But in the top of the sixth, Newk gives up three straight singles and the Phils jump ahead 1-0. Nothing to worry about, I know we're coming back, and we do—that very same inning. With two out, Pee Wee blasts one to right field and it's gone! It's gone! The crowd goes nuts— we're yelling louder than anyone—'cause the Bums have tied the score and there ain't no way we can lose today. "I love you, Pee Wee! I love you!" Bobby's screaming. But then Robin and Newk get tougher, and no one scores in the seventh, and no one scores in the eighth. In the top of the ninth the Phils manage a single and I hold my breath, but it's okay 'cause Newk holds steady and puts out the side, and now—now we're coming up at the bottom of the ninth and all we need is a run, one little run, and we've forced 'em into a playoff.

Now the fans are really nutty. You can't believe the noise. One long roar. Cal Abrams is up. The count goes to 3-2, and then Roberts walks him. Boom! The joint explodes. Man on first, no out, Pee Wee up. Everyone's on their feet for Pee Wee, who's already got two big hits today. Pee Wee's our hero, Pee Wee can't miss, and then, sure enough, Pee Wee smacks it to left—a clean single—and Abrams stops at second. Unbelievable! Two on, no out, and look who's coming to the plate:

The Duke! "Come on, Duke! Moider it, Duke! You can do it, Duke!" Duke steps in, Duke watches as Roberts shakes off one sign, then another. Now Roberts is ready. He stretches, he sets, he looks at his runners, he delivers a fastball down the pike that doesn't fool Duke. Duke slaps it into center field—it's a hit! It's a hit—and here comes Abrams wide around third and he's being waved home—he's gonna score and we're gonna win—here comes Abrams, but here comes Richie Asburn, the center fielder, who was playing shallow. Now he has the ball and he's firing to the plate, and here comes Abrams—run, Cal, run!—and my heart is in my throat. Abrams is nailed at the plate. Abrams is out by a mile. The whole borough of Brooklyn groans.

Still, we got two outs left, and Jackie Robinson's up. But Roberts ain't pitching to Jackie. He walks him to load the bases. Now it's up to Furillo. Furillo can win the game for us. Just a long fly ball. But Carl fouls out behind first base and we've got only one more chance. Hodges. "Come on, Gil! Come on, Gil baby!" I ain't giving up and Bobby ain't giving up, 'cause the bases are still loaded and all Pee Wee has to do is travel ninety feet from third to home. Big Gil digs in there and here's the pitch and *smack*, there it goes, high, high in right field, and we're screaming, we're screaming for a grand-slam home run, but it comes down too short and Del Ennis pulls it in and the game's going into extra innings. Someone behind us yells, "Ya bums!"

I want to forget about the tenth inning. I want to forget about those leadoff singles by Roberts and Waitkus, but most of all I want to forget about that sucker pitch that Newk threw to Dick Sisler, the pitch that Sisler unloaded not very far from us in the left-field seats, putting the Phils ahead 4–1. After that, nothing. We couldn't touch Roberts. He mowed us down in the bottom of the tenth, one-two-three.

I couldn't speak, couldn't even move. I just stood there, trying to believe it. I kept thinking—*if; if* Abrams hadn't taken such a big turn at third he might have scored in the ninth; *if* Hodges had put a little more muscle into that last . . . but I had to stop the ifs. I had to face facts: We had lost the pennant, and down the aisle I heard Hilda cursing, and when I looked at Bobby I saw his eyes were filled with tears. Our heads were hanging low; now we just wanted to leave, to get out and go home. On the way down the ramp it was so sad and quiet except once in a while you'd hear someone let out the war cry, "Wait till next year!"

Dreaming...

ONE

IT ALL BEGAN one day when I was playing with the boys in the playground of P.S. 105 at 59th Street and Fort Hamilton Parkway. A lot of the guys from the neighborhood were hanging around—it was a Saturday afternoon—and naturally we didn't wanna do nothing but play stickball, which got a little boring because whatever team I was on would win. I don't say that to boast, but I could whack that hard little pink rubber Spaldeen to Coney and back. I could send it sailing over fences and roofs 'cause one thing I had was power. Brute power. And after a while all the guys—even the ones a lot bigger than me— would take turns pitching, just to see if they could get it past me, but they couldn't. Which is why I was such a happy little guy. I was sure God had blessed me.

Now I wasn't born beautiful like some people, though you wouldn't call me ugly. Just plain-looking, and definitely on the short side—picture, say, the way Roy Campanella and Yogi Berra were short—which is good for a catcher. Which is what I was. And how I got my name Squat, 'cause even when I wasn't playing ball, I was practicing my squat, beating my fist against my make-believe glove, getting ready for the pitch. Yeah, I was sure God loved me because He gave me at least one thing I could do good —play baseball—and if that took the place of being graced with lots of brains and blond hair, I was happy to accept. Deep down, I knew I was going to be a star for the Dodgers.

I knew that because even when I was only eight years old people would come by just to see me hit and they all said I'd be playing for the Bums, and in Brooklyn, especially back in those days, people knew their baseball because Brooklyn was baseball-crazy. Brooklyn had a great team—the greatest and most beautiful team in the history of organized sports. And it seemed like baseball made everyone happy, and it seemed like the world was less complicated back then. But what did I know? Baseball. And Brooklyn loved its baseball, from the majors to the mudholes.

I was out there in the playground on this particular morning putting on a show. Big Mickey Bernstein reared back and fired the ball, inside and high. I connected and kissed it goodbye. Then J.D. Washington, who was blacker than midnight and faster than Jackie Robinson, tried to fool me with a curve. They're still looking for that one. I was having a good day. Nothing bothered me, not even the biggest guy in the neighborhood, who everyone called Wiggy 'cause he was a little nuts. He pitched the way his old man drove a hack. Wiggy had muscles on his muscles. He was fourteen, and when he wound up to throw I could hear him suck in his breath—he made a noise like a steam furnace about to blow up—and the ball came in at a million miles an hour and went back out at a trillion.

This was going on for a while when I noticed there was someone watching me who I had never seen before. I noticed this kid leaning against the wall of the school. I knew he wasn't from the neighborhood because he was wearing these fancy blue flannel pants, and no one in our neighborhood wears pants like that on a Saturday afternoon. He was also wearing this pale-yellow shirt which looked pretty swanky. He had these bright-blue eyes which were very strong and looking right at me, like he was studying me or something. I took a few glances over at him and I saw that he was a lot taller than me and looked like maybe he could be an athlete. His hair was blond, which was something you didn't see too much in Borough Park, which was my neighborhood. He was real handsome, this kid, and I figured he was pretty cool because he didn't make any moves, he just watched me put on my show until everyone got ready to choose up sides for another game.

I was one of the captains, and Wiggy was another. We flipped for first choice and I saw the blue-eyed kid moving towards us, like he wanted to play. He wasn't dressed for the part, and I knew no one was going to choose him until the end because he didn't belong there. So when I won the toss—don't ask me why—I chose him. Maybe I felt sorry for the way he looked and everything. I could tell the kid was real grateful to me and I told him to go ahead and get up and hit first 'cause I wanted to see what he could do.

Wiggy was ready. He grinned his mean fearful grin. The kid stood in there, looking unafraid. He was clutching the broomhandle bat, getting himself ready. Wiggy wound up, and the ball came in like a rocket, right into the kid's left thigh. Oh, I could feel it sting. But the kid was still standing there, ready for another. I don't think he understood what was happening, that this was Wiggy's way of introducing him to the neighborhood. The second pitch was another zinger, and it got him right on the ribs, but the kid stood his ground and shouted to Wiggy, "Throw me a strike, will you?" I could hear right away that he didn't have no Brooklyn accent. He sounded like he came from somewhere fancy, you know, those places where everyone talks like they're in the movies. Wiggy wasn't paying any attention. He was glad he had the kid rattled. He took his time, and when he delivered again he really grunted and groaned and let go of this gung-ho fastball which went right for the kid's Adam's apple, blew his wind away and knocked him to the ground. I was scared because I thought maybe the kid was dead. I ran over there, but suddenly the kid was up and jumping on Wiggy, who was pounding his fist in the kid's face. Some of the other guys had run over there to kick the kid in the ass—because they didn't like anybody intruding in our neighborhood. I wasn't liking this whole thing, I wasn't liking it at all, because really, the kid hadn't done nothing.

"Leave him alone!" I was shouting. "Get away from him!" And when they heard me, they thought I was a traitor or something and they got on my back, which was a big mistake on their part. Maybe I wasn't too good at school and maybe I was shy with the girls, but I was good with my hands. And fast. Suddenly I was in the middle of this fight, slugging it out with my pals, trying to get them to leave this kid alone. I pulled J.D. off him. I leveled Mickey with a strong left which my dad had taught me to use. I got scratched by Wiggy, which got me very mad, and I don't remember too much of the rest except that I was swinging real hard and I got Wiggy in the stomach, which finally brought the fight to an end. When Wiggy folded up, holding his tummy and crying like a baby, the other guys got the idea that I meant business. The game was ruined. The guys left, telling me that they weren't playing no more and that I was a turd and didn't belong in the neighborhood. They even called me a pansy. I was going to call 'em something back, but I remembered that I could hit the ball farther than them, which is all that mattered. I was also real worried about the kid, who hadn't gotten up yet, and who was bleeding on the lip pretty bad.

"Anything broken?" I wanted to know.

"It's nothing," he said.

"Gotta be something," says me, "or it wouldn't be bleeding."

He tried to smile, but I could see that it hurt him. I could also see that his fancy pants were ripped around his knee and his yellow shirt was stained with blood.

"You don't live around here, do you?" I asked.

"No."

"Why don't you come over to my house? My mom's real good at fixing up bleeding. She used to work over at Kings County Hospital."

"I don't want to bother her."

"Wouldn't be no bother. She likes my friends."

"You didn't have to help me that way," he said as he slowly picked himself up from the pavement. "I would have taken care of those guys."

"Are you kidding? They were murdering you. What are you doing here, anyway? Don't they have stickball games where you live?"

"Not as good as these."

"Where do you live?"

"Brooklyn Heights."

I guess I raised my eyebrow, 'cause the kid said, "Something wrong with Brooklyn Heights?"

"No. I only been there once and it seemed real rich, all the houses were awful fancy. You live in one of those fancy houses?"

"Sort of, yes."

"And I bet that's why you don't talk like the rest of us."

"Maybe." Now he was smiling.

"What's your name?"

"Bobby."

"My teachers call me Daniel and my folks call me Dan, but

everyone else calls me Squat 'cause I'm a catcher. One day I'm gonna catch for the Dodgers. I'm gonna replace Campy. What do ya think about that?"

"I saw how far you can hit."

"I was just so-so today."

"I've been planning on playing on the Dodgers myself. I've been practicing a lot lately."

"What position?"

"Outfield."

"Can you throw?"

"Like Furillo."

"Can you hit?"

"Like Robinson."

"You're all right, kid." I called him "kid" not because I was any older but because we were in my neighborhood and I felt kinda in charge. "Let's go see my mom so she can fix you up."

We walked down Fort Hamilton Parkway. The afternoon was growing a little chilly, and the streets were still crowded with guys playing stickball and lots of them shouted for me to get into the games, but I said no because I wanted to get home so Mom could look at Bobby.

We got to our apartment building at 56th Street, right above a candy store. Upstairs Mom was busy cooking a big stew and Rich, Jerry and Peter, my little brothers, were pulling at her apron, asking her to do different stuff. Mom was patient with them, the way she was patient with everyone, and when she saw Bobby, all bloodied, she dropped everything and got out the soap and ointments and sponges and Band-Aids and made him feel much better. She wanted to know why we got into a fight, and I told her it wasn't a fight, it was baseball, and she said we should learn to play nice. When she was through, Bobby told her thanks. "I appreciate your kindness," he said. He sounded like a grown-up, and he kissed her on the cheek. Mom liked that a lot, she thought Bobby was really something special, and she gave us milk and cookies and then I grabbed a couple of gloves and a bat and a ball and out we went to this vacant lot not far from the BMT station at 61st Street and threw the ball to each other and pitched and hit for another couple of hours. Bobby was feeling fine, except I saw that as a baseball player he was just okay—nothing more than okay. There was no way this kid was ever gonna make the Dodgers.

"I don't see how you hit the thing so far," he said to me after I belted one real good.

"Me either," I confessed. "I just do it."

"Wish I could."

"You're all right," I told him. "You can play."

"You think so?"

"You need to practice a lot."

We played together for a long time. He talked more than me. He had a real good personality. You wouldn't have figured that two hours ago he almost got killed in a fight. He asked me all kinds of questions about myself and my folks. He also wanted tips about baseball. I could tell he was a classy kid. We stayed there, swinging and catching and hitting, until the sun was long gone and we could barely see the ball. We were having such a good time that we didn't notice the dark.

"Wanna come back to my house? Mom will fix you dinner."

"Sure," he said.

We were starved, and Dad was home, back from the Brooklyn Navy Yard, where he worked, and I introduced Bobby and Bobby was polite and asked my dad lots of nice questions about his job and the ships down in the Yard. Pop was real surprised that a kid this young was asking him this stuff. Everyone was impressed with Bobby.

"Shouldn't you call your mother and tell her where you are?" my mom asked him.

"She died some time ago," Bobby answered, "but I will call my father. Thank you."

Naturally we felt bad, we felt sorry for him. I knew some guys who didn't have fathers, but I didn't know anyone without a mom. He made his call and we sat down to eat.

My dad was talking about baseball, because the 1949 season was about to start.

"How do you kids think the Bums are going to do this year?" Pop asked.

"Oh, there's no question about it, sir," Bobby answered quickly. "We're sure to win."

"How do you figure that after coming in third last year?" Pop was baiting. He wanted to see how much Bobby knew.

"I would guess, sir, that Roe, Hatten and Branca could each win fifteen games, maybe more. This rookie pitcher Newcombe is supposed to be very good. And the new outfielder from last

24

year, Snider, shows a lot of promise. I also have a great deal of faith in Mr. Shotton, don't you, Mr. Malone?" he asked my dad.

"Shotton's a bum," said Pop, smiling. "What does a manager have to know? He fills out the lineup card every day and that's it. He don't have to be no genius."

Bobby laughed and agreed. Bobby was a very agreeable kid. We talked a lot more, and Bobby showed that he knew every Dodger and every Dodger statistic imaginable. He knew a lot more than us, which was good, since I had seen he wasn't such a hot player. After dinner, my mom said she wanted to mend Bobby's pants and see if she could get the bloodstains out of his shirt.

"That would be wonderful," he said. I thought it was strange and so grown-up to use the word "wonderful."

I loaned Bobby my bathrobe to wear and we went to the bedroom that I shared with my three brothers. It was pretty small, but Bobby was happy to see all my issues of *Sporting News* and all the pictures of the Dodgers on the wall. I also had a baseball with all their autographs. He said he had one, too.

"The Dodgers are the greatest team in the world," he said. "The Dodgers are my heroes. That's why I must become a Dodger."

I didn't say nothing. I didn't want to make him feel bad.

"You don't think I can make the Dodgers, do you?" he asked.

I felt real nervous. I couldn't say anything.

"That's okay, Squat," he blurted out. "Deep down I know I'm not really all that good. Just fair. But I am good at something, and that's business."

"Business?" I asked him. I hadn't heard too many kids our age talking about business.

"Sure, business. I have a good head for business. That's what people are always telling me, just the way, I know, people are always telling you how you can hit. And right now, my business sense is telling me we ought to put these two things together."

"What do you mean?"

"My thinking and your hitting."

"What are you thinking?"

"That I should be your agent."

"Agent?"

"Like movie stars have agents. Guys who talk for them. Guys who negotiate for them. You see, Squat, you and I should be in business together. You're the best hitter I've ever seen. Maybe you're the best-hitting kid in Brooklyn. I know, because I've been to all the different neighborhoods. I've been walking around after school and on Saturdays and Sundays, just watching and sometimes getting into games."

"Don't you have friends over there in Brooklyn Heights?"

"Some, but I like the neighborhoods like this one a lot more. Everyone's out on the streets and it's easier to talk to people. Anyway, I've been around Brooklyn, and I know we can make a mint."

"How?"

"I set you up. We go to different neighborhoods, to every part of Brooklyn where kids are playing stickball or softball or hardball —it doesn't matter, because you can hit anything."

"That's right." I liked the way Bobby talked.

"And we make bets on how far you can hit, and every time we win because no one will ever guess. We'll let them choose the pitchers or you can fungo and it won't make any difference. I'll cover all your bets and we'll split the winnings. Do you think that's fair?"

"I think that's wonderful," I said, using his word.

"I've had this idea for a long time, but I've been looking for the right hitter."

"You've never been anyone else's agent?"

"Never. But don't worry. We can't lose."

"When do you want to start?"

"Monday," he said. "Right after school. I'll meet you here."

Then Mom came in with his clothes. Bobby thanked her like a gentleman, thanked her for her first aid and her food, and told Dad how much he enjoyed conversing with him. A half hour later when he heard honking outside, he told us that was his ride. Running down the staircase, he reminded me about Monday. I told him I wouldn't forget. Then me and my whole family gathered at the window of our tiny living room to watch a man in the street greet Bobby. The man was wearing a uniform and he opened the door of a long black limo for Bobby. "Wow!" I couldn't help but say. Bobby got into the car and seconds later was whisked away into the dark night.

TWO

"*THIS NEIGHBORHOOD'S NOT* so hot," I warned Bobby.

"I've been here before," he said to me. "It doesn't bother me. The kids are Dodger fans around here just like the rest of us."

"Don't kid yourself, kid," says me. "They may root for the Bums, all right, but they ain't any more like us than a fastball is like a change-up."

"I like when you talk that way, Squat. You're always thinking about baseball. You're always on the job."

"I talk about baseball 'cause I love it. Don't you?"

"I love it, too. But I'm also beginning to see some of its business potential." That was how Bobby was talking back then.

"What does 'potential' mean?" I had to ask him.

"How much money you can make."

We'd have conversations like these almost every day, which was how we got to know each other. But on this day, I wasn't too interested in talking. We were somewhere in Williamsburg and the territory was getting grim and there weren't too many people on the street. I ain't scared in the city. I'll walk anywhere. But it helps if there's lots of people around.

"You know where you're going?" I asked Bobby, 'cause I didn't.

"Of course. There's a park up ahead. You're about to face some serious opposition, Squat. We've been all through the white neighborhoods. That's been the easy part. Now we're going to see how we fare elsewhere."

"Don't sound too brainy of an idea to me, kid."

"Trust me, Squat. I'm here to help us both."

The park was full of beer bottles. The grass wasn't grass; it was weeds. Up in the sky, the clouds were flying by. Felt like rain. I was hoping it would pour so our hustle could be called off. I smelled trouble.

There were four black guys in the park. Big. They were fooling around with a ball and a bat and there was no doubt that they knew what they were doing.

"You guys wouldn't be interested in betting, would you?" Bobby came on just like that. Boom—right between the eyes.

"What you got in mind?" asked one of them.

"My pal Squat can fungo the ball further than any one of you guys. It's as simple as that."

The dudes laughed. Real loud. Which sorta got me angry. But on the other hand, these guys had long muscular arms. I wasn't all that sure how I'd do.

"I think we can handle this," said the same big guy. He and his pals whispered among themselves, and then he came back with, "Twenty bucks. Put up or shut up."

This was something new. We had been going a dollar or two a hustle. Once we got five over on Linden Boulevard, but that was just luck. And I was happy with the earnings so far. Fact is, I was overjoyed. I had saved enough to buy myself a new bat and new glove and almost had the money for a big-league chest protector. But twenty bucks! This was a different story. This was making me very nervous.

I looked over at Bobby. He didn't blink an eye. He reached into his back pocket and came up with four five-dollar bills—just like that. "Where's yours?" he asked. The guys grouped together and came up with twenty.

"Who wants to hit first?" I asked.

The spokesman took the bat. He was going to do the hitting. He threw the ball up in the air—his toss was gentle and just high enough—and I saw his muscles ripple as he swung the bat and sent the ball soaring down the long street, maybe three sewers away. Bobby and the other guys were down there to mark the spot where the ball had landed.

My turn. I swallowed hard. I was good at hitting my own tosses; I hadn't been beat yet. But I knew this was going to be close. I breathed deeply and I belted one, almost to the identical spot as the black guy. I strained to see what was happening down there between Bobby and the others, but I couldn't make nothing out. Seconds passed, and then I heard some bad cursing—Bobby cursing, them cursing—and so me and the other batter raced down there, but by the time we arrived Bobby and the guys were pushing each other.

What was I supposed to do? My agent was fighting for me, but it was four against two, so instead of immediately jumping into it, I started screaming about what if Pee Wee and Campy started fighting, or Robinson and Furillo. The Bums would never win a game, and what the heck was Bobby cursing about anyway?

"They're calling it wrong," said Bobby. "We won by a good two inches."

"If it was that close," says me, "we gotta call it a draw."

"You're crazy," Bobby yelled. "We won fair and square. We get the twenty."

"It may be the last thing you'll ever get," said one of the guys.

Bobby made a move to fight. Bobby was that way. He'd pop off at the slightest thing. Crazy. I ain't that crazy. I didn't want no fight with these boys over anything.

"Take another step," one of the guys said as he brought out a switchblade which sprang open at the flick of his wrist, "and I'll cut you."

Bobby didn't look scared, and that scared me. He was nuts enough to take on this guy. I was sure we were at the end of the road.

"Listen, man," said the batter who had belted the ball either two inches more or less than me. "I don't have eyes for any fight. Besides, if we start cutting, my man here"—he pointed to me— "might get messed up, and the Dodgers would be missing out on a sure Hall of Famer."

I beamed. Everyone beamed. Bobby returned the compliment, asked the guy if he wanted an agent. The guy said no. His real game was basketball. Suddenly things had cooled. We started talking sports, and then we were friends—all six of us—and we forgot about the bet and I sighed and thanked God for sparing my life and Bobby's.

I'd have to thank God again, because we'd get out of several tight spots—though there was one time when we got bruised pretty bad: Bobby had used the wrong word in Spanish and some kids in East New York thought we were calling them queers and they proved to us that they weren't. They not only beat us up, but they robbed our money and our shoes and we had to walk home barefooted.

We always went back to my place. Bobby said he loved it. He was getting to know Mom and Dad more and more, and they were nuts about him, and even though we were curious about exactly where he lived and what his father did, we didn't poke into his business. Once I had asked him something about that and he changed the subject right away. Whatever it was, I could see that he didn't have a family like ours, and it made me feel great that he liked Mom's cooking and Dad's Dodger talks.

Pop was in a real happy mood that night and everyone was eating up a storm and it was like Bobby was part of the family. Dad went around the table asking each of us about our day—Dad was like that—and when he came to me I told him the truth about the fight we almost got into. He raised an eyebrow. He had very bushy eyebrows.

"Stay out of fights whenever you can," he said, directing his comment at Bobby. "But it's also good to show that you're not afraid."

Bobby smiled, seeing that Pop, in his own way, was telling us that we both had done good. Bobby always used to say that Dad amazed him 'cause he talked to his kids so much. What he mainly talked about, though, was baseball.

"They're Fascists," Dad would say. "Nothing but cold-blooded Fascists." He was talking about the Yankees. That was his word for them—Fascists—and that's where me and Bobby picked up the tag. For the rest of our lives, the Yanks would be the Fascists. Pop was reasonable about a lot of stuff, but not about the Fascists. They were the enemy. They didn't like the little people. They only played for money. The Bums, on the other hand, *were* the little people; the Bums played for the love of the game; the Bums were the salt of the earth, and they let blacks play for them and the Fascists didn't. Then Pop would start telling Dodger stories about the olden days, when Casey was manager and Uncle Robbie and Leo the Lip fighting with Larry MacPhail and getting kicked out of baseball for a year. "The Bums were always colorful," Dad would say, telling us about Zack Wheat, Brooklyn's greatest star from 1909 through 1926, who had a lifetime average of .317. And then he'd bring it all to life for us—that terrible moment in the '20 World Series when the Indians' Bill Wambsganss made an unassisted triple play against us and we went on to lose the whole thing.

Bobby would surprise us. He'd know a lot of this already, and he'd fill in some of the facts for Dad, but he'd do it in a good way so Dad wouldn't feel bad. In fact, I could see that Dad respected Bobby's interest in history. Bobby made my pop feel important.

Everything was going great that night. We were eating chocolate pudding for dessert and Dad was still talking about the Dodgers. "That team's got a lotta heart. Even when they lose, they got heart. That's why the people of Brooklyn love 'em so much. Now if only those crooked politicians running this borough had half the brains of those baseball players, we'd be in a lot better shape."

Bobby turned white. Just like that. None of us knew why, but we understood that Pop had said something wrong, because Bobby stopped eating and stopped talking and a few minutes later said he had to run. He didn't forget to thank Mom and Dad for dinner, but when he did, his voice was sorta shaky, and he ran out of the apartment real fast, and he didn't show up the next day or the day after that.

THREE

IT DIDN'T TAKE us long to figure it out. Pop felt read bad that he hadn't put two and two together—Bobby's last name and the name of the Borough President of Brooklyn. It just never occurred to us.

I waited and waited, but Bobby didn't call, and after a couple of weeks I really missed him a lot and didn't have the heart to go out and play ball by myself. I sure didn't have the nerve to hustle alone, so I went down to Borough Hall and finally got someone to give me the home address of Robert J. Hanes, Senior, who everyone called the Judge, even though he wasn't no judge. I waited till the next Saturday—I needed a while to build up my courage—and I took a bunch of buses and got off at Henry and walked over to Montague. I was a little lost. Suddenly the neighborhood started looking different, not anything like the Brooklyn I lived in. The houses were out of the history books in school. Reminded me of a faraway country like England or France. The streets were very clean, and lots of the houses had shutters all painted nice and pretty, especially where Bobby lived, on Willow Street, and especially Bobby's house, which was four stories tall. I stood there for a long time, sorta expecting a horse and buggy to come bouncing down the block. Didn't see any stickball players around. Finally I got the nerve to ring the bell.

The guy who opened the door was wearing a uniform. He looked down on me. I was short and I was wearing dungarees.

"Yes, young man?" he said. "What is it that you want?"

"Can Bobby come out and play?"

"Is Master Robert expecting you?"

"Bobby. I'm Bobby's buddy."

"Please wait where you are."

He shut the door in my face. A minute later the door opened again and there was Bobby. Smiling. I could tell how happy he was to see me.

"How'd you find the place?" he wanted to know.

"You're famous."

"Thanks for coming. I missed you."

"Then why didn't you call?"

"I don't know. I felt lousy. I felt . . ." He struggled for the right word.

"Well, I'm broke. I'm down to my last nickel," I lied. "And I need you."

"Come on in," he offered. He knew I was anxious to see his house, but I could tell that he was nervous about it. He introduced me to the guy who answered the door. Ralph. This time Ralph smiled at me; he figured I was tight with Bobby. Ralph, Bobby said, was the butler and the driver and the cook.

There was a big entryway with a living room on one side and a dining room with fancy chairs on the other. All the floors were shiny wood and on the walls were real old-time pictures of Prospect Park and the Brooklyn Academy of Music and guys in battle uniforms and a painting of the Brooklyn Bridge while it was only half-built. Sort of spooky but classy at the same time.

"Who lives upstairs?" I asked.

"Us."

I didn't figure just one family could live in this whole joint. "Who's us?" I wanted to know.

"Me and Father and Ralph. We each have our own floor."

"Holy cow."

The third floor was Bobby's. He had his bedroom and then he had his Dodger room. I couldn't believe it. A room with nothing but Dodger stuff—Dodger pillows, Dodger pennants and posters, Dodger yearbooks, dozens and dozens of Dodger scorecards, Dodger bubblegum picture cards, old-time Dodger photos of the guys my pop talked about: Buckwheat and Lippy Leo and Dolf

32

Camilli—photos of the new Dodgers, even this huge painting someone did of Ebbets Field. There was a big window against the wall with a view of the East River with Manhattan across the water. I kept thinking of my brothers and me squeezed together back in our place in Borough Park, and how I wished that they —and my folks—could see this.

"Now that you've seen it," he said, "let's get out of here. That okay with you, Squat?"

I did sorta wanna stay longer, but Bobby seemed in a hurry. He took off his sweater and put on a genuine Dodger warmup jacket and we skipped down the stairs and just as we were about to go through the front door the Judge appeared. He was tall, the tallest man I ever saw. He scared me. He scared Bobby. I could see it, feel it. He was wearing a suit with a vest and a gold watch chain and he had this fatso stomach and his chin was real loose and fleshy and his eyes were small and his hair was gray and he looked tired. I figured right away that Bobby must have gotten his good looks, his blue eyes and blond hair, from his mom, because the Judge didn't have any of that stuff. When he spoke, it sounded like he was making a speech.

"Where, if I may ask, are you going?"

"With my friend, Squat. Squat, this is my father. Father, this is Squat."

He didn't look at me, but that was okay. The quicker we got out, the better.

"When do you intend to be back?" his big voice boomed.

"Early."

"Have you completed your school assignments?"

"It's Saturday. School's not until Monday."

"My question stands."

"No, sir. I thought I'd do my homework tomorrow."

"See to it that you do."

And with that, the Judge turned his back on us, handed Ralph his large leather briefcase and said that he wanted a Cutty on the rocks up in his study at once.

Outside I felt a million times better. What a relief to get away!

"See what I mean?" Bobby asked me as we walked down the street.

"Geez," was all I could say in reply.

Bobby showed me the neighborhood. We went on the Esplanade, which reminded me of a boardwalk except it was cement.

"Let's look for a game," I suggested, seeing that there wasn't much daylight left.

"It'll be tough finding a game around here. Why don't we just walk?"

And so we walked, for hours and hours, letting Brooklyn get dark around us. We walked downtown and saw all the people going into the Paramount. I think *The Asphalt Jungle* was playing. We walked all the way back down Flatbush, past Atlantic, down Eastern and Washington, along by the Gardens, which smelled wet and green from yesterday's rain. Then, at Montgomery, we turned left. We didn't say anything. But we knew where we were going. It was like a magnet.

It stood in the night so dark and lonely. Such a beautiful ballpark. Right there in the neighborhood—like a candy store or a school. Like a friend. It had real personality, Ebbets Field did. And Bobby and I were thinking the same thing: We were sad that there wasn't no game. And the more we stood there, the sadder we became, until Bobby said, "Why don't we go in?"

"You're nuts," says me.

"It'll be a snap," he promised, and he started walking around the outside of the joint, looking for ways to sneak in. Why not? I figured. On Bedford Avenue, right where there's an ad for Botany Wrinkle-Proof suits, the place where fans would line up for bleacher tickets, we saw above this fence—about sixty feet high —a very small opening that led to one of the ramps. Bobby didn't even ask. He just looked around and started climbing. "You look out for cops," he told me. "And wait till I get in. Then I can look out for you."

He was a good climber and did it in a few minutes. He made it look easy. Now, I'm a power hitter, but climbing ain't my strength—I always hated those jungle gyms in the playgrounds. But naturally I had to follow the leader. I nearly slipped a couple of times, but Bobby egged me on. Once I got to the hole, I saw I couldn't squeeze through. I wasn't exactly fat, but I wasn't exactly thin either. Bobby was a toothpick next to me, and this opening was tiny. "No way," I said, and turned to climb down. Bobby insisted, and I finally let him convince me. Head first, I went in; I ripped my jeans and scraped my thigh—it stung like crazy—but Bobby pulled me through. And there we were! In Ebbets Field, alone at midnight! It was all ours!

Naturally we were on the lookout for guards and guys like that.

We tiptoed up the ramp and went right to the center-field bleachers where we always sat. Geez, what a sight: the field lit by the light of the moon. The grass was sort of messed up by the heavy rains, and the infield had a few puddles. Still, we were imagining Snider chasing down flies and Jackie ripping into second. "Want to do it?" Bobby suddenly asked.

"Do what?"

"Go down on the field."

And before I had a chance to answer, he was already making his way around the ramps, down to the lower boxes and over the small fence. I chased him all the way, even onto the field, chased him around left to center to right—and I was Furillo! I was a Dodger!—chased him around the bases, one time, two times. Somehow I couldn't even feel my scratched-up thigh. He went to the mound and I stood in the batter's box. He was Roberts and I was Campy—Campy was my favorite on account of us both being catchers. I took Campy's stance, with my butt sticking out, with the bat straight up, letting it wave back and forth ever so slightly, getting ready for the pitch. Bobby wound up, he delivered, and with my imaginary bat I socked the ball deep deep deep into right field—up higher and higher—and Bobby announced it all, like Red Barber, and I trotted around the bases and 32,000 fans were screaming and waving and Bobby was laughing his head off. Geez, it was really something the way we were in Ebbets Field that night.

Later we found a way to climb to the top rim of the stadium. It was a little scary, but we did it, and we were actually up there, right under those huge banks of light, looking into the street, over the rooftops of Brooklyn. Far, far in the distance were the giant buildings of Manhattan. The view was really something— all the roofs of the apartment houses and the spires of the churches—and we sat down, right over the entrance, right above where it said EBBETS FIELD. If we craned our necks, we could see the white letters and the awning below.

"I was really mad," Bobby told me.

"At who?"

"The Judge."

"How come?"

"Because he's a hypocrite."

"What's that?"

"He says one thing and does another."

"What d'ya mean?"

"Like going to the Dodger games. He says he likes the Dodgers, but he never goes till the end of the year. He doesn't know Pee Wee Reese from Jake Pitler. He doesn't care about baseball. All he cares about is cement, and getting votes."

"Why does he care about cement?"

"Haven't you noticed, Squat? The name Hanes is written on practically every corner of Brooklyn. My family's been in the cement business for years. That's what my grandfather did. He made millions, and so does the Judge."

"What's wrong with that? Everyone wants millions. That way you don't have to work or go to school or nothing."

"But he works anyway. He works all the time. He has two jobs. The cement and the politics. He's a big shot, he loves being a big shot, and he's always in meetings. Even on Sundays he has meetings. I hate them. I hate meetings. I hate cement."

"I see what you mean, kid."

"People are always coming around to ask him favors. And his picture is in the paper all the time. That's about the only time he's in a good mood. And he thinks it makes me happy because he wakes me up early and shows me the paper—first thing—as if I care. I wish I didn't even live here. I wish I lived in Montana. I wish I was a Canadian Mountie."

"But that way you'd never see the Dodgers. And this year we're sure to win the pennant, ain't we?"

He smiled. "You're a real pal, Squat. And I'm going to tell you something right now," he said as he looked south, toward Gravesend Bay. "You and I are going to make a killing together. And don't you ever forget it."

FOUR

NO ONE TOLD me that airplane engines were so loud, and there I was sitting alone in the back of the plane, the first plane I had ever been on, with the noise screaming in my ears. Naturally

I was a little scared, but I wasn't about to let on, because I was also happy, maybe happier than I had ever been in my life, because I was on my way to Montreal. Montreal! The Dodger farmclub—their best farmclub—where Robinson came from. I had been signed by the Dodgers and I was going to play minor-league ball in Canada and I was only eighteen. Nothing could stop me now, nothing in the world.

I looked out the window. I couldn't be sure, but it looked like Brooklyn down there. I smiled. The sky was so blue and the world seemed so peaceful down there. I liked that world. It had been good to me. My dream was coming true. I hated to leave my folks and my brothers, and I hated to leave Bobby, but he was going off to some big university in Michigan anyway. I never even thought of college; this was all I wanted. We promised to write each other, and I knew we would, because we were real interested in seeing what happened to each other. He expected me to be the new Campy, and I guess I expected him to be President of the United States one day.

The stewardess came by and asked me if I wanted a drink—I felt great that I looked old enough—and I said no, that I was in training, that I was a catcher and about to play ball for Montreal. She was taken a little by surprise, and I actually surprised myself, 'cause usually I'm so shy around gals, and the only times I had the nerve to make a move was when Bobby was around. He had enough sweet talk for everyone, and sometimes we'd double-date and go to Coney, but the best times we had together were when we were hustling or going to ballgames. During the summers we were together all the time, living the life of a Bum in Ebbets Field. The greatest time was in 1955 at Fascist Stadium.

I thought about that day as the stewardess brought me lunch. She said she put on an extra roll and an extra piece of pie because athletes needed nutrition. I thanked her and tried to eat, but I was too excited thinking about Montreal and remembering the way Fascist Stadium looked on the afternoon of October 4, 1955. Bobby and me were sitting out in left field watching our boy Podres shut out the Yankees, and Hodges, who everyone called the goat of all those past Series, batted in both our runs. We had finally done it, finally won our first World Series, and Bobby was so happy he took us out to eat at this fancy old-fashioned-looking joint in downtown Brooklyn called Gage & Tollner where the headwaiter wore a monkey suit and called Bobby by name. The next year we won the pennant again, but Larsen pitched that perfect game that I don't wanna talk about and the Fascists won the Series in seven.

Our senior year—this last year—was the big one. I was at New Utrecht High and Bobby at his high-class prep school. This was my third season on the varsity club, and I had already broken all the records for total hits and rbi's and homers when I was a junior. I was voted all-city twice and I could see I was getting stronger and stronger. I took real good care of myself and stayed out of trouble. My peg down to second base was like a rocket, and I knew how to handle my pitchers. I knew the game, and mostly I could relax at the plate—hitting or catching—which is something my pop taught me. Just relax and enjoy it and let your natural juices flow. I was going great.

But Bobby was worried: in the same year, 1956, Walter O'Malley, the owner of the Dodgers, who Bobby never trusted because he reminded him of the Judge, sold Ebbets Field. Everyone was saying he was going to move the team. The Dodgers played some games that season in Jersey City, just as an experiment. Bobby went nuts when this happened. He screamed and wrote letters to the paper and told me that O'Malley wouldn't get away with this because the Bums didn't belong to him, they belonged to all of Brooklyn. He even tried to get his old man to do something, but by then the Judge had resigned and wasn't riding so high. There was talk about his having taken kickbacks, and even though he was never dragged to court or put in the slammer, his reputation was bruised and my mom and dad wouldn't even talk about it with me on account of how we all felt about Bobby.

Then two big things happened, one right after the other. The word was out that O'Malley was pulling up stakes and taking the Dodgers to L.A. Oh, that hurt. It hurt everyone I knew, but I think it hurt Bobby the worst. "O'Malley's making a fortune here," Bobby would say. "He's always drawn over a million at the gate. What else does he want?" "More," I'd tell him. "He wants as much as he can get." And sad to say, I was right. It was a bad, bad time for all true lovers of the Bums, and I'm not sure I would have ever gotten over it if the second thing hadn't happened right away: The Dodgers signed me up.

One of their scouts had been following me during my whole high school career, and it was him who came by and talked to me and my dad about signing me and shipping me out to Montreal.

That might have been the best day of my life. When the guy came to our apartment, half the building knew what was happening, and the neighbors were all in the hallway, and my brothers were screaming and you might have thought that I had hung the moon.

But when I called Bobby that night to tell him, I could hear that he was straining to sound glad. I knew he wasn't jealous or nothing; Bobby was behind me all the way. But this California business really had him upset; he took it personally.

"You sound like something's wrong," I had to tell him.

"What could be wrong?"

"I dunno. You tell me."

"I guess it's just that part of me hates to see you playing for O'Malley. You won't be with the Dodgers because there won't be any more Dodgers. You'll be in L.A."

"I know, Bobby, and you know that I'd rather be here in Brooklyn, but the world is funny. You understand that. And I ain't never been to California, and Campy ain't getting any younger and—"

"Of course. Of course you're right, Squat. It's the chance of a lifetime. You deserve it. You have to grab it. And I don't want to ruin this thing for you, I really don't. I only wish . . ."

"Nothing's perfect, kid."

"Except your home-run swing."

"Get outta here," I said to my pal, happy that he was finally coming around.

Now I finished off the second piece of airplane pie and looked out the window. The stewardess took away my tray and I stretched out, closed my eyes and drifted off to sleep, worried and excited about what was going to happen to me alone up there in Montreal. Canada seemed so far away, so cold. . . .

. . . I felt the plane drop. I woke up, scared, but the stewardess was there, saying that we were about to land. Now I was real jittery. I reached in the pocket of the warmup jacket I was wearing and couldn't find the piece of paper with the address of the team office. I was supposed to take a cab there, but where was that slip of paper? I started getting a little panicky, and I stood up in the aisle because I figured it might be in my pants pockets, but now the plane was coming down fast and I nearly fell down and I had to get back in my seat. I still couldn't find the address. I could picture myself stranded in the airport forever and never getting to play. Maybe that sounds funny, but I was only an eighteen-year-old kid who hadn't ever been away from home before and here I was going into some foreign country and I had no idea where to go. We hit the ground flying and the wheels were screeching and I wasn't feeling good. I needed to get that address 'cause I didn't know anyone in Montreal. Everyone was filing outta the plane and the stewardess looked at me and she could tell something was wrong. She asked me if she could help, but I was too embarrassed to admit anything, so I just told her goodbye. My stomach was turning cartwheels—I was scared about this address, scared about this new place, scared about playing minor-league ball—and when I started walking off the plane I kept my eyes peeled on the steps so I wouldn't trip and break my neck. When I got to the bottom I looked up and, holy cow, there was Bobby! Bobby was right there! Bobby was wearing this classy blue blazer and his eyes were roaring blue and he had this row of kids holding up a huge banner with bright-red letters saying BROOKLYN LOVES SQUAT! There was no one in the whole world I'd rather have seen. He took me over to these reporters he had gathered up who knew all about my high school records— Bobby had told them—and some guy was taking pictures of me. Then Bobby led me to a limousine he had rented for the day. It was gleaming silver and long as a city block.

"Now why'd you go and do something like that?" I asked him.

"I was afraid you'd never find your way to the office. Just trust me, Squat. I'm here to help us both."

FIVE

BOBBY DIDN'T STAY for more than a day or two, but during that first season he came back to see me play a good half-dozen games. He knew everything I was doing. He saw how I was tearing up the league. There was even an article about me in the New York *Daily Mirror* which predicted that I'd be called to L.A. in no time at all. While the Dodgers wound up their last year in Brooklyn, I wound up with the best slugging percentage in the history of Montreal. I led the league in homers and doubles, was second in rbi's and threw out so many guys trying to steal second that after a while they gave up trying.

Bobby was doing good, too. He told me he was in this very cool fraternity and he was voted president of the whole freshman class and there were all these parties and gals and why didn't I come up sometime during the winter to visit him 'cause he was meeting the Judge in Mexico for Christmas and wouldn't be back to Brooklyn for a while. The winter was sort of a nervous time for me—I was living at home and working out at the gym and mainly waiting to hear whether I was going back to Montreal or moving out to L.A. with the Dodgers—and so I figured it'd be good to get away. I had never been on a big college campus and I wanted to see Bobby's setup out there. I knew it had to be slick.

It was. When I got to Ann Arbor there was snow on the ground and there were lots of tall trees and big buildings which looked something like the Brooklyn Museum. I saw all these girls walking around with books under their arms. They looked very smart and beautiful. Bobby's frat house was big and swanky. He took me around to all the guys and introduced me like I was a star. They were wearing their collegiate plaid shirts and I was wearing my genuine Montreal warmup jacket, which was satin if I ain't mistaken.

"Let me tell you gentlemen about Squat," Bobby began after gathering everyone in the living room. "Squat's fame, Squat's proficiency at slamming the ball from one corner of Brooklyn to another, is legend. You are looking at a man whose prodigious talents on the diamond are certain to propel him to even greater fame." That's how the kid was talking. I was embarrassed, but I was loving it, and soon the guys were asking me a million questions about baseball 'cause they'd never met a real pro before. And listening to myself spit out the answers, I was pretty amazed, 'cause I seemed to know a lot. But then again, I guess I've always known a lot about baseball, being a catcher—the catcher is actually the head guy out there. So I did a lot of talking, which is pretty unusual for me, but these frat kids wanted to know stuff and I saw that Bobby was having a ball listening to me—he always liked my Brooklyn accent—and he was sorta showing me off.

Bobby then took me up to his room, which looked very fancy with all this woodwork but then I saw the Dodger things on the wall and right away I felt at home. Pictures of Ebbets and the Bums and even a picture of me in my Montreal uniform.

"How do ya like it up here, kid?" I asked.

"It's all right."

"You learning lots of stuff?"

"It's not like that, Squat. Primarily, it's parties and drinking and girls."

"You're kidding."

"Not at all. My main activity is this fraternity. Did I tell you I'm going to be rush captain next year? I'm the youngest guy in the history of the frat to be picked. That means I'll recruit new members. And we're very choosy. Not everyone can get in. It costs a great deal of money and you can't be a drip."

"But ain't you studying *something*?" I had to ask.

"Business, but it's easy."

"Is that what you're going to do, be a big businessman?"

"I'm not sure what I want to do. Right now I'm primarily interested in taking advantage of my position."

"What does that mean?"

"Getting as much pussy as possible."

That was Bobby.

"How about you, Squat? Those little French honeys must be chasing after you in Montreal. You're a baseball hero up there."

"It ain't like that, believe me. Besides, who's got time to worry 'bout dames?"

"I've heard that line before, Squat. You're getting too old to keep using it."

"When they call me out to L.A. and I'm actually on the Dodgers, maybe then I'll start worrying about girls."

"Haven't you noticed, Squat, that this campus is overflowing with beautiful women?"

"Sure, I noticed. What do you think, I ain't normal?"

"I know you're normal, which is precisely why I've set something up for you."

"Please, kid. Gimme a chance. I just got here."

"We'll take a nice leisurely stroll around campus so you can relax. The party's not till tonight."

"There's a party?"

"For you. I intend to take full advantage of your celebrity status."

It was cold walking around the college, so we ducked into this student hangout called Drake's. Everyone in the joint knew Bobby, and he invited them all to the party—Bobby could never resist asking anyone to a party; he'd invite the whole world if he could. As we walked back outside it started snowing and I could smell chimneys and burning wood. Bobby had to pick up a pair of shoes that were being fixed. Inside this little shoemaker's shop, six or seven students were waiting in line while an old man with wild white hair ran around, searching for shoes. He was real hassled.

"Nick!" Bobby shouted to the guy. "You're getting rich. Look at this crowd!" All eyes turned on Bobby as he went to the counter and jumped over to the other side. Then he put his arm around Nick and announced, "Everyone here to pick up shoes, see me. If you're bringing in shoes for repair, see Nick." And for the next ten minutes, Bobby worked beside the shoemaker—taking cash, hunting for shoes, giving change—until the store was cleared of customers. "Nick is the last craftsman left in America," Bobby said after he had introduced me and sung my praises. "Nick's from Flatbush," Bobby added. "He left only because the Bums lost the '53 Series. Isn't that right, Nick?"

"That little son of a bitch Billy Martin," said Nick, who sounded a lot like my pop. "He singles in the bottom of the ninth and the Yanks win. Can you believe it?"

"Clem Labine was the reliever," Bobby reminded us. "The Fascists beat us in six that year."

"I rebuilt your heels," Nick tells Bobby, "and I shined 'em up with a special wax, but this time I ain't charging you."

"That would be like not paying Heifetz to play his fiddle," said Bobby. "Artisans are to be rewarded." Bobby took out a bill and stuffed it in Nick's pocket, then made me give Nick my autograph. "It'll be worth hundreds of dollars someday," Bobby was saying. "Especially after Squat is inducted into the Hall of Fame."

At the party that night there was brew, broads and lots of baseball talk. I was in heaven. Bobby was working the room, filling up glasses, kissing girls on the cheek and slapping guys on the back. I was drinking a little and my date had a nice shape, but she was sorta silly and didn't care nothing about baseball. I didn't have to pay much attention to her 'cause Bobby kept on bringing everyone around to meet me. He fixed it so that I was the big deal at the party. He was playing all the records I liked—the Drifters and the Five Keys and all those smooth sounds which reminded me of the guys who would sing on the streetcorners of Brooklyn—and when he saw I wasn't crazy about my date he got rid of his and had some guy take mine back to her dorm. There we were, with the party over, the two of us all alone in the living room of the frat house, which reeked of beer and cigarettes. Three A.M. I was spread out on the couch and Bobby was spread out on an easy chair.

"You'll be rich, Squat." He burped. He was real drunk, and I was a little drunk.

"You're already rich."

"But what difference does it make? What does it get me?"

"Things."

"What good are things?"

"They're fun. Cars and boats. Things like that are fun."

"Yes, but what am I going to do? What am I going to do once I get out of here, Squat?" Bobby was in one of those kind of moods.

"Business," I told him. "You'll be a genius at business."

"Wrong, Squat. I hate details and I'm not sure I have any true feeling for finance."

"People. People love you, kid. And business ain't nothing more than people."

"It's not that simple. You wouldn't think so, but I'm burdened with a number of problems."

"Problems? Come on, Bobby. You got money, looks and brains. Any problems you got, kid, you made up in that fancy head of yours."

He laughed and lit a cigarette. He threw me the pack and I lit up, too. I didn't smoke, and I coughed on my first drag and put it out.

"I need to find something that has nothing to do with the old man. But that'll take work, and I'm not sure if I really want to work."

"Good point."

"Which makes me think that there's only one thing left for us to do, Squat."

"What's that?"

"Go outside right now and play some baseball."

But before we did, Bobby took out this bottle of booze and had a swig and passed it to me and I took a big slug just for old times' sake. It burned my throat and tasted awful and my head was really reeling 'cause I had been up so long. I saw Bobby's eyes laughing and I saw him get a couple of mitts and a hardball. We put on our coats, and outside—oh man—outside it was freezing with the snow still falling, thick pieces of wet snow, and I thought to myself: I'm in Michigan, I'm in college, I'm drunk and soon I'll be famous, soon I'll be with the Dodgers, and if it wasn't for Bobby and all the confidence he gives me, I would have never made it, never in a million years. The cold on my nose felt so good—so clean and so clear—and there was Bobby, throwing the ball to me. We were both in the middle of the street, playing catch, with me going way far back and hauling in the ball and firing it with all my might. Bobby was screaming at me that I'm a major leaguer and the snow was landing in my nose and in my mouth. Snow was on my shoes and my socks were wet and the street was so peaceful and quiet with the frat houses all lined up in a row. I wasn't worrying about nothing 'cause we were raising hell and yelling our fool heads off, joking about this time or that time when we hustled in East New York or Ridgewood.

We were so happy out in the middle of the snowy night, hooting and hollering. This crazy energy was going through my body —the kind of energy that had Bobby written all over it—and, now that I think about it, I was probably carrying on and yelling too loud to realize where I was standing.

I was standing in front of a driveway, waiting for Bobby to throw me the ball. I was jumping up and down to keep warm. I didn't see the car backing out of the driveway; the car didn't see me; the windows were packed solid with frost. And then *boom! Crack!* I was hit. Knocked down. I groaned: Oh God. Exhaust fumes running up my nose. My legs crumpling. This awful crunch, bones crushed like chalk. Hearing 'em crack. Twigs snapping. Cold steel. My head was resting on a sheet of soft snow, and there was Bobby racing toward me, his eyes wild, hollering "*No! No! No! No! No!*" He was scared, and then my eyeballs turned another way and I saw that I was underneath this car, and my legs, sweet Jesus, where were my legs? What happened to my legs? And Bobby was still yelling "*No! No! No! No! No!*" and then the pain screamed through me, the pain put out my lights and I felt my legs melting, melting, melting into the snow.

SIX

THEY SAVED ONE, but they couldn't save the other. They left me with only one leg. But if you saw me walking around, you'd have to look hard to notice my limp. This fake leg works almost as good as the real one. Bends at the knee and everything.

Bobby had the Judge fly in this character with a little beard and a thick accent all the way from Switzerland. All he did was make legs. I was laid up in this hospital in Ann Arbor and all of a sudden he walked in the room and started ordering everyone around, and Bobby—who had a cot and was sleeping right next to me every night—told me who he was. Bobby said this doc was some kind of genius and that he'd fix up everything.

We didn't talk about the accident. I was having all these crazy dreams and all these crazy thoughts, and part of me was mad—madder than I'd ever been in my life—mad at me for drinking or mad at Bobby for getting me drunk. But it wasn't the drinking, it was the idea of playing baseball on all that ice, or coming out to Michigan when I should have been back in the gym in Brooklyn, and now what was gonna happen to me? What did I have to live for? Everything was over—that's how I felt sometimes—that car backing out of the driveway smashed every dream and every hope I ever had. And sometimes in the middle of the night in that hospital room I cried to myself—I didn't want Bobby to hear—I sobbed for hours and hours, even though when I talked to my folks I told them they didn't have to come out 'cause I was getting the best treatment in the world. Which was true.

When I first came around, I didn't know anything; couldn't figure out what I was doing in a hospital bed. Then I panicked. I grabbed my right leg and nothing was there and a half hour later they were explaining to me how the tires had crushed me, how both front and back wheels had backed over me. "But I'm a catcher," I wailed. "I'm about to play for the Dodgers. I'm a catcher and I need my legs, I gotta have my legs," and my voice got real loud and they must have given me some kind of calm-down shot 'cause I went out after that.

The main thing I remember in those first days is the fear. The fear wouldn't leave me, it was all over, up and down my neck, inside my spine. The fear said: You're nothing now; you're through. I couldn't play, and if I couldn't play, I wasn't worth a nickel. And it seemed wrong, unfair; why should I have such rotten luck? And there was nothing Bobby could say, and he knew that, and I figured he felt as bad as me. But it wasn't him who had a leg chopped off, it was me, me who had been gypped out of a career and maybe even a shot at being the greatest. . . . But I had to try to stop thinking that way 'cause I was driving myself nuts.

One morning the sun poured through the window. First time I had seen the sun since I was in the hospital. I opened my eyes and saw that Bobby's cot was empty. The sun hurt my eyes. I was about to call the nurse to come close the blinds when Bobby came through the door carrying a newspaper. His face was real sad, and I knew something else was wrong. He handed me the paper, which was folded to a story about Roy Campanella. Campy had been in a terrible car accident on Long Island. My hands were shaking as I read the details. He might be in a wheel-chair for the rest of his life. There was a picture of what happened to his car. A shiver passed over my heart. I thanked God that at least I'd be able to walk with a fake leg. And then I wondered how I would have felt about Campy's terrible disaster if I hadn't been run over. Would I have been even the tiniest bit glad 'cause my chances of making the team would be better? I didn't want to take advantage of my hero, who was the greatest catcher in the history of all baseball. Campy was crushed, just the way I was crushed, but worse. But at least he had had a chance to play. Now there'd never be any chance for me. I kept this up for days —staying down, feeling sorry for myself, crying into my pillow at night.

The Swiss doc with the beard finally came and took my measurements like he was fitting me for a suit. He told me that he personally was going to make this leg. He was a real nervous fella, but Bobby kept telling me he was world-famous, and when the leg came Bobby and him were the only ones I let in the room. It fit real good; it was even the color of real flesh.

The big problem was what was gonna become of me. Bobby or his dad was paying for the hospital and the Swiss doc, but I couldn't stay there forever.

47

"Why not?" asked Bobby, who hadn't been to school since the accident—three weeks ago. "The Judge could get you into the university here. You might even like it."

"Come on, Bobby," says me. "I ain't exactly what they call college material."

"There's not much work. You could slide by. I'd get you in our frat and—"

"I don't belong in no frat."

"I guarantee you, Squat, I'm going to find something for you."

"Stop worrying, kid. I can take care of myself."

We'd have talks like that now and then. We were usually pretty calm, but once in a while Bobby would start yelling about O'Malley, how my accident and Campy's accident had something to do with O'Malley moving the Bums out of Brooklyn. How that was causing disturbances all over the universe. I thought it was a goofy idea, but I didn't say nothing 'cause maybe it made Bobby feel better.

The more I stayed in Ann Arbor, though, the more I knew I had to get out. Bobby couldn't do anything for me except worry, and I didn't need that. I just needed to be home. I missed my folks and my brothers, and a few days after my fake leg was hooked up and I could walk with it, I had Bobby make me a reservation and take me to the airport. He didn't want to. He wanted to keep talking till we got the thing worked out. But as far as I was concerned, there was nothing to work out. It was over. Part of my life was over, and all I knew is that I wanted my mom's cooking instead of that hospital rot.

Winter worked its way through Brooklyn, and when the nice weather came, I felt better. Not great, but at least I started limping around the old neighborhood and I stopped thinking about shooting myself and other such pleasant thoughts which had been bouncing in and out of my brain. The physical therapist I had been going to helped a lot. Spring warmed me up, and I felt some of the old me creeping back. Everyone around Borough Park was glad to see me out. They were real encouraging, and the energy was definitely coming back to my body. I could feel my muscles again, and in July, when Pop said there was a job down at the Navy Yard where he worked, I took it. It was just lifting heavy boxes and stuff, but I could do it; I could do it as good as any guy with two legs, and that made me feel proud.

Once in July I even stopped by a playground on Fort Hamilton Parkway and started hitting the ball to a couple of little boys. I saw that I still had my power, and that got me scared and happy and sad, and I wondered if I should try coaching kids or something, but no, I knew not to. I knew to stay away from baseball. There was still so much pain.

Funny how you can get used to anything. Even a fake leg. Sometimes I'd think about it and decide that my life wasn't so bad after all. My family still treated me like a king. I had all my meals and I didn't have to pay no rent and if I was a little lonely or down, everybody would try to chase those blues out of my head.

During the vacations or holidays Bobby'd come buzzing out to Borough Park in his black Thunderbird convertible and drive me around Brooklyn and tell me about college and how he hated it. He kept telling me that if he went into business it was only to make money, to make enough money to buy the Bums and move 'em back to Brooklyn, and I'd smile and think to myself—yeah, just the way he bought me my leg.

SEVEN

ON FEBRUARY 23, 1960—two years after my accident—Bobby flew into town and came by with Ralph to get me in the limo. We drove over to Flatbush, not saying a word to each other, our heads hung low. We stopped in front of Ebbets Field. We got out. It was so eerie and strange and cold. We sat behind the Dodger dugout and watched the crane, which had a wrecker's ball painted to look like a baseball, honest to God. We watched it go to work. For hours we watched the place being demolished, and we didn't talk, couldn't talk, because of all the sadness and the sounds and memories that were running through our brains.

I could still picture 32,000 people screaming for Furillo to fire it home. I could picture the ballpark all dressed up for the World Series—with the bunting, the flags, the place packed solid. And when the seats crumbled under the wrecker's ball, I thought of

Campy and my own accident and I winced. I felt like I was being wrecked—and the whole world around me. The ballpark was coming apart, they were really tearing it down, and when they started whacking at the Schaefer scoreboard, I couldn't stand it anymore. I got up and left, and Bobby followed me outside. Looking at those beautiful old white letters that said EBBETS FIELD, we bit our lips and fought back the tears.

"Well, at least we paid our respects," Bobby said when we were back in the limo. "At least we attended the funeral."

And the next funeral I went to was just as sad, but very different. That was the Judge's funeral in 1965.

EIGHT

"WOULD YOU LIKE some more, Dan?"

I nodded, and Mom dished out another portion of corned beef and cabbage. Mom wouldn't ever call me Squat.

"It's real good," I told her. She stood at the sink washing the dishes. Pop and my brothers Rich and Jerry had eaten an early dinner, then gone to a Mets game. I wouldn't go. I hated the Mets.

"Talked to Peter this week?" Mom wanted to know.

My brother Peter had just gotten married. He was twenty-two —four years younger than me—and he was a bookkeeper. He married this nice girl named Beverly and they were living somewhere on Long Island.

"No," I told Mom, "but I'm sure he's doing fine."

"What did you think of Beverly's sister Nan?"

"Nice. Very friendly."

I knew what Mom was getting at. She wanted to know why I didn't go out more with girls. Which was a normal thing for a mother to wonder, except that I wasn't entirely straight in my head about this fake-leg thing. And I'd been sticking around the house now for a long, long time. My life could have been a lot worse, but I also knew that something was gonna have to happen.

"Your father tells me that everyone down at work says you're the best worker there, Dan. He says they call you Muscle Man."

"They kid me a lot, Mom." I looked at her. Her hair was real gray and tied up in a bun. Her eyes were soft and pretty, and she sure had a Brooklyn accent, but her voice wasn't hard or anything; her voice was full of love. I finished my second helping and she put down a plate of fresh-from-the-oven brownies along with a cup of hot coffee. She poured in a lot of cream, just the way I like it.

"But I guess," she said, "it must get a little boring for you, just working with your muscles like that."

"It's good for me."

"Sure it is. It's been real good for you. But I'm just wondering how long you should do it."

"Pop's done it his whole life."

"Your father never graduated from high school the way you did. And besides, the world's different now. Things are better than when he was your age."

"I don't know what other kind of job I could get," says me.

"It's not just the job, Dan. It's the idea of changing things around. See what I mean?"

"You mean moving out of here?"

"We love having you. We'll always love having you, but . . ."

"I'm getting too old."

"You're our son, and we're proud of you, and . . ."

"I hear you, Mom. I know you mean well."

"I was at the grocery store on Thirteenth Avenue the other day and I happened to pick up one of those Hollywood magazines they have by the checkout counter and whose picture do you think I saw? Bobby. Your friend Bobby Hanes. He was with a very lovely actress and the writeup said he was living somewhere down in Florida and had many businesses. They called him a playboy, but I could see that it was the same old Bobby. It made me wonder, Dan, how come when he calls on your birthday or just to ask after you, how come you get so upset? Wouldn't you like to see him? Don't you think he could help you find something more exciting to do?"

"I don't need no help. Especially from Bobby."

"Are you angry at him?"

"I ain't angry, Ma. It's nothing like that. It's just that when he calls and tells me that he's in Hawaii having a party and that he's sending me a ticket and why don't I take off a week, I don't feel right accepting. And I know it'd be dumb to accept because I see that we just went different ways—that's all."

51

"If you don't want Bobby to help you, Dan, then you're going to have to help yourself."

"I'm trying."

"You're going to have to try harder."

"What do you mean?"

"A different job. A different place to live."

She stopped with the dishes and sat down next to me. Her eyes told me how hard this was for her. I could feel her using all her strength, feel her going against herself.

"You can stay here as long as you want," she went on. "I don't have to tell you that, Dan. And maybe if your father knew I was talking to you this way, he'd get mad. I know he could never say this to you because he worries about you so much, but I know how strong you are—not the muscle kind of strong, but strong all over, Dan, and I know that you're not being everything you can be. Everything you were meant to be."

"Everything I was meant to be changed that night in Ann Arbor, Mom. You know that."

"I don't know that. You're still thinking of the muscle kind of strong, the baseball kind of strong. But what about the rest of you, Dan? The rest of you is strong."

"I ain't no genius, Mom."

"You're as smart as you need to be. As smart as anyone needs to be. You've got a fine head on your shoulders, and you don't need to apologize to anyone about anything. Just start following your heart, Dan, and using your head, and everything's gonna turn out just fine."

She smiled at me and kissed my forehead. I couldn't sleep that night, because her words kept going round and round.

Finding a new job wasn't easy, and it was kinda scary. It took over a month, but when it happened I was very proud because I had enough money to get a one-room apartment of my own over on Atlantic Avenue on the outskirts of Brooklyn Heights. Sometimes I'd walk down Willow Street, past Bobby's townhouse, which he still owned but never used. He hadn't called me in a long time, which was fine by me, because Mr. Grabelsky, my boss, was teaching me the diamond business and I'd work late almost every night. I was real anxious to do good and learn a trade. Mr. Grabelsky had a place in one of the big diamond exchanges on 47th Street over in the city. That whole block is nothing but jewelers; it's one of the main jewelry streets in the world—at least that's what everyone says. Grabelsky had been there forever and knew everything. His older brother, who had been his partner, had just died, and he needed someone young to help out. He said I was very smart. Those were the words he used. First he taught me about diamonds—how to look at 'em, weigh 'em and sort 'em—and then he taught me about gold—buying and selling and mounting—and after six or seven months at this I was feeling so good I even had a few dates. Nothing too serious. Some girls I met down at the Exchange. Just real enjoyable companionship where you go out and eat spaghetti and maybe take in a movie.

The weekends could be a little rough, though, specially if I didn't go see my folks. I might make the mistake of taking out my scrapbooks and looking at all the pictures again. I might do that for hours, for days, and that usually meant that I couldn't sleep at night and my stomach would be churning and I'd go fix myself a cup of hot chocolate and watch some dumb cowboy story on TV to try and knock all those thoughts out of my mind. *I have a life to live, this here is my life*, I kept thinking to myself, but that didn't always work. I was gaining too much weight and maybe you could say I was a little lonely, so when, a year or so later, Mr. Grabelsky gave me two weeks off I guess I shouldn't have been so surprised that I was sitting next to Bobby with the sun beating down on my brain as we roared up the California coast in his black Porsche convertible, past the beach near San Luis Obispo, heading fast and furious for some place called Big Sur.

NINE

"I FEEL USELESS," Bobby kept telling me.

"How can you say that, kid? You just got done telling me about these freighters and these oil deals and all these other business adventures."

"Ventures, Squat. They're ventures."

"They're making you more filthy rich every day, and I don't know what you're bellyaching about," says me. Bobby seemed real different. He was struggling with himself. He didn't seem as happy-go-lucky as he used to be.

"These were things which I just fell into," he was telling me. The wind was blowing in our face. The Porsche—which he picked up in L.A. just before he got me at the airport—smelled of new leather. I thought we were going to hang around L.A., but he said we had to hit the road.

"You got the magic touch," I said.

"I'm little more than a passive agent. These deals come to me. Money begets money. It's still all the Judge's doing."

"But the Judge is dead and you're the guy making the decisions."

He took out a joint and lit it. This was something new. It smelled sweet and disgusting, and when he offered me some, I said no maybe a little too loud 'cause he looked hurt—like I was trying to remind him of Ann Arbor or something. I ain't no prude, but dope does nothing but make me sleepy.

"I own a chain of health spas in Texas," Bobby started explaining. "Not because I care about health spas or, perish the thought, even know the first thing about them. I made the acquisition simply because one of my many financial advisers—a man who has more degrees than a thermometer—suggested it might be a smart move. It was. It earns enough these days to support a small Central American country. But what am I to think? What am I to feel? I did nothing more than listen to the right man."

"That took brains."

"My social life is just as dismal."

"What about all these magazines that show you running to parties with the beautiful ladies? Ain't that fun?"

He yawned in my face. "High society is overrated."

"You sound like you really been on a big bummer."

"Which is precisely why I need this vacation. You'll love Big Sur, Squat. The mountain air will do wonders for our heads. We'll analyze our problems and have them resolved by the time we pull into San Francisco."

"I don't have no problems."

"You're lying through your teeth. You were not meant to be a jeweler. You were meant to work with me, and you know it."

"There's nothing I could do for you, kid," I said, looking at how the day was all sun and light, sky and road, looking at those waves rolling to the shore over by the side of the highway, thinking how strange it was to be here in California with crazy Bobby, who had grown this big beard which was more red than blond and made his eyes look more green than blue.

"We'll come up with something sensible, Squat. Trust me. I'm here to help us both."

The inn at Big Sur was really something. Very rustic. At night came the fog and the mist, and we ate in this restaurant made of glass and wood beams, right in the middle of a forest. Bobby was drinking brandy and smoking a Cuban cigar and wearing a yellow plaid shirt and old blue jeans.

"I could go back to school," he was telling me. "Maybe I could become a lawyer, maybe a doctor. Save people's lives and make my own fortune. But what's the point? There'd be no point. Except that every man must make his mark."

"How big does the mark have to be?" I wanted to know.

"Large enough to change the world."

"Ain't it enough to be happy?"

"No. I'm already happy. I've always been happy."

"Then what are you looking for, kid?"

"I want to be happier."

The next day we were sitting on a wild, deserted beach. Bobby was drinking a beer. I was watching seagulls.

"It may be something as obvious as banking," Bobby was saying. "I could buy a bank somewhere in the Great Pacific Northwest and lead a simple, tranquil life, get married, have kids—you'd be the godfather, Squat. I'd put up a white picket fence, and within a few years—"

"You'd blow your brains out," I finished the sentence for him.

That night the car broke down just north of Carmel. It was raining bullets. Bobby fooled with the engine. I fooled with the engine. But the engine wouldn't turn. We left the car by the side of the road and hitchhiked to a gas station. We were soaked to the skin.

"I'll sue the Porsche dealer," Bobby was fuming. "The first thing tomorrow morning I'm slapping the dealer and the manufacturer and the entire nation of West Germany with a multi-million-dollar suit. The bastards will never know what hit them. Here I buy a spanking-new car for a small fortune just to avoid this kind of crap!" He kicked a tire with all his might. I think he hurt a toe, but he wasn't about to admit it. I didn't say nothing.

We went to four gas stations before we found a mechanic. The guy drove us back in his pickup, but he couldn't get the Porsche started either. The car would have to be towed. "Fuck it," Bobby spit out as rainwater dripped down his beard. Then he handed the mechanic a hundred-dollar bill and said. "Have this shit-heap hauled off. I'll call you tomorrow from San Francisco and tell you what to do with it."

There were no cars around to be rented, no planes to be taken. Only the bus. "Relax," says me when I saw that the color in Bobby's face had turned a brighter red; his blood was really boiling. "We'll enjoy the ride," I told him.

The ride was another bust. First off, the bus—a Golden State Cruiseliner—was two hours late. It creaked and coughed its way up the coast, with me and Bobby nauseated and about to puke. The scent of fumes was all up in our nose, and then, in the middle of some valley, the bus broke down.

"We don't have nowhere to go anyways," I reminded Bobby, trying to be a pal.

"What are you talking about, Squat? We have to be in San Francisco tonight."

"What for?"

"So I can make arrangements for the Porsche."

For an hour we stood by the side of the road while the driver fooled with the engine. Bobby, in his usual style, started talking to all the other passengers and trading stories. Then he said everyone should play charades. He acted out the title of the movie *Bus Stop*. That cracked up the crowd, and someone asked whether Bobby was a famous person. I said yes.

"If the Judge were here," Bobby said to me a little later, "the Marines would already be helicoptering us out."

Somehow we got to Salinas, but in Salinas they told us we had to change buses; the six P.M. wouldn't be leaving till eight. We checked the other lines: nothing going north till ten. Finally at a quarter after eight, some joker told us that the Golden State San Francisco Cruiseliner Special was canceled; not enough passengers. That's when Bobby chartered us a private plane and pilot, flew us back to L.A. and bought the bus company.

It didn't start out that way, believe me. Bobby just wanted to go beef to T.R. Simpson, president of Golden State Transportation. By then, I was ready to head back East. Things were getting a little too nutty, and I was tired of living off Bobby. But no, Bobby said I had to stay for this meeting. "You saw the beginning of this thing," he said. "Now you'll stay for the end."

Simpson was an old grouch. He had ruddy cheeks and crooked teeth and a Masonic diamond stickpin in his tie. He looked like a raw meatloaf. We sat in his office in Burbank. The coffee he served us tasted like the yellow air outside.

Bobby told him the long sad story. He didn't leave out anything. And when he was through, he asked the guy how such a sloppy operation could hope to make money.

"Frankly, Mr. Hanes," said Simpson, leaning back in his exec chair, "your complaint doesn't surprise me. There was a time when we ran a clean ship and even made money, but those days are over. There's no way to compete with the giants—Greyhound and Continental."

"You must be kidding," answered Bobby. "The California coast has to be one of the most traveled lines in the world. There must be room for—"

"I'm afraid, Mr. Hanes, that you don't know what you're talking about. The giants have money and marketing plans. We have nothing but a tired tradition."

"Fuck the giants," said Bobby. "I'm an old Dodgers fan, Mr. Simpson, and back in Brooklyn that meant rooting for the Bums, the underdogs. We hated the Yankees because the Yankees were United States Steel."

"United States Steel owns this country, Mr. Hanes, and, in case you haven't noticed, the Dodgers are living in Beverly Hills. I'm sorry you had an unpleasant trip, and I'll gladly refund—"

"So you've given up."

"I haven't given up. I've merely faced reality. It's impossible to—"

"Nothing is impossible."

"If you don't mind my saying so, you're young and rash and more than a little naive."

"You're sitting on top of a goldmine," Bobby barked, "and you're too lazy to mine it."

"I'd mind my own business if I were you."

"Not only do I intend to mind your own business, Mr. Simpson, I intend to buy it."

Bobby stormed out of the office, and when I caught up with him in the hallway, he was fuming, talking about how the Judge built up the cement business, how it was rough and tough and took guts and vision. "But the challenge was there, Squat, and the challenge is what had him working night and day." I ain't ever heard the story that way before.

"But you don't know nothing about buses, do you, kid?"

"I'll learn."

The next afternoon accountants and lawyers and marketing experts showed up at our hotel suite. Bobby had flown 'em in from all over. And after a few days of research, they all said no; don't do it, Simpson's right, Golden State is a dud. But Bobby wasn't listening. Bobby thanked the boys for their advice, he told 'em they'd be paid, and then we went out and swung a deal with Simpson.

Naturally Simpson was in hog heaven. He thought he had a sucker. Meanwhile, Bobby started selling a slew of stocks and bonds and buying a fleet of old buses. Me, I was just sitting around the hotel watching him make a hundred phone calls an hour. He liked when I watched him. He said he operated better with me there. By now, though, my vacation was over. When I told Bobby I was leaving, I really thought he'd cry.

"You started this scheme with me," he kept on saying, "now you've got to finish it. I'm putting you on the payroll. I need you. You're the one who's going to keep me from going off the deep end."

Fat chance, I thought to myself. But something inside me did wanna stay to see what would happen. Something inside me also wanted to go back to New York; after all, Mr. Grabelsky was counting on me. I called him that night and leveled with him.

"Stay," he said. "Stay all summer if you want to. Business is so terrible I don't even need to be here." So I stayed.

Bobby changed. He shaved his beard. He worked. Like a bull, he was on the attack. "I'm putting my name on these buses," he told me late one night in the bar of the hotel where we were living, "and there's no way we can crash." He planned new routes, he mapped out marketing plans, he fired the old ad agency, hired another, fixed up the financing, picked out fabrics for the bus seats, talked to government big shots. Meantime, I was making sure he got to all his appointments on time, making sure he woke up in the morning and went to bed by a reasonable hour at night. I'd guess you'd say I was like his secretary. Not the kind who types, but the kind who tells him where he has to be and what he has to do. I'm pretty good at that kind of thing; I don't forget anything. Mainly, though, I was around for the sake of old times and good feeling.

By the end of the first month, he was more sure of himself. He was acting a lot older than a kid who wasn't even thirty. By August 15, the first new Hanes bus was ready to roll. The others would be ready a few weeks later. The fleet had been repainted and decorated in blue and white (Dodger blue, Bobby said, even though we never went to Dodger Stadium—that would have been against our religion; they weren't the *real* Dodgers). Bobby was also antsy. He had a right. Only God knows how much loot he had poured into this thing. "If we're going after the competition," he'd say, "let's go for their nuts."

The first L.A.–San Francisco run—the maiden voyage of a Hanes bus—was set to leave on a Saturday morning. A celebration had been planned. The press was coming. And now Bobby really had the jitters: all this work, all this planning, all these days and nights—this was for real.

I had to be the one to tell him. Everyone else was scared. Simpson's old vice president, a good guy who Bobby had kept on, called me with the news. His voice was shaking. It was late Friday night—that was part of their stragegy. I couldn't believe it. Sure, I had heard some rumors, but I never thought it'd come true.

"Which suit will look more dignified tomorrow?" Bobby asked me when I walked in his bedroom. "I'm torn between the black pinstripe and the chocolate-brown. Which do you think will show up better in the newspaper? Did I tell you that the Sunday paper is running a feature on the bus business, and the whole thing is built around Hanes?"

"Bobby, they're striking."

"Who?"

"The drivers."

"They can't."

"They are. They say you got to midnight to meet their demands."

"You mean that crap they presented me with two weeks ago?"

"Yeah."

"That was outrageous. I threw them out of my office."

"That's why they're striking, kid."

"They want to break me before I get started."

"Something like that."

"What time is it?"

"Ten."

"I've got two hours."

"You better call Malmgreen," says me. "The union boss you ticked off."

"Give me his number."

"Stay cool, Bobby. You don't wanna blow this one."

"I'm not using a lawyer," Bobby said to Malmgreen a few minutes later. "I'm not using a negotiator. I'm talking to you man to man. Now are we going to make a deal tonight or are you going to keep acting like an asshole?"

Malmgreen wouldn't budge; Bobby wouldn't budge. Bobby was convinced that the union was just testing his will. Some test. I talked to Malmgreen, and he said he'd give us a two-hour extension on the deadline, but by two A.M., after Malmgreen had nixed the sixth compromise that Bobby had put together, we knew it was over. "No need to worry," Bobby said. "Not now. The ceremony is tomorrow at nine. We should leave here by eight-thirty. See you then, Squat."

I started to say something, but I held my tongue. Who knew what was going on in that screwy brain of his?

There were a couple of reporters and photographers at the depot. The big-shot politicians, once they heard about the strike, dropped out. They weren't about to get on the union's bad side. So we were left with a few friends, lots of employees, 101 passengers—winners of a free trip in this contest Bobby had dreamed up—and no driver. I still didn't have the foggiest of what Bobby was gonna do.

There was a small speaker's stand draped with a flag of the new Hanes bus emblem. Next to the stand was the big blue-and-white bus. Bobby was wearing the chocolate-brown suit. He looked real handsome, and, believe it or not, he was in high spirits. My stomach had turned into a Boy Scout's knot. When everyone started asking him questions about the strike, he avoided them. He just went right into his speech—which I told him to keep short and simple—about the free marketplace and how wonderful competition was. Then, before anyone knew it, he put on a Hanes driver's hat, waved for me to come along, slipped behind the wheel and took the 101 contest winners up the coast, joking and carrying on like life was just one long terrific party.

That night we flew back to L.A. and had a private meeting at Malmgreen's apartment. Malmgreen was a big strapping guy with green bug eyes, but Bobby broke his jaw anyway with one beaut of a right hook. I didn't know the kid had it in him. Then we took Malmgreen to the hospital and before the doc arrived Bobby slipped this creep fifty very crisp thousand-dollar bills. The next morning Malmgreen was able to move his mouth enough to settle the strike.

By then I was pooped. My brain had been working too fast. I was tired of playing hookey. I had to get back to New York. So I went. My brother's wife, Beverly, had just had a baby, a boy named Joey, and I wanted to see him. I was an uncle. I missed my folks, who were happy to see me and hear my stories. Joey was a doll. In October, Mr. Grabelsky gave me a raise, and by the time I turned around another year had passed and Bobby, that maniac, had already bought his thirtieth bus.

Scheming...

ONE

"**Y**OU'RE NOT GOING to believe this, Squat." He said it just like that—no hellos or nothing, breaking into my life at three in the morning after God knows how many years.

"Believe what?"

"The Germans are buying the Dodgers."

"You've flipped out."

"I couldn't be more serious. Can you believe it?"

"I can't believe anything right now. Where are you calling from?"

"The sky."

"I gotta go back to sleep. I got work tomorrow."

"Did you hear what I said before?"

"The Krauts have invaded L.A."

"Worse, they've bought the Dodgers from the O'Malleys. I just spoke with my man in Munich, and he happened to mention it to me in passing. Just like that. The Schmidt Conglomerate. Swallowed it whole, the team and the stadium both. Squat, do you know what this means?"

"Better sauerkraut at the ballgames?"

"We have to do something about it. We have to act fast."

"We? What we?" I wanted to know.

"You and me. It's a travesty. And there's no one who cares anymore except us. No one willing to say, 'This is enough. Things have gone far enough.' What the hell did we fight World War II for? What's the world coming to anyway? I need to talk to

you, Squat. I've needed to talk to you for a long time. I'm . . .
I'm . . ."

"You don't have to say it, kid. Just tell me where you are."

"In my jet thirty thousand feet over Kansas."

"And where are we gonna talk?"

"Tonight, at the Palm, at nine."

How could I go back to sleep? I'd been having a bunch of bad dreams anyway, the kind where I'm a big-league baseball player and the stands are packed and everyone's yelling for me and everyone knows my face and my name and even my batting stance, just the way they did in high school.

That kind of dreaming wasn't gonna get me nowhere. I looked over at Pee Wee—Pee Wee was the cat I picked up on the streets and nursed back to health—who was curled around my feet, and I started thinking about Bobby and wondering whether I was glad he was storming his way back into my life, even if it was only going to be for an evening. Sure I was, 'cause there are pals and then there are pals. Some pals you meet for a beer and they tell you about their job and how they got the hots for some gal. And if you're lucky, they'll ask something about you—maybe. But then there are pals where you don't have to say nothing. You look at each other and you understand. No matter how much time has passed. Which is how it was between me and Bobby.

Even if nine or ten years had gone by, even if we had only seen each other at Christmas or on my birthday, it didn't make no difference. Sometimes Bobby'd just disappear for a while. He had to go off and fool around with the buses or the freighters or maybe find some new toys. He had to make more money. For a long time he didn't wanna think nothing about Brooklyn, nothing about his past.

Same with the Dodgers. We had both been ignoring them for nearly twenty-five years. We hated them being out in L.A., and we tried to act like they weren't even the Dodgers anymore. I don't mean that we were ignorant. Sure, I was kinda half glad when they beat the White Sox in the Series of '59. I was pulling for Larry Sherry, who was a helluva pitcher, but I was also pulling for that whole Coliseum to collapse. And I kept my eye on Maury Wills. I seen how many bases he stole out there, how he broke Cobb's record in '62, and I loved that, I loved it when we zapped the Fascists 4–zip in '63. And wasn't that Koufax and Drysdale something? I mean, the way the Fascists couldn't get more than four runs in four games. And in the Series of '65, when Koufax wouldn't pitch on his Jewish holiday, he reminded me of guys I knew from Borough Park or Bensonhurst. That took some guts. And it was real beautiful when he came out for the last game with the Twins, with only two days' rest, and blanked 'em 2–zip. But the next year when the Birds swept us in four, I was thinking—yeah, that's what L.A. deserved, 'cause when the Bums moved out there no one would call 'em the Bums anymore, 'cause they weren't the Bums, they were a different team, especially when Koufax retired, because he was really from Brooklyn. He was the last link.

Then those bad years—'67 through '74—when Bobby and me didn't care, or said we didn't care. We were looking out of the corner of our eyes, though, and we were seeing a bunch of bleached-blond-headed surfing boys who didn't look nothing like Bums. And really it wasn't till the Fascists beat them those two Series in a row—'77 and '78—that I stopped and thought about the old Dodgers, because Junior Gilliam died and I could remember when he was Rookie of the Year in '53 back in Ebbets Field. He was a beautiful second baseman, and I started thinking—maybe he was the last link.

But the rest of them out there for all those years—Tommy Davis and Willie Davis and Mike Marshall and Garvey and Lopes and Russell and Cey—they were a different breed, a different team. They belonged to another city and another time with a different ocean and different little kids rooting for 'em. Me and Bobby, we were grown-ups. We were forty-something years old, and I was a real good jeweler and diamond trader and I thought I had my life pretty settled. Then why couldn't I go back to sleep? Why was I so excited about Bobby coming to town?

The Palm is one of these strange joints that's supposed to be very high-class even though they throw sawdust on the floor. They get the big-money crowd—I seen that as soon as I walked in—and there's cartoons of famous mugs on the wall, old politicians like the Judge and Italian signers and Jewish comics. It's real loud and the waiters are real tough and everyone's in a hurry, putting away their lobsters and steaks and throwing around their credit cards. Me, I'm standing there watching this zoo and remembering the last time I saw Bobby, which was when he took me to a fight at the Garden. That's when he told me that he had this slew of guys running his companies and they each got at least $200,000 a year and didn't I want a slot 'cause there's a million things he could find for me to do. Naturally I said no; I didn't want no free rides.

Now when he walked through the door he was smiling from ear to ear and he sure didn't look any older, just tanner. He'd grown his beard back, which was even redder with little flecks of gray. Maybe his eyes were a little bloodshot but they were still laughing to beat the band.

The host made a big fuss over Bobby, and people turned and stared and a few called out his name. We went to a table where the waiter's name was Solly and he and Bobby got to talking about Joe Black and the 1952 Series against the Fascists. Solly was telling me how he's waited on Presidents and Mafia dons, but no one he liked better than Bobby. And Bobby was telling Solly about me and my career up in Montreal.

"You look terrific," Bobby said after Solly took our order. "You look strong as a bull. I presume you've been working out?"

"What else have I got to do?"

"Come on, Squat. Don't tell me you've been down."

"I been sideways."

"I know what you mean. It's our age."

"Tell me what you've been up to, kid."

The drinks came. Booze for Bobby. Club soda for me. "It's business, Squat. Business here and business there. And when you break it down, business is nothing more than the 'ness' of being busy."

"You got a girl?"

"Fleets of them, just as I have fleets of buses, and next week a book bindery in Yugoslavia and someone tells me I'll be buying a forest in northern Italy."

"You like any of the girls?"

"I like them all, and I don't love any of them. They keep me company or they drive me crazy and sometimes I confuse one for the other."

Now he was looking a little misty, and I was starting to see why he called me in the middle of the night. It was the old deal: He still didn't know what he was doing.

"Someone showed me this article about you in *Fortune* magazine, Bobby. Nice pictures."

"I didn't even read it."

"You're lying."

"Okay, so I read it a few dozen times."

"I also found out what you said last night about the Dodgers is true. My brother called this morning before I left my place and said he heard it on the radio."

"I haven't been able to think about anything else, Squat. This thing has my mind moving at a million miles an hour."

"You really think it makes that much difference? I mean, what does it matter if the team's run by some private family or some big machine? They're still stuck out there in L.A."

Our steaks arrived, and Bobby talked between bites. "It makes all the difference in the world. It's one more blow to everything we once held sacred. It's part of a hideous process which will finally result in doing away with players. Soon we'll go to the ballpark and there, down on the diamond, instead of human beings, will be a massive TV screen, and we'll be watching computer baseball. Can't you see it, Squat? It's part of the pattern begun when Robert Moses built highways leading out of Brooklyn so anyone with money could escape to Long Island. Those were the roads that ruined the old neighborhoods. Then O'Malley made his move. And if everyone was afraid to hang around Brooklyn, he was the most afraid of all; he hightailed it out all the way to the Pacific Ocean. Since then it's been nothing but plastic dreams and plastic grass, faceless suburban stadiums where Interstate 801 meets Interstate 802. And now the faceless stadiums will be occupied by faceless teams run by faceless owners, international conglomerates like Schmidt's which couldn't care less about the game. It's a crime, Squat, one of the great crimes of our time, and it's up to us to do something about it."

I was thinking that maybe he was drunk, or maybe just high on his own bull. "You know this guy Schmidt who bought the team?" I asked him.

"There's no one to know. He's a robot, the invention of the conglomerate's space engineers. He cares as much about baseball as the executioner cares about the guy in the chair. One of his financial experts tells him that American leisure-time entertainment is a good investment. They look over at Southern California and see that it's been hit hardest by the gas crunch. They see that the area is still without mass transportation, that everyone still has to get to the games by car. The Dodgers have been losing since 1982. They also see that, as a result, attendance has drastically fallen. So the price of the team, they conclude, is undervalued, and they're convinced they can buy one of the most valuable franchises in sports relatively cheap."

"You never looked into it? You weren't tempted yourself?"

"Not really, Squat. Not until now. The Dodgers aren't even the Dodgers to me. You know that."

"Then why are you talking about all this stuff?"

"Because I need you to help me get them back, to keep them out of foreign hands."

I saw he was serious. We were done with our steaks and he was ordering fancy cognac. "Hey, Bobby," I had to tell him. "I don't know nothing about these things. This is your high-class finance."

"It's as simple as the nose on your face, Squat. I want to buy the team from Schmidt, I want to buy it worse than anything I've ever wanted to buy in my life. Only you can understand that, Squat. But I'm handcuffed. Not because of money, but because of my name. If Schmidt knows I'm behind this, he'll either refuse to sell or send the price through the ceiling."

"How do you know?"

"I've had a couple of run-ins with him before. One was business, the other personal."

"A dame?"

"A dame."

"Don't go into details."

"I won't, but believe me, this is one time we can work together, Squat. One time when you'll see how much I need you. I want you to buy this team for me."

"What are you saying?"

"I want you to front as the head of a group of independent businessmen—from the diamond industry, say—who want to see the team back in American hands. And before you go over there and meet with him, we will have launched a major public-relations campaign in California to show him that the fans are resentful of foreign ownership. He'll worry that attendance will drop even more. He'll be convinced he made a bad deal, and just when he's having his gravest doubts, you'll be there with the cash. It'll work, Squat, because you're so square and honest, and because you're baseball. He'll believe you."

"And how you gonna get the league to approve the deal?"

"The deal will be done before the league sees it. And they'll be delighted. They'll be happy to have the Dodgers reclaimed by American money."

"You really want the Dodgers?"

"More than life itself."

"And what about L.A.? L.A. don't bother you?"

"I've been living out there three or four months a year, Squat. It's tolerable. The weather's nice. You'll like it."

"Me?"

"Of course you. Who else is going to run the ball club? General manager, field manager—you pick the position."

The Palm was emptying out now. My head was spinning so fast it hurt. I felt my life leaping out of my heart, into my throat. I saw everything changing. I wasn't drunk, but I felt like I was. Bobby did that to me, sitting there and smiling with that crazy gleam in his eye. His eyes were doing a little tap dance for me.

"This is what we've been waiting for, Squat. You and I back in the baseball business again!"

"I don't know, kid," says me, shaking my head.

"I do. Just trust me—"

"I know." I had to laugh and finish off the line. "You're here to help us both."

TWO

AT FIRST I wasn't gonna do it. It was too much like make-believe and costumes. My life was normal, and I liked it that way. I had my folks and my brothers and I liked watching my nephew Joey grow up—we were real close. Sure, I had this fake leg, but I got along just great on my own. I had my job and I had my routine. This other thing was Bobby feeling sorry for me again, Bobby cooking up something to make me feel better. Which ain't what I wanted. I didn't need no glamour, no Palm Restaurant and no private planes.

But then I got to thinking: Here it was 1985, and how much longer did I wanna go on helping Mr. Grabelsky run his little jewelry booth at the diamond exchange? Did I like fighting my way through the subway mobs every day, eating my corn-beef hash at the luncheonette and going to the movies on the weekends? No. I was really sorta bored. I put up with it 'cause I didn't think I could do any better. And maybe—I was thinking to myself

—maybe this is what Bobby was telling me. The same thing Mom was telling me: to break out of my shell, kick in the door and say, here I am, and the heck with this routine, and I ain't afraid of nothing, 'cause I'm still the kid who can murder the ball whenever I please. Why not be as crazy as Bobby? Isn't that what I always wanted anyways? Just to close my eyes and let it happen —to forget what I was or what I could have been?

The next day I quit my job. It was tough, but I did it. Then I had lunch with Bobby and a few of his public-relations boys. Bobby was boasting about me and then got me to do some talking about baseball. The boys ate it up.

The next day we flew to California in Bobby's plane, *The Bum*. L.A. looked the same as last time except maybe the air was dirtier. At least it wasn't winter there. We had a bunch of hush-hush meetings with more public-relations guys. Everyone was nervous. Everyone was also a little scared of Bobby, except me.

Couple of days later there was an ad in the L.A. *Times* from a "citizen's group" that hated the idea of the Dodgers' being bought by foreigners. The ad was planted by Bobby. And the day after that there was a story on TV that said a big boycott of the Dodgers was being planned. Some big movie stars were part of the boycott.

I was staying with Bobby in a swanky house he had bought up in Bel-Air. Pools and tennis courts, the whole works. He didn't play much, though; he mainly talked on the phone, talking real fast and liking the fact that I was around listening to him talk. He always looked at me out of the corner of his eye when he talked. After each call, he'd half-explain what was happening—how he was putting together this financial package. But I ain't sure he was all that sure of the details. As best as I could understand, what it came down to was getting a heap of cash together and borrowing a heap more.

After about a week, I was really getting into the part I was playing. It was like a movie or something. Everyone was telling me how good I was. Lots of the money figures were still giving me trouble, but Bobby had them all written down, and he said that it was good if I sounded confused when I talked with Schmidt.

The boycott business was also starting to look serious. It was all over the papers and on the tube. Even Bobby was wondering how much of it was made up and how much was real. Maybe the fans out there really *were* fuming. This guy who Schmidt got to run the Dodgers was talking a lot to the press, sounding scared and saying that foreign ownership didn't mean nothing. That's also what the commissioner—W.W. Percano—said. Anyway, the thing was steamrolling, and I was thinking that I was almost ready, and Bobby and the boys thought I was ready, too.

They wanted to buy me a suit for my trip. They wanted to take me to Beverly Hills. But I said no, that ain't me. Bobby said I was right, so we went to some discount house and I picked out the suit myself. Light blue, like the ocean on a pretty day. Pick another, said Bobby. I did, and the second one was the color of a salmon. Black shoes, white shirts, the kind that didn't need cufflinks 'cause I hate cufflinks. And my tie was the kind where the knot's already made for you. I felt snappy, I felt ready. I slept good that night in Bobby's guest bungalow out by the pool, and the next day I flew to Germany.

Everything was legit. Bobby made certain of that. He really had gotten together a group of guys in the jewelry business with money to form this group. Some of 'em had big names, and they all knew what Bobby was up to, and they were happy to go along. There were also a couple of big bankers in on the thing. They were pals of Bobby's. Actually I think Bobby controlled their banks. Anyways, I was sure that it was all on the up-and-up. Because he wanted the team for real. And he knew that the deal would have to stick.

I felt real proud to be flying first-class. The seats were big and there weren't that many of us and right away the gal serving booze called me by my last name. I was sipping a little wine and snipping at the sirloin and having a big time. But when it came time for the movie, I couldn't even watch 'cause I had my papers to study and my job to do. I had to memorize how I was going to buy this baseball team.

It was January and Berlin was freezing. The snow never let up and I couldn't see much of the city, but it seemed real modern and there were lots of Mercedes Benzes buzzing around. My hotel room had its own fireplace and there was a terry-cloth robe for me hanging on a hook in the john. Very swanky. I slept all that first day and dreamed I was climbing a mountain and when I got to the top Bobby was there, waiting for me, holding a Dodger pennant. The next morning I swung into action, just like we had planned.

I woke up early and took a shower and put on the salmon-colored suit and decided to wear this V-necked sweater I had brought along. I was ready to roll. Naturally the taxi driver on the way over there didn't know a blessed word of American, and that was driving me a little nuts 'cause I could have used someone to talk to. I wanted to ask him whether the Germans liked baseball and whether he had heard of the Dodgers. I had this briefcase on my lap with all these notes inside and my head was full of what I had to say. I was nervous, real nervous. Suddenly I was thinking—what am I doing here? How can I pull it off? My stomach was a mess, and, if you'll excuse me for saying so, I felt the runs coming on.

The cab stopped in front of this glass building a hundred stories high. So modern it'd scare you. I paid the hack, got out, walked in the lobby, which was all chrome with no pictures or nothing. My stomach was still screaming, but then—don't ask me why— my head and my heart started screaming back: Why not? Why not me? I can do it. I can do anything I wanna do, I can be anyone I wanna be. As I took a few deep breaths I could feel all this courage flooding through my chest. I held my head high and I marched into the elevator and punched the button for the top floor, the executive suite. When I got out there was this waiting room that looked like a space station. The secretary spoke a lot better English than me and said that Schmidt was waiting for me.

His office was the size of a small gym. On the wall, instead of pictures of flowers and birds and little kids, were these black-and-white photos of factories and assembly lines and engines and computer parts. His desk was as big as my old apartment back in Brooklyn, but there was nothing on it except a thin gold pen. He looked something like a pinhead. His mustache looked like a gardener had cut it. I mean, this character was really neat. He had this real light German accent, and he talked like an IBM typewriter.

"I know you must be a busy man, Mr. Malone, and you've traveled a great distance, and if you care to outline your proposal for me, I'll be happy to entertain your ideas."

Entertain my ideas?

I knew it was time for me to talk. I sat down across from this cold-blooded gent and I did talk. I talked turkey. I thought about how much Bobby trusted me and how much he was counting on me and soon none of the stuff I was saying sounded ridiculous.

"You know what the publicity has been like in the L.A. market,

Mr. Schmidt," I said to him, happy I was using the word "market." "It's been real rotten. Nothing against you personally, sir, but no one out there likes the idea of anyone but a bona fide American owning the Dodgers. And because the team's been losing so bad recently, why that only makes it worse. The way I figure it, you'll be lucky to draw a million fans next year, and I say that, believe me, not to be nasty but only truthful, because even your local TV money ain't gonna be more than a third of what it was only three years ago, and—"

"Get to the point, Mr. Malone."

I stopped, I swallowed hard and I said, "We got the cash. Yeah, we got the connections and we got the cash to take this problem of the team and the ballpark off your hands right now."

"What do you mean by 'cash'?" he wanted to know.

"Cash is cash, Mr. Schmidt. Cash is as real as the hair on your mustache. Cash is when we sign the preliminary papers and I pick up the phone and have my bank transfer the money to your bank. Today. That's what cash is."

"Exactly how much cash are we talking about?"

"Half the purchase price."

He blinked his eyes real fast. He tapped his gold pen on his bare desk. He looked down and then he looked up. I could see the offer got to him; I could practically hear his heart hammering. The surprise was working. He was thinking hard, he was believing me. And right then and there I realized that though it'd take weeks to work out the details with lawyers and accountants, I was actually about to do it. Me. Squat, from Borough Park. Me who had barely made it out of New Utrecht High, me who hadn't ever made more than eighteen thousand dollars a year in my life. I was about to buy the Los Angeles Dodgers for over seventy million.

THREE

SOON AS I left Schmidt's building, I forgot everything I had memorized. All the numbers and the percentages and the stock plans that Bobby taught me came tumbling out of my brain like rainwater. And none of it mattered no more 'cause Schmidt believed me; Schmidt had listened to me talk for over an hour, Schmidt had bought my line.

I was happier than I'd ever been in my life, so happy and so proud because I could see that there were certain things I could do very well besides murder a baseball or weigh a diamond. I could look a big-shot businessman in the eye and get him to take me seriously. Oh man, I was feeling my oats. Flying home the next morning I even got plastered. I got bombed on the plane, put on the earphones and felt myself bouncing to the beat of the music just like the old days back at the Brooklyn Paramount when Bobby would find us a couple of gals and we'd dance in the aisles. And geez, I was thinking how long it had been since I danced with a dame, and then I saw that the lady next to me, who was wearing a man's suit and had the face of an angel, was smiling. Smiling at me. And she smelled like the first day of spring and I took off my earphones and introduced myself.

"I'm Squat," says me.

"I'm Jeanine."

"What do you do for a living, Jeanine?" I asked, feeling no pain and seeing that she was loaded with class.

"I'm a lawyer. How about you, Squat?"

"Me, I'm . . . I'm a . . . an independent businessman."

"What kind of business?"

"Sports. Yeah, I'm in sports. I used to be in jewelry, but now it's sports."

"What aspect of sports?"

Oh man, she was really interested and I was offering her champagne and she was accepting it. "The kind of sports," I said, "where I gotta fly around. Like I'm just coming back from Germany where I had this big meeting."

"That sounds intriguing," said she. "What was the meeting about, if I may ask?"

"Well, it's like this, Jeanine. You see . . . I dabble, I buy things here and there . . . and yesterday, well . . . yesterday . . ." I took another gulp of champagne and said, "Yesterday I bought myself the Los Angeles Dodgers."

Her eyes lit up. Her eyes were dark and beautiful, like the sky we were flying through. Her eyes said she believed me, just like Schmidt believed me, just like everyone was believing me. And now I started talking to her a lot, and I told her how I played ball myself, and then I mentioned this accident, and I tapped my leg, and I wasn't ashamed or nothing. I asked more about her and she told me that she worked for this big corporation and fooled around with contracts and had gone to a fancy school, but she loved sports and told me about when she played baseball as a little kid and was mad that the girls couldn't play with the boys. She said she always wanted to play with the boys.

Hours flew by and we were still gabbing, and when we landed in New York I decided not to fly out to L.A. but stay over in the city and see my folks and maybe offer Jeanine a ride over the bridge in a cab. She said swell. In the cab I leaned over and kissed her. Just like that. I stayed with her and all her high-class modern paintings down in her Village apartment with the record player blasting the music you hear in concert halls. And we danced, real slow. It was so beautiful. She was very kind, and I couldn't believe I was doing it, couldn't believe I was making it, now letting her see me in bed without my fake leg. This was my gift to myself for pulling off the deal. Jeanine said I was down-to-earth and sexy. Jeanine said I was cute and I was real honest. Which made me tell her about Bobby and how it was really all his money. Which made her like me more for being even more honest. I couldn't do nothing wrong with this dame. And afterwards, she said, "Thank you," just like that. And I was lying there thinking of this whole trip, knowing that this was one of the biggest thrills of my life. Which was even more reason to believe in Bobby and the crazy things he made me do.

I thought of asking Jeanine to marry me. And I probably would have if she hadn't told me that her husband would be flying in from Chicago the next day. I tried to act like I wasn't surprised, but she saw the look on my face and she said that made her like me even more.

"Does he treat you good?" I asked, expecting her to say no.

"Yes. But you're different, Squat. You're something special. And I hate to see you go, but the Dodgers are waiting for you. You'll make a woman very happy someday."

I told her she had a box seat at Dodger Stadium anytime she was in L.A.

I slept like a log on the plane out to the coast, and when I woke up we were landing. My heart started beating real fast. I was bringing home the bacon. And there was Bobby, waiting for me at the gate, and he had Ralph with him. Ralph looked terrific even though he said his ulcers were flaring up. Ralph drove us back to Bel-Air in the limo, and he seemed as proud of me as Bobby.

"You did it," Bobby was telling me in the car.

"It was a setup, kid. You set me up."

"You're a wheeler-dealer, Squat, and I assure you, you can do anything you want to, anything in the world."

I had to tell him about Jeanine, and naturally he loved hearing it. He slapped me on the back and said he wasn't surprised, that a jet-setting businessman like me was bound to get dozens of dames.

"Come on," says me. "I was just lucky."

"Lucky hell. You're hot. You've always been hot. It's just taken you this long to figure it out."

Maybe the kid had something there, I was thinking to myself as we shot up the San Diego Freeway, heading toward those rich hills where we and all the movie stars lived. It was one of those winter days in L.A. where you can see mountains behind mountains, and some of those mountains were all white with snow. And maybe I was something special, maybe Bobby really did need me the way he used to need me back there when we were hustling in Brooklyn.

"What do you think?" Bobby asked.

"It's big."

It was nighttime and Bobby and me were alone, sitting inside the Dodger dugout and looking out on the playing field of Dodger Stadium. The grass smelled cool and wet and I was watching those palm trees just beyond the fences swaying with the breeze. Bobby had his feet propped up and I was thinking—geez, how could one guy own a joint this big? I couldn't believe it, even now, those thousands and thousands of empty seats and all the lights and the scoreboard and giant instant-replay TV screen and the parking spaces outside. O'Malley once owned all that stuff, then Schmidt, and now Bobby. I was feeling great, knowing that I had done my part and pitched the deal right.

"Remember the night we climbed the fence at Ebbets?" he asked me, reading my mind.

"You know something, kid, that night I was thinking how the Dodgers belonged to us. I was really thinking like that. We had the whole place to ourselves and it was so crazy I was sure I was dreaming. Now that I been to Germany and back and actually talked to Schmidt in the face and seen that he was ready to sell, now I feel like it's still a dream—you taking over this joint and owning the team—but the dream ain't gonna end 'cause we ain't sleeping. The dream's gonna go on for a long time, and I'll just have to get used to it."

"It is quite amazing, Squat. It's quite a ballpark."

"I don't like it," I said quickly. "It's big and clean and everything, but it ain't Ebbets. It'll never be Ebbets."

"Everything's different, you and me and the Dodgers. But the differences are not necessarily bad."

I thought about what Bobby said. Was he different? Maybe. Calmer? A little. At least tonight, sitting here in the dugout. At least he had finally got something that he really wanted, really cared about. We stayed still for a long time, just looking around that huge stadium, thinking back to Brooklyn and ahead to next season, still trying to get it through our thick skulls that this was ours, that we had done it. I closed my eyes. A cool breeze was blowing all over my skin. I'd never felt better, and I took out a minute to give thanks for the good things that had happened to me—like hooking up with Bobby.

Then Bobby bounced up. He had found a ball and a bat in the corner of the dugout. His eyes were doing that little dance of theirs when he said, "How 'bout it?"

"Why not?" I answered. It had been a long time. Too long to think about, but somehow it seemed okay tonight. The right time and the right place, with Bobby walking out to the mound and me digging in at the batter's box. He took off the tweed sport coat he was wearing. He did a couple of deep knee bends. I took a few cuts. Felt the same. Felt great. The bat seemed real light. Maybe I had gotten stronger, but looking around that ballpark—with all its upper decks and the light of the moon shining down, the heavens full of stars and the infield dirt perfectly smooth—I felt like I was part of it all. Bobby and I were in the center of it all, where we were meant to be.

"Ready, Squat?" he screamed, and his echo circled out to center field.

"Ready as ready can be," I yelled back.

Barehanded, he wound up big and threw a wild one over my head. I laughed and limped after the ball, threw it back to him. "Take your time. Give me something good, kid."

He studied me, studied the plate. He knew he couldn't pitch too good, but when Bobby puts his mind to something, you never can tell. He wound up again, gave it a real big delivery, kicked and came off the top of the mound with all his might. I saw it coming in. I saw it was good, it had speed. I saw it and followed it and met it with every ounce of muscle in my fingers, my wrists, my arms, said hello and goodbye with one solid slam, a blast that cracked the night like thunder, that sent the ball sailing, with Bobby and me watching it rise, rise, rise—thinking about all those other times—following the path of the ball, up higher and higher, holding our breath 'cause it seemed too good, too strong —farther and farther out there in deep left field, up, up, up, sailing toward the top deck, out of sight, up there with the stars and the moon, traveling into space. Me and Bobby were jumping up and down and screaming like kids. That was the biggest and best hit of my life.

FOUR

BOBBY WANTED ME to go with him to New York to meet the Commissioner. He said it was important I come along. At first I figured he was saying that just to make me feel good. But then I seen he was serious. I seen he was maybe a little nervous about the meeting, and he could use the company. Plus, he said, I was an executive with the ball club, and I had every right in the world to be there.

Rumors were flying in the press about the team's changing hands, but Bobby's name hadn't come up. Not yet, anyways. But the Commissioner knew. Like Bobby said, the Commissioner knows every time every owner goes to the john.

"The Commissioner," Bobby was telling me as we were winging our way back across the country in *The Bum*, "is a tight-ass. They've all been tight-asses, all the commissioners. They're cautious and conservative and love to hobnob with power. That's their big thing—political power. W.W. Percano is the worst of the lot. He dreams of those days when the President or the Speaker of the House or an influential senator comes to a ballgame with him. In fact, I wouldn't be surprised if he has his heart set on becoming a politician himself. Depending upon the year, he might even make it. He has the politician's gift for saying nothing and doing nothing and acting like everyone's friend. I hate the asshole."

"How does he feel about you?" I wanted to know.

"He doesn't love me, that's for sure. He probably would have tried to block our scheme if he had learned about it in time. He thinks I'm a wise guy and he thinks wise guys are bad for baseball. I even suspect that he would have tried to block the sale if we hadn't done such a bang-up job with the public-relations campaign in L.A. But right now he wouldn't dare go against public sentiment—which will be very strong, especially when the story breaks that the Dodgers are back in American hands. He doesn't like it, but I'm certain that he knows that now he has no choice but to play ball with me. And surely the thing which bothers him most is the fact that I'm alone, that I'm independent, and that I really don't need him. He knows he can't control me—he'll never be able to control me."

The next day, in the limo going over to the Commissioner's office, Bobby got stoned. That sorta worried me, but I figured the kid knew what he was doing. He was nervous, and this was his way of relaxing. When the limo pulled up to Rockefeller Center, my stomach turned a couple of cartwheels, maybe 'cause I was feeling what Bobby was feeling. I knew this was a big deal.

The Commissioner looked like an owl, if you can feature that. His head was long and round and bald and his skin was very wrinkly and saggy. His office smelled like the old-fashioned lotion that the barber slaps on the back of your neck after a haircut. His fingers had just been manicured, and when you shook his hand you knew he had spent a lot of time in the shower that morning.

"Everything said in this office," he told us right off the bat, "will be held in strictest confidence."

"Why?" Bobby wisecracked. I could see that this was going to be trouble.

"Discretion, Mr. Hanes. I am a believer in discretion."

"And I," said Bobby, "believe in candor."

"Quite," coughed the Commissioner.

Me, I was a bug in the rug. I was feeling real excited just being there and watching the mental action.

"Mr. Hanes"—this was Percano talking—"let us minimize the possibility of misunderstanding between us. Let us, as gentlemen, speak, as you suggest, frankly, remembering, if you will, that it is my duty to act solely in the best interest of the game of baseball."

Bobby turned and winked at me, and Percano saw the wink. Bobby wanted him to see it. Bobby was toying with the guy, which, to me, didn't seem the smart thing to do.

"You asked me here, Mr. Commissioner," said Bobby, "and I came, anxious to show your office all the respect it's due. I know there are questions you want to ask me, so please, sir, fire away."

The Commissioner opened his middle desk drawer and fished out a pipe, which he stuffed and lit. He let us wait. I used the time to look around the office, which had pictures of Percano with the last three Presidents. There was also a shot of Percano hauling in a big fish and a color photo of his wife, who looked like Mamie Eisenhower.

"My sources have indicated," said the man, "that you have made an offer to the Schmidt Conglomerate of West Germany for control of the Los Angeles franchise. My sources further report that the offer was made by a group headed by Mr. Malone but, in fact, financed by you, Mr. Hanes."

Bobby said nothing. Just grinned, which naturally drove the Commissioner a little buggy.

"And?" Bobby finally asked.

"Come now, Mr. Hanes. There is no reason for us to play games. I want to know whether this was, in fact, your offer, whether it has been accepted, and what the terms of that offer cover. Having determined what transactions have occurred, we will then do what we deem necessary."

"Who is this *we?*" Bobby challenged.

"This *we,* Mr. Hanes, is *me.*"

"I am not at all sure, Mr. Commissioner, whether this is a propitious moment for me and Mr. Malone"—I liked the way he included me—"to reveal the details of our offer."

"You understand, don't you," Percano shot back, "that no franchise change of hands can be realized without the full consent of this office and the approval of two-thirds of the owners of the National League teams?"

"Mr. Malone and I have read the rules, Mr. Commissioner."

"I have other pressing matters to deal with this morning, Mr. Hanes, and I would appreciate your detailing the proposed purchase of this franchise."

Percano leaned back in his chair and puffed on his pipe, trying to look calm, though I could feel that Bobby was definitely rattling him. Bobby felt it, too, which was probably why he reached in his coat jacket, pulled out a joint and lit up. I wanted to hide under the desk.

"I find your action offensive," said the old man.

"I mean no offense," Bobby lied.

"You are only hurting yourself, Mr. Hanes. I can assure you of that."

"When I am ready, Mr. Commissioner, I will present you with the facts and figures."

"I suggest, then, Mr. Hanes, that you ready yourself immediately. I have already called a National League meeting to be held here in New York precisely at nine-thirty tomorrow morning in the conference room of this office. Each owner, or a legally authorized representative of the owner, will be in attendance. The sole purpose of the meeting is to evaluate your proposed purchase of the Los Angeles franchise. This will be your one and only opportunity to make a formal presentation. If more than a third of the owners are not satisfied with the full package you detail—the financing of the team, your executive organization, your plans for promotion, your own personal experience in these matters and the experience of those working for you—then whatever has taken place between you and Schmidt will not be worth the paper it is written on. I wish you luck, Mr. Hanes, though I'm certain you'll do just splendidly. I imagine you've been working on this presentation for weeks. In the meantime, I'll be happy to have my secretary show you to the door. I'm not sure that in your present state of illegal inebriation you'll be able to find it. Good day, gentlemen."

And with that, the old geezer gave us the heave-ho.

You'd think Bobby would be blue that night. You'd think he'd be worried. But he wasn't. He was just mad that Percano was such a creep. I almost told him that it wasn't all Percano's fault, that Bobby had asked for it. But I clammed up 'cause I knew that Percano reminded Bobby of the Judge—I saw that the minute we walked into the office—and I also knew that the whole thing had been a trap. Percano had tomorrow's meeting planned all along. Even I could see he was trying to ruin the deal.

"You did well in there today." Now Bobby was talking to me over dinner at some swanky Italian restaurant.

"I didn't do nothing," says me.

"You looked tough. And it makes me feel good, Squat, to see you out of the corner of my eye looking so tough."

"The really tough guy is the Commissioner."

I wanted to say more, but I stopped myself. Bobby was nervous enough without me telling him how I was scared. "But what about that stuff for tomorrow?" I asked instead. "All those facts and figures and marketing business that the owners wanna hear. How're you gonna have time to pull it together?"

"It's nothing to be concerned about," he said coolly. "In fact, I'm thinking about having you give the presentation."

My heart hit the floor. "Don't even joke about that, kid. I ain't saying nothing to those owners."

"You sold Schmidt, and you can sell them. The pitch is virtually the same. And I have a feeling that they'll love you. You don't realize how your sincerity shines through, Squat. You have rare integrity, unhampered by the lusts the rest of us share for outrageous luxury and wealth."

"You got the wrong boy. First off, I forgot everything I said over there in Germany. And second off, I ain't ever talked to more than two or three people at one time. I don't do good with crowds, Bobby. I promise."

"We can review the facts together."

"*You* can review the facts. I'm going to bed early. I'm bushed."

Bobby saw that I was serious, and he laid off. "What about all those experts back there in L.A.?" I asked him. "Ain't those guys supposed to know something about baseball management? I mean, those advisers you told me were pulling down five hundred a day to tell you how all this stuff works."

"What do they know that we don't? High-priced bullshit artists —that's all they are. Most business is bluff. Surely you've learned that by now, Squat. The owners themselves are pretty much in the same category. It's a different level of bullshit, to be sure, but it's bullshit nonetheless. I've talked to many of these chaps over the years. I've run into them in some of the better boardrooms. They also consider themselves experts—experts on finance, on promotion, on the recruiting of a team, and naturally on the strategy of the game itself. They're experts the way the Judge was an expert—by virtue of the fact that they bought themselves not simply a toy, but the entire toy factory. They're experts because they can fire you if you demonstrate their lack of expertise."

I loved it when Bobby talked like this.

"For the most part, these are the men who have ruined the game," he went on, puffing on his thin cigar and sipping his brandy. "They've yanked out the grass and glued down the plastic. They've been intimidated by the greed of their players, the greed of the free-agent system. They, and their public-relations flacks, have turned the game into a suburban lawn party, and nothing's real anymore, not the way it was real when we were kids."

"But that's 'cause we ain't kids, Bobby."

"Speak for yourself, Mr. Squat. This whole baseball business has shaved at least twenty years off my life. I've never been happier about anything I've bought. I'm a teenager again, Squat, and so are you, and this is what we were always meant to do. This is our destiny. Nothing can stop us."

"Except that meeting tomorrow."

"We'll be brilliant, I assure you."

"I still don't know what you're going to say."

"Neither do I, which is what makes it all so exciting."

The conference room was as big as a basketball court, and all the guys were already there, sitting and staring at us. They looked a little puffy—red in the cheeks and fat in the tummy. Percano was sitting at the head of the table, grinning like the cat who just swallowed the canary. Next to him was Roy Trapp, the president of the National League, but really the boy who carries the Commissioner's water pail—at least that's what Bobby said. I figured, just smelling out the scene, that Percano must have just put the bad bite on Bobby, 'cause this group seemed mighty grim. More and more, it was looking like an ambush.

We sat down and then Percano started up. "Gentlemen," said he, "as we have already discussed, we are here to consider the matter in which the Los Angeles franchise, held by the Schmidt Conglomerate of West Germany, was—"

"Listen, men." Bobby suddenly shot out of his chair, taking me and everyone else by surprise. "I'm sure you're tired and bored with these kinds of meetings, and besides, everyone knows that if you don't approve my deal I'll hire four dozen lawyers and sue organized baseball and undoubtedly win. I don't have to tell you the antitrust and restraint-of-trade decisions have all been going against the major sports leagues recently. So instead of meeting here and listening to me go over two hours' worth of tedious facts and figures, I move we adjourn to the bar upstairs—which I've reserved for our private use this morning—and I'll be happy to answer any and all of your questions, personal or private. Will anyone second my motion?"

And before the Commissioner had a chance to open his mouth, Charlie Greenstreet, owner of the Miami SunKings, seconded the motion and everyone was up on their feet, chattering and happy, something like little schoolkids running out of the classroom at the first ring of the bell.

We went up to a private club with all these big glass windows and the city surrounding us. The men sat at tables and Bobby stood in the middle of the floor, walking around, talking and doing a little dance for everyone. He didn't seem worried at all. "The only real issue," he began, "is whether I can help you boys make more money next year. That's all there is to it. If L.A. collapsed as a franchise—and that seemed as certain to me as the German occupation of Poland—then each of you would be the big loser. The gate at Dodger Stadium, of which you get forty percent, has always been the biggest in the league, and, if these past four years are any indication, it will continue to decline at an alarming rate. Foreign ownership will only accelerate that decline. I modestly propose that I'll be able to turn the team around. And as to the most critical question—am I financially strong enough to take on this club—after five minutes, I think you'll no longer have any doubts." Bobby took five minutes to rattle off the money facts, proving that the team would be, as he put it, "far from cash-poor." When that was done, he dipped back into the bull: "There is an issue here, though, that goes deeper than the soundness of my fiscal prospectus, copies of which will be arriving here in a few minutes from my accountant's office. That issue is loyalty. That issue—if I might use an old-fashioned term—is patriotism." Geez, was he ever playing to the crowd! "That issue is the integrity of a tradition—the Dodger tradition —which is as important to me, as pure and sacred, as the dreams of a little boy who sits at his first baseball game, certain that life is full of wonder, grace and honor."

Quiet. Then one guy started clapping—I think it was Greenstreet—then everyone, louder and louder. Bobby gave the bartender the nod and the booze started to flow. Bobby made his way from fat cat to fat cat, working the room now with his special brand of high-class polish. He had talked to them as a group; now he'd nail them one by one. He told Pete Blatsky, who owned the Cubs, about all his memories of Wrigley Field and how he would legalize pinochle gambling in the grandstands and how Blatsky's father Saul was the greatest paper-cup salesman in the history of America. He congratulated Jason Honnerstein of the Pirates on the birth of his first grandson and asked to see pictures. He talked horseracing with Jim "Bucks" Baxter of San Diego for a half hour

—I don't know where Bobby learned this stuff from, but Baxter owned a couple of nags and was crazy for the trotters. Bobby was in top form, especially when he told Tug Leavis of the Reds that the Cincinnati–Dodger rivalry would have to be revitalized, not only for the sake of attendance—both clubs had been hurting at the gate and in the field—but because it was a matchup made in heaven. He told Harris Dives, who looked like a walrus and who owned the Giants, the same thing. For a long time, Bobby and Charlie Greenstreet, the only other guy there in his forties (everyone else looked like he was pressing seventy), talked about Jamaican grass and Cuban cigars and traded a few cock-and-bull stories about broads—that's Greenstreet's style—but with J. Peterson Vaux, a dead ringer for an undertaker, Bobby asked a bunch of questions about the Rotary Club, because Vaux, who ran the Cards in St. Louis, was the Rotary national president. "Freemont!" Bobby went after Freemont Mintz, with his wavy blue-gray hair and white cowboy boots. "I was just comparing the Astros the other day to the 1955 Dodgers. I sincerely believe that they merit such a comparison," and for a long time Bobby talked about the man's team that had been doing so good the last three years.

At one point the Commissioner tried to shut off the bar and get the guys talking again. He said there had to be more questions about Bobby's financial stability and ability to take over a big-league baseball team. But no one was listening, not once Bobby was on the loose, slapping backs and filling everyone's ears with everything they wanted to hear. He had done his homework after all. He knew wives' names and pitchers' era's from thirty years ago. He told a funny joke about a girl sportswriter in a locker room, and the joint howled while the Commissioner scowled. And then, just when I was feeling a little left out, he stopped the party and introduced me as his "lifelong pal." All of a sudden my stomach got real queasy and he said I was from the streets of Brooklyn and had a better feel for baseball than anyone in the room. He told 'em how I had gone to Germany and closed the deal for him. He talked like I was some sort of hero, and naturally I turned red, but I could see how glad everyone was to have the Dodgers back in American hands, in Bobby's hands. They believed in his bull and his bank account, and when I looked around for the Commissioner and his man Trapp they were nowhere to be found, which didn't matter much because the party went through lunch into the afternoon. A couple of the guys—Bucks

Baxter and Tug Leavis—had to be helped to the elevators, and another one—I think it was Blatsky—fell down 'cause he was laughing so hard when Bobby told the story about how the people who lived high in the apartments on Bedford Avenue overlooking Ebbets one day in the '40s shined mirrors reflecting the sun into the eyes of the Cubbies who were trying to bat. This was a real important game, and the umps went nuts and they threatened to forfeit the game against the Bums, which is when the ump behind the plate got hit in the back of the head with a balloon filled with water. And Bobby, he was playing like he was the ump, then he was the fans, then he was the people with the mirrors, then he was the Cubbies trying to hit. Not always, but sometimes, Bobby could be everything—and this was definitely one of those days.

FIVE

DODGERS BOUGHT BY AMERICAN TYCOON!
N.L. OWNERS APPROVE SECRET PURCHASE BY BOBBY HANES;
GERMANS SELL FOR REPORTED $80 MILLION

I looked out the window of the little jet as we were pulling up to the terminal, and there were all these press people, and one of 'em was holding up the L.A. *Times* with those headlines screaming across the top of the page. We were just pulling in from New York and Bobby was a little bombed—he was entitled—and I was feeling great. As soon as we got off the plane we were mobbed by these characters screaming questions at Bobby, taking pictures and treating him like he was the King of Sweden or something. He loved it.

By now, everyone knew everything, and they were asking if he was worried that Percano would still try to queer the deal. They wanted to know how much cash we put up for the team and would there be a new manager and whether we'd be dipping into the free-agent market. "I've absolutely no money left," Bobby said. He was grinning and wearing his World War II leather bomber jacket and a red silk scarf. "Besides," he had to add, "free agentry is little more than highway robbery. There are other ways to build a great baseball team." They asked him how, and he wouldn't say except that the Dodgers had a winning tradition and it wouldn't be long before they'd be winning again.

"Is it true that you sabotaged the Commissioner at the meeting yesterday?" one of the writers asked.

"Not in the least," Bobby lied. "This entire enterprise has been conceived and realized in a spirit of cooperation and mutual respect. This is more than a financial investment for me. I didn't buy the team to make money. No, this is an investment in something greater than dollars and cents; it's an investment in the future of . . ." And Bobby was off, lapping up the questions and loving the attention. That day it was all over the radio and all over the TV and everyone was happy, everyone thought we had done great. In one paper there was a front-page picture of Bobby with his hands clasped over his head like a prizefighter: HANES'S TRIUMPH!

While the press stuff went on for the next couple of days, me and Pee Wee, who I'd brought out from Brooklyn, went searching for apartments. I couldn't live with Bobby anymore in Bel-Air. I had to have a place of my own. I settled on Silver Lake, which is this quiet neighborhood not far from Dodger Stadium. There were loads of brown people around, which reminded me of Brooklyn, but in other ways it was different. There were all these hills and cute little houses with tiled roofs and stucco walls and tiny gardens and giant skinny palm trees everywhere you looked.

I found a small house to rent on Westerly Terrace. It had two bedrooms, a fake fireplace, a backyard and this big picture window which looked out on a row of those palm trees, way off in the distance, which always gave me a thrill. I hadn't been there more than a day when Bobby showed up.

He was still wearing his leather bomber jacket, still high from all the excitement and news about him. He came in and gave the place a quick once-over, peeped into the bedrooms and examined the furniture. He shook his head.

"Don't like it?" I asked.

"It's not that. I just don't understand why you'd take a place this small when you can come over to the other side of town and pick out anything you want and charge it to the club. It's a business write-off anyway. You do understand that, don't you, Squat?"

"I understand that I gotta fall asleep at night, and to do that I gotta be comfortable, which means having my butt resting where it belongs."

Bobby stopped and closed his eyes and turned his head up to the ceiling. "Either you're an idiot or a genius," he said.

"Ain't either one. I'm just a kid from Brooklyn."

"Who's about to become a general manager of the Los Angeles Dodgers."

"Is that what carrying your attaché case is called?"

"I love you for your humility, Squat, just as I loathe you for your low opinion of yourself."

"You're nuts. I'm crazy about me. I think I'm doing swell. I got a little kooky flying back from Germany, but I've settled back down here and maybe I'll even be able to keep you from flipping out."

"I *love* your house!" Bobby started shouting. "I *love* it! I think it's perfect, Squat, and it's modest and sincere and all of your best qualities. I wish *I* could live here. Hell, I might. I might rent a house across the street. I might even start taking the bus to the stadium."

"You're full of more crap than the city cesspool. I heard you complaining that there wouldn't be enough privacy for you on the Dodger team plane, and I seen those catalogs for new Lear jets you been looking at."

"Hurry, get dressed, Squat, because we're about to fly through the clouds. I've called my first major news conference for noon today at the ballpark, and I don't want to be more than an hour late."

"Thought about what you're going to say, kid?" I asked as we were about to walk into the room where the press was waiting.

"I haven't the faintest idea."

It was a circus inside. More cameras and cables and sound men and photographers, and at the front where Bobby was going to stand were about thirty mikes all squeezed together. He kept on his bomber jacket and walked right through the room. Light bulbs were popping in his face. The noise got louder. He smiled a big broad smile, held up his hand for everyone to shut up and then started in on his act.

"Thanks so much for coming out today," he said. "Thank you for your interest and thanks for your continued support. I'll be brief; I know you have questions and I want to get to all of them.

I'd simply like to say that the Dodgers are back in safe hands. At a different time and in a different place, this ball club was my first love. And so it remains. And so it will be forever. You can understand, then, that today represents the realization of a long and beguiling dream which has lingered not only in my imagination, but in the imagination of my close friend and associate, Mr. Squat Malone." I felt goose bumps all over, embarrassed, proud and happy. Which was when a bald-headed reporter with granny glasses jumped up and asked the first question.

"You must know better than anyone," said this guy who looked very antsy, "that the Dodgers' fortunes have fallen faster than any team in sports in the past five years. It has been widely rumored that your purchase was more emotional than practical —that is, you bought the team for strictly sentimental reasons. In the light of this, Mr. Hanes, and the fact that major-league baseball has generally suffered a severe blow from the astronomical rise in fuel costs in the past decade, how do you propose bringing people back to Dodger Stadium especially when the markets hardest hit have been precisely those, like Los Angeles, which are dependent on automobiles?"

"I'm not a negative thinker," Bobby shot back. "So let me only say that people will come see a winning team—they'll come if they have to take the bus, if they have to hitchhike, if they have to bounce over here on pogo sticks. Our objective will be to win ballgames, and once that's accomplished, I feel certain that your question will be irrelevant and, perhaps, so will you." Bobby was smiling. Somehow he said this without sounding mean, and the room rocked with laughter.

"Let me see if I can find a friendlier face," Bobby said, scanning the press until he stopped at a woman with long, beautiful, curly red hair and dark black-framed glasses.

"There has been a long string of inexperienced club owners" —she rose and spoke in a very businesslike voice "—who have tried and failed at what you're doing, Mr. Hanes. And the pattern is usually the same: An extremely wealthy individual seeks diversion from his primary means of income—oil or hamburgers or bus lines—and toys with a baseball team. But because of the individual's lack of experience and specific know-how of on- and off-the-field management, the enterprise collapses within a season or two and, once again, the team is sold. Why should we believe that your experience here will be any different?"

"As you are well aware," Bobby came back, "there has been an outpouring from the people of Southern California against the foreign money controlling the Dodgers. A number of grass-roots groups—true-blue Dodger fans—have been publicly protesting the transaction for months now. I certainly don't think I'm fooling myself by saying that there is a tremendous popular sentiment favoring this sale. I know I have the goodwill of those fans, and I'm certain that they see this as much their victory as mine."

"It's been reported," she kept pushing, "that you manipulated that so-called popular sentiment."

"Reported by whom?" Bobby was getting mad.

"Reported by me, for one."

"And what were your sources, may I ask?"

"My original question was never answered, Mr. Hanes. And my original question was: How will you overcome the inexperience that has plagued other first-time owners?"

"What am I supposed to say to you—that I'm smarter than the others, that I'm slyer or shrewder, that I have more money and insight into baseball, that I plan to make brilliant trades, so brilliant that I'll be remembered forever in the annals of the game? You've asked me to boast, and if I refuse, you'll claim I'm ducking your question."

"Then you have no answer," she raised her voice.

"You have no question," he raised his.

"I will repeat my question for the third time, Mr. Hanes. Why should the people of Los Angeles, or for that matter, baseball fans everywhere, believe that you really know what you're doing?"

Oh God, I was thinking to myself, this gal's really going for the throat. The room was so quiet you could hear the fluorescent lights buzzing. I saw Bobby's face tightening.

"Are there other, more specific questions?" Bobby asked.

"Then you do not intend to answer mine," the lady shot back. She was still standing up.

"I consider it beneath me."

"Do you consider it beneath the million or so viewers whom my station represents?"

"I will answer professional, not personal, questions. This press conference was not intended to indulge the gossip columnists among you, but to accommodate the legitimate sports reporters."

Right about then I leaned over and asked a guy next to me who this dame was. Oran Ellis, he said, from Channel 2. He looked at me like I should have known her, like everyone knew her.

"How much money," this Ellis gal was asking, "do you plan to spend on new talent for the team? And what positions do you intend to strengthen—and when?"

"If I revealed that, I would be depriving you of stories for the rest of the year."

"Then you don't know, or you haven't thought about it."

"I didn't say that."

"What did you say, Mr. Hanes?"

"Only that you're dominating the questions and that your questions are stupid."

"You are insulting."

"You are embarrassing yourself. You have pretenses of being a sports journalist, and yet if I were to ask you the simplest question about the very team you cover, I would wager a considerable sum that you wouldn't have the answer."

Now no one in the room was saying anything. Everyone understood what was happening: Bobby had dared her.

"Go right ahead, Mr. Hanes," the Oran Ellis lady challenged.

"I'd be interested in the most basic information on the history of the Dodgers. Nothing esoteric. Nothing obscure. Nothing more, say, than the first time the team won the pennant."

A second didn't go by before she took off her glasses—I saw now that she was really pretty and probably not even thirty years old—she looked him in the eye and rattled off, "Not counting their crown in the American Association in 1889, the Dodgers won their first pennant their maiden season in the National League in 1890. They beat Chicago by six games. Bill Mc-Gunnigle was the manager. They also won the crown in 1899 and 1900 under Ned Hanlon and in 1916 and 1920 under Wilbert Robinson. Any other queries about early Dodger history, Mr. Hanes?"

Now Bobby was smiling—what else could he do?—but inside I knew he was a little sick.

"She's obviously a sexually frustrated woman," Bobby was saying when we were alone in his office. The press conference had just ended.

"I thought she was pretty sharp."

"How can you say that, Squat? The woman's a bitch, a trained and merciless bitch."

"Come on, kid. She's paid to do that stuff. It's a job. Like the wrestling matches. She's supposed to give you a hard time."

"She's hopelessly attracted to me, and this is her only way of dealing with her emotions."

I laughed out loud.

"Stop it, Squat. You're no better than she is."

"You're taking this too seriously. You did good today, believe me."

"I did?"

"You knocked 'em dead. You showed 'em you were tough, and that you weren't taking no bull. Which is why they'll be back for more and they'll put your puss all over the paper tomorrow and everyone'll be talking about you and the Dodgers and maybe we'll sell some season tickets, which is why you should really give that Ellis lady a commission."

"What she needs is a good stiff—"

"Don't be nasty, kid. It ain't your style and it don't do you no good."

"I didn't know that you were in the practice of defending the honor of lady reporters."

"Bad vibes are bad for everyone. I'm just saying that you had one job to do and she had another."

"I could undoubtedly get her fired if I wanted to. I could buy that two-bit TV station and yank her off the air so fast her head would spin."

"I think it ain't so two-bit. I think it's the biggest TV station in town. But go ahead and buy it anyways, kid, 'cause we don't have enough to do with the Dodgers now."

Bobby broke the seal on the Scotch bottle and poured himself a healthy hit.

When I went home that night and sat around my little house, I was still thinking about it. Thinking about Ellis's questions and Bobby's answers and wondering if maybe she didn't have something there. I wondered so long and so loud that my brain was all disturbed, so I decided to take a walk over to Silver Lake, which I think is really a reservoir that just happens to look like a lake. I couldn't get her face out of my head.

Her face was different with and without her glasses. With glasses, she was all business, tough. Without 'em her features softened. I saw that the lake was calm and the moon was a little sliver, and my mind was still on her. Very classy dame, this Oran Ellis, and she didn't back down an inch—which took guts—and she did seem to know her stuff. I mean, look at the way she knocked out everyone with her answer. I couldn't take this thinking no more, so I went back to the house. I turned on the news and there she was. Right there on Channel 2 at eleven-fifteen, staring into the camera and looking better than she had that afternoon. She was wearing a green silk blouse, and I could see that she was sorta busty. She had beautiful green eyes and that red hair, which was now sitting in a bun on top of her head. The guy who reads the news was saying, "I understand, Oran, that Los Angeles was introduced to the new owner of the Dodgers today. You were there, and why don't you tell us about it?"

"That's right, Larry," she said as she straightened up her notes and started talking with a whole lot of poise. Underneath her, the words SPORTS EDITORIAL flashed on the screen. "Robert J. Hanes, Junior, an internationally known businessman, gave the official word today at Dodger Stadium: He's now running the ball club. Hanes, whose bus line in California has become the most profitable in the state, hopes to repeat the feat with a baseball team which shows all the signs of permanent disability. The price of the team has still not been made public, though rumors have placed the figure between seventy-five and eighty million. There was a time when the Dodgers were called the most lucrative sports franchise in the country, but today the transaction raises a number of questions. First, does Hanes, who has never operated a sports team before, have the know-how to run the club? Second, is he willing to spend the necessary money on player acquisition and free agents? Traditionally, the Dodger organization has been reluctant to shop the open market, preferring the slower but less costly process of cultivating player product from their own farm system. That system has ceased to work, and one would have to go back to the last half of the '60s or perhaps the '30s to find a Dodger squad this undernourished in talent and spirit.

"Not all the signs are gloomy, however. Demonstrations of displeasure with the West German conglomerate's prior purchase of the team may well mean that the public will greet Hanes as something of a hero—if indeed those demonstrations were genuine. But whether such popular affection will turn to ticket sales remains to be seen. And finally, the question tonight must remain: What can Mr. Hanes do about the Dodger dilemma?

"I remember Mr. Hanes's mentioning you this afternoon, Mr. Malone." Man, her voice sounded sweet.

"Squat, call me Squat. Mr. Malone is my dad back in Brooklyn. Used to work at the Brooklyn Navy Yard. For over thirty years. Me, too. Not for that long, though. But that was just after my accident." Nuts! I heard myself blowing it. I was sounding like a moron.

"And Mr. Hanes has appointed you general manager of the team, Mr. Malone?"

"Squat. Everyone calls me Squat. He told me I could do anything I wanna do with the team. You see, I play ball. Or at least I used to. I was a catcher, and a lot of people had me tagged as Campy's replacement. Pretty fair hitter, too. Bobby and me, we been tight our whole lives, though naturally he's a lot different than me. I probably know him better than anyone, and you could have really lit into him on the tube tonight, the way you did at the press deal this afternoon. I thought there were very hard feelings between the two of you, but now I'm glad to see you cooled down."

"I like to think of myself as a responsible reporter, Mr. Malone."

"Squat. You sure are, Mrs. Ellis."

"Miss."

Boy, was I glad to hear that! "Oran—you mind if I call you Oran?"

A few seconds ticked by and she said, "Of course not. By all means. You're sweet to phone. In fact, this is one of the nicest calls I've received in weeks. It's wonderful to know that my work is appreciated, especially by a sports executive. Thank you, Mr. . . . Squat. I hope we can get to know one another better. In fact, I'm making myself a note right now to call you in the next week or so. Perhaps we could have lunch."

"When?" I blurted out, and I almost said, "Tomorrow," but stopped myself in time. I was going too fast. I told her goodbye and got off the phone.

Lunch, I sat there thinking, she was going to call me for lunch. No girl ever invited me to lunch before. Never. And especially one that looks like this gal. Oh man. There was no way I could fall asleep. I was bouncing around the house. Finally, I picked up the phone and called Bobby.

"Didn't wake you, did I, kid?"

"No. I'm going over figures for the food concessions."

"You didn't happen to watch the tube tonight, did you?"

"Of course I did. I was on every report. I had all my video recorders humming. I have everything on tape."

"See that dame Oran?"

"Every minute of it."

"She could have been a lot nastier."

"The woman's a hypocrite."

"You got her wrong, Bobby. I think she gave you a fair shake. Matter of fact, I did something crazy—I called and talked to her down there at the station."

"I know."

"How do you know?"

"I spoke to her after you did."

"You called her or she called you?"

"She called me looking for an exclusive interview, first thing tomorrow morning."

"And?"

"I told her I'd think about it. I told her to call me later in the week."

SIX

I WATCHED HER on the news every night; I seen her covering basketball and hockey and interviewing the players and giving her own opinions. She was for real, this lady; she could nail anyone she wanted to, especially the coaches, who'd be bulling a mile a minute. She wasn't afraid, and she acted something like a star—not too snotty, just real confident—and I also seen that she had all the facts and figures right there at her fingertips, and that's why I had to respect her.

At the same time, I was trying to figure out what my job was. I had this big office, which made me feel sorta ridiculous. Bobby was down the hall and for the first two days he was on the phone every minute and I couldn't even get to talk to him. He was working hard. He had shaved his beard. I had the roster of all the players, and Bobby told me to figure out what changes I'd make and what moves I'd recommend, and then we'd talk as soon as he worked out the food concession business and the broadcasting rights, which, naturally, was stuff I didn't wanna mess with. Whenever I'd walk to his office, he'd be busy—still on the phone, or meeting with someone—and tell me nicely that we'd get together later. So I'd go back to my desk and think a while about why the Dodgers had been such a lousy team and I'd figure out who I'd can and who I'd try to buy. It was just like being a little kid playing. Some of the other execs working there would come in and talk to me, 'cause they knew I was close to Bobby. These guys were all worried about their jobs, and they tried to tell me that the team couldn't get along without them. I was nice to all of 'em, 'cause I hated to see grown men squirming like that, but I really didn't have nothing to say except that soon I'd be meeting with Bobby and knowing more about what I was doing.

I was also worried about Oran Ellis. She hadn't called and I was getting a little antsy, and I didn't know whether Bobby had given her that interview. I figured I could talk him into it. He usually did everything I asked, since I hardly ever asked anything. But maybe I should wait for her to call me—that's how I was thinking. After all, she was the one who was after this Dodger story.

The hours passed slowly that first week, but I knew how to be patient, I knew Bobby had all this pressure on him, and I hung in there, and I finally did call Oran at the station but she was out on a story so I left my name and number. By then—this was Friday —I had cooked up a couple of dynamite trades in my head, and I was real anxious to tell Bobby about my ideas. At the end of the day I walked down the hallway to his office. His door was half open but he was on his speaker phone, the kind that broadcasts everyone's voice all over the place. I stopped just before I walked in; I recognized the voice coming out of the box. Schmidt. He was talking to Schmidt. Something told me to freeze, so I stayed in the hallway, where Bobby couldn't see me, and I heard every word that was said.

"You're a good sport to call," Bobby was saying, acting real nice. "I would have never suspected you of being a gentleman, Konrad, but now you have forced me to reassess my opinion."

"The least I could do was offer you my congratulations on your astute purchase. Nothing pleases me more than to see you in control of the team."

"True gentlemen are never sarcastic, Konrad."

"Sarcasm is not my style, Mr. Hanes."

"I can understand why you'd be peeved about the way we went about making you our offer, but—"

"Peeved? Far from it. You don't think for a minute, do you, that your Mr. Malone was convincing? He was quite amusing, but let me assure you, Hanes, that Mr. Malone and his quaint Brooklyn manners were nothing more than a joke to us. We saw your fine hand behind this scheme very early in the game. And to be quite candid, we were anxious to be fooled, simply because we were anxious to sell. I had come to the conclusion that we had drastically overpaid for the club weeks before you initiated your so-called public-relations effort to turn public opinion against us. We hadn't anticipated the ten-percent leap in real-estate taxes, which, on a property such as Dodger Stadium, is a most radical increase. In fact, we were worried about the prospects of finding a buyer for the park and the club—worried, that is, until your preposterous Mr. Malone came along. So I did want to call you and, once again, thank you for helping us out of this unpleasant and potentially unprofitable situation. It is good to know that we have American business friends, such as yourself, willing to—"

Bobby started to say something, but I had heard enough. I turned around and headed back to that bare office where I had been goofing off all week and picked up the phone and called my dad in Brooklyn and told him I was coming home.

"Why?" he wanted to know.

"Can't talk about it now, Pop."

"Anything wrong?"

"Everything's wrong. I'm coming home and that's all there is to it. I can't talk now."

I felt like hell. Bobby had fooled me. He fooled me that I had fooled Schmidt. All this was just a game to those guys, and I didn't understand the game, and I didn't know how to play it. I felt real dumb and real useless and real used. And worst of all, I had fooled myself into believing that I had actually done something for Bobby like helping him buy the Dodgers when all the time everyone was looking at me like I was some kind of dumb joke. How could I have been such an idiot? What did I know about high finance? I didn't belong here. And if I wasn't so proud, I'd be crying, because where I really belonged was down on that baseball diamond—that's where I've always belonged. I didn't wanna be no mascot. I didn't need Bobby to feel sorry for me and give me these phony-baloney jobs. I could work on my own and make a decent living and get along just fine. I hated this free ride and tagging along like I was a cripple or something.

Forget it. Forget the whole business—this Dodger Stadium and this Los Angeles and these palm trees. I went home and I packed and I didn't say nothing to Bobby. In the back of my brain, I had seen it coming. I had known I was just here like some kind of toy for Bobby. Because Bobby had been holed up in his office and the reason he didn't have time for me was 'cause he had nothing for me to do. Let him fly around in his airplane and live in swanky houses, because I had seen enough of that stuff to last me the rest of my life. I was getting out and nothing was going to change my mind. The phone rang. It was Bobby.

"I've been looking for you."

"I'm leaving."

"I don't understand."

"I'm going home. I'm going back to Borough Park."

"You're kidding."

"I already made a reservation for the first thing in the morning."

"What the hell is going on, Squat?"

"Ask Schmidt."

"Schmidt?"

"Ask him what he thinks of me. Ask him how I bought the team."

"Shit. You heard him talking to me."

"I didn't have to hear him. I knew before. I knew I wasn't no executive, and I knew I wasn't fooling no one, and I knew that you knew. Everyone knew, and now I'm sick and tired of thinking of me flying over there and back and being so proud and all the time it was a joke."

"Squat, listen to me. Schmidt's trying to save face. We've had a running feud for years, ever since I bought a Japanese transistor plant away from him at an incredibly cheap price. He's never forgiven me, and he'd say anything to make me think that he screwed me. There was also this lady. He'd never admit that I—"

"You can save your bull, Bobby, 'cause I already seen what I did and I know I got no business here." And I hung up, just like that. A minute later, the phone was ringing again, and I knew it was him, so I let it ring. I wasn't changing my mind—I got my pride. I looked through the window of the living room, up at the palm trees way out there in the distance, and I couldn't hold it back anymore, so I cried. I put my face in my hands and I cried for a very long time. I felt like a dumbbell, a grown man like me, crying like a baby.

I must have fallen asleep there on the couch, 'cause when I heard the ring of the phone I reached for it automatically and said hello before I remembered that I didn't wanna talk to no one. But by then it was too late, and I heard Oran asking me if I wanted to meet her for a drink. At first I said no, and then I said yes, and she gave me the address of a bar and grill on Melrose Avenue in Hollywood. She said it was a nice old-fashioned place.

I liked the joint because it reminded me of New York. It was narrow and dark and not too fancy, and a hockey game was on the color tube. I got there a little early 'cause I didn't like the idea of her having to wait alone in a bar. Never can tell what might happen to a dame in a situation like that. I ordered myself a beer and drank it real slow 'cause I didn't wanna get drunk. I wasn't sure that I really wanted to be there, but I was leaving tomorrow morning, and this was the only time I'd ever get to talk to this Oran lady, and I figured I owed it to myself.

At five after ten Oran showed up carrying a big briefcase and wearing a man's suit, except that it had a skirt, and of course men don't wear beautiful white blouses like the one she had on. Also men don't smell like lilacs and roses, and when you shake a man's hand the skin doesn't feel so smooth, and most men don't have long curly red hair. And neither do most women—not like Oran's.

"Squat," said she, looking me in the eye, "finally we meet. I'm glad." She talked just like that. Real enthusiastic and everything. I was still feeling glum, so I didn't say much.

"You look a little down." She smiled at me.

"Like something to drink?" I changed the subject.

"Vermouth on the rocks, please."

A classy drink, I thought, and called the cocktail waitress over to our table in the corner.

"I'm leaving tomorrow," I said, figuring I might as well level with the lady.

"I heard something about that, Squat."

"What do you mean? How'd you find out?"

"You forget. I'm a reporter, and the Dodgers are my beat."

"Who could have told you? No one knows except Bobby."

The vermouth arrived, and she took a sip. "I spoke with him late this afternoon."

"He talked to you?"

"He said he was granting the interview only at your insistence."

"You're putting me on."

"Those were his exact words."

"Geez, I wouldn't have figured that. How'd the interview go?"

"Miserably. He was quite hostile."

"That's 'cause he figured you're out to get him."

"Or because he was so depressed about you."

"He talked about me, huh?"

"He talked of nothing else."

"What'd he say?"

"I got the whole story—all-city catcher at New Utrecht High, brilliant rookie season in Montreal, the best baseball instincts since Reese. He puts you in the same category as Campanella."

"Bobby's the best bull artist there is."

"You've shaken him up by quitting. He's afraid."

"Bobby? He ain't afraid of nothing."

"He's afraid of this baseball team he's bought. He's afraid that he doesn't know what he's doing. And that's one of the reasons he's afraid of me. I've sensed his fears, and he realizes that. He may be over his head this time. Baseball's a tricky business."

"Not for Bobby. Bobby can do anything he wants to do. He's a genius. Anyone who knows him will tell you that."

"But you're leaving him in spite of that."

"What did he say about my leaving?"

"Simply that you had gotten mad and quit. That you didn't feel useful."

"You're too young to remember this," says me, "But when we were kids there was a song called 'The Great Pretender.' Real pretty song. Well, that's me. That's just how I felt. Pretending that I was doing something when I really wasn't doing nothing."

"Sounds like me when I began covering sports."

"Come on. You must have been one of those tomboys. Not that you don't look good. But I figure you were a big sports nut even when you were a kid."

"Oh, I was. I've always loved sports, always been competitive, good at tennis and swimming. I was a guard on the girls' basketball team at the University of Missouri. But none of that mattered when I decided to become an on-the-air reporter. I had had no formal speech lessons, I knew nothing about broadcasting, and my only experience was writing for the college paper."

"So why didn't you just get a job on a newspaper?"

"That didn't seem like enough. It seemed too easy. And besides, I wanted people to look at me."

Now here's an honest dame, I thought to myself. "That must have been easy to pull off."

"It wasn't," she said. "I fumbled around for years at local stations in the Midwest, trying to feel my way around the camera. No one took a female sports reporter seriously in those days, and the going was rough."

"But you made it."

"Not entirely."

"You got a big job."

"At a local station. I'm still at the local level, and L.A. is not New York. National television news is run out of New York."

"So you ain't happy here."

"It's a step for me. It's major-league reporting—the Angels and the Dodgers, the Lakers, the Rams, the Kings, UCLA and USC. L.A. is a big sports town, though my audience is still regional. But here I am talking about me when I came to find out about you."

"You're not married, Oran, are you?"

"I was."

"Oh." I felt silly now that I had asked the question.

"No harm in asking," she said. "We've been divorced four years. He was a decent guy, a lawyer, but he resented the time I devoted to my work."

"He was jealous of your job."

"Yes, in the extreme. It didn't help that I made more money than he did."

"Some men are like that. Some men don't respect dames. But me, I see them as the same as us—except for certain things which we all know about." Now she was laughing and finishing off her vermouth. I ordered her another one, and she wanted to know about Bobby.

"We're all a little nuts," I said, "but maybe he's a little more nuts. Good at heart, though. A good kid."

"But not enough to keep you around?"

"I'd stay if I belonged. But I ain't interested in being no 'Great Pretender.' "

"Do you think he's pretending, Squat?"

"Bobby's different. Bobby's always pretended, but once he pretends that he's someone, he actually becomes that person, or does the thing he needs to do. That's why this Dodger thing ain't gonna do him in."

"You have more confidence in him than he has in himself."

"The only thing he's never done that he wanted to do was play baseball real good. He wasn't bad, just average. But average never made him very happy. He wanted to be great."

"The way you were great?"

"I could hit the ball. I could definitely get around and hit the ball."

We talked for an hour like this, and I gotta confess that it was one of the most amazing conversations that I ever had with a lady. This Oran was easy to be with. Real open and honest, like she had no secrets and wasn't trying to hide nothing. I could see she was on the make—for a big story, a break to get more people looking at her. She definitely liked to be looked at, and I definitely liked doing the looking. When it got to be about midnight, I asked her if I could give her a lift home, but she said she had her car. I still didn't know exactly what to think, but I could tell she liked me. She had to like me to be talking the way she talked. But I also knew—after all, I wasn't born yesterday—that she was using me to find out stuff about Bobby. For every question she asked about me, she asked ten about him. Even though I was still ticked at him, I wasn't about to say anything bad.

"I hate to see you leaving the organization, just when we're getting to know one another," she said as I walked her to her car across the street in the lot. It was a little chilly, and I would have liked to put my arm around her, but I didn't.

"Those are the breaks," says me. "Maybe we'll meet up one of these days."

She took my hand and shook it, and her skin was as smooth as a baby's behind, and the moon was shining in her eyes.

It wasn't my alarm that woke me up the next morning, it was the sound of a helicopter roaring over my house. I figured the cops were chasing some bum, but the terrible noise was getting closer and closer and then I heard someone shouting really loud, through a bullhorn, screaming so loud that I could hear the voice above the chopper blades. Bobby was yelling, "You asshole! You come out of that house with a suitcase and you'll be shot on the spot! You're not going anywhere! Who do you think you're fooling? You want this team as much as anyone. *More* than anyone. Who do you think you are to act like a prima donna?"

I put on my bathrobe and walked out on the front lawn. This chopper was hovering over me by about twenty feet and I saw Bobby in his leather bomber jacket with the bullhorn at his mouth and he was still screaming, "Okay, so I ignored you a little last week, but I was busy, and I apologize, and I just came over here to say that I need you, honest to God need you."

Everyone—all my neighbors—ran out of their houses. They were all running down the block to see this strange show. "I need you, Squat," Bobby was still yelling, and the helicopter landed on my lawn. I got in, and we went up—up, up, up—over the hills of Silver Lake and Echo Park, over Chavez Ravine and Dodger Stadium, over the freeways and past the skyscrapers of downtown L.A., with me and Bobby shouting at each other over the roar of the blades, trying to figure out who was going to be on first and who was going to be on second, and what we were going to do with this second-division ball team.

SEVEN

I HAD FORGOTTEN the way the red dirt in the infield smells, how it kicks up when someone goes in for a slide at second base. I had forgotten how gorgeous those new bats look—blond and brown and black—stacked in the rack. They're like cannons, just standing there, waiting for the sluggers to grab 'em and blow the pitcher off the mound.

Here I was—in Vero Beach! At Dodger spring training! You can imagine what was going on in my mind and in Bobby's mind when we walked around the place. This was Dodgertown, which was a magical name to us when we were kids living through the freezing winters in Brooklyn. We'd dream of the Dodgers playing down here, and there were memories and photos all over the place of Erskine and Preacher and Cox and Labine when they used to train down here in the old days.

I had to pinch myself. I was here, Bobby had gotten us here. This was the real deal. Baseball. The Dodgers in their white-and-blue uniforms. Everything I dreamed of when I was a kid—the big leagues, the team I loved with all my heart. And there I was, out on the diamond with the rookies and the veterans on the first day of spring training. Everyone was treating me nice 'cause they knew who I was—they knew I had played and that I was tight with the boss and that I had something to say about this ball club —and it only took an hour for me to wander over to the batting cage with everyone kidding me. "Go ahead, go ahead, Squat," they were shouting—and sure, sure I had to step in and take a few swings. Oh man. It was like life came back to my body, the blood rushing through my brain. I held that bat and blasted the first pitch—okay, it was a lob, but I still blasted it, sent it sailing out, out, out, over the fence. Everyone was cheering me, and I think I let out a little hoot. I'd been working out at the gym now for so many years—lifting weights and building up my arms and chest—and I knew that, even at my age, I was strong, maybe stronger than anyone on the team. On about the third or fourth pitch, I hit another one out, and I spotted Bobby over behind third base grinning from ear to ear—like he had done it, not me —and I knew it was right that I was back in baseball.

Those first hours of spring training were so delicious. I felt like a hero. Even Oran was down there, and she had seen me hitting. Afterwards I went around the field and gave tips to the guys, which came natural, 'cause they were all asking me stuff and they liked the way I got out there with 'em and had something to say about sliding or stealing or hit-and-run and just about anything. I gotta admit that I do know the game.

At first, I was a little worried that Blank Hendricks, who had managed last year, wouldn't take to me and might be ticked that I was giving out all this advice, but when he saw that I was on his side, when I told him I was definitely recommending that Bobby keep him this season, he started liking me. Don't get me wrong. Hendricks was no genius field manager, but he could figure out a batting order and none of the guys hated him, so I thought he deserved another year. We had enough to fool with without changing skippers. Besides, even though Blank was kind of a blob of a guy, he was a nice blob.

By the end of the afternoon, I was pooped. I had been running around like a little kid, and my good leg was aching and I thought maybe I had overdone it. I went back to my room, where I was gonna nap before dinner, and there was this note from Oran under my door that said she wanted to see me that night. My heart started beating a little faster, but I stopped myself from getting too worked up 'cause I knew she just wanted a story. She was looking for an angle, which was Oran's business. I called over to her motel.

"You were fabulous today," she said to me, which is just what I wanted to hear.

"Thanks. It felt so good to see some real baseball. I forgot how much I love it."

"You've been stuck in the office."

"Geez, you're right. Too many charts and projections and computers and scouting reports. I didn't wanna hear nothing more about contract negotiating, 'cause that's Bobby's business anyway, not mine. Mine's down on that playing field."

"I've been surprised that Bobby hasn't done more negotiating. I would have guessed he'd initiate a more aggressive acquisition program."

"We decided to go light at first. Blank is gonna stay"—I heard myself giving her one good story—"and we ain't going to rush in and try to conquer the world right now. Besides, Bobby's singing the blues about money."

"He's posturing, trying to protect himself in contract negotiations."

"Maybe, but he ain't buying no players, that's for sure."

She sounded disappointed, like she had expected word of a juicy trade.

"Can we meet for dinner?" she asked.

"Sure." I didn't hesitate. "After my nap."

I tried to sleep, but I couldn't. So much going on up there in my noodle. Thinking about Oran, thinking about Bobby, going over the past weeks in L.A. Bobby had been pretty good about paying attention to the team. He hired this new staff of college-educated guys, a few of his old frat brothers, and stuck 'em in different positions like promotion and ticket sales. For the most part, though, he was on top of things himself and concentrating on learning the ways of big-league baseball. Me, too. After our little blowup, I was in on all the big meetings, and when they were over I'd tell Bobby who I thought was bulling and who was being straight. He'd usually listen to me and usually I was right. I even was the one that found the new TV announcer, who'd never be as good as Barber or Scully—those guys were geniuses—but he knew baseball, and it was actually Oran who tipped me off to him. You see, Oran and I had become friends by then.

I never took advantage of Oran. Maybe I could have, and maybe I couldn't. But she and me talked about that very early on, and we decided that if we started rolling in the hay that would probably foul up the good vibes between us. I also remembered that I had to be careful about what I told her. I just couldn't run off at the mouth and start blabbering about the team. I knew I was what she called a "news source," and that was okay; we could use the press to sell tickets, and knowing Oran was like having a friend in court. Not that I went around talking to Bobby about her. Whenever her name came up he'd usually say something nasty. He hated the idea of her covering the team.

I just couldn't nap with Oran and Bobby bouncing around my brain. Finally I showered and dressed and went to the restaurant.

She was already there, wearing a pink skirt and this T-shirt top which had me squirming a little. We sat on the patio and the Florida breezes were blowing all over the land, real sweet and easy.

"I meant to tell you," I said while we were waiting to order, "that I liked how you uncovered that big scandal in the junior colleges. Imagine, those jocks taking courses that didn't even exist. I loved the way you nailed 'em, and I seen that you weren't afraid, even when you were talking to the deans. I hope you got a big raise."

"I didn't. Unfortunately, the men I worked for are not as enlightened as you. In many ways they remind me of Bobby. I suspect that they're afraid of me."

Here we were, together for only two minutes, and we're talking about Bobby. "You think about Bobby too much," I had to tell her.

"It's hard not to, being here in Dodgertown. You have to admit that he *is* all over the place, inviting every reporter he can corner into his office for an interview. Everyone but me. He's a hopeless ham. He can't get enough publicity."

"He's just trying to help the team."

"He wants his picture in the paper—it's as simple as that. He cares less for this team than you imagine, Squat. In fact, I have a theory that within two years he'll lose interest and sell. He'll be bored playing with his toy, and he'll buy himself another. Mark my words. As soon as the going gets rough, he'll get out."

"You got him wrong, Oran. He's been doing good. Once in a while he'll fool around with his freighters or his oil deals, but mainly he's thinking about the team. I been real proud of him. He's stuck with it."

"Where was he last weekend?"

"Oh, that was just one of those times when he took off and went to Mexico with some dame for a few days."

"I see," she said with ice in her voice. A couple of seconds passed, and then she added, "Anyone I know?"

"You're pumping me too hard."

"I'm just doing my job," she said too loud.

"That's what concerns me about you, Miss Ellis," Bobby said, coming from nowhere, standing right next to our table, looking cool in his resort duds. "You take your job far too seriously."

He took a table in the corner and had dinner with some pretty blond babe, and for the rest of the night I could see that Oran was having a tough time not looking over there.

The biggest day was the opening game of the Grapefruit League, the kickoff of the exhibition season. This was really something special, 'cause the Yankees were coming to Vero Beach. Everyone was up for it, and as I looked around the field watching our guys take batting practice, I realized how, in just a few weeks, I had become comfortable with them and how they liked me and kept asking me baseball questions. But I also realized that this was the first game the Dodgers were playing for Bobby and the first time he'd be watching *his* team in action.

Him and me got to the ballpark early. I could see he was a little nervous, and I could understand it, 'cause after all we were playing the Fascists. Playing the Fascists was always serious business. Bobby's eyes looked real serious, and he was suntanned in the face. He was dressed all in white, with this wide-brimmed white hat and his blond hair flowing out on the sides and the back. He had started growing his beard back, which was only a couple of weeks old and gave him sort of a tough cowboy look. Bobby was always growing and shaving and regrowing that beard.

We sat behind third base, in the middle of a big crowd that was already there even though the game wouldn't start for another half hour. The crowds were always good at Vero Beach. There were kids and their daddies, but mainly the old people, the retired folks who lived around there. A lot of them came from New York, and they loved watching these games and throwing around the bull 'cause they had so many memories. I could see how Bobby was losing his nervousness about the Fascists just by being around these old guys. He loved them a lot. And he'd start talking to them and they'd start telling him about the old days in Brooklyn. This one came from Park Slope, and that one lived on Fourth Avenue. They were excited and naturally they knew who Bobby was from the newspapers and naturally he loved being recognized, but he also loved the Brooklyn stories, especially when they talked about the old Dodgers, how Lefty O'Doul had won the game that day with a clutch hit against the Giants in 1931. "Yeah," Bobby would add, "the year he came over from the Phils." And then they'd ask us questions about the current team. They'd want to know, for instance, whether Blank would be back as the manager. Bobby wouldn't answer directly, he'd use it as an excuse to tell a Brooklyn story of his own, and, believe me, Bobby could tell a story.

"When I think of Dodger managers," he said, "I always think of my favorite, the most outrageous of them all, Leo the Lip. Naturally he was somewhat before my time, but when Leo was with Brooklyn he was a holy terror. He wasn't just a manager and he wasn't just a player, he was both. He had guts. And no one in the history of the game did anything gutsier than Durocher when, in the bottom of the ninth with the score tied against the Cubs in Ebbets and the winning run on third, Durocher pulled the next hitter, who was none other than Dolf Camilli—Camilli, mind you, who was leading the Bums in homers and rbi's. Leo pulled him for a pinch hitter and the crowd went crazy booing. They started throwing bottles and sticks and small children into the infield. They couldn't understand what Leo was doing. Here was the team's leading hitter up with a golden opportunity to win the game, and he wasn't going to hit. The Lip was sending in a pinch hitter, and the pinch hitter was none other than—listen to this—Leo Durocher!

"Imagine the reaction. The fans rained down their wrath, the fans were crazed beyond reason, they wanted Leo's head on a platter, but Leo wasn't afraid. Leo did what he thought was right. And he chose his bat, and he took a few cuts, and he marched up to the plate, and he snarled at the pitcher—it was Vern Olsen, I believe—and he laid down a perfect bunt on the first pitch—the squeeze play was on—and the runner came roaring in from third, and the play at the plate was close, but he was safe, and we won the game. In less than a second the fans went from sour to sweet, mobbing the man they had been prepared to murder only minutes before. Now that was Brooklyn."

You should have seen these old people's faces. They started applauding Bobby, like he was an actor or something—which he was—and I loved it that he made them so happy, and he loved them because they made him less nervous. Now we were ready to play ball.

Seeing those gray visitors' uniforms of the Yanks did something to me and Bobby. Changed the mood again. Our mouths were getting a little dry, especially when the Fascists scored a couple of runs the first inning. Their slugger, Newt Cane—a meatball potatohead from Texas or Oklahoma or someplace—got hold of an inside curve and hit it out. Cane was one of those farmboy freaks who was strong and mean and either fanned or hit the thing a country mile.

They scored again in the second inning—a walk and a couple of singles. Our pitcher, Tom Alvarado, was young and fast and wild, and this was just a tryout. I kept reminding Bobby that the game didn't count. But in the fourth—we still hadn't scored—when Blank pulled Tom after he had given up another three runs, Bobby started mumbling how Tom had been left in there too long. Bobby also didn't like the way Blank was using pinch hitters, and he didn't think Howie Fassbinder should have gone in for Alvarado.

"Blank missed at least two golden hit-and-run opportunities," said Bobby. "These fucking Fascists are running over us like we're tin soldiers."

In the seventh inning it got bad. We were losing 9–zip, but the worst part was that we hadn't gotten a hit. Mick Greene, a run-of-the-mill southpaw, was throwing fire, and, as the game went on, Bobby began to give me strategy messages to take down to Blank. I wouldn't do it. I told Bobby that was bad business. The game was only practice, and he couldn't start up like this—not now, not in the first contest of the Grapefruit League. And when I wouldn't budge, and when the Yankees scored two more runs in the eighth, I saw Bobby starting to lose control, yelling stuff to Blank in the dugout, telling him who he wanted out on the mound.

By the top of the ninth the Yankees scored four more on three stupid Dodger errors, and I realized that me and Bobby were seeing for the first time how miserable this season might be for us. We didn't have no pitching, no fielding, no hitting. Which don't leave much. I tried to stay cheerful and kept saying how exhibition games are like jokes, but Bobby wouldn't say a word. He was sitting there fuming, watching Newt Cane again, who was up to bat and had already smacked two homers, a triple and a single. Cane was brutal, and by this time I wasn't paying that much attention when I saw him swing a little late. Suddenly the ball came whizzing right at us and I tried to stick out my hand and catch it but it came at me like a rocket and hit the side of my throat and knocked my breath away, knocked me off my seat. At first I couldn't breathe, but Bobby was there calling for a doctor and this guy came hurrying over and lifted me up and saw I was all right. But by then Bobby had charged down to the field and jumped over the railing and gone for Newt's throat, and they were wrestling on the ground with the umps trying to pull them apart. That night the Commissioner issued a statement saying that Bobby would not be permitted in any major-league ballpark, including Dodger Stadium, for the first two months of the regular season.

EIGHT

"*THIS IS PERHAPS* the most undistinguished Dodger team of this century. They're pathetic, Squat, and I'm afraid they're only getting worse."

Oran was talking to me. We were sitting at a table in the private club high in the stands that overlook right field at Dodger Stadium. It was the end of May and the sun was shining brown rays through the smoggy air. We were lucky to be sitting in this air conditioning. On the field, we were getting beat by the Padres. What else was new? We had wound up in last place in the Grapefruit League, and now, in the regular season, we were in the same spot. Fact is, we were so deep down there in the dark cellar that I was thinking maybe we'd never find our way out.

"There's a bright side to this," I said, trying to convince myself. "The team's spirit ain't all that bad, and, besides, there's more to this game than winning or losing."

"Yes, there's attendance. The average gate thus far is the lowest in the history of the Los Angeles franchise, already twenty-five percent lower than—"

"Know something, Oran? If you weren't so pretty, I'd belt you, I really would."

She smiled. She was wearing this yellow summer dress, and her hair was so red you wouldn't believe it. Such a pretty dame, but she could drive you nuts with these stories she was putting on the tube—all real downers.

"I can't blame you, Squat. You work for the man and you are right to remain optimistic. I admire that. But you also must understand that I wasn't hired by the station to tell fairy tales. I'm not in public relations. I'm in hard news."

I looked out on the field. Bottom of the seventh. We were still behind 3–1. The fans were standing and stretching and singing "Take Me Out to the Ballgame." All six thousand of 'em.

"Oran," I told her, "you got lots of influence. Lots. You give those reports of yours every night, and whatever you say, the folks believe. Am I right or am I right?"

"I have a certain influence, but that influence is based on credibility."

"Don't fling those big words around."

"The audience believes me because I tell the truth."

"What's the truth? You can say the Dodgers stink, but I see that the guys are trying hard and I think they'll get better. Or you can say the Dodgers stink and are getting worse every day. Say the first thing and fans stay away. Say it a nicer way, though, and everyone's happier. Right?"

"I could have been a cheerleader in high school if I had wanted to. But I didn't. Hanes doesn't need me to flack for him. He has his own flacks."

"You calling me a flack?"

"Of course not, Squat. You're a strong and independent soul, but you're also blinded by Bobby—just as he's blinded by himself."

"You talk too fancy."

"You don't want to understand. You refuse to see him for what he is."

"You think about him too much, baby. You write about him too much."

"He's a major story. Ever since 1958 the Dodgers have consistently been the hottest ticket in this town. Now that's ending, and your Mr. Hanes is acting the part of the undertaker. He's planned the funeral."

Now I was really getting mad, 'cause I honest to God didn't think she knew nothing about Bobby. "He wants to win more than anything in the world," I told her. "He didn't come to L.A. to lose. Bobby ain't no loser."

"Certainly. He sees himself as the great macho hope of modern baseball. He's going to save the Dodgers, breathe new life into them. But tell me, what's he's really done? In one dazzlingly impetuous move, he paid an inflated price for a deflated team. He kicked out the Germans and reclaimed the Dodgers for America. But then, faced with running the club, with spending money on new talent, with wrestling with the day-to-day complexity of management and—"

"Honey, I hear you on the tube all the time. I know your line."

"You tell me, then. Has he been paying attention to the team? Has he been working on trades, on developing the farm system, the—"

"How could he do any of that stuff? He ain't even allowed back in the stadium till next week. You're forgetting that Percano barred him from the office."

"Is his telephone at home not working? Is he unable to have meetings in his house?"

"He's been a little down, but you can understand that. He went away for a while to forget about that Percano thing. He felt real out of it."

"He's afraid."

"He *ain't* afraid!"

Now she smiled, and the air conditioning blew a whiff of her sweet-smelling perfume my way. How could I really get ticked off at Oran? All she had to do was look at me.

"What's he going to do, Squat? You tell me."

"We got plans."

"Spell them out." She took out her notepad and pen.

"To win some ballgames."

She laughed. "One season," she said. "Now I'm giving him only a season before he quits. Yes, I'm revising my prediction. He won't even last two years. And what's more, he'll find a way to sell for a profit. No matter what, though, he won't stay. He doesn't have the temperament for this."

"He'll surprise you. Bobby's gonna surprise everyone."

Down on the field we were coming up for our last licks. Harv Binder, the best hitter we got at .268, was up first. He fell down striking out. Oran didn't say nothing, just made a little note. Next two batters dribbled out to the pitcher. We lost again.

"Everything'll be different next week," says me, "when Bobby gets to come to the ballpark and run the club in person."

"Different," Oran said, "but worse."

I still wasn't convinced, 'cause I knew better, I knew Bobby Hanes better than anyone in the world, and it was only a question of time before he would do the right thing, whatever that was.

Later that night, with Oran's words still shooting through my brain, I went to Bel-Air to see Bobby. He had just gotten back from some swanky island. I hadn't heard from him in a week, and I was sorta worried. When he opened the front door for me, I could see by his red eyes that he was ripped. He hugged me, and his breath stunk of pot. Other than that, he looked good. His beard was bushy again, bleached by the sun.

"Just who I wanted to see," he said, leading me into the huge den with all the wood and the bookcases. This was really a spiffy house. "Someone sent me a heretofore unknown picture of the Judge with General Patton. Can you believe it? Let me show it to you."

I looked at it. They were shaking hands and beaming at the camera.

"I've been thinking," Bobby went on, "about what the Judge would say about this Percano feud. Naturally he'd think I acted foolishly. He'd say the whole purchase was self-serving—that's just the word he'd use, 'self-serving.' And I'd argue with him, I'd defend myself for hours on end, but after the debate had ceased and I'd be alone, I'd hear that phrase again and again reverberating through the echo chamber of my mind—'self-serving, self-serving'—and I'd know he was right. The Judge might have been a tightass, but there was no fooling the old bastard. He could always nail me anytime he wanted to."

"No one's gonna nail you once this team starts winning, kid."

"Your optimism is heartening, Squat. If only it were rooted in some reality."

"You'll feel a lot better when you come down to the ballpark next week."

"The Dodgers need to catch fire. Or we need to light a fire under their ass. Or fire them all. Which is probably what we should have done to begin with. Except that I'm not sure what ten million in the free-agent market would have gotten us. A couple of wise-asses. Two or three golden boys who, in between their TV commercials and talk-show stints, might have consented to play a few games for us. Ah, to be a superstar in today's market—to demand five-year contracts and ten percent of the team, security for life and peace of mind for all eternity! Can you see me, Squat, dealing with one of those clowns? Or his battery of lawyers and agents? No, I was wise to stay away. And I'm beginning to think the more I stay away, the better off I am."

"That's crazy talk," I said, thinking about Oran's prediction. "We've just gotten started."

"Of course, of course. What's the big deal? Who cares if we have a mere twenty-five million in yearly expenses? So what if salaries are costing me a meager five million, if the Dodger jet requires a million and a half to run, if the bill for Vero Beach was a modest two mil? Hell, it's all peanuts. Baseball is nothing but peanuts, and who wants to worry about peanuts? Only elephants or fools. Which makes me think that I may sell this team at the end of the season and buy a circus instead, dress up as the ringmaster, complete with my top hat, my whistle and my whip."

"That ain't funny!" Now I was mad. "I don't like it when you talk that way."

"Where's your sense of humor, Squat?"

"Baseball is fun, Bobby, but it ain't no joke. It's serious."

"Then perhaps we've made a serious mistake."

"Buying this team was the best thing you ever done, and don't ever forget it. You owe it to yourself and to the Dodgers to give it your best shot, and if you don't—"

"What then? Will I burn in hell? Will I be beaned by baseballs forever? Will I be evicted by the Almighty Umpire in the sky?"

"You'll hate yourself."

"You see this too personally, Squat. You're getting too involved. This is one of several investments I've made. If it works, fine. If not—"

"It ain't no investment, and you know it. You know darn well what the Dodgers mean. They're everything we ever wanted to be, Bobby. If we stop believing in the Dodgers, we might as well stop believing in ourselves."

"Horseshit. You've been seeing too many Disney movies. Now let's switch over to a little reality," he said, cutting off the conversation by flipping on the TV. It was newstime and there was Oran, sitting at one end of the desk, waiting to give her report.

"If you were really interested in helping us, Squat," said Bobby, "you'd stay away from that bitch, she who bears only malice for me and the Dodgers. She takes what you say and then twists it, turning the public's mind against the team. She's a wicked woman, a false friend and a swift pain in the ass."

"I talked to her today about not being so negative," says me. "I put it to her real straight, and I'm hoping something sunk in."

Just then Oran began her report. She had on her glasses, and behind her was a chart with lots of numbers. She explained: "The sinking saga of the Los Angeles baseball franchise continues." *Oh God*, I moaned to myself. "Just for the sake of comparison," she went on, "I've pulled together some statistics. Since financial information is a tightly held secret within the Dodger organization, these are merely estimates. Certain facts, though, are public. Such as attendance. This curve, for instance, represents the total gate over the past five years, which you can plainly see has dipped . . ."

"Goddamn bitch!" Bobby was shouting at the tube. "Does she have nothing better to do than bore sports fans to death with this drivel? Is this how you turned her around, Squat? Listen to how positive she is!"

"The Dodgers," Oran was saying, "once the most celebrated money-makers in modern baseball, are in the ironic position of becoming perhaps the most celebrated money-losers. And if there is any solution to this dilemma, surely it rests with Bobby Hanes, whose time in the penalty box, you will remember, expires this coming week. We're all looking forward to Mr. Hanes's next move. Will he be able to bring his winning ways to the Dodgers, or will he—as so many sophisticated observers are predicting—write it all off as a bad investment and return to the somewhat less arduous task of driving buses?"

Bobby flipped off the TV and went to the bar, where he poured himself a big shot of booze. He slugged it back and started stalking the room.

"I don't like the way this thing is going, Squat. I don't like it one bit."

"This two-month-fine business has been tough on you, kid. That's all." I tried to calm him down.

"What do I need this kind of pressure for?"

"It's not pressure, it's pleasure. It's baseball, Bobby, and we love it just the way we always loved it."

"Love changes, Squat. Love can turn cold. And sometimes when a love is driving you crazy, you realize that it's not love after all. It's just some mad obsession. It's childish, and it needs to be forgotten or destroyed."

"*Never*," was all I could say before I got up and left the house, driving out of those swanky hills, smelling the sweet night and trying to keep my head from busting wide open.

NINE

TO CELEBRATE HIS first day back on the job, Bobby held a press conference. He figured that if he was coming back, he might as well come back with a bang. And to make sure that it wasn't just another routine press conference, he decided to make an announcement. He decided to can our manager, Blank Hendricks, something which I learned at the same time as the reporters.

The conference was held in his big office, and when he walked in thirty minutes late he was wearing a Dodger uniform. He didn't say anything about it; he just had it on—with a cap and cleats and everything. Naturally the press started asking him about the getup and Bobby said, "This represents my commitment to the Dodgers. Today I am a Dodger."

Oran, who was sitting next to me, frowned, even though I whispered to her that he looked pretty good in that uniform since he wasn't fat or nothing.

Then he said Blank was out and Jim Cobb was in, and in walked Jim Cobb, who wasn't wearing a uniform yet. Bobby said all these glowing things about Cobb—how his talents had not been appreciated in Seattle last year and how lucky the Dodgers were to have him. And then, in his usual manner, he got off the track by talking about the great Dodger managers—Uncle Robbie, Casey, Leo, Shotton, Dressen, Alston and Lasorda—and he said how they had all won at least one pennant, and so would Jim Cobb.

"That's wrong," Oran spoke up, rising to her feet.

"What's wrong?" Bobby wanted to know.

"Those managers you mentioned. They did *not* all win pennants for the Dodgers."

"What are you talking about?"

"Stengel. Casey Stengel never won a pennant for Brooklyn."

Bobby pulled a book from a shelf behind his desk and looked through it furiously and when he came to the right page I could see that she was right because his face was turning pink. He yanked off his cap and stared at her and didn't say anything—he didn't have to; everyone knew. He started to talk about the promotional push he was about to put on. The plans were real sketchy, except he sounded excited—which was a good sign, I thought. Except for the news about Blank, there wasn't much to the press conference, and twenty minutes later everyone filed out and me and Bobby were alone.

"You could have mentioned something about Blank to me," I said to him.

"I was going to, Squat, believe me, but this was one decision I wanted to make on my own. You were the one who convinced me that I had to rekindle my interest in this team, and this was my way of doing it."

"You think Cobb's that good?"

"He's cheap—that's one thing in his favor. Actually, I don't have much faith in any manager. With few exceptions, baseball managers are emotionally retarded. And the reason for this is simple: They must wear uniforms. Now think about that. Imagine how the basketball coaches—at ages fifty-five or sixty, with their bellies protruding and their skinny legs showing—would look wearing shorts and sleeveless scoop-necked T-shirts. Or imagine football coaches decked out in full regalia."

"I ain't sure you gave Blank enough of a chance," I had to argue back.

"I can't afford to run a training school for managers. They're going to have to practice on their own time. In spite of appearances to the contrary, this team is not a charitable institution, and as long as we continue to get plummeted by our noble opponents, we're going to respond, and respond immediately."

"What's this publicity stuff about?" I asked, changing the subject.

"I've rehired the same public-relations firm that did such a bang-up job on the anti-Schmidt campaign. I'm paying them fifteen thousand dollars a month, and I'm looking for quick results. I had them working through the weekend on the thing, and tonight, I'm pleased to say, you'll see the first phase of this plan put into action. Tonight we play the Mets. Tonight I get to see my team for the first time this season, and tonight, dear Squat, I want you to meet my newest flame."

The game was slated to start at eight, and at a couple of minutes after eight the stadium went black. I was sitting just above the Dodger dugout, waiting for Bobby. I didn't know what was going on; I figured it was a blackout. But just then these floodlights—the kind they use up on Hollywood Boulevard on opening nights—started going nuts, swinging back and forth over the stadium and across the sky. Then there was this music, like marching music. Then fireworks shooting off in the sky—red, orange, green, crazy purple fireworks, rockets and starbursts—then the lights back on and Bobby was at home plate in a tux with a Dodger cap on his head, and standing next to him were about ten of the biggest stars in Hollywood. Bobby took the microphone and said how this was going to be the beginning of a new era of "glamorous victory" for the Dodgers. He introduced all of his "friends." I was practically hiding under my seat, not 'cause it was so creepy—which it was—but 'cause there weren't more than ten thousand fans in the seats. And I was wondering to myself: Don't Bobby see that he's talking to himself?

Bobby trotted across the field and came to the box and sat next to me. He put all his movie-star friends around us. Then he whispered in my ear, "This is who I want you to meet." He pointed to the young woman out there singing the national anthem. She was pretty the way that maybe poodle dogs are pretty, except her figure was real perfect and her voice wasn't all that bad. Her name was Darlene, and I had seen her on TV. When she was through, she came to our box and sat on the other side of Bobby, and he introduced us. He introduced me to all his pals, and I nodded my head and shook their hands, but what was I supposed to say? They were very big stars, and sure, I was impressed—who wouldn't be?—and they were smiling and asking Bobby a lot of questions 'cause they were happy to be in the owner's box. Tonight Bobby was the biggest star of all. A few minutes later an engineer type brought a tiny TV set and put it right next to Bobby's seat. The game was being broadcast back to New York, and Bobby wanted to see everytime the camera was on him. I was getting a little sick to my stomach.

I tried not to get down. I knew Bobby wanted to believe in this team and this city. He thought he was doing the right thing. Movie stars couldn't hurt nothing, and, wouldn't you know it, the team actually did play a decent game. We beat the Mets 4–2. You'd think we had won the Series the way Bobby carried on. He was sure that he and his famous pals had made the difference. He thought the Dodgers had won the game for him, and maybe they had. He put his Dodger cap on Darlene's head. She threw her arms around him. "This was the most exciting night of my life," she said. "This was exquisitely thrilling." I wanted to puke. On her. But I didn't say a word as the gang moved down to the locker room, where Bobby spread around his congratulations like blueberry jelly, putting it on thick. He took his movie stars by the hand and introduced them to the guys, and everyone was having a real big time. Except me.

"Mark this day," Bobby was saying. "Mark this as the moment of truth. I have every confidence that this team is destined for greatness, and though it may surprise the rest of the league—and especially the Commissioner—it will not surprise me when we start setting records." I could see all the players smiling, and I could feel them liking Bobby, just the way the movie stars like Bobby, the way everyone likes Bobby. He was standing there and the bull was flying and you want to believe him because he's telling you how great you are, he's real confident and handsome and he's got fifty million bucks and you just know that he's got this crazy power and he can do anything he wants.

Sure, I could feel it. I had seen Bobby's power for many years now. I wanted to go to the party he was having at some swanky club. I wanted to make love to a movie star. I'm human. I wanted to believe that all those lights and fireworks were going to turn this season around. I wanted to believe that Oran, with all her predictions, was dead wrong.

But I couldn't. Because I knew the team, and I knew Bobby. I saw that we had no pitching—only two decent starters and a shaky bullpen. I saw the squad had no real leader. And this new manager was really just some guy on the skids. The team would be all right if we were playing triple-A ball, but not in the majors. I knew too much about baseball to fool myself.

So I didn't go to the party. I didn't go near it. I tried not to be mad at Bobby. Maybe I was just hurt that he didn't ask me nothing about firing Blank and hiring Cobb.

I went back to my place in Silver Lake and fed Pee Wee and read *Sporting News* and concentrated on the statistics and didn't even think about what Oran must have said on the eleven-o'clock news. I just wanted to sleep, but I couldn't. I was getting angrier and angrier, and then I thought about calling her up and telling her that she was right, that Bobby was a first-class jerk who had no business owning a baseball team. At least not this one, because this wasn't even the Dodgers anymore. This was some outfit who just happened to be wearing Dodger uniforms. It was a disgrace. A real disgrace. It was show biz, it wasn't baseball, and I felt bad being a part of it. Me and Bobby were betraying the old Dodgers and the old Dodger spirit. It wasn't bad enough that he had bought the L.A. Dodgers, but now he was turning them into the *Hollywood* Dodgers. That stunk. That was as phony as a bottle of spotted ink. But what could I do? I thought I had some influence, but then he goes off and hires a new manager without saying a word to me. Could I quit? How could I do that when I was the only one around who even had an outside chance of keeping him honest? No, I had to stick around—at least for this season. I had to see it through—at least that's the line I kept feeding myself, hoping that, somewhere in Bobby's heart, I'd find that old Dodger feeling again.

"It will not surprise me when we start setting records," is what Bobby had said. And he was right: We set a record for losing; we lost the next eighteen out of twenty, and that season we lost more games than any team in Dodger history. And if that wasn't bad enough, at the end of June we began to see these commercials on TV, each one different, with a movie star like John Disc walking through the gates of Dodger Stadium with all the other fans, saying, "You might think that making a movie is thrilling, but I'd rather be with you out at Dodger Stadium, watching the most surprising team in baseball." It got to the point where I wouldn't even turn on the TV; I was scared that I'd see one of those jackass commercials—there were about eight of 'em, with the cream of the Hollywood crop—or, even worse, I was scared I'd hear Oran making fun of the commercials on her sports reports. She could do that, because Bobby told the agency not to put any of the ads on her station.

After the All-Star break, things got so bad that Bobby got married. Just like that. He called me up at midnight to tell me, and before I could say anything back, he put Darlene on and she said, "Squat, I just want you to know that I think you're darling. You're so precious, and I know how much you mean to Bobby and never —never ever ever—would I dream of interfering with your friendship. In fact, I just told Bobby the other day that I wish we could adopt you, I really do, because you're one of the dearest and cutest men, and I know that someday soon some lucky girl is going to gobble you up, and I don't want you to worry, you sweet thing, because Bobby and I will always take good care of you."

What could I say? Take a flying leap, lady—that's what I wanted to say. But she had landed him, and it was dumb to say anything, so I didn't. I just sat there with the phone to my ear and felt my skin crawl, thinking that she was Bobby's newest toy. She was his way of forgetting about the Dodgers. The next day, when Oran heard about it, she called me.

"Will it last?" she wanted to know.

"Once upon a time, I thought I knew him," says me. "But no more. He might be married to this broad for one day or one million days."

"You still don't like her?"

"She's a phony."

"What about her career? She has a fabulously successful recording career. Is Hanes going to force her to stop singing?"

"He says they're going to do everything—he'll run his businesses and she'll run hers and they'll travel together whenever they can."

"Did you mention the team to him?"

"What's there to mention? He knows what's happening. That's why he hasn't been to the ballpark in two weeks. He don't wanna see anyone, especially me. He don't wanna think about it. He wants to forget it's there. Now he says he's going to Greece for his honeymoon and won't be back for a month."

"Who's going to run the club?"

"What's there to run? I'm the one who deals with the players. I'm the guy they talk to 'cause they think I'm a pipeline to Bobby. And you know something, Oran, I've learned to like a lot of those guys. They've grown on me and I hate to disappoint 'em, I hate to even tell them what Bobby's doing."

"What about Cobb?"

"That creep has to go."

"Does Bobby know that?"

"I tell him all the time."

"And?"

"You ain't gonna report this?"

"Not if you tell me not to."

"I'm looking for someone new right now. Bobby gave me the word."

"That's a big responsibility he gave you. I presume that means the two of you are working well together."

"Don't mean nothing except it's something he ain't interested in fooling with himself. It wasn't any big discussion. He just told me to go out and do it. We don't have any talks anymore. You'd think he would have mentioned this marriage business to me ahead of time. I mean, we been pals for thirty-five years. We been bachelors together all that time. But no, there's this one phone call out of the blue and that's it. Pretty strange, wouldn't you say? Makes me think that there's something he doesn't want to admit."

"What's that?" she asked me.

"That he still don't know what he's doing."

I heard Oran sigh. Then I sighed. It felt like the whole world was sighing.

TEN

YOU THINK BASEBALL is glamorous? You think it's all kicks? Well, don't try a season on the road. Don't even try a week, just try a day, and you'll see what it's like.

What it's like is Room 318 of the Holiday Inn in Pittsburgh.

The room's got one bed and two dressers and one color tube and a pitcher of water and lots of plastic glasses and a painting of a sailboat over the dresser. When I look outside to see Pittsburgh, I see a Texaco station on one corner and an Exxon station on the other. Also, there's a Denny's around the corner. There's always a Denny's around the corner.

This was a typical morning: I got up and while I was in the shower the phone rang and I had to hook on my fake leg and limp over to find out that Cobb was mad because two of the boys hadn't come back last night and he wants to suspend them, but he won't do nothing till he can talk to Bobby. That's impossible, I told him, 'cause Bobby can't be reached, Bobby was still on his honeymoon in Greece and he ain't taking calls, even mine. Then Cobb started cursing Bobby, which was two-faced since he'd never have the guts to say this to Bobby's face. So in a nice way I told Cobb to get lost. Then the phone rang again and it was Tom Alvarado, who was one of the guys out all night, telling me that his piss is burning to beat the band and what should he do. He admitted he was wiped out—him and Ted Fromp, an out-fielder—and he didn't even remember the names of the girls. I told him he needed a skin doctor, and he said he didn't know any in Pittsburgh. I called Jesse, our trainer, but his room didn't answer and later I learned he had to fly back to L.A. because his wife was having an operation. So I called the Pirates' trainer, and he gave me a name, and I called the doctor and made an appointment for an hour from now and told Tom. He didn't wanna go alone. He was embarrassed. So I went with him. This, mind you, is Tom Alvarado, who weighs 180 pounds and, on the right day, is the most ferocious flamethrower on the team. By the time we had cured his VD and taken a cab back to the motel, my morning had been murdered and I still hadn't eaten breakfast.

The phone was ringing off the wall as I stepped back into my room. It was some creep from the local rag wanting to know whether Bobby was selling the team and was it true that Cobb was out. I told the guy to buzz off and remembered that I had to make a half-dozen phone calls about new managers before the day was over. After that it was Benny Stern, the pitching coach, telling me that Hart Fredericks, today's starter, was a little shaky and sore, and I said bull, just get the trainer to pop his arm and break the adhesions, but then I remembered that Jesse was gone so I told Stern to find a doctor. But now Stern wanted to know if he could have a five-hundred-dollar advance until next month 'cause his son needed tuition money at UCLA. I knew the real reason—the boys tell me everything—was because last week Stern had lost three Gs to the poker sharks. I told Stern I'd get back to him, and three seconds later it's Moon Weller calling me, saying, "Can you get me a couple of dozen tickets for tonight, Squat? Because my whole family's here in Pittsburgh and I promised them."

I tried to nap. I slipped in a cassette tape of Sam Cooke singing "A Change Is Gonna Come," which is one of my favorite oldies. I tried to doze off behind the music, but there was a rap at my door and Cobb had come to see me to discuss strategy for tonight's game and that took another hour and by that time there was no time left.

I took a cab to the ballpark and walked around batting practice and gave a few tips—the boys were still asking me for tips—and when the game began I was sitting above our dugout keeping a box score the way I've been doing ever since Ebbets Field. I studied the game, and once in a while Cobb would look at me, and because I knew the signals, I'd give him a few and he'd be happy to use them—to bunt or to hit-and-run—because he figured they were coming from Bobby. At nine-thirty, we were losing by six runs and had gone through three pitchers and it looked like we might have to use Alvarado, even if his pecker was falling off. And I'm thinking to myself—what's the use, because the season is over here in August. The Dodgers were dead as a door-nail. The hot dog I was eating tasted like rubber, and my stomach was turning to rust. The road will do that to you. But I hung in there and marked the last three innings.

When I got back to my room and started putting my key in the lock, I heard this noise inside, and then music—my music, my tape—Sam Cooke singing "Shake." Oh God, now this, I thought, now I'm being robbed! I didn't think about being shot, I didn't think about being knifed in the stomach or hit over the head with a tire tool. I was so mad, so fed up with this whole rotten day, that I took my good leg and kicked the door so hard that it crashed open and I said, "Okay, you creep, put down my stuff before I break you in half!" And there, instead of a thief, was a smiling bearded Bobby, reclining on my bed, listening to my music.

"Glad to see you haven't lost your courage, Squat."

"Geez," was all I could say. My heart was beating real fast. It took me a while to notice that the room stank of pot.

"Sorry I missed the game. We ran into some rough weather just outside of New York. I thought we might have to turn around. You know, Squat, those Lears aren't all they're cracked up to be."

I was still shaking my head. I couldn't believe this.

"You're not going to inquire about my honeymoon?"

"How was your honeymoon, kid?"

"Strange. Marvelous but strange. Darlene is much more than meets the eye."

"I figured."

"She's a free spirit, I'll say that much for her. And I certainly learned a great deal from her. New places, new experiences. Dazzling—that's how I'd describe her. Daring, and quite delicious. The time we were together—how long was it, Squat, four weeks? five weeks?—will not soon be forgotten."

"How much is she going to take you for?"

Bobby laughed. "I knew I needed to see you, Squat. I knew it had been too long." He got off the bed and stood next to me, gently patted me on the back. I looked in his eyes which were sparkling and stoned and confused in his confident way. Bobby was always Bobby, a little kid acting too old for his age or a grown guy acting too young. And now that I had been with him for a couple of minutes the old feeling came back, the thing that a reporter back in L.A. had once written—that as soon as Bobby walked in a room you felt like you had downed a slug of whiskey, even if you hadn't.

"So how much is she gonna get you for?" I asked him again.

"Very little. She's rich. She's singing in Japan right now. The divorce will be painless. No judge will feel very sorry for her. Besides, that's not her style. She prides herself on independence. Only once in a great while does a man come along who's capable of dissuading her of that notion. Though, as you can see, the dissuasion has a limited duration."

"You're okay, kid?"

"Fine, never been better. I spent a glorious month dining with kings, courting the fallen and fake aristocracy of imperial Europe. I gambled and I won."

"Won what?"

"Confirmation of the fact that life is even more wondrous than

I had imagined. More wondrous and various and provocative. Did you know, for example, that in Erina, Italy, a small jewel of a village on the Riviera, prostitution is only legal if the prostitute —man or woman, mind you—goes to bed with a married couple?"

I managed a weak smile. I didn't really wanna hear this stuff. "I've been trying to get in touch with you," I told him.

"I heard the end of the game on the radio. I've been following the team. I've had reports wired to me."

"I know. But I still couldn't get you on the phone."

"That was my intention, Squat. You had to see that you could run this team by yourself. I had to find a way to prove that to you."

"Horse manure," says me. "I ain't running nothing, kid, 'cause there ain't nothing to run."

"What did you think of the TV commercials?"

"I thought they stunk. Who cares about a bunch of movie stars grinning and saying that baseball is so *divine?*"

"Everyone cares. The world loves movie stars."

"The world ain't baseball fans. Baseball fans sweat in their beer and burp real loud. They only wanna see one thing—their team winning. Anything else is bean dip."

Bobby started walking around the room now. He flung his brown blazer over a chair. He looked out the window. "The commercials have resulted in an increase at the gate," he finally said.

"Five percent. Exactly five percent. And you know that five percent of nothing is nothing. Which is exactly what's happening this year. Nothing."

"Patience, dear Squat. We must have patience."

"I'm tired, Bobby. I'm telling you right now that I'm tired. Tired of beating my head against the wall and pretending this is really a baseball team when deep down I know better. I also wanna tell you that I'm tired of making excuses for you." I said it, and I was glad.

"I don't need you to make excuses for me."

"I think you do."

He was silent, but I kept talking. "You made a promise, but you ain't keeping it."

"What promise did I ever make?"

"To run a baseball team."

"Squat, you're going to have to see this thing in perspective. This is only the first year. This is our virginal season. Our plans have yet to blossom. When I get back to L.A., I'm meeting with the public-relations agency to go over a new series of promotions—"

"Don't talk like that, Bobby. Just don't. Because you'll get me mad and I don't wanna be mad at no one. I don't wanna think about how you used to talk against the gimmicks in baseball."

Now he started stalking the room again. He put a joint in his mouth and lit up.

"I wish you wouldn't do that," I said.

"I'm not sure I'm in the mood to hear you moralizing."

"It ain't that. But this happens to be my room and I don't want it stunk up any worse than you already done."

"I'll get you another room if you wish."

"I know, kid, you'd buy me the whole hotel. You got a heart of gold."

"Stop it, Squat, I'm as tired as you are. I've been on airplanes for the past two days."

"Rough life you lead, ain't it, kid?"

"The strange part is that I was convinced that this team would be a way for us to work together, Squat. That was my sincere belief."

"I ain't interested in no movie-star teams. I don't wanna kiss no one's behind and I don't want no one kissing mine."

"Talking about behinds, did you ever get to screw that bitch?"

I knew he meant Oran, and I knew I had to count to ten. I counted to ten and said, "I happen to respect that lady."

"Even though she's practically single-handedly responsible for the demise of this team?"

I laughed in his face. "You're really grasping for straws, ain't you, kid? Oran just reports what she sees, and when it comes to you, she's been right. It tears my guts to say that, but it's the truth. She had you pegged from the beginning."

"Somehow that woman's gotten you very mixed up, Squat. You continue to view this game through the eyes of a boy. You ought to try looking at it through the eyes of a man, a man who knows the difference between fantasy and reality."

"I'm there every day, Bobby, and you ain't. You're the one who's flying in the clouds. I'm down there on the field. I've stuck with it."

"Then you know it's not working."

"It's not working because you don't want it to work. You've given up—just like Oran said you would. It could be just as good as you want it to be—and you know it, Bobby, yes you do."

"It's just another business!" He was yelling. "Nothing more and nothing less, and I'll sell it tomorrow and it won't make the least difference, not the least! And if you want me to, I'll get you a job on another major-league baseball team. You don't have to worry about selling jewelry again. Just trust me, Squat, I'm here to help us both—"

That's when I slugged him in the face, in the right eye, and I know it hurt him real bad 'cause he went down in the corner, knocking a lamp off the dresser and breaking a bulb. When I went over to him he kicked my leg out from under me—now he was furious and so was I—and I was on the floor and my heart was hammering like hell—I wanted to murder the bum, I really did—and I reached over and got my fake leg and I smashed it against his side, and I knew it hurt 'cause that plastic is hard as steel. I smashed the leg against Bobby, again and again, and he tried to stop me. He stuck his fingers in my eyes and he landed a left to my chin, but I was still smashing him with my fake leg and screaming, "You're a liar, you're a rotten liar, you said you'd do all this stuff and you ain't doing nothing! It's all bull and tricks and gimmicks, and you fooled me like you fooled Schmidt and the owners and Percano and everyone! You even fooled yourself!" He hit me again, this time in the neck, right in the Adam's apple, and I couldn't say nothing, I was hurting and bleeding where the light-bulb glass had cut my skin, and he was hurting and bleeding and twisted. Suddenly he started crying, not crying but sobbing and shaking and saying to me, "Oh God, Squat, I hate what I've done. I hate this team, I hate L.A., I hate my friends out there and the smog and the stadium and the stupid color TV screen thing and I don't care, I've never cared if the team wins, because they're not the Dodgers, they're fakes, and they've made us fakes, and we need to get out. Don't you see that we need to sell, right away, tomorrow, tonight? Get me the phone and let me sell. I'll do it in a minute and we'll all feel better because I hate everything about it, I really do." He was still sobbing and we were sitting there on the floor, leaning against each other after having beaten our brains out, all black and blue and bloody, and I said:

"You don't hate nobody, kid. You love people more than anyone in the whole world, and everyone loves you and wants to be around you. You'll make it work, you'll see, because none of this was an accident. There's a plan somewhere out there in the sky, and you're the one—the only one—who can make it come true. You haven't seen it yet 'cause you've had all this other stuff on your mind. You thought it might have been buying buses or running for President or something like that. But it wasn't. The plan is something different. And whatever the plan is, you'll do it. I know, because you've got the magic in your heart."

"The plan is to get out."

"We'll never get out. We're in it to stay. The plan is just to go somewhere else."

"Where?"

"Home, Bobby. Don't you think it's time to take us home? Ain't that what you've wanted to do all along?"

"Brooklyn? Are you talking about going back to Brooklyn?"

"There's no place else for me. I don't think there's no place else for you either," I said as I looked at his face, all stained with tears and blood. "And there sure ain't no other place for this team."

Moving...

BACK TO BROOKLYN. Over the bridge. I decided to walk, just for the hell of it. The water didn't smell too polluted today and the bridge wasn't too crowded with cars. I just wanted to be alone for an hour or two before I caught up with the team, which was staying out near Shea. So I had taken a cab from my hotel in midtown to the foot of the Brooklyn Bridge.

There's something about that bridge—all the dirty bricks and cables, that beautiful old design—which always gets to me. It was the first bridge to Brooklyn and it'll always be the best—so solid and straight-ahead. When I got to the highest part and looked over at Brooklyn I could see the tops of factories and the smokestacks and the spires of churches and so many apartment buildings and I thought of all those people who live in Brooklyn and don't have no baseball team, because if there's any place that deserves one—that needs one—it's Brooklyn, where baseball was invented, where we know the game better than anyone in the whole wide world. I started walking faster and faster 'cause I was getting closer to Brooklyn. I was excited and thinking that it was beautiful over there, it really was, and when I arrived on the Brooklyn side, I looked around and saw that no one was looking at me, and I bent down and kissed the ground. I know you'll think I'm nuts, but this was my turf and it was so good to be back. The sidewalk might have been a little dirty, but I kissed it all the same, with both lips, with my eyes shut. And when I opened them, I saw some lettering right there in the concrete. It said: ROBERT J. HANES CEMENT.

In the early evening everyone met up at Shea—me, my family and the ball team. Natch, I was something of a star with my folks. They hadn't seen me for a while and they were giving me lots of attention, but Cobb was also there and he wanted me to go over stuff and everyone else had questions for me, the players and the trainers and the coaches.

I put my family right behind the first-base dugout and sat between Mom and Pop, who looked a lot grayer than last time. They saw how Cobb kept popping up and asking me things. Cobb was real nervous, because there were still rumors about his being canned. Of course the rumors were true; I just hadn't been able to find anyone to replace him yet. My folks were also impressed that I had this telephone hooked up to the bullpen and to Bobby in California. Bobby was out there in Bel-Air with some lady friend of his, but he still took the time to talk to Mom and Dad and tell them that he missed them. We were having a pretty good time except that near the end of the game Pop said that this was the worst Dodger team since Uncle Robbie had that string of losers in the '20s. I knew he was right, but I still wish he hadn't said nothing. Especially since the Mets whipped us 9–1.

That night I went back to Borough Park with the folks. I know this sounds corny, but I liked sleeping in my old room. My folks hadn't changed a thing; even my old Dodger pennant was hanging over my bed the way it always had. It looked so weird to see BROOKLYN instead of LOS ANGELES above the Dodgers' name, weird but right, deep-down right, the way "L.A."—replacing the beautiful "B" on the front of the caps—was deep-down wrong.

It was tough falling asleep, 'cause I had so much on my mind. Mainly Bobby. And our fight. And me trying to decide what to do next. Would he ever move back to Brooklyn? Could he take the team out of L.A.? Sometimes I thought it sounded so crazy that I'd laugh out loud. Other times I was so sure it was right and sane that I'd want to scream, "Do it! Do it! Do it!" 'Cause if he didn't do it, what was the use of hanging around?

The next morning Mom saw I was down. Pop saw I was down. She made me my favorite breakfast with eggs and potatoes, and he started talking baseball. Since Pop had retired he didn't do too much except walk around the neighborhood and shoot the breeze, and he wanted to know if I'd come along. I couldn't, I told him; I just had to be by myself today. I'd mess around the place for a while, read the paper, get all the sports news, and then it'd be nine o'clock in L.A. and I'd call Bobby and he'd give me the shot in the butt that I needed.

"Did I wake you up, kid?" I asked him.

"I'm talking to Paris on the other line. Wait a second." Then I was on hold, which I always hate. When he came back, he sounded worse than me.

"What did Paris tell you?" I asked.

"I lost a freighter last night two hundred miles outside the Persian Gulf. A freak accident. I'm waiting for the details."

"Sorry to hear that, kid. I hope no one was hurt."

"All hands were saved except me."

"Big losses, huh?"

"Extraordinary losses, yes. I need a sedative to calm my frazzled nerves. Sometimes I fear my world moves too quickly."

"*Now* you worrying about that?" I almost laughed, but stopped myself. The kid was in a lousy mood.

"Where are you?" he asked.

"Home."

"That must be nice."

"Yeah, I wish you had made the trip with me. I'm about to go on a walk and catch up on the sights."

"Don't neglect the playground at P.S. 105."

"Sure thing."

"When are you coming back?"

"Not till the end of the road trip. We're in Philly for three days, then Atlanta, then Miami. It'll be another two weeks."

"What about replacements for Cobb?"

"Still looking, but it don't make good sense now. There's nothing left of the season, kid. It'll cost you money."

"Money? When has that ever been a concern of mine? You know the line that your dear friend Miss Ellis likes to use—'rich beyond reason.' Yes, I'm rich beyond reason and therefore money matters not."

"If it didn't matter, you wouldn't be so sick over your freighter."

"I'm tired of your team, Squat. I'm telling you that right now." His voice was real severe and sober.

"What do you mean *my* team?"

137

"You care for it, you run it, you bleed for it. As far as I'm concerned, it's the most expensive write-off in the history of taxation. The prospects for its future are bleak, and we must face that fact with some degree of maturity."

I hung up on him. Just like that.

Fuck him. Excuse me, but that's just how I felt. One day fireworks, the next day fiddlesticks. Enough of that crap. Why should I get sore? Why should I give myself ulcers? Why should I go over that fight we had in Pittsburgh when I was convinced that I had him convinced? By tonight he'd change his mind again and be selling tea to the Chinese. "I'm going for a walk, Mom. Be back later," says me, and I was gone, down the steps, out the building, on the streets. Hello, Brooklyn. Hello, Fort Hamilton Parkway. How the hell you been?

I strolled over to Thirteenth Avenue, which is my favorite shopping street in the world 'cause of all the stores and people. I was in a buying mood. I didn't worry about Bobby no more. It was a perfect afternoon, sunny and warm, and I wanted to get presents for everyone I loved. Flowers for Mom. And this here fifty-dollar *Encyclopedia of Baseball* would be perfect for Pop, with all the statistics from the old days, and maybe I should buy another copy for myself. Why not? I was making good money. What else was I gonna spend it on? I better not forget Pee Wee, 'cause Pee Wee had been staying with Oran so long he had forgotten all about me. So I bought Pee Wee this squeaky little mouse that he could kick around the house, and pretty soon I was loaded down with presents from Thirteenth Avenue—scarf for Oran, sweaters for my brothers—gifts for everyone except Bobby, 'cause I guess I was still mad at him. But that wasn't right; I had to bring Bobby something, something from Brooklyn.

Easier said than done. What can you get a guy like Bobby? I couldn't think of anything he didn't have. The kid was impossible. So I started walking home, and getting down again, remembering what a pill Bobby was. I was walking slower and slower 'cause my leg was giving me a little trouble and the packages were weighing me down and I was tired of thinking of him and trying to figure him out and I stopped to rest. Suddenly I realized that I was standing in front of the playground of P.S. 105 at 59th Street and Fort Hamilton, which is just where Bobby told me to go.

A bunch of kids were playing ball and running around, and I saw that two guys were playing catch on the far side of the yard.

They were black. One was very dark and muscular and tall. The other was shorter and lighter and heftier. They were using decent gloves and they knew what they were doing. Something about them made me stop. Ain't sure why, but I put down my packages and leaned against the school building. I watched. I couldn't keep my eyes off them. They were just throwing the ball, but they were doing it with such poise and polish. The tall one seemed more nervous, wound up; the shorter one was easier with himself, more relaxed. But there was something about them, something about them both that was driving me crazy, that was . . .

Then I saw it: Campy! The short one threw like Campy, looked like Campy. And the tall one was a dead ringer for Jackie Robinson. I rubbed my eyes. I pinched myself. I looked again. Campy, so quiet and smooth and sure of himself. Jackie, so eager and anxious and cocky. And dark. And jumping out of his skin. I felt my heart hammering inside my chest. I was scared of having an attack. It was crazy, but it was happening. And the more I watched them, the surer I was. But how could it be? Roy Campanella played for the Dodgers from 1948 to 1957 and that was it. Jackie was there from '47 to '56 and then no more. But here were these two stars, right before my eyes. I had to say something.

"Hey guys."

"Us?"

"Yeah."

"What are your names?"

"What's it to you?" said Jackie.

"Wise guy, huh?"

"Listen, chief"—Jackie talked real fast in a high-pitched voice —"we're not interested in buying no smack, no coke or no smoke, so peddle your wares somewhere else."

I laughed real hard. Can you believe the kids were taking me for a pusher? It was probably the limp. "What would you do if I told you I worked for the Dodgers?"

"Shit a brick," said Jackie.

"Then start shitting," says me, pulling out my card, which Bobby had made up for me: D. MALONE, VICE-PRESIDENT, LOS ANGELES DODGERS. Now the kids were real quiet.

"My name's Bo Solomon," Campy told me.

"And he's the baddest catcher in the history of New Utrecht High," said Jackie.

My heart stopped. My mouth fell open. I *knew* he was a catcher. But New Utrecht! Holy smoke!

"Sonny is no slouch himself," said Bo. "This is Sonny Muse. He plays infield, usually second base." What else? Bo's voice was so soft it was hard to hear him. His face was plump and open and sweet. Cheeks like a baby. He talked through his smile. Muse was still glaring at me.

"We're both all-city," said Sonny. "Last year we hit over .400."

"Was it your last year?"

"We're only juniors. Gonna be seniors in September."

"Let me just take a look at your swings," I said. "Pick up that bat over there."

Bo was first. He held the bat straight up, his fists at waist level, he crouched, and then he waved the stick back and forth, ever so slightly—just like Campy!

I knew Sonny's stance before he showed me: the bat way up high, his fists level with his neck, the crazy batting stance of Jackie.

I couldn't stand it anymore. I had to ask 'em. "You guys ever heard of Campanella and Robinson?"

"Naturally," snapped Sonny. "What do you take us for?"

"They played for the Dodgers," added Bo.

"Sometime last century"—that was Sonny.

"Ever seen old movies of them playing?" I asked.

"Why?" they wanted to know.

"Oh, it don't make no difference. When can I see you two play in a game?"

"How come?" asked Sonny. "You gonna sign us up?"

"Maybe."

"Nothing's happening now," said Bo. "It's summer. We both have jobs. We're just waiting for our last year of school to start."

"How about tomorrow?" I kept pushing. "Can you get together a decent sandlot game tomorrow? I just wanna see you play for a couple of hours."

"Sure, we'll fix it up," said Campy—I mean Bo.

I hated to miss the Phillies, but this sandlot game was a lot more important. We set a time and a place, an empty lot not far from Sunset Park that I knew like the back of my hand.

"See you guys tomorrow," I said, feeling in my heart that I had finally found Bobby the Brooklyn gift I'd been searching for.

TWO

WHEN I WOKE up the next morning, I was nervous. I opened my eyes and saw that I was in my old bedroom in my parents' place in Brooklyn. Had yesterday really happened, or were Bo and Sonny part of a dream?

I ate breakfast with the folks, and when Mom said she was going to Mass, I told her I'd come along. It had been a long time. I figured I needed it. The sandlot game wasn't till two. Mass would do me good.

Our neighborhood church looked the same as it did when I was a kid—even the smells hadn't changed—and I sat there thinking about miracles, thinking about the time I was at New Utrecht High and the scout from the Dodgers came by and signed me up. I guess you'd call that a miracle, too.

I got to the sandlot early, right after lunch. It was exactly the one I remembered—long and narrow and going slightly uphill, just wide enough for roughly the right distance from first to third. If you ran out of the base lines, you were in the gutter.

Bo Solomon and Sonny Muse arrived first and didn't say much to me. They looked serious, like they had a job to do. The others —there were six guys on each side—came along a few minutes later. Bo was behind the plate and Sonny covered most of the infield. I wished Bo had been wearing his catcher's gear, 'cause I'd be able to tell more about his moves, but still, I could see. He called to the pitcher in a real level, easy way, and he reacted quick as a fox, and Muse made two spectacular stops at second. They both were smooth, strong hitters, both had good power, and after an hour I was convinced all over again: These two guys were as real as the Brooklyn Bridge and just as beautiful. Solomon was solid and Sonny was fiery hot, and now I knew they were no dream. Afterwards they came over to me and wanted to know what I was thinking.

"The big time," I told 'em.

"You sure?" asked Sonny. " 'Cause we don't need any jive."

"I'm straight as an arrow," I said. "I mean what I say and I deliver what I promise."

"What are you promising?" Sonny wanted to know.

"Nothing. At least not now. You both got to finish high school. I ain't touching you till then." They frowned. I could see that they were disappointed. "That's the least you gotta do," says me. "I couldn't live with myself if I ruined your education now. And even if the Dodgers do work out for you, that don't mean that you ain't going to college."

"What about L.A.?" Bo asked.

"Things are real complicated now. Too complicated to explain. All I can do is ask you to see that I ain't lying and to trust me. 'Cause I'll be back, and when I come back it'll be with the boss, Bobby Hanes, and we'll see you play during the year, we'll come to a game, and by then other scouts will be after you—they probably been talking to you already—and all I can say is that me and Bobby are about to do something which I can't even talk about, not now, but you'll be reading about it in the papers, and when you do, remember me and what I'm saying to you now— that we'll be back to get you guys."

After that I took 'em downtown to eat desserts at Junior's and we talked baseball and I finally had to tell 'em how I played at New Utrecht and Montreal. You should have seen their faces when they found out. I asked about their families, which didn't have much money but lots of pride. Bo was a sweetheart, and Sonny was a wise-ass and a hothead and kept wanting to know about the bread and telling me how he wasn't gonna be screwed, but I could see under all his heavy hipness that he was soft and sweet like his pal the catcher. These guys were something so special I wanted to hug them both.

Soon as I got off the plane in L.A. I headed for Bobby's house in Bel-Air. The long road trip was over, and I was glad. Looked like we might lose a hundred games this year, which was unbelievable. But I wasn't thinking about that; I couldn't afford to; my mind wasn't on 1986. It wasn't even on 1987. I was gunning for 1988, I was living for 1988, 'cause that was gonna be the year the world would start spinning a lot faster, and when I told Bobby about Bo and Sonny I knew he'd flip.

At his place I saw that all the fancy landscape lights were lit, which meant he probably had company. It was about ten o'clock, and when I rang the doorbell a woman answered, who was blond and pretty and built real good and had this squeaky voice that asked, "Yes?"

"Squat!" I heard Bobby yelling from the den. "Come on in. I'm in the middle of an interview."

I followed the lady and her swing inside. Bobby was in his lounging jacket sitting in his big armchair, puffing on a pipe, which was something new. "Patty, this is my man Squat. Squat, this is Patty Sides, who's just been hired over at Channel 4 to cover sports. She's a whiz, and we're right in the middle of a wonderful conversation. Sit down and listen. You might learn something."

I didn't like the way that sounded, and I didn't like the way this woman looked, especially now that I knew who she was. Also, it was strange that she was answering the door for Bobby, like she was the maid. Her hair was bleached, not like Oran's hair, which was real natural red. And I could hear by the way she was asking questions that she didn't know anything about sports or the Dodgers or Bobby. She had been hired just for her looks, and she was wearing this blouse, which was opened three buttons down and, as far as I was concerned, showed too much for her own good.

"You were saying, Mr. Hanes, that you're much more optimistic about next year."

"Exactly, Patty. This year has been an experiment, a time to get my feet wet and test the waters. I may or may not decide to jump in next year."

"Do you enjoy owning a baseball team, Mr. Hanes?"

"I love it. It's a stimulating experience. Wonderfully instructive and challenging."

"There's been a lot of talk about your personal life. One magazine listed you among the top ten eligible bachelors in America. How do you feel about such a rating?"

"Love it, *adore* it. If there's to be gossip, let it be about me."

"Do you prefer women who are interested in sports or those who . . ."

I couldn't stand it. I went outside and walked around the pool and waited till this joke of an interview was over. I couldn't believe that the TV stations were hiring Playboy bunnies to cover sports. It was an insult.

"Come say goodbye to Patty," Bobby called to me twenty minutes later.

"See you around," I told her, and when I looked at the business card that she had put on top of the TV set for Bobby, I saw she had written her home number under the one for the office.

"Patty!" Bobby shouted at her before she left. "Forgot to tell you something. An item you may be able to use on the news tonight. I've fired Jim Cobb as manager and will be using Bull Jacobs, the third-base coach, to manage for the rest of the season."

"Gosh, that's a *fabulous* scoop. How could I possibly thank you?"

I was gonna say something, but I didn't. When she left, I looked at Bobby and told him that he was really nuts.

"We put up with Cobb for far too long, my friend," he said. "We would have fired him long ago were it not for your need to be perceived by everyone as a nice guy."

What could I say? I was disgusted. The only reason I hadn't fired Cobb was 'cause I hadn't found anyone any better. But I didn't start up with Bobby. I could see he was in one of those moods.

"What did you think of Patty?" he wanted to know. "Lovely, isn't she?"

"She looked like a bubblebrain to me," I had to say.

"Don't look for brilliance in sports reporters. Look for sincerity."

"What'd you mean when you told her that maybe you wouldn't be 'jumping in' next year?"

Bobby started sniffing a lot, and I figured he might have been snorting some of that cocaine before I got there. The reason I say so is 'cause he was talking so fast.

"While you've been mothering our valiant boys in blue," he started speeding along, "I've been repairing freighters and the damage done to my mind in recent months. I've been seriously thinking about our Dodger problem, and I've been asking myself a most provocative question—what would the Judge do in a situation such as this? For one thing, dear Squat, he would take a sheet of paper"—Bobby stopped stalking around the room long enough to sit at his desk and take a sheet of paper— "and with a ruler divide the sheet in half. Thus." Bobby did it. "And on one side he would print the word 'Positive' and the other side 'Negative.' Then he would proceed to categorize the elements of the problem. Take the Dodgers. What is positive about this particular property? I will write down the words 'Childhood curiosity satisfied.' How about 'High visibility for RJH, Jr.'? We must put that down. And certainly 'Demonstrates courage' belongs there, and 'Creative outlet,' and 'Diversified interest.'

"What shall we write on the other side, Squat? 'Negative cash flow. Net corporate loss.' That's two. 'Overweaning ambition.' That's three. 'Losing proposition from start to finish.' That's four, five, six, seven, eight, nine and ten. That's everything, Squat, and by now I know it, I feel it right here in my heart"—and he banged his fist against his chest—"though it pains me, it really does, to tell you this. I've invited them all in again, all the outside experts, the money men, the analysts, and they tell me that the mess will only get worse, and they advise me to get out, to get out now while the getting is good.

"You know what the Judge would say? He would not be angry —that's for certain. He would be realistic, because the Judge was always realistic, and he'd tell me that I attempted to turn the dreams of my youth to an adult reality, and therein lies the Lesson, the Simple and Sane and Most Spectacular Lesson of your life, he would say, the Lesson you should have learned years ago, but alas, the Lesson which will now cost you five or ten million dollars, the Lesson which says you can't do everything you want, especially when what you want is, in the end, quite silly."

I didn't say nothing. Didn't mention Bo or Sonny. I couldn't. I was choked up and sick at the same time. I didn't want to waste my energy arguing or begging or fighting. I just wanted to get the hell outta there. And I knew where I had to go. I had to go to Oran.

I got in the car and drove like a maniac over to her station's studio on Sunset where I knew she'd be getting off work. I just made it. When I pulled into the parking lot she was stepping into her car. I honked and she turned and smiled and I could see how glad she was to see me. And then, just when I thought she was reaching over to kiss me, she hauled back and slapped me across my cheek. It stung like hell.

"What was that about?"

"Patty Sides and Jim Cobb."

"Oh God."

"I just saw a replay of the tape. Do you know how I feel? Do you have any idea? There I am, reading the news at eleven, giving the scores and scraping the bottom of the barrel for the smallest crumbs, and on Channel 4 this cheerleader is telling all of L.A. that you guys have canned Cobb and that Hanes is hinting about selling the team."

"Let's have a drink and talk about it." I wanted to calm her down. Her face was as red as her hair, and her voice was furious.

"You should have heard my bosses," she said, "and seen the smirks they gave me. They've been waiting for this to happen. Now they have a reason to can me. Do you realize what this is going to do to my career? I've always considered the Dodgers my specialty. I've studied the Dodgers the way a surgeon studies hearts. And now—"

"A drink. I'll explain over a drink."

She cooled down a little. She had me follow her over to the joint on Melrose where we first met. We went to the same table by the bar, and this time I ordered a Scotch and she got a martini straight up.

"I had nothing to do with it," I told her. "You gotta believe me, 'cause it's the truth. Firing Cobb is stupid. I got common sense, specially baseball sense. Why would I fire the guy with three weeks left to play?"

"Do you realize the interview he gave her was the first he's granted in over two months? I know he doesn't like me, but why does he want to wreck my career?"

"I don't think he looks at it that way."

"Come on, Squat. The man knows precisely what he's doing."

"He might, but she doesn't. I was over there, I heard the interview—"

"Then why didn't you call me with the news about Cobb?"

"I didn't think there was time."

"You just didn't think at all!" She was steaming again.

"Maybe you're right."

"I know I'm right! And the questions she asked him! Pee Wee would probably ask tougher questions than she did."

"How is Pee Wee?"

"Wonderful. He's been sleeping with me every night."

"Maybe I should go back to your place and get him now."

"Maybe so," she said, and we finished our drinks and left.

Following Oran over there, my mind was working overtime. I had a lot of ideas running around trying to catch up with themselves. We got to her apartment in West Hollywood, and Pee Wee was all over me. Such a great cat.

"I'm worried," Oran told me as she fixed a big pot of coffee. We sat at her kitchen table and started getting real sober.

146

"Worried 'bout what?"

"Sides."

"She's nothing. She's a Barbie doll."

"Barbie dolls have been big business for decades. They sell."

"Your ratings are still good, aren't they?"

"Our eleven-o'clock news is slipping. They don't know who or what it is—news, weather or sports. But I'm the easiest target, especially now that Channel 4 has come up with Sides. There's no telling what will happen."

"You need to relax."

"You wouldn't say that if you really understood the politics at the station."

"Tell me more about them," I urged her, knowing that's exactly what she wanted to talk about—her job and her bosses and her professional problems. And talk she did, for nearly an hour, throwing back the coffee and getting real wired. I was patient, I felt what she was going through, and I was thinking, thinking, thinking. Things were coming together, beginning to make sense. I started getting this idea. This very big idea.

"Listen, Oran," I finally said to her, changing the subject a little, "how can you worry about a dame like Sides when you know more about the Dodgers than anyone around? I bet you can even give me their 1946 roster."

"Stevens, Stanky, Reese, Lavagetto, Walker, Furillo, Reiser, Edwards," she shot back, smiling. I knew that'd make her feel better.

"What about the pitchers?"

"Choose from Herring, Hatten, Higbe, Lombardi, Behrman, Melton, Gregg and Casey."

"You know your stuff."

"So do you, Squat." Now she was getting nice again.

"I wish you could have seen Ebbets Field."

"I feel like I've been there. I've gone through hundreds, maybe thousands of pictures."

"You were born too late. It was really something."

"It'll kill you if he sells the team, won't it?" she asked. This was the opening I'd been waiting for.

"He won't sell," I told her flat out.

"You've been saying that for so long, Squat. Surely by now you see that you've been deceiving yourself."

Now I was ready. My plan was set. I gulped hard and I looked her in the eye and I said, "Listen, Oran, I gotta tell you something that's been burning inside me for a long time. So long I can't stand it no more."

"What? What is it, Squat?"

"He ain't selling, I know he ain't selling, 'cause after next season he's moving the team back to Brooklyn. We're going to be Bums again."

She jumped out of her chair—just like that—and stood in front of me. Her green eyes were so bright and wild.

"*Brooklyn!*" she screamed.

"You got it, baby."

"It's the most phenomenal, most amazing . . . what am I going to do with the story? Are you kidding? Are you sure? How can he do it? . . . He'll never do it . . . but even if he doesn't . . . the story, it's the biggest story in ten years!" Oran was so excited she didn't know what to do. "You realize," she kept on chattering, "that I can't sit on this. You wouldn't expect me to sit on this, Squat, would you? There's no way this story can be kept quiet. Especially since he's probably giving it to Sides right now."

"Not a chance. You heard what he told her tonight. He's feeding her the wrong line. He's acting like he's gonna sell."

"Why?"

"You know Bobby. He wants to spring the surprise of the century. He wants to fake out everyone."

"Then why are you spilling the beans?"

"Two times he's fired managers without my knowing. Never said a word to me. Both times he picked the successors without my advice. The first time I decided to forget it. But now that it's happened again, I ain't happy at all. If he can pull an end run around me, I can do the same with him."

"But how can you be sure he's actually going to try to make this move?"

"Because I know Bobby. I know him better than anyone in the world. And we've been talking about it for months, talking about it our whole life. And then the other night in Pittsburgh he came out and told me," I lied, remembering that Bobby had never committed himself. But the lie was okay, 'cause I knew that's why Bobby needed me, to do the committing for him. "Yeah," I kept on telling Oran, "I know the inside of Bobby's brain like a jeweler knows a watch—every tick and every tock."

"Do you realize what the story will mean? It won't be simply a good scoop, like the firing or hiring of another manager. It's even more than a major sports exclusive. It's a major *news* exclusive. Do you have any idea how much time I'll get on the network news? Three, maybe four minutes. And they'll have to use me, because no one will know what to do with the story. It's not just the exposure, Squat, not just the air time, but it's the impact this will have on the boys in New York. They'll see this as one of the most important pieces of reporting in the last ten years. They already know how I've covered this beat. They've been worried that I've overdone it, pressed too hard . . . well, now they'll see the results for themselves. That is, if the story is real. Because if it's not, I might as well start applying for a cub reporter's job on the Hicksville *Gazette* right now."

Did I really know what I was doing?

"It's real," I told her. "Bobby's doing it."

"If this story turns out to be a dud, Squat, I don't have to tell you that—"

"Pour me a little more coffee, baby, and I'll give you the rundown."

She poured and I babbled. I told her how the story of my life with Bobby was all leading up to this one thing. I told her that's what we were put on earth to do. I went on and on, about the Judge and when Bobby was a kid. I didn't leave out nothing, and as I heard myself, I knew I was right, I was convincing myself. And when she asked where we were going to play, I said I didn't know, but it'd be in Brooklyn, not next year but the year after next. It would take that long. And when she asked about league approval, I said it could be worked out, 'cause Bobby could do anything in the world he wanted to. And I believed it. I believed everything I said to Oran. "Don't concern yourself with no exact players or ballparks or nothing like that," I said to her. "You just gotta get this story out and credit some mystery source the way you guys always do."

"And when they run to Bobby for verification?"

"He won't deny it. He can't."

"Are you sure, Squat? Are you really sure?"

"As sure as there's a God in heaven—that's how sure I am that Bobby Hanes is gonna bring the Dodgers back to Brooklyn."

THREE

"ARE YOU ANGRY? I trust you're not too angry." That was Bobby talking to me on the phone the next day. I was back at the house at Silver Lake.

"Why should I be angry, kid? It's your team. You hire and fire whoever you wanna hire and fire. That's the whole fun of having a team, ain't it?"

"Why are you so goddam reasonable, Squat? I don't trust this mood of yours."

I smiled. I did feel awful good. "The sun's shining in my face. Who can ask for anything more?"

"You weren't talking this way last night. Last night you ran out of here as though my house were on fire. I tried calling you, but you weren't there. What happened to you? Where did you go?"

"I had to think."

"And what conclusions did you come to?"

"That you're a great man."

"Even if I've concluded that it's best to sell this baseball team?"

"You gonna do what's right, kid. I know that. You're a real important person in this world. There's big plans for you, and I'm just happy to be hanging around now 'cause it's gonna be so beautiful later on."

"Squat, what in thunder are you saying? Have you been toying with drugs? You sound like you're floating."

"Maybe I'm a little tired, but I'm feeling good and in a little while I'm gonna run over to the ballpark."

"Listen, that's my other line buzzing. It's Geneva. I have to run, but I want to talk to you more, we need to talk seriously. I'm not quite certain whether to put the team on the block before or after the end of the season. Questions like that must be answered, and answered quickly."

"Go talk to Geneva. Give her my love."

When we got off the phone, I wondered again—was I nuts? For a long time I thought about calling Oran and telling her to stop the story. For a long time I was sure I had gone off the deep

end. Was the roof gonna cave in on my head? I asked Pee Wee.
Pee Wee just purred, and instead of calling Oran, instead of going
over to the ballpark and seeing the guys, instead of thinking anymore about Bobby, I took a nap. Slept all afternoon.

I woke at six and flipped on the tube. I didn't wanna miss it.
There was a new pretty-boy anchor man, one of those Tarzan
types. "Channel 2 has an exclusive story tonight in the world of
sports," he said. "A real bombshell. Let me move quickly to Oran
Ellis with the details."

Oran was dressed in hot yellow, and she wore her hair long to
her shoulders. She stared into the camera and didn't blink or
hesitate for a second. She ripped right into it:

"I have learned that the Dodgers will be leaving Los Angeles
after the 1987 season. Robert J. Hanes, the ball club's owner,
intends to relocate the franchise in its original home, Brooklyn."

She kept on talking, mentioning this reliable source, but I
didn't hear nothing else. My brain was screaming with her first
words—*The Dodgers will be leaving Los Angeles! The Dodgers
will be leaving Los Angeles! Original home, Brooklyn! Original
home, Brooklyn!*" And to hear it coming out of Oran's mouth,
right there on the color TV. The words: Dodgers. Leaving. L.A.
Going. Back. Brooklyn. 'CAUSE IT'S TRUE, OH SO BEAUTIFUL AND
OH SO TRUE, SO CRAZY AND SO PERFECT! BACK TO BROOKLYN! BACK
TO BROOKLYN! PRAISE GOD, THE BUMS ARE MOVING BACK TO
BROOKLYN!

"I'll have you murdered," Bobby said. He called me after the
newscast.

I laughed.

"*How in the name of reason can you be laughing?*" He was
yelling.

" 'Cause it's funny."

"You're a goddamn manipulator, Malone. You're working behind my back, you're undermining my empire. You think you've
got power that you don't have. You think you're going to pull
something off and all you're doing is making a fool of yourself, a
goddamn pathetic fool. Who the hell do you think you are, anyway?"

"Squat."

"You're through!" He was still screaming.

"You're great, Bobby. You're a great man."

"Fuck you!"

"Did I ever tell you that I love you? Did I ever tell you that you're a terrific guy?"

"You've been feeding that bitch lies."

"You're wrong. I told Oran the truth. Don't you see it, kid? This is why you bought the team in the first place. This is why you've been so miserable here. You've always known that you had to get out. We've both known it. Besides, something happened in Brooklyn that I need to tell you about, a miracle, believe me, kid, a real miracle. This thing's getting bigger and bigger. Can't you see how it's got us going?"

"I hear you talking crazy, Squat. I sincerely believe you've gone mad. Meanwhile, I do not have that privilege. Instead, I have to turn off my phones and lock my doors and prepare some sort of answer to this absurd story."

"You don't have to say nothing. Not now."

"Quiet, Squat! Do not tell me what to do! I don't need your advice! I don't want to hear another word out of you! I want you to remember where I found you and where I can . . ."

He stopped himself. I listened to him breathing. A few seconds passed and he started up again. "You've made a mistake, a very grave mistake, and so has your Miss Ellis, because when I'm through with her, she'll be elected to the Sports Writers' Hall of Fame as the reporter who committed the blunder of the century."

Click. He was gone. Dial tone in my ear.

Could he back out? Could he tell the press that he wasn't moving, that he was staying or that he was selling? Before, I was figuring like this: Once he heard the news and it was out in the open, once Oran put it on the air, he'd have to go with it. He'd see it was right. He'd get the old feeling back. But now I was hearing something else. Now Bobby was screaming his head off that I betrayed him and that he ain't moving nowhere, and I had to wonder whether that's baloney or whether that's for real, 'cause if it's for real all bets are off, and Oran, poor Oran . . .

"Where is he?" Oran was calling me the next day.

"You mean Bobby?"

"I'm not talking about the Pope."

"Tried his house?"

"On the phone and in person. I've been there three times today. No sign of him."

"Don't worry."

"I've been fed to the network all day. The story's everywhere from Sacramento to Singapore. It's serious, Squat. I've got to find him. I need confirmation. I'm even being interviewed by other journalists. Major columnists. *The Wall Street Journal*. *Sports Illustrated*. My phone hasn't stopped ringing. If I can't find Hanes, I may have to ask you to make a statement."

"You got the wrong boy."

"You aren't telling me the story's fake, are you?"

"I ain't doing no talking for Bobby."

"Don't pull the rug from under me, Squat. Not now, for heaven's sake."

"I ain't doing no pulling and I ain't doing no pushing. All I'm saying is that everything's fine. And when Bobby gets ready, he'll come out and talk."

"The story's in the *Times*—New York and L.A.—and the Washington *Post*. Page one. And they use my name. They call it my story. You should see what's happening over here at the station. They're treating me like some sort of conquering hero."

"Heroine," I reminded her.

"Not for long, though. Now they're starting to get nervous. They want to hear something from Hanes, and so do I. We need to have a statement!"

"Give me two hours."

I tried, but I couldn't find Bobby. All the numbers and all the secretaries and all the private lines didn't answer. I even called the airport to see if the Lear was still there. It was, but Bobby wasn't. So I was a little shook, 'cause half the world was calling me—the players and the management and the announcers and my dad, everyone was calling me and I was telling 'em that I couldn't say nothing, couldn't deny it and couldn't confirm it 'cause Bobby was the man, he was the one. And I was sounding real calm, but as time ticked by I was feeling a little shaky. Maybe I hadn't understood him after all. Maybe my dreams were getting me confused.

"Well?" It was Oran again, two hours later.

"No luck."

"Shit."

"He'll turn up."

"It's being carried on all three network evening news shows. All three. My bosses are insane. Now they think I've made it up. I want you to talk to them. You have to say something, Squat."

"We'll ride out the night and by tomorrow we'll have the word from Bobby."

"I might not make it through the night."

Click. All these people hanging up in my face.

That evening I watched the news. "An unsubstantiated rumor," they said. One bozo even called it, "a possible error on the part of a Los Angeles sports reporter." Oh Jesus. I took my phone off the hook. I couldn't stand it no more. I had to get out, so I decided to take a walk. I went around Silver Lake, smelling the sweet grass and the dog crap. I was too nervous to go on walking, so I went back to the house, fed Pee Wee, put the phone back on the hook. Then the players started calling me again and I took the phone off the hook again. I watched TV for a while. Doris Day loves Rock Hudson. I turned off the TV, put the phone back on the hook. I worried. Oh man, I was worrying my head off. What was I doing? What had I done to Oran, to Bobby, what had I done to myself? I fell asleep with my clothes on.

Ring-a-ding-ding. I reached for the phone. What time was it?

"Tomorrow at noon." It was Bobby. It was the middle of the night. His voice was like sandpaper.

"What's tomorrow at noon?"

"The press conference at the Bonaventure Hotel."

"What you going to say?"

Click. Dial tone in my ear.

It was rough getting through breakfast the next morning. The phone wouldn't stop. This one, that one, Tom Alvarado and the New York *Daily News* and the Chicago *Trib*. Sometimes I heard myself talking and I had to remember that it was me—handling problems and the press like I had been doing it my whole life, putting these people off. In between there was also Oran, who sounded like she had been eating uppers instead of eggs for breakfast.

"What's he going to say?" she wanted to know.

"I don't got the faintest."

154

"You've talked to him. I know you've talked to him."

"He only said a couple of words to me."

"What were they?"

"Fuck you."

"He's really infuriated about the leak?"

"Yeah."

"But is he going to do it? Is he going to move the team?"

"You still don't got no faith in Squat, do you?"

"You don't sound as confident as you did the other night."

She was right, but I said, "I know my man."

"I'll see you at noon. You'll be able to recognize me because I'll be the one with a dagger behind my ear instead of a pencil—just in case he changes his story."

You've seen hotels like the Bonaventure. They're everywhere. I guess they're built so people can feel like they're flying through space or floating around the moon. But I'm one of those guys who likes the earth, and I ain't crazy about all those towers shooting up and elevators going through the roof, and the big courtyard in the middle which reminds me of the old apartment buildings in Brooklyn except no one's hanging their laundry out at the Bonaventure. The joint makes me nervous.

I was having a hard time finding the room where the press conference was being held, because the way this hotel was put together was really nuts if you ask me. So I was turning this way and that way and now I was worried I was gonna be late. Then I saw a guy with a minicam and I followed him 'cause I figured he was heading in the right direction and there we were in this big room with all the chairs set up and a place up front where Bobby was gonna stand. All the big reporters in town were there and Oran was looking very foxy in a gray suit. She already had her place down front and next to her was Patty Sides in pink—real shocking pink—and even though I didn't like her it was hard not to look at her. All the guys were looking at her and the place was buzzing, the room was charged up with this electricity 'cause of all the reporters—dozens of 'em—and their lights and wires and mikes, with more and more people arriving, the room getting packed solid, no more seats left and newsmen standing in the aisles and against the walls and someone carrying in extra chairs but it was no use 'cause everyone in town was here.

I was asked a zillion questions, and I smiled and didn't say nothing. It was already five after twelve, and then it was fifteen after twelve, which was about when he should have arrived— that's his style—but now it was twelve-thirty and the crowd was getting annoyed and Oran gave me a look from across the room —I was standing in the back—and I could hear her heart beating from sixty feet away. I heard my own heart, too. I kept stepping outside and looking down the hallway. Where was he? He hadn't ever been this late before. Twelve-thirty-five, twelve-thirty-six. How much longer were these folks gonna wait? I heard some of them saying that they were about to pack up and head out when he bounced in the room wearing a black terry-cloth jogging suit.

It looked like there were a couple of hundred-watt bulbs lit up behind his blue eyes. He went right to the mike and stroked his beard, which was shining red in the TV lights. "I must apologize for being late this morning, but I had some urgent last-minute business with the Egyptian government—nothing about baseball —and I ran over here as soon as I could."

"Buying the Sphinx, Bobby?" one of the wise-guy reporters shouted out.

"No, just one of the smaller pyramids," Bobby shouted back.

Everyone laughed. Then there were a few seconds of silence, and then Bobby asked, "Is everyone waiting for me to say something? You know me, I'm not much on prepared statements. I'd rather throw it open to you people, give you a chance to make news. Are there any questions?"

The room went up in one great roar. The reporters leaped to their feet.

"Yes, Miss Sides?" said Bobby.

My heart was sinking.

"Mr. Hanes," started Sides, "it's been reported that you have decided to move the Dodger franchise from Los Angeles back to Brooklyn." Her voice was so squeaky it sounded like it needed to be oiled. "Is it true, or is it just one of those silly rumors?"

That did it. Now I was sure he was gonna deny it. Now I was sure he was gonna humiliate Oran, crap on me and return to his senses. Now I was convinced that moving back would be nuts, and that I had been nuts, and sure, it was impossible.

"Is it true?" this dame was asking him. "Or is it just one of those silly rumors?"

Bobby's smile got bigger. He let a couple of seconds tick by. He was loving this moment. He knew how casual and cool and sexy he looked up there, his blond hair, his black jogging suit. At this moment he was the happiest man on planet earth.

"Like most rumors," he finally said, "this one represents incomplete information. The fact of the matter, Miss Sides, is that I will not merely move the Dodgers back to Brooklyn, but I will rebuild Ebbets Field for them, for all of us—brick by brick."

I nearly fell over. Oran's face turned pinker than Patty Sides's dress.

"You've toyed with the press now for months," Oran spoke up before any other reporter had a chance. "Is this Ebbets Field business another one of your jokes?"

"Miss Sides," replied Bobby, ignoring Oran, "did you have a follow-up question?"

"Yes," said Patty. "When are you planning on—"

"Moving to Brooklyn or to Bellevue?" Oran cut in. "Because obviously this is another madcap publicity gimmick, a way to use the press—"

"I had the floor," snapped Sides.

"Then why don't you start mopping it up?" Oran bit back.

"Miss Ellis," Bobby said, "if you find these events too stimulating to handle, you should take a sedative beforehand."

"I want specifics, Mr. Hanes," Oran was asking. "I want to know exactly how you propose to . . ."

Back and forth, between Bobby and Oran, between Oran and Patty, the fireworks continued, but I didn't listen after a while. I really didn't hear nothing. Only those first words. Moving back. Rebuilding Ebbets Field. It was so perfect, it was the best thing Bobby ever said! And I knew what he was doing, I knew what he was saying. He was saying to me: Okay, Squat, you think you're gonna dare me into moving the Dodgers back to Brooklyn, you think you're gonna get me to do something I was too scared to do. Well, I ain't scared, Bobby was saying, and just to show you, I'm going even further. I'm going back all the way and putting us back where we *really* belong. How's that?

Oh man, Bobby was great! Bobby was fantastic! I was standing in the back of the room, and now my smile was as big as his, and he was watching me enjoying him. He saw how I was listening to him field all those questions—he was throwing around the bull so beautifully, and naturally he didn't give Oran no specifics. He didn't give 'em 'cause he didn't have 'em. She was trying to nail him, but she couldn't. And I could tell, in her own way, she was loving it. Everyone was loving it, 'cause it was the most wonderful story any of those creepy reporters had ever heard. Bobby was talking about the old days, about the way the ballpark felt and how ballparks don't feel that way anymore. He was gonna change all that. He didn't care how much it cost or how crazy it sounded. He was dedicating himself to doing nothing else. "Facts!" his voice boomed. "Who cares for facts? The facts will come later. The truth is that what we need in baseball is feeling, a real feeling for the game and the players and the community, which, more than anyone else, owns the team, spiritually and morally. There was once such a community, and it was called Brooklyn, and I contend that when those people were deprived of their team, baseball lost its soul. We have spent these many years since searching for that soul, and until it is found, until it is returned to the body to which it belongs, the world will never be at peace, the heavens will never be at rest." Everyone was eating this up, no one was minding if Bobby wanted to play God. My heart was singing again. Bobby was my pal again. I believed in him again. I knew he was gonna do it—do it for me, do it for Brooklyn, but mainly do it for himself. I was feeling warm and proud all over. I felt like screaming and crying, 'cause I knew we were together again, and nothing could stop us now!

FOUR

THEY SAID IT wouldn't be snowing this early in the year in Berlin, but I didn't believe 'em, so I packed heavy clothes, and man, was I smart. It was some cold October in Germany, and here I was in the middle of a snowstorm, in the back of a cab, riding over to Herr Schmidt's place.

This was my idea, not Bobby's. We were sitting around after the last game of the season, discussing the problem at hand. Lots of people still didn't believe Bobby was gonna do it; they didn't think Bobby would leave L.A., 'cause L.A.—no matter how lousy things had gotten there—was considered one of the big sports towns in all the world. And, after thirty years, how could the city be without a baseball team?

"That's just tough," Bobby was saying. "Didn't O'Malley just pull out because he felt like it? Did he ever worry about the fans he was leaving behind?"

"I think that's just the point, kid," says me. "We ain't interested in pulling an O'Malley. That's how everything got messed up to begin with."

"The focus, Squat, must be on the future, not the past. From now on, Los Angeles is the past, Brooklyn is the future."

He was spinning around like a revolving door.

"But maybe there's a way we can keep everyone happy," I said.

"A noble ambition, but one which has more attraction for you than me."

"You gotta dump Dodger Stadium, don't you?"

"It's a prime piece of real estate, and it will sell."

"And I been thinking of buyers. You see, kid, in my humble opinion, it's real important to be smart about this thing. And there ain't no reason why we gotta have half of California hating us."

"Exactly what do you have in mind, Squat?"

"I wanna sell Dodger Stadium back to Konrad Schmidt."

For a second I thought about what I had said: *I* want to sell Dodger Stadium. What did I mean, *I* wanted to sell it? But Bobby was chuckling and seemed real happy.

"It's an idea so sensational I'd like to claim it as my own," he told me.

"Feel free."

"You're starting to hustle the hustlers, Squat."

"Just trying to earn my keep, boss."

That was less than a month ago, and now here I was back in a blizzard in Berlin, marching into the man's office and looking at his little mustache—he must have had it clipped every hour on the hour—and remembering what he had said about me over the squawk box in Bobby's office.

"You are here on another mission," he told me in that almost perfect English accent of his. "I welcome you, Mr. Malone, and I certainly commiserate with you. You have a most difficult superior with whom you must contend."

"Bobby? No. Haven't you heard, Kon, the kid's really working for me. I just don't like to hurt his feelings or nothing, so for the sake of appearances I lay low."

He managed the tiniest smile I'd ever seen in my life. "But you did not come to Germany to joke, Mr. Malone. Just as the fate of the Los Angeles Dodgers is no joke. And this business about transferring the team, I must confess, confuses and intrigues me."

"That's great, Kon, 'cause that's exactly what I came to talk to you about."

I pulled out the facts and figures. I had pages of them—how many people and how much money and the leisure team industries in southern California and the history of the ball team there and the profit that had been made in the past three decades. I had charts and graphs and all sorts of proof, and when he asked me how I could verify this stuff, I showed him my source— which was the six-month survey Schmidt had commissioned before his conglomerate had originally bought the team. Now his smile got about a quarter inch bigger.

"But that was before you and your Mr. Hanes took over, when the team had not quite fallen to its currently abject position."

"Which is why there's this beautiful opportunity, Kon, the opportunity of your lifetime. Don't you see? L.A.'s mad at us, the way Brooklyn was mad at O'Malley when he pulled the plug in '57. We're gonna move the Dodgers, and that's that. While we're getting it together in Brooklyn, no one's gonna come near Dodger Stadium next year. We're planning on taking that season on the chin, 'cause there's nothing else we can do. But once we're outta there—in 1988—we'll be leaving behind us one of the hungriest baseball towns in America, a town that's gonna be looking for a team. And that's where you come in. 'Cause that team could be your team, Kon. Call 'em the L.A. Schmidts or the L.A. Sauerkrauts. Call 'em anything you like, because they'll be money-makers. They'll be heroes—this new team of yours. The league's gonna give you approval—Bobby can guarantee it, the other owners love Bobby like a son—and no one will fight the idea of replacing the Dodgers with another National League team in L.A. It'll happen, Kon, I'm telling you. If it ain't you, it'll be someone else, probably the Japanese, which is where I'm going next."

"Tokyo?"

"Tomorrow night," I lied.

"An expansion team in Los Angeles. Is that what you're proposing?"

"It'll be the biggest goldmine anywhere outside of South Africa," says me, fingering the stacks of facts. "You know the L.A. market better than anyone, Kon."

160

"I would be purchasing the Los Angeles baseball facility and the right to play in the city, a berth in the National League. Is that what you're saying?"

"Right. We're giving you L.A. All we're taking is a few not-so-hot players and that one little name—Dodgers."

"Your proposal is quite absurd, Mr. Malone."

"I thought you'd like it, Kon."

And by the end of the week, the deal was done: Schmidt snatched back Dodger Stadium and a slot in the National League —all pending approval.

I gave Bobby credit for the deal, not because I was modest, but because I was truthful. It *was* his pitch. Sort of. And if he and Schmidt didn't hate each other, Bobby would have sold him in person. He wouldn't have needed me. So I wasn't fooling myself, I was just happy to be helpful and to keep things moving along, into November, when the big winter meeting was coming up and Bobby was going to have put on the performance of his life. He was going to have to sell the owners on Brooklyn. Sure, I did okay with Schmidt, but now it was time for the heavyweight event.

"He intends to move them anyway?" Oran asked me over a plate of mushu pork in Hollywood. "No matter what happens with league approval, he's going to move the club?"

"Yeah," says me, "but he doesn't wanna mess around with the courts. You remember what happened with Al Davis when he first wanted to pull the Raiders out of Oakland. He didn't give the other owners no respect. Didn't even ask them. He said, 'I'm going to L.A. and that's it, and I don't need no approval.' Well, everyone got ticked off, 'cause, first of all, he was making money in Oakland—least that's what everyone said—and now he was depriving the city of a team, just like O'Malley. We don't want none of that. We gotta spend money on ballplayers, not lawyers."

"It sounds like you're in charge of this operation, Squat."

"I don't know nothing about this complicated stuff, I promise you. I'm just trying to keep everyone happy, that's all."

"I'm certain that you and Bobby and Patty Sides will all live happily ever after."

"We don't see her much anymore."

"You will when she starts broadcasting the Dodger games," said Oran.

"I thought that would make you happy. Now she'll be out of your hair. Your competition's eliminated. And besides, who wants a job broadcasting for a team that's bound to lose another hundred games?"

"She'll be going to Brooklyn with you."

"By then she'll be a movie star, and we don't allow no movie stars in Brooklyn."

"What's his plan to get league approval?" Oran asked, always looking for a story. "How's he going to deal with Percano?"

"The same way you're going to make it to the network. By being sweet and kind and courteous."

"Tell me the plan."

"You'll be in Washington next week. You'll see it for yourself."

We broke open our fortune cookies. I read Oran's: THE LOYALTY OF A FRIEND IS TWICE THE STRENGTH OF AN ENEMY'S SCORN. She read mine: YOUR LOVE LIFE WILL DRASTICALLY CHANGE—SOONER THAN YOU THINK.

We drank tea and she kept on questioning me. "I don't know how he's gonna hustle the owners," I told her. "I really don't have the foggiest."

"If you knew, would you say?"

"If it helped us both, sure."

"And if it only helped one of us?"

"You're the one."

"You mean if it came down to between Bobby and me, you'd side with me?"

"We're all here to help each other," I explained. "That's the way I look at life."

"And what if the Brooklyn venture fades after a season, or never really materializes? What if the obstacles prove to be too great, even for the great Bobby Hanes?"

"That's what I mean. It ain't just him. He's got all of us working for him."

"Percano may well be a problem," she said. "The man has enormous power. That's why I'm so interested in Bobby's strategy. All evening I've been writing an editorial about the situation in my head. Would you like to hear it?"

"No."

And for the next half hour Oran delivered her theory of baseball ownership—how everything was working against Bobby's winning over the establishment. The idea of leaving Los Angeles without a major-league team was unacceptable, she said. Which is when I remembered how it had slipped my mind to mention my Berlin trip to her. Oh well. I figured she already had enough to worry about.

FIVE

FOR SOME REASON there were all these bird cages in the lobby of the old hotel in Washington where we were staying. From hanging around Bobby all these years, I already knew this kind of joint—sorta crummy, but it gets away with it 'cause people think it's fancy. Sometimes crummy is exclusive. Sometimes it's also weird, specially with these birds singing in their bird cages, tweet tweet tweet.

Now we were walking through the lobby with the big chandelier hanging down and roses in the carpet when who did we see but the Commissioner himself, W.W. Percano and his wife. His wife looked like she belonged in one of the bird cages 'cause she looked like a bird. Her nose was more a beak than a nose, and she chirped instead of talked.

Bobby kissed her hand. "I'm so glad you could come down for the meeting," he said to her, ignoring the old man. "These get-togethers can be so terribly dull without the presence of at least a few lovely ladies."

She blushed. Percano stared at us. He still looked like an owl, and he was mad. Bobby's charm was working on his old lady. She thanked Bobby, said she was pleased to meet me. Bobby started telling her about the history of the old hotel, when it used to be really something in the old days, before Washington became so . . . so "popular." She quite agreed. She remembered those days. She remembered Bobby's dad. Back in New York, they were in the same social circle. Percano hooted out something or other—that they were late, that they had to go. "What a shame," remarked Bobby. "I would have liked to have had you both up for a drink." Percano didn't say nothing. He blinked his eyes. I expected to see him and the Mrs. spread their wings and fly away.

163

"Do you know what he's thinking?" Bobby asked after they were gone.

"Ways to screw you."

"That's a generous reading of the situation."

Upstairs Bobby was still in rare form. He smoked and drank and took calls from halfway around the world. He bought a boat, and a pile of silver. And sold a forest. And kept on getting happier, and wouldn't tell me what he planned to do at these meetings. This was one of those times when I kept quiet. I just listened to him make his calls, and when I got bored I went to my room. Oran kept calling me and I kept telling her I didn't know, I honestly didn't know what he was going to do.

That night me and Bobby went to dinner in the crummy fancy hotel dining room and there was Oran with a slinky dress and a famous senator—I couldn't think of the bum's name— feeding her face. Bobby didn't like that. And there was Percano and a bunch of the owners and their wives at a big table and we went over with handshakes and hellos. Bobby was acting like he owned the hotel and the whole District of Columbia to boot.

We sat on the other side of the big dining room, far away from everyone. Bobby sipped on a martini he ordered and he asked me, turning toward Oran and her date, "Do you think she's sleeping with him?"

"Beats me."

"You seem awfully interested."

"No more interested than you, kid."

"You're certain you're not sweet on her, Squat? Because if you are, that's perfectly all right with me."

"Glad I got your permission."

"I just don't trust her. Not with you. Not with him. Not with anyone."

"You and Oran remind me of each other."

"What do you mean by that, Squat?"

"Just what I said. You're both winners."

"Should I be flattered?"

"I'd rather you'd be worried about these meetings. 'Cause I sure as hell am."

The boardroom of this hotel was aching with age. It looked sick. Sitting in these great thrones of cracked leather were the powers that be, the owners of the National League, puffing on cigars and looking bored. Percano gave the official long-winded welcome. He gave a regular political ad; he warned them about the dangers facing baseball—"frivolous franchise hopping" is the term he used. He said there was no place in the sport for impulsiveness. He said that the authority of this great body had to be respected, and obeyed. He quoted the President, said how the President had praised him, had praised all the owners and the hallowed traditions of the game of baseball and bull, bull, bull. . . .

Me, I was looking around the room. Hello, Roy Trapp, President of the League, who was about to nod off. Percano carried this cat around in his back pocket. Hello, Greenstreet. He was stoned. Hello, Blatsky and Honnerstein and Mintz, sitting on their fat wallets, trying to pay attention to the owl. Hello, Tug Leavis, who looked like he needed a drink. Hello, Bobby, who was sitting and grinning like he was holding a fistful of aces.

"Tomorrow morning," Percano was hooting, "you gentlemen will face a number of grave decisions. I trust that you will not be swayed by . . ." A schoolteacher, that's what the Commissioner was. The junior high school principal.

The speech droned on, and the rule changes were discussed, and when it came time for preliminary talks on the franchise changes everyone looked really tired and bored, and Bobby said that the whole crew—including Percano and Trapp—were invited up to his suite for lunch. Lunch was being brought to the conference room, the Commissioner complained, but by then we were all on our way, anxious to see what the kid had in store.

Lunch was liquid. And man, the guys could drink. I think lunch is the time of the day when richies drink the most, 'cause it seems respectable or something. Bobby knew this and had three waiters going around filling up glasses. Bobby was working the room, helping the boys down their drinks and drown their sorrows, listening and laughing, and then, at about two o'clock, he held up his hand and said he wanted to say something.

"We've been waiting for the horseshit to start flying," said Harris Dives of the Giants. Dives really looked like a walrus this time; his mustache had gotten bushier. "Just make your pitch short, Hanes."

"Gentlemen, gentlemen," Bobby protested in his calmest voice. "I've come not to bury Percano, but to praise him." That got a laugh from everyone except Percano.

"But I do want to say a couple of words." Bobby started walking around the room, stopping here and there for the sake of drama, putting his arm around the guys, sitting on the edge of a chair, getting real serious and sincere. "I'm not going to give any lectures, and I will be brief. A mood has been established this afternoon, and I'd be the last to violate that mood. Besides, this isn't the kind of group that's going to respond to hyperbole. Each of you knows the ways of the world. You've made your fortunes by doing what feels right, by having the courage to compete in the jungle of the marketplace—and by surviving in that jungle. In your own ways, you're pioneers—in the end, you realize that you're always alone. I like to think that I'm no different. I like to think that, like you, I've bought a baseball team not because I myself love the game, but because I have a responsibility to those who also love the game—the fans for whom we operate and play and struggle to win." Bobby's blue eyes were shining, and he was talking with his hands, gesturing like a preacher. He was saying, "These teams are ours, and they are not ours. They're everyone's. Naturally we have our indulgences"—and he stopped and put his arm around Tug Leavis's meaty shoulders—"and certainly we are entitled. Tug here bought the Reds so his grandson Tug III could be the batboy when Bob Targan beats Hank Aaron's home-run record three or four years from now. Isn't that the truth, Tug?" Tug was too bombed to reply. "We know that Pete Blatsky here," Bobby went on, "bought the Chicago franchise because he and his brothers and his cronies from the beer plant have been playing pinochle at Wrigley Field for twenty years and one afternoon the security guard said there was a tough new nongambling policy in the ballpark and Pete got pissed—you guys know what Pete's like when he's pissed—so he bought the team in order for his card game to go on undisturbed. Do I have it right, Pete?" And Pete burped his approval.

"None of us are any different," Bobby was saying. "We're in it for the kicks and the power plays, the ego trips and the small bits of glory along the way. We're in it because it's crazy and fun and no one—let me repeat, no one—is going to tell us why or how or where we should run our ball clubs, because you understand better than anyone that none of this would be possible were it not for our own private dreams, dreams which have been there since we were little boys, dreams which will not go away, not until we do the impossible and make those dreams come true. And we know in our hearts that we are not merely dreaming for ourselves, but we are dreaming for millions of others.

"But what is the dream? It's not a chart or a graph or a page of facts and figures. It's not a marketing strategy or a financial plan. God knows it's not a way to get rich. It's precious, this dream; it's unique. It's something dear to all of us, something we have been selected—by ourselves and perhaps a force greater than ourselves —to protect. We are defenders of the dream, and my dream is here." And now Bobby put this big picture on an easel in front of the room. It was a drawing, in color, very true-to-life and scary, because it was Ebbets Field, in the exact location where it used to be—McKeever and Sullivan—with all the old bricks looking new.

"What was said about this ballpark by Branch Rickey in the '30s will still be true in the '90s. 'You can turn on the lights in the middle of the night in Ebbets Field,' Mr. Rickey boasted, 'and two hundred thousand fans will show up just to see what's happening.' There's still half a million people who live within walking distance—that's *walking* distance—of the ballpark. The borough of Brooklyn is still the fourth-largest city in America. And furthermore, to restore baseball to Brooklyn is to restore sanity to America. It's to take us back to where we once belonged, and where we need to go. It's where past and future meet. It's a community waiting to be healed, a city waiting to be revitalized. I have lived with this dream for decades now, and I can see that it is real. As real as this rendering. It will be the same, the same wonderful warm baseball park called Ebbets Field. The plans and the projections are all sound and logical. It can be completed in eighteen months, in time for the 1988 season. But it will also be different; it will be better. The surrounding area will be cleared for a half-dozen huge parking garages. The city has already promised to cooperate. The citizens themselves are delirious. And as to the question of Los Angeles, that, too, has been considered. They are baseball fans in California—loyal and true—and we are proposing that the L.A. franchise, along with Dodger Stadium, be bought by a financially sound international concern with prior experience in the market. These details will be provided to you in tomorrow morning's meeting. But now I only want to emphasize that this whole transaction can be made simple if we finally allow Tucson the team it so deeply deserves. The Brooklyn club would stay in the Western Division and Tucson would join the East. That way, things will remain balanced.

"I know what you're thinking: Up until a few years ago, L.A. was your most profitable stop on the road. Aren't I ruining that for you? And what kind of crowds can we expect to draw in Brooklyn? Will the fans really turn out? These were questions I asked myself. And rather than accept my own answers, I'd prefer that you take the answer found on this piece of paper." Bobby pulled an envelope from his coat pocket, opened it, read from this sheet. "In my hand is a proposed contract from a local New York TV station offering the Dodgers eight million dollars for the 1988 season. I don't have to tell you that this is the richest contract of its kind in baseball history. The TV boys are as hard-nosed as they come. They're giving nothing away, and certainly the unprecedented size of this contract reflects the most realistic, no-nonsense assessment of baseball in Brooklyn. Gentlemen, I'm talking big business, big business for all of us.

"But I've talked enough. Now it's time to spread the joy and the fun, to pay tribute to each of you for sharing my vision. I can only return the favor by returning the vision—your vision—in a slightly different form."

And with that, Bobby opened the door to his bedroom, and there was a lineup of costumed mascots—like the life-sized Mickey Mouses and Donald Ducks you see walking around Disneyland—only these characters were Cardinals and Braves and Pirates and Cubs, and each character strolled over to his respective owner and shook his hand, and each owner howled—everyone was howling except Percano, even Trapp was howling—especially when the characters started unzipping and stepping out of their costumes, and underneath they were ladies—beautiful, sexy ladies—who were practically naked except for a trace of the original costume: the Pirate lady had on nothing but a black buccaneer's mask; the Cub lady had this furry little tail taped on her rump; the Astronaut wasn't wearing nothing but silver space boots; the Indian brave was all dressed up in her birthday suit and a war bonnet; the Cincy chick had on one red sock; the gal from the Phillies had this cracked papier-mâché liberty bell ringing deep down in her cleavage. This was really something, this was more than anyone had expected, even me, and by now the owl had taken off in a huff, but the owners, they weren't going anywhere. The owners were having a ball.

The party went all afternoon, and late that night, down in the lobby, when I ran into Oran the first thing she asked me was whether the long meeting meant we were going to have a hard time getting league approval tomorrow morning. What could I say?

"Well," she pressed me, "did Bobby speak today?"

"Yeah, he spoke, all right."

"Was he effective?"

"I ain't sure what the right word is."

"What was his presentation like?"

"If you can feature a combination of the Sermon on the Mount and a Roman orgy, you'll be pretty close."

Oran got ticked off 'cause she thought I was putting her on. But next time I saw her, a day later, she was holding a copy of the New York *Post*, and the headline on page one was screaming in blood-red ink:

> *IT'S OFFICIAL!*
> *BUMS BACK IN BROOKLYN!*
> Hanes Says Ebbets Ready by '88;
> NL Expands; New Teams in L.A., Tucson

Closer...

ONE

I T WAS COLD and gray and mushy in Flatbush. Last week's snow had turned to slush. Everyone was bundled up like polar bears, and I was looking out of the window of the cab—we weren't about to take a limo—watching all the streets: Carlton, Vanderbilt, Underhill, Grand, Classon. I was wishing the weather wasn't so lousy, and I was wishing that Oran could have been here to cover the story instead of stuck back in L.A., 'cause, after all, this was the day we'd been waiting for.

I saw it there at the corner of McKeever and Sullivan. Ebbets Field Apartments. Big and ugly and tall, a bunch of twenty-five-story buildings stuck together. How come, I was wondering, these things looked like they were designed by escaped convicts? We were definitely doing the world a favor by tearing 'em down. They were only one-third occupied anyway, and every other window was boarded up or broken. Seemed very seedy and sorry to me, like no one cared anymore, like this part of Brooklyn—like so many parts of Brooklyn—was down in the dumps.

Bobby and me, we knew all that, but we didn't talk about it too much, 'cause what was to be gained? We had a job to do, and we knew we had to stick with it. Worrying about stuff outside our control wouldn't help. Besides, today Bobby was making his big announcement with the press there and the Governor and the Mayor and the Borough President; today Bobby was telling every-one about this incredible deal he had cut, this beautiful partner-

173

ship between the city and the state and himself to do what almost everybody said was totally bonkers. I didn't get all the details, I just knew that the President got involved 'cause he needed the New York vote and he thought everyone was gonna love this back-to-Brooklyn business. Which is just what the other politicos thought. Specially after talking to Bobby and seeing the look in his eyes and knowing that he was willing to put his money where his mouth was. Besides, in New York, who didn't want the Dodgers back in Brooklyn?

That's what I was thinking when we arrived and Bobby started shaking hands with all the big shots. I wasn't paying too much attention. I was looking around this huge apartment complex and trying to really believe that Ebbets Field once stood on this very spot, trying to believe that it was really going to stand here again, and that this area—from Empire to Eastern, from Bedford to Nostrand—was going to be rebuilt with stores and restaurants and parking garages and that the center of it all was going to be here, exactly where it once was—Ebbets Field—because these architects that Bobby had dug up somewhere in Cambridge claimed they could duplicate it with a few little changes in material. These guys were hysterically happy, because they saw it as the challenge of a lifetime.

I was looking around at the press and the politicians, and I still wasn't sure whether it was all for real when I saw a sign, right here in front of the Ebbets Field Apartments, that said, PLEASE —NO BALL PLAYING ALLOWED.

I was surprised that there wasn't a bigger crowd. But who wants to stand outside in the middle of winter? The bigwigs were standing next to Bobby, getting ready to make their speeches, but Bobby went to the mike first. I was standing with the press. Everyone was snapping pictures, and the cameras started to roll, and Bobby was saying that this was the start of a big adventure and everyone was going to live happily ever after because something ugly was coming down and something beautiful was going up and all of Brooklyn would be proud. Then he said that the tenants here would be temporarily relocated in these next few weeks in a mostly unoccupied city project in Bensonhurst, but then, after that, they'd be moved to a brand-new complex that the Dodger organization would be putting up with the city in Bay Ridge which would have a lot bigger apartments than the ones here, and the rent would be the same, so everyone would make out, no one would be hurt. Just then the army of angry tenants —blacks and Puerto Ricans and white people—came roaring around the side of the building and started pelting Bobby and the bigwigs with eggs, one after another, and, believe me, these people could throw, and they were shouting about how they didn't give a shit about a lousy baseball team and they didn't wanna be moved around like they were cattle, and this is where they lived and they didn't wanna know nothing from no Dodgers and no rich man's memories. Bobby was trying to tell 'em that it wasn't about rich men, it was about all men and women, 'cause the Dodgers stand for . . . and pow! an egg in his puss, with yolk dripping down in his beard, and pow! another egg in his ear, and pow! an egg right at the knot of his tie. The bigwigs were ducking out and the press was having a ball—the cameras were catching everything—with ladies and kids and rough-looking teenagers mad as hell. Then I heard the roar of sirens, cop cars and cop vans, and someone threw a rock at a cop—I saw the cop hit the ground, his face a bloody mess—and the other cops were boiling. Bobby was still talking, still trying to tell 'em that everything was cool, but now I saw that I had to get him outta here, and he wasn't budging, no matter how hard I tried to drag him away. Then a nasty rock got him in the neck and cut him. The cops were doing some serious head-busting, and Bobby still wouldn't budge, so I hauled off and clobbered him. He went down and I dragged him to a cop car and we went speeding off, sirens blaring. The riot was still going full force behind us, and I closed my eyes and thought to myself that this was one strange way of bringing peace and brotherhood back to Brooklyn.

"I didn't have a chance to show you my surprise," Bobby said when he came to in Kings County Hospital.

"Enough surprises for one day," says me. He was real groggy and they had his neck all bandaged up where they had put in the stitches.

"It's the surprise I mentioned before we left the hotel. I've been working on it for months, and today was the day I wanted you to see it." His speech was blurred and his eyes were swollen. He could barely lift his head off the pillow. The nurse asked him if he wanted another pill, and he said yes. I've never known Bobby to turn down dope.

"Was anyone seriously hurt?" he wanted to know.

"You."

"A few scratches, nothing more. But what about the tenants and the mayor and—"

"Cops messed up a couple of the people who live in the apartments. It was just on the TV news."

"Oh shit."

"You remember what happened?"

"You floored me—that's what happened."

He did remember. I was hoping he wouldn't. "I had to. You were about to be murdered."

"By the very people who would benefit from our plan."

"They don't see it that way, kid."

"Brooklyn may be somewhat rougher than we anticipated."

"They don't call it a jungle for nothing."

"Elysian Fields," he started slurring and drifting off behind his painkillers. "The Garden of Eden. Paradise Lost and Paradise Regained. Oh dear Squat, what in the name of heaven are we doing here?"

Ralph, whose hair had turned snow-white, picked us up at the hospital the next day. Bobby told him to drive us to the surprise. The surprise was on Willow Street. I saw that poor old Ralph was crying. We were back at the house where I hadn't been for more years than I could remember. It looked the same, with the brick and the painted shutters, all old and beautiful and so very classy.

I helped Bobby up the steps, 'cause he was still feeling a little shaky and his neck was all bandaged. He wasn't saying much, but he didn't have to, because when he opened the door I saw that the whole joint had been redone. All painted fresh and white and the wood floors were gleaming. The furniture was new and modern, and he told me the fourth floor was all for me, my own apartment in the townhouse, and Bobby, he was going to be on the third floor, and the second floor was for offices—we each had an office so we could work here whenever we wanted. This was really something, completely redesigned except for two things: The little room across from Bobby's bedroom on the third floor, the Dodger Room, was the same as it was forty years ago. The same pennants and the same posters, the same pictures of Van Lingle Mungo and Skoonj Furillo and Preacher and the Barber. The same Dodger pillows and the same shiny blue satin Dodger jacket. It was good that he did this, but I wasn't sure about his old man's study: There it was, down on the first floor, waiting for the Judge to come in and sit down and start working. All his books and his big fat highback chair, even his ashtray and the old-fashioned couch and telephone. It was like a museum, and maybe a little too weird for me. But I didn't say nothing, 'cause I knew I was the only one he could show it to, maybe the only one who really cared. But could I live here? Could I move in with my bags and my baseball books and Pee Wee?

"I need the company, Squat," he said.

It was sorta sad the way he put it, and I felt bad, but I had to tell him, "Geez, this is beautiful here the way it's all old and new and everything, Bobby, but I think I'm just going to get a place over in the old neighborhood, somewhere in Borough Park. Know what I mean?"

He looked at me, and I could see he understood. I was real relieved, 'cause I didn't want to hurt him. He had Ralph bring some brandy, and the three of us toasted the memory of the Judge, who, Bobby said, "will always be the master of the house." I wasn't so sure about that, but Bobby and Ralph were, and when Ralph left, Bobby lit up and got stoned and started describing the Judge's first race for Borough President when he'd jump on the trolley cars with little Bobby racing behind him and give speeches to the people going to work. Then Bobby would start reciting the speeches himself, imitating the old man, and he was good at it, real good. This was how we talked for a long, long time, so long, in fact, that I could hardly keep my eyes open. I asked Bobby whether he'd be okay. He said yes. And then I left for my folks' place, where I was going to sleep. I wasn't there to see what happened to Bobby the rest of that night, but I heard about it from two different sources.

After I left, Bobby took these pills which the hospital gave him. I don't know the name, but the kind of pills that get you up. He couldn't sleep, so he walked around the house, upstairs and down, looking at all these rooms that he had done over. He tried to read, tried to watch TV, tried to look at last week's computer sheets from all the businesses. Nothing worked. He remembered that he had been cooped up in the hospital for two days and that he needed to get some fresh air. So he drank a strong cup of coffee, got dressed—a cashmere turtleneck sweater to cover his bandaged neck, an old pair of jeans and jogging shoes, a Navy pea jacket—and went outside into the night.

His brain was crowded, but he didn't want to think, 'cause thinking made him nervous. He didn't want to think about the tenants or the people who wanted to kill him. He just wanted to walk and breathe, look at these swanky old streets of Brooklyn Heights and not worry about mashers or muggers or gangs of crazy-mean teenagers, not worry about anything except walking, driving all doubts from his mind, walking and clearing the decks.

Had he chewed off more than he could swallow? he thought. One step after another—that's all he was doing. Looking up and seeing the darkness of the covered sky—no stars—smelling the fragrance of the winter night, focusing his eyes straight ahead. Seeing the trio of men at the end of the block. Coming towards him. He heard them laughing. Were they carrying guns or knives? Would his life end here, just a few blocks from where he had been raised as a kid? How would the obituary read? They came closer and he could see their eyes and their teeth—they were young and strong—and he thought about turning and running, but he just smiled at them and they smiled back and laughed and kept walking, and so did he, ashamed at all the fear that had built up inside him. He kept walking until he reached the entrance to the Brooklyn Bridge, which reminded him of everything strong and solid and old about the borough. He thought of those times when the Brooklyn boulevards were really boulevards, when the parkways bloomed with flowers and the avenues were lined with mansions.

He looked up through the maze of girders and cords and cables, looked down into the dark East River. There wasn't much traffic on the bridge—just a car every once in a while. He heard a foghorn far off in the distance. And then he heard footsteps behind him, which were also far off. He tried not to think about the footsteps. He remembered what happened only a few minutes before. He just kept walking a little quicker. He got to the top of the bridge and the footsteps sounded like they were hurrying behind him, but he told himself not to worry. He didn't even bother to turn around, even if the footsteps were now only inches away, even if they had caught up with him. Finally he couldn't take it anymore, and he spun around, and there . . . there he saw a young lady in a white trenchcoat. She was beautiful and he was sure that she was for sale and right away he thought about buying her. He figured that's why she'd been hurrying after him. And why not? Why not have a whore for the night—three or four hours of fun. Bobby was ready to take or be taken, when he all of a sudden realized that the gorgeous gal beside him was no street-walker, she was Oran Ellis.

"Ellis," he said. "Aren't you afraid of walking alone at night?"

"Not in the least, Hanes. Are you?"

"Of course not. I'm just surprised to see you here. I hope you weren't thrown out of your job. You haven't decided to put your business on the streets, have you?"

"My business is your business, Hanes. You know me, I'll follow a story anywhere. I've rented a basement apartment in a town-house on Willow Street only eight doors down from you. We have the same taste in neighborhoods, and I see we're both fond of late-night strolls."

"What about L.A.?"

"I've quit. I've been meaning to for months, and I suppose you were the excuse I needed. After all, how could I possibly drop you?"

"Squat never said a word to me."

"Squat doesn't know."

"Do you have another job?"

"I'm looking, and I don't anticipate any problems." They kept on walking toward the lights of Manhattan.

"And you've been following me."

"For nearly a year. How's the neck?"

"I'll be fine, but what about you—you're really not afraid of Brooklyn?"

"No more so than you. If I needed help tonight, I knew all I'd have to do was shout and you'd protect my honor."

He looked at her. Her eyes were real soft and her hair was blowing in the wind. She leaned against the railing of the bridge and said, "We each have a job to do, Hanes, and I'm not one who gives up easily."

"Did anyone ever tell you that you're a pain in the ass, Ellis?"

"I know you're under pressure, and I want to say that I'm sympathetic."

He laughed in her face and began walking again, this time real fast. "You sound like I have a terminal disease."

She began to say something, but stopped herself. "I just meant that you've hit a nasty snag."

"What gives you that idea?"

"You could hardly call the incident at the apartments minor.

Now the New York press seems to be reevaluating you. They're not quite as excited—or perhaps the word is 'gullible'—as they were initially."

"And you," he told her, "you've moved three thousand miles just to see me crucified."

"I'm just looking for the facts. I intend to be as objective as possible."

"Objectively, you're full of shit."

"May I quote you?"

"Until your typewriter keys fall off."

"There's no need for you to get excited."

"You're the one who's worked up, Ellis, not me." They stopped again, seeing that their bickering wasn't getting them anywhere. They slowed down a little, and as they started walking down from the top of the bridge, they saw a bald-headed black man playing a golden saxophone. He sang through his horn and ignored Bobby and Oran, who side-stepped him as they passed by. The music was sexy sad, but no one said anything. Oran looked up and saw the dark clouds racing across the moon. She turned her eyes back on Bobby. Now it was freezing. Would he put his arm around her? Would she let him? Did she want him to?

They reached the end of the bridge. They were in Manhattan. Where to now? Who would make the first move? What would it be?

"Let's take a cab," said Bobby.

"Fine." Oran was ready.

There was a taxi waiting at the foot of the bridge. Bobby opened the door for her. Oran got in, and he followed. "Just drive," he told the driver. "Go up to Central Park." Still no talking. He sat next to one window, she looked out the other. They sailed up the island.

Bobby had the driver drop them at the Plaza Hotel, and from there they strolled up Fifth Avenue to another swanky East Side hotel. The place was small and cozy, and the walls were covered with suede. A high-class piano player was noodling some tunes in the corner. Bobby got them a booth and ordered a bottle of Dom Pérignon champagne that cost $250. Oran laughed, though inside she loved it. For the first time that night, she took off her trenchcoat. She was wearing a light-brown skirt and a tight green sweater. She was looking good.

"I've been doing research on your father," she said to Bobby.

"What have you found?" Naturally he was interested.

"It's hard to put together an accurate composite picture. The pure facts can be cold."

"He was cold."

"Is that how you view him?"

"Are you working on a story?"

"No, I'm drinking very expensive champagne with you."

"He was nearly as complicated as I am. Nearly as enigmatic and nearly as wealthy."

"But not quite as modest."

"Even less so."

"And you loved him?"

"How do you feel about your father?"

"I adore him." And for a long time she told Bobby about growing up in Denver. "My dad," she said, "is the most respected homebuilder in the state. He has absolute integrity. He's the last of a dying breed. He's one of those men who could build his houses singlehandedly if he had to. But he really wanted to be a writer. He loves history and literature, and I suppose some of his ambitions rubbed off on me, because I . . ." And she was telling him the story of her life, and when he saw how talkative she was, he got talkative, too. He started opening up. Bobby explained about the Judge and the Judge's important friends. And then he began telling Dodger stories, and naturally she knew of every player he mentioned, and he wanted to know whether she'd like more champagne. Just a little. They drank until two in the morning, when the bar closed.

Out on the street it was really cold, and in the cab back to Brooklyn he lit a joint and handed it to her. She laughed. Why not? She inhaled hard, and suddenly they were shooting back over the beautiful old battered Brooklyn Bridge, and she was sitting next to him, they were very close, and at the far end of Willow, close to Montague, he reached over and kissed her, and she let him. Just like that. They got out at his townhouse. He asked her in. She said sure.

They went into the living room, and he started a fire in the fireplace. They sat in different chairs.

"You amaze me," he said to her.

"Oh." She was cool. They were both being cool.

"You know something about this sport, and about this team."

"Thank you," she said suspiciously. She didn't trust him when he was trying to be charming.

"And yet you have a problem."

"I do?"

"You're still local, you're not network."

That got her mad. Why was he doing this? Why was he starting up again?

"Fuck you," she told him.

"How can I argue with a woman who uses language as eloquently as you?"

"The networks are nothing but—"

"Choosy, quite choosy. That's why they're about to hire Patty Sides away from me. They want to use her on the Game of the Week next year."

"I don't believe it!" Oran shouted. "I can't believe it!"

"It's true, though it pains me to be the one who has to tell you. She was stolen from right under me."

"Tits and ass, they're just interested in tits and ass."

"The men want to do the talking when it comes to sports. Patty understands that, and someday you will too, Ellis."

She got up to leave. He stopped her. "You have to see my Dodger Room before you go."

She wanted to get out of there, but now she was also curious. The room amazed her. She couldn't stop looking around at all the stuff. She sat down on the floor, on a 1955 Dodgers souvenir pillow; she went through the stacks of baseball cards. He sat down next to her. He moved closer to her. They were touching. And when she came to Sandy Koufax's card, she stopped and smiled.

"The finest Dodger pitcher of them all," she stated firmly.

"I'm not certain," Bobby was quick to say. "There's Erskine and Newcombe and certainly—"

"The '63 Series, the greatest Series of them all."

"There you *are* wrong."

"Wrong? When they swept the Yankees in four games. When Koufax won the first and fourth games, beating Whitey Ford twice. How could that be wrong?"

"There were greater Series," said Bobby.

"Perhaps '65 when Sandy shut out the Twins in the fifth and seventh, striking out twenty-nine in three games."

"You're moving in the wrong direction."

"What are you talking about?" she wanted to know.

"Come back to Brooklyn. We're in Brooklyn. You're with me in Brooklyn." Now he actually put his arm around her. Now she looked in his eyes, which were smiling at her.

"You don't like these Series because they took place in L.A.," she told him, not moving away. "You're prejudiced against that era because it happened in California."

He just kept looking at her. He kissed her forehead. He kissed her ear. She didn't do anything. She was liking it. "The best years, the only years," he said, "were the Brooklyn years. They had the excitement and"—he stopped to find the right word—"the intimacy which makes life worthwhile. Without intimacy, nothing is real, nothing is right."

Oran knew a line when she heard one. And this was a line. She wanted to pull away, she wanted to argue about Koufax and the 335.2 innings that he pitched in 1965, but now Bobby was touching her, and she wanted to be touched by him again. Right here in the Dodger Room with the pennants and the pictures of the old players. She wanted to be touched by this man who was stubborn and strong and whose heartbeat she could feel against hers, here in the room of a little boy, because that's what he was. She knew he was harmless and cute like a little boy, sweet and charming, even though his charm had power and he had power — that's what she liked and hated and now he went to close the door, now she couldn't keep any of the statistics straight—Drysdale's 2,486 career strikeouts, Maury Wills's 104 stolen bases— now she couldn't fight, didn't want to fight, just wanted to let him, and let him, and let him . . .

. . . "Are you shocked?" she asked him afterwards, not even bothering to cover herself.

"A little," he said. He was naked, too, next to her on the floor with all the old Dodger souvenirs. He stuck an original Van Lingle Mungo bubblegum card on his forehead.

"What are you shocked about? My wanton behavior?"

"No," he answered. "The spectacular nature of our lovemaking."

Another line, she wanted to believe. But she knew he was right, and she closed her eyes and sighed and then remembered about Patty Sides.

"This will in no way affect our professional relationship," she said, sitting up, searching for her clothes, which were thrown around the room.

"Not in the least," he agreed.

"Don't be smug about it," she warned.

"Not in the least," he repeated. "You're nervous now, but you needn't be. You merely did something which comes naturally to all women. You submitted to—"

"Submitted! Oh Jesus! I can't stand it. You see this all in terms of strength and submission. Is it inconceivable to you that maybe —just maybe—*I* am the one who is strong and *you* are the one who has submitted?"

"If that's how you prefer to see it."

She began to get dressed in a hurry. "You're going to need to find some strength, Hanes, if you hope to get through your last season in L.A. There's talk that the team may not even show."

"Daily chroniclers like yourself, Miss Ellis, have short memories." Bobby was still reclining on the floor, still naked. "You might remember some years back when Finley's Oakland A's were not competing. Finley decided to sell his stars and invest nothing more in the squad. He cut his staff back to the bone and actually reduced his losses. In one of those lean years—even with attendance at its lowest—he may have even made a little money. Who knows? The point is that by drastically cutting costs it's feasible to operate a losing team on something much less than a disastrous deficit. A minimum gate can have all sorts of positive effects—less security is required, fewer maintenance men, a payroll that can be cut in half. No, this lame-duck season won't be the end of the world for us."

"But what about your first year in Brooklyn? Surely if you're going to make some kind of showing you'll be forced to go into the free-agent market. And all the inside reports claim that, in spite of the joint-venture partnerships you've established with the city of New York, you'll be so strapped financially that big spending on players will be impossible."

"What are you doing, conducting an interview?"

Oran was still only half dressed. "Am I right or not?" she still wanted to know.

"I told you over a year ago that I don't intend to tinker with the free-agent market. Unlike the Fascists, we will never be a bought team. Besides, both the prices and the egos of the players are ridiculously inflated."

"And what about your ego, Hanes?"

He kept on smiling. "My ego is under control."

"All egos aside," she kept on, "where is the talent going to come from? How are you going to build up this team in time for '88?"

"By ignoring reason, my dear lady. By following instinct and adhering to divine will."

"Then money really is a problem."

"This was a profitable franchise when O'Malley pulled out in '57, and it's my contention that it will be a profitable franchise when we return."

"Please stop talking in quotes, Hanes. I don't intend to use any of them." She put on her sweater and brushed back her hair with her hand.

"Are you sure?" he asked, finally standing up. "Are you sure that this isn't just one of your devices"—he pointed to the scattered pillows on the floor—"of fishing for a story?"

She flew into another rage. "Listen, Hanes, there's no one in sports more frustrated right now than you. And the reason you resent me is simply that you can't accept the fact that a woman sees through you. You can't accept the fact that a woman understands baseball as well as—perhaps even better than—a man. But I see you for what you are—the laughingstock of both leagues, a man who's accomplished the incredible feat of bringing a team to a city where there's no place to play. You've blown it, Bobby Hanes, and you've blown it on page one of every important paper in the country."

"Don't underestimate me, Ellis. You've done it once, don't do it again. If anyone has made an ass of herself, it's you. Your predictions about me, your entire analysis of who I am, were so wrongheaded that they chased you out of L.A."

"The Dodgers will never play in Ebbets Field. There will be no Ebbets Field. Not by 1988, not ever."

"Listen, goddammit, *if I have to tear down those apartment buildings with my bare hands, I'll do it!*"

And that was the headline—the quote from Bobby—that appeared in the next day's afternoon edition of the New York *Examiner*, the paper Oran had been working for for the past two days.

TWO

THE BIG MEETING happened four days later. By then I knew what was up. I knew Oran was living down the street from Bobby. I had heard two long versions of their meeting on the bridge—hers and his—and it didn't surprise me none. I guess I had it figured out a long time ago. I knew what all that fighting had been about, and I was glad to see that they had decided to be honest for a change. Anyway, I made up my mind to leave the two lovebirds alone on Willow Street. I got myself a nice roomy apartment not far from the corner of Thirteenth Avenue and 50th Street, in the heart of Borough Park, near Mom and Dad, which is exactly what I wanted. I was back home.

Far as Oran went, well, she knocked me out. She really did. I mean here she was, on the case, with a new job and a big scoop only hours after arriving in the city. She got this exclusive quote from Bobby, the first after the riot. I think they both liked her story—Oran because it was a hot scoop, and Bobby because they used a huge picture of him on page one. Meanwhile, Oran was looking around for a spot on the tube. She could do newspaper stuff, but she didn't want to, at least not for long. She wanted to be back on camera as fast as possible.

I was trying to find a few pieces of furniture and move into my joint before Bobby had time to change his mind and transfer us back to L.A. I guess I was still a little worried about Bobby's determination to pull this thing off. I only stopped worrying when he mentioned the big meeting.

He said he was going back to talk to the apartment tenants. I told him he better go in a Russian tank. He said he didn't need no protection, that he was setting up this meeting in a church over on Lincoln Road. He was inviting all the tenants, and the press, and he promised me that by the time the meeting was over the problem would be solved. Sure, says me, the same way suicide solves the problem of living.

When I got to the church that night I thought they had already murdered him. There were swarms of cop cars and press trucks, a fire engine and an ambulance and a chopper checking us out from above. Inside, the church was packed solid. The press was jumping around, cornering tenants for interviews, popping pictures and setting up their gear. Oran was there, looking cute in this khaki-colored safari suit. I told her she looked like a war correspondent. She said she was.

I didn't like the look on the faces of the tenants. Their eyes were wide and angry and they seemed ready to kill. Some of them liked the press being around—you should have seen 'em waving at the camera—but others said this was just between them and Hanes and no one else's business. I thought I saw some mean-looking stuff bulging out of the pockets of a few of the teenagers—sticks or clubs or who knows what. The cops were inside and out, but they weren't searching anyone. You know cops; sometimes they just like to stand around and look mean.

Bobby was late, the way he's always late, and he arrived in a big huff wearing a red plaid shirt and green worker's pants looking real handsome and tough with his neck still bandaged and his beard uncombed and wild and a bunch of big cardboard sheets under his arm. He went right to the pulpit and started preaching.

"You might not know this," he said, "but I love you."

That didn't go over all that well. The tenants yelled back different versions of "Fuck you, you asshole."

Bobby's smile got bigger. "The reason I love you is that you are not only everything that is beautiful about Brooklyn, but because you have been living on hallowed Brooklyn ground. Whether you know it or not, you have been keeping the faith in your own way. You have been receiving the vibes—those incredible Dodger vibes—and they are deep inside you, so deep that you'll never be able to leave the land which you love so well."

Bobby waited for encouragement. He got none.

"Now the fact of the matter is that I don't want you to leave. I want you to stay right where you are. I *need* you to stay where you are. Because if you're forced to go, this dream of mine is as good as dead."

Everyone looked confused and on guard.

"Yes," Bobby kept on, "I want you to stay with me this evening, and I want you to stay with me a year from this coming April when I bring the Dodgers back home. I want you to stay as my partners, as my guests. I want you to stay as my hosts."

187

The crowd was still mixed up—like me.

"Here's where I want you to stay." And he took out one of those huge cardboard sheets and put it on an easel next to the pulpit. It was a drawing of the inside of his new Ebbets Field, only there was a big change. He went to the picture and started pointing and explaining. "You probably know that every stadium that has been built or redesigned in the past fifteen years has provided executive suites, enclosed rooms which are bought and decorated by the biggest, richest businessmen around. These are the suites from which they watch the games and entertain their friends. Such suites have always made me more than slightly sick. Not only is the concept snobbish, it is an insult to the average fan. It's a perpetuation of an archaic class structure which has no place in popular sports, an ugly throwback to the days when the emperor sat in his golden throne watching the lions dine on the Christians while servants peeled his grapes. No, the new Ebbets Field is going to defy this venal tradition; no fat-cat suites. Such a notion would be incompatible with everything that the Dodgers represent.

"But then, as I lay in the hospital, enjoying the rest that you so generously granted me"—the tenants laughed a little—"it occurred to me that there were special fans who deserved special treatment, and perhaps the concept of spectator suites was not in and of itself repulsive; perhaps it was just the application of the concept which was wrong. I had this vision, this beautiful and blindingly clear vision of you, each of you, coming to the Dodger games, coming to every one of the Dodger games—which, after all, will be played in your very home—and coming not as average fans, but superfans, coming as VIPs, coming not only free of charge—that goes without saying—but coming to sit in your very own suites, which, as you can see, will be built just below and above the upper deck—everywhere but right field, where the original slanted wall and scoreboard will be preserved. These suites are the kind for which businessmen normally pay fifty thousand dollars, or sixty thousand, or sometimes even a hundred thousand. And then the suite owners are obliged to purchase tickets as well. In your case, you will never pay for anything, since this is your home. Of course, there won't be enough individual suites for everyone, and you'll have to double up, but it will be worth it. Your seats, your food will be free; you will be kings and queens in your own palace. Just as the press has been interviewing you and putting your pictures on television and in the newspapers in these past days, they will continue to do so—especially when the season begins. You will be the toasts of the town.

"I realize that having to move not just once, but twice, is a difficult thing for anyone to do. And it would pain me—pain me as much as it would pain you—if I didn't sincerely believe that, in the long run, you will be better off because of these moves. You will be celebrated and honored as the borough's first and foremost Dodger fans—those who were willing to sacrifice their homes, no, to *share* their homes—so that the rest of Brooklyn might rejoice in the greater glory of the miracle of this Second Coming!"

And someone shouted out, "Amen! Amen!" and I saw in their faces, in the way they were coming up to look at the picture of the suites, that they were interested in everything Bobby had to say.

"A lifetime pass to Ebbets Field"—Bobby still pitching—"and not only that, but your names engraved on the outside of the suites—engraved for all eternity to see that here were selfless souls who contributed to the greater good of mankind."

He went on like that for another half hour. He sold them. Of course he had to cut a deal with the tenants' lawyer to kick in a healthy cash settlement for each family, but that was okay; that was expected. Afterwards, everyone was happy. Bobby was beaming. Only Oran was glum; she thought this whole thing was underhanded. I told her it was funny. She said I had a warped sense of humor. Couldn't she see that she was fighting a losing battle? She said the word "losing" wasn't in her vocabulary.

The next day Bobby hired something called an "urban relocation firm." They took care of smoothing out everything; they got the trucks and the packers and before four or five weeks went by the move was under way; the tenants were starting to leave. By then Oran was reporting on-the-air for a New York TV station. It was still local, but it was the Big Apple. Even though she wasn't about to admit it, she knew she had an inside track on the biggest sports story since David took care of Goliath in the first round.

Then there was the day they tore it down. Bobby demanded that they use a wrecking ball painted to look like a baseball. And when that round sphere of steel started swinging into the apartments, oh man, what a sight! The ball only did part of the work; naturally there were other instruments of destruction. But to see that baseball going back and forth, knocking out windows and taking out the top two stories, was really something. It was a little after New Year's and a gigantic crowd had come to watch the wreckers. Seemed like half of Brooklyn. At first, Bobby had wanted to put himself on the end of the baseball and ride the first swing into the side of the building, but the demolition boss talked him out of it.

It turned out that they didn't even need the ball, but Bobby made them use it the way it had been used to tear down Ebbets almost thirty years before. The real way they were going to destroy these apartments was very simple: dynamite. They were going to blow up the joint from the inside, and naturally Bobby had to be the one who set it off.

He wrapped his fingers around the handle and held them there for a long time. He closed his eyes, and I thought I heard him mumble something like a prayer, but I couldn't be sure. There was a lot of excitement and confusion. I saw him press his fingers against the handle until his knuckles turned white, and then he opened his eyes and let out a scream and pushed down the handle against the box with a murderous vengeance and my ears were shattered by a tremendous *BOOM!* The earth shook and huge billows of smoke and dirt flew into the air, and right over there, right before our eyes—hundreds of feet away from where we were fenced off—the giant apartment buildings ached and sagged and finally gave way, slowly, slowly, collapsing to the ground, into a heap of rubbish. It was maybe the most beautiful thing I had ever seen in my life, the way the bricks and board and glass and steel and plaster all went down into a pile, and suddenly I felt almost scared by all that power—the power of the explosion, the dynamite, Bobby's power to push down the handle and make this happen, and even my power, and even Oran's power, because, just as sure as I was standing there, I knew all these powers were tied together and I felt like all these powers were one.

The days flew by. It got colder, and on the afternoon of the ground-breaking ceremony it rained buckets; cold freezing rain turned to hail, the kind that slaps you in the face and makes you mad. It was a mean day. The same crew of reporters were there, but, due to the cold, hardly any spectators. Bobby was wearing this wide-brimmed floppy rain hat, looking silly and distinguished at the same time. They gave him a shovel. He was supposed to dig a little dirt and that was it. But he also wanted to make a speech. Bobby always wants to make speeches. He told me he was going to announce how, in only sixteen months or so, this ballpark was going to be built, how cooperative the trade unions and the construction firms—all Brooklyn-based and Brooklyn-owned—had been. How Ebbets was being built by Brooklynites for Brooklynites. How the design—so close to the original—was being hailed as one of the great architectural breakthroughs of our time, just because it was a step backwards. How the suburban stadiums and the freeway ballparks would be outmoded within a few years. How everyone would be coming home, how we'd be building roads back into Brooklyn, reversing the work of Robert Moses, who led our people out of the holy land into the desert called Long Island, how this single stadium was going to change the face of the borough, renew it, reinvigorate it, make it fresh and whole and happy again. He was going to say all this, but the hail was socking us in the face, and Bobby couldn't say anything, not a single word, and it was hard to tell because of the rain, but it looked to me like he was crying too hard to talk.

THREE

JANUARY GOT COLDER and I got more and more worried about the player situation. There were Bo and Sonny, but they wouldn't be enough, and besides, I didn't want Bobby to know about them yet. Once he saw them, he'd feel less pressure about getting good players, and that would work against me. I kept in touch with the boys and told them what was going on. Like a lot of the players, they liked me, they trusted me, and they weren't about to sign with anyone else. Besides, I promised them they'd be going to Vero Beach in March.

The problem was finding and developing talent. Every time Bobby heard the words "free agent" he'd throw a fit, so I just stopped saying it. On the other hand, I couldn't shut up completely. I knew it was my job to keep bugging Bobby—everyone else was too scared—about putting together a decent team by '88.

"There are non-traditional paths which we have yet to travel," Bobby said to me one snowy afternoon in his townhouse office.

"What are you talking about, kid?"

"Truly imaginative scouting."

I almost mentioned Bo and Sonny, but I held my tongue. "I been looking," I said, "and I gotta confess that it ain't no easy chore."

"*Where* have you been looking?" he asked.

"Here and there."

"I suggest you expand your horizons."

"To where?"

"Places where baseball is as much a passion as lovemaking. Places which burn with diamond fever, and yet have not been exploited, soiled and spoiled by the crassness that has so pervasively invaded the game here in the States."

"Where are you talking about?"

He pointed his finger to the window toward Staten Island. "Cuba!" he said.

Two days later we were thirty thousand feet in the air, tearing our way through some really raunchy weather, in the little Lear jet. I would have been scared—that plane never made me feel too safe—if Bobby hadn't pulled out this old record and put it on his stereo setup:

Say, did you hear the news about what's happening in Brooklyn?
We really got the blues about what's happening in Brooklyn.
It ain't official yet, we hope official it won't get,
But beware, my friend, and let me warn ya,
They're thinkin' of takin' the Bums to California.

Let's keep the Dodgers in Brooklyn,
A house is not a home without some love,
Don't let them leave our premises, L.A. would be their nemesis,
'Cause Brooklyn fits the Dodgers like a glove.

The song was half sung and half talked by this guy who wasn't no singer, but a comedian from Brooklyn called Phil Foster. His voice sorta stunk, which made it more beautiful, and his accent was even thicker than mine, and it all came back, everything that was happening in my life in 1957. I listened hard, real hard, over the roar of the plane, and I laughed—me and Bobby were cracking up. I remembered that I was the one who first bought the record and gave it to Bobby—we were just teenagers—and now, on our way to Havana, he fished it out of nowhere and started playing it.

Brooklyn would be like a pair of socks that's holey
Without Jackson and Cimoli,
Like a bed without a pillow
Without Erskine and Furillo,
Like a ship without a harbor
Without Podres and the Barber,
Like the sun when it don't shine
Without Zimmer and Labine,
Like the birds without a bee
Without Alston and Pee Wee

. . . So send the Phils to Trenton, the Giants to St. Paul,
But keep the Dodgers in Brooklyn,
The greatest borough of all!

And when the record was over, we played it again, and then again, and when Foster said "Erskine," he said it the way it should be said—"Oiskine!" I was feeling great, I was thinking how good it was to remember the old days; I was sure that we were going to make the new days the old days, 'cause the old feeling was a good feeling, it was the first feeling and would always be the best feeling.

Castro looked a lot older to me in person. His face was all lined and his beard needed to be trimmed something awful. Bobby's beard, next to Fidel's, was very respectable. They stood there looking at each other for a long time while I was thinking—holy cow, is this really happening?

It was, even though it had taken Bobby two days of ferocious telephoning and incredible bullshit-blowing to set up the trip. He wouldn't tell anyone what it was about. He said he had come to talk turkey with Fidel and wouldn't deal with no one else, not even their baseball czar, who was a young good-looking guy named Luis who spoke fast English and liked Bobby right away. Luis had heard of Bobby, but he wouldn't say whether Fidel knew

Bobby's name or not. At first, Luis said meeting Castro was impossible. He said Fidel didn't have time and that Fidel couldn't be bothered.

"If he's the sort of baseball fan he purports to be," said Bobby, "he'll see me."

"What are the details of your proposal?" Luis wanted to know.

"You're a great guy, Luis, and I know you'll understand that this is one instance where I can only negotiate with Castro."

Luis smiled and shook his head. I could almost feel him fighting off Bobby's charm. But it was no use. Bobby was filling Luis's glass with wine, walking around our suite at the Havana Libre—which used to be called the Havana Hilton—saying how Castro would love our proposal, he'd be so pleased with it he'd surely give Luis a raise just for introducing him to Bobby. Luis laughed and left, saying that he was sorry, but that seeing Fidel was impossible, it really was.

The next morning he called us at nine and we were in Castro's office by ten. We walked in and there he was in his green fatigues and combat boots. Luis was standing next to him, just like I was next to Bobby, who was dressed in this white suit looking like a big-game hunter. Man, it was weird. We all shook hands. Fidel had a very strong grip. His eyes looked right through you—bright and clear, but no brighter or clearer than Bobby's.

The office was plain and stark, and for the first time in my life I think I exaggerated my limp, 'cause I figured it might impress Castro. We sat down in these wooden chairs across from his desk. He didn't even have a roll-around executive chair, just a secretary's chair with no arms. He looked at us for a long time, then said something in Spanish, which Luis quickly translated.

"The Premier would be curious to know if you can provide him with the names of the pitchers who were in the bullpen for the Brooklyn Dodgers during the deciding playoff game with the New York Giants in the Polo Grounds on October 3, 1951, when Bobby Thomson came up to bat in the ninth inning."

Holy Jesus, I was thinking to myself, I can't believe this guy. I was wishing Oran was there. What a story she'd have!

"Ralph Branca," said Bobby. "Branca came in to pitch to Thomson."

Fidel shook his head sternly and started blabbering in Spanish. Luis translated: "Yes, of course Branca was the pitcher. That is common knowledge. But who were the other pitchers in the bullpen, the pitchers whom the Dodgers could have sent in, but chose not to?"

Bobby closed his eyes. This was a tough one. He looked at me, but I didn't say nothing. I wasn't sure that I knew myself. This Fidel was rough. Seconds ticked by. A full minute must have passed before Bobby finally blurted out, "One was Carl Erskine, the other Clem Labine."

Castro leaped up, ran around the desk, opened his arms, embraced Bobby and kissed him on both cheeks. He told Luis to tell Bobby, "You're the first man I've met who could answer this question. Now we can talk baseball."

Bobby looked happier than I'd ever seen him, and when Fidel broke out the cigars, Bobby fished in his pocket and came up with an 18K gold lighter in the shape of a baseball bat.

"A most beautiful ornament," said Castro through Luis.

"Please accept it with my compliments," offered Bobby.

"I couldn't," smiled Fidel.

"You must," Bobby insisted.

Castro took the lighter and examined it like a kid examining a toy. He fingered it and he flicked it, lighting all of our cigars. "You are most generous, Señor Hanes."

"Please ask Fidel to call me Bobby," Bobby asked Luis.

"Yes, Bobby," Fidel went along. "I have read about you in the newspapers. I see that you have many troubles with your baseball team."

"The Dodgers have always had trouble," Bobby answered. "This is nothing new, Fidel. It's part of the tradition."

"But there have always been two Dodger teams, have there not?" asked Castro.

"Exactly!" Bobby beamed.

"The first team was the one which interested me. That was the team with what I would call revolutionary fervor. But alas, that team has been long dead. You bought the second team, the one in that strange state of California. I know what you're trying to do now, but I wonder whether it's ever possible to rewrite history."

"I believe, along with you, Fidel, that we make our own future. I have faith in the inevitable progress of history. I don't have to tell you that there are material forces at work greater than ourselves. Such forces initially attracted me to that first team, Fidel. That was the team of my childhood, the team of my dreams."

"How well I can understand." Castro looked up to the ceiling and closed his eyes as he spoke. "And how well I remember the day that Señor O'Malley's plan to build a new stadium at the corner of Atlantic and Flatbush Avenues in downtown Brooklyn was rejected. I knew that was the end."

"I am greatly impressed," said Bobby, "that your command of Dodger history is so vast. I had always heard that you were a Yankee fan, but I never believed it."

"You are right. It is a false myth perpetuated by the capitalist media. True, that I was once a resident of New York City, but how could I ever root for the team called the Yankees? The very name was repugnant to me. So naturally I would find their greatest adversaries irresistible. They were called the Bums, and they were the underdogs, and they were heroic, they were the Yankee-killers, the first team to end the curse of discrimination against blacks. And though it is always ignored in the foolish history books of American baseball, it is nonetheless absolutely certain that it was a Cuban, from this very city of Havana, a black Cuban, a brilliant and fleet-footed Cuban outfielder, who is more responsible than anyone for the first and most glorious World Series victory of the Brooklyn Dodgers."

Fidel stared at Bobby with a twinkle in his eyes; he was waiting to see if Bobby remembered, and sure enough, Bobby did: "Sandy Amoros!"

"Amoros!" shouted Fidel. "Amoros was the one. I will never forget the 1955 World Series—"

"I can see it now, Fidel," Bobby interrupted, with Luis translating a mile a minute. "Series tied up at three games apiece. Final game, Yankee Stadium, Dodgers ahead two–zip, trying to win their first World Championship after having lost to the Yankees in '47, '49, '52 and '53. Now it was the bottom of the sixth inning and the Yankees were up." Bobby paused to give Luis time to catch up with his translation, even though it looked to me like Fidel was understanding the English pretty well. "Podres is on the mound for the Bums. He walks Billy Martin. Gil McDougald beats out a bunt. Berra's up. He reaches for an outside pitch and whacks it down the left-field line. Everyone in the park can see that it's going to be good for extra bases; two runs will probably score. But Amoros, Amoros—"

"Amoros," Fidel filled in as Luis continued translating, "races over like a speeding panther and makes a spectacular catch!" And with that Castro came from behind his desk and did a nifty imitation of the running catch.

"But then what happened?" Bobby asked.

"What do you mean?" Fidel looked confused.

"What happened next in the game?"

Fidel started thinking, but Bobby answered his own question. "Amoros whips the ball back to Reese, who in turn throws to Hodges to double McDougald off first."

"Ah, how right you are! I had forgotten! It was a double play!"

Now Luis was really happy; he saw how Bobby had scored with Fidel. I was happy, Bobby was happy, Fidel was falling down he was so happy. "And we went on to win the game, and the Series," Castro continued, "and the Cuban was the hero. Edmundo Isasi Amoros hit .333 in those seven games." Now Fidel stopped to suck on his cigar. He slowly blew out the smoke and looked at us with misty eyes. "But that was long ago," he sighed.

There was some silence, and then, seeing this was the right moment, Bobby gave Castro a soulful stare and said, "I have yet to explain the purpose of my mission."

"Wait," Fidel cautioned. "Before we talk business, there is something I wish to show you."

We rode to the ballpark in a jeep—Fidel driving, Bobby next to him, Luis and me in the back seat. It was a Russian jeep and uncomfortable as hell. I was bouncing around like a jumping bean back there as we drove through the center of the city, which was all sunshine and ancient American cars.

"You can see that we were very modern and exact in our specifications," Fidel said through Luis as we made our way into the stadium, then down to the playing field. Attendants were running around nervously, all excited that their leader had showed up. On the field a team was practicing in workout clothes. When they saw Fidel, they stopped playing, but he waved to them and shouted something and they started up again.

"Magnificent!" Bobby declared, looking around the joint. "This is the finest baseball facility I've seen in years." It was nice and clean and green and open. "How's attendance?" Bobby asked.

"Full for every game," replied Fidel.

"What's the price range for tickets?"

"There is no price. This is a game of the people," Castro explained. "How can I charge my people—farmers and factory workers—admission for one of the great pleasures of their lives?"

"What about player salaries?" Bobby wanted to know.

"The players are content without inflated paychecks. They are paid with the respect of their fans. They are rewarded with a sense of their own pride."

"If only the major leagues worked that way, dear Fidel, my life would be so much easier."

"There is every indication that your system is falling apart."

"The system is being threatened," said Bobby, "but the system is strong. I can assure you that the system will survive in spite of its weaknesses."

"And one of its weaknesses is undoubtedly the ball."

"The ball?"

"You play with an inferior ball," Fidel announced in the middle of the field. He made a gesture and one of the nearby players handed him a ball. "This is the finest baseball in the world," said Castro. Luis's translation was fast as lightning. "It is made in a factory right here in Havana, the most modern and efficient hardball factory in the world. You see, when the Revolution came, our normal supplier of baseballs—the U.S.A.—was no longer available to us, and so we learned to make them ourselves. We now manufacture a ball which has no match anywhere, not in your country, not even in Japan. See for yourself—the stitching is the strongest, the bounce the truest. You must try it." Now Fidel made another gesture, and two of the players handed over their mitts. Castro put one on and gave the other to Bobby.

There they were—Fidel and Bobby—standing in the middle of Estadio Latino Americano in Havana, Cuba, at high noon, playing catch. Castro stood a little bit behind the pitcher's mound and Bobby was at first base, and as they threw the ball to each other, they kept up their conversation, with Luis in the middle, relaying the messages back and forth.

"Can you feel the superior quality of the ball?" Fidel asked.

"It feels fine," Bobby assured him, showing off his best form as he caught and zipped the ball back to Castro. "But it's not so much the quality of the ball itself, Fidel, as it is how far your boys can hit it."

Castro howled. "Look at the farthest point in this ballpark," he said, turning and pointing to deep center field. "Last week one of our hitters sent the ball at least a hundred and fifty yards beyond that point, out of the park. I know. I was here watching the game."

Now Bobby laughed and said, "Must have been a pretty soft pitcher."

"We have no soft pitchers in Cuba," answered Fidel, getting a little ticked and throwing the ball to Bobby with a whole lot more speed.

"I know your pitchers use a great deal of finesse." Bobby threw it back with just as much force.

"Not finesse, my dear Bobby, but *speed*. Brute force. In Cuba, we throw hard and we hit hard." His next toss to Bobby really had something on it—to prove his point—and, throwing back the ball, Bobby returned the favor, saying:

"Surely you wouldn't compare your players to ours. I know there are a few men down here of possible major-league caliber, but wouldn't you say that the majority would be playing minor-league ball in the States?"

"No, I would not say that at all," Fidel shot back. I could see that he was feeling the sting of the ball that Bobby had just fired to him. He took off his mitt—his palm was flaming red—and shouted, "El Tigre! El Tigre!" And suddenly from the outfield a tall, light-skinned, big-muscled guy came charging toward us. He had a lean frame, but strong. His face was happy and handsome; he had a wide nose and high cheekbones. I could see how relieved Bobby was to have this break. His hand was as red as Fidel's.

Castro called to another player, a pitcher, who took the mound as El Tigre picked up a black bat and went to the plate. We moved to the sidelines to watch the show.

I don't have to tell you that I know something about hitters. I seen all kinds. But El Tigre had the most natural instincts of any of 'em. Effortless. Which was the key. Not straining, but letting that ball come to him, letting his muscles just flow. He was beautiful. His stance was simple and straightforward, his eye was deadly and his swing was like music, like the prettiest melody you ever heard. He kept on whacking 'em out. Man, this guy had poise and he had power and after about fifteen minutes of fireworks, Fidel held up his hand. He grinned at Bobby, who turned to him and grinned back. Then Bobby walked to the plate, where he embraced El Tigre and kissed him on both cheeks, Latin-style. He brought the slugger back to where we were standing with Castro and he said to Luis, "Tell the Premier that it's time for us to do business."

"First we must have lunch."

"Perhaps the Premier would care to spend the afternoon with me in my house in Jamaica?" Bobby asked. "My Lear is waiting. It's just a short hop away."

Castro laughed. "You may have a Lear, my friend, but I have an air force."

And he called one of his boys and an hour later the four of us—me, Bobby, Luis and Fidel—were zooming around in a sleek Russian bomber, munching on some spicy rice and drinking wine.

"This is a nice way for you to see our island," said Fidel, looking out the window.

"You're a man of action"—Bobby was talking loud over the jet engines—"and I have a feeling you can appreciate the way I've taken action." Bobby couldn't hold back anymore. "I am not only moving my team back to Brooklyn, but I'm rebuilding the stadium, which I know houses many memories for you. Ebbets Field is going back up, Fidel, but I need to put a decent club in there in 1988. That's why I've come to Cuba, and, if I'm not mistaken, that's why you showed me El Tigre. He moves and hits and responds like a Dodger. He *is* a Dodger. And I need him, Fidel, I desperately need him to carry on the tradition of Sandy Amoros in the very ballpark where that tradition was first established."

"I know you're having trouble with your club," Fidel answered, "but you can hardly expect us to solve those problems for you. What are we to gain by giving up our best player?"

"The respect of the world. The respect of every American, North and South. You'll never have a better opportunity to prove to us that a Cuban, born and trained in Havana, can turn major-league baseball on its ear. El Tigre is sure to set records. He'll attract enough goodwill for your country to last a century. He'll be admired and loved by children everywhere. He'll become a national hero without losing his national identity."

"How can I be sure of that?"

"Send along a chaperon. Give him a spokesman. I'll pick up the tab."

The jet came in for a landing, and everyone became quiet. Everyone was thinking. A few minutes later we were on the ground, but no one got up to leave. Fidel licked a new cigar and lit it. "My man Luis," he said, still speaking through Luis, "is probably the best sports executive you'll ever encounter. I have had him study the methods of all the great Dodger front-office men—Fresco Thompson, Red Patterson, Buzzy Bavasi, Al Campanis. He has built the Cuban baseball league to be the finest anywhere. But I would not be displeased if he had a chance to see the American system for himself. It is corrupt, yes, but there are technical aspects worth observing. And if he was with El Tigre in America, he could report directly to me and, even more important, make certain that the untarnished image of a patriotic Cuban ballplayer remains intact. What would you say to taking Luis into your organization on temporary loan?"

Bobby lifted his glass of wine and toasted Fidel. "You are a man of wide and daring vision."

"I am not quite as insane as you are," Castro told Bobby, "but there is no true Dodger fan who can resist the idea of the Dodgers back in Brooklyn."

They drank to each other's health, and the deal was done, even though Bobby had to promise Fidel a series of a half-dozen exhibition games between the Dodgers and Cuban All-Stars, with the money for worldwide TV rights split down the middle. The last question I remember Castro asking before we left the next night was, "What do you think a minute of commercial time during these games will bring?"

FOUR

I KNOW BROOKLYN ain't paradise, but on the right Sunday morning when you're walking down Emmons Avenue in Sheepshead Bay and you see all those boats bouncing in the water just as the sun's coming up, with the smell of fresh fish from all the markets strong in your nose, you're happy to be here. At least I was. Oran had called to invite me to an early-morning breakfast. She said I could pick the time and the place. So here I was, not far from the docks and the bridge that goes over to Shore Boulevard, in a little coffee joint that overlooks everything. The java was piping hot and the hard rolls were the best anywhere and everyone was talking about last night's fight at the Garden and the big splash in the paper about us getting back from Cuba with El Tigre and Luis.

Oran got there a little after me. She was wearing a cherry-red blouse and fancy blue jeans. She kissed me on the cheek, and she smelled good. We ordered eggs.

"You look happy," I told her.

"That's just a front," she said. "I still feel betrayed by the trip. One of you two could have asked me along."

"Is that why you asked me to breakfast—to complain?"

"You knew it was a big story, Squat."

"We tipped you off about when we were arriving at the airport with Luis and El Tigre, didn't we?"

"Me and a half-dozen other reporters."

"We called you first. Right from the plane. We couldn't let you cover it alone 'cause we needed the publicity."

"Did you have to talk Bobby into including me, or was it his idea?"

Here we were, talking about Bobby again. "He ain't against you," I said.

"Then why hasn't he returned my calls? I've phoned him at least a half-dozen times in the last twenty-four hours."

"He's recuperating from the trip."

"I wish I could believe that."

"You know Bobby," I said just as our eggs arrived. "He has strange ins and outs." I didn't mean that the way it sounded.

"He has a strange attitude about women, especially those involved with baseball. He contends that we can't begin to comprehend the game. Why else would he promote the career of a cheerleader like Patty Sides? In his mind and in the minds of millions of men who follow the sport, she is living proof of the fact that female sports reporters are basically there to be seen, not heard."

"You think about that dame too much."

"That dame, as you call her, is probably pulling down a hundred and fifty thousand dollars a year and has a reasonable chance of becoming the first female play-by-play baseball announcer in network history."

"She'll never make it."

"You're right, but only because of a wattage shortage in her brain. If she were only barely literate about the sport, she'd be calling those games in a minute. Now she's allowed to say brilliant things like the day is cloudy or that the pitcher has long arms."

"Forget her."

"Has Bobby?"

"What do you care?"

"I don't."

"Then why you asking?"

"I'm a reporter. It's my job."

"It's gossip."

I watched a couple of beat-up fishing boats leaving the docks. I mopped up what was left of my eggs with half a kaiser roll and took a slug of coffee. I felt my good mood moving away from me. I was getting a little tired of Oran. Why had she asked me to breakfast anyway? What was with this gal? When she excused herself to go to the bathroom, I started thinking—what has she ever cared about except getting inside info outta me? I'd be an idiot not to see that. She was cold-blooded, this broad; she was cold-blooded and calculating and it was the network and her big stories and nothing else. It wasn't about us being pals. The only real pal she had was her job. And here we were sitting in the middle of Brooklyn and she wasn't even looking at Brooklyn. Which really ticked me off, 'cause she was missing the whole thing—the scene and the feel and the smell and the sights and, hell, she called herself a reporter. What was with her? Bobby. She was interested in getting to Bobby in all kinds of ways. And I was getting tired of that stuff, real tired.

"Come on, Squat," she said when she got back from the bathroom, "you look like you've been thinking too hard. Let me show you why I invited you to breakfast."

She paid for the meal and put us in a cab and gave the driver an address on Nineteenth Avenue and I said to her, "What do you know about Nineteenth Avenue? Nineteenth and where?" And she said, "Around Benson Avenue." And I said, "That's right there in Bensonhurst. What do you know about Bensonhurst?" And she said, "Be patient, Squat. We'll be there in a minute." Patient? Why should I be patient? I was tired of being tooled around, and why should I have to kill my morning like this with her playing with me like I was some kinda toy? But naturally I didn't say nothing, 'cause she was a lady and I like to think of myself as something of a gent and I was wondering who she knew in Bensonhurst.

We got out of the cab on Nineteenth Avenue. Bensonhurst looked the same as always. We walked up the stoop and Oran knocked on the door of one of those two-family houses—real narrow and close to the house next to it—with white curtains covering the windows. The door opened and there was a girl who was maybe twenty-five years old with a pretty face and jet-black hair. A pretty face but not a beautiful face, and I was trying to guess whether she was Italian or Jewish—I always get the two mixed up. She was taller than me and she was wearing a sweatsuit and looked trim. Her eyebrows were dark and her eyes were soft brown and liquidy. She told us to come in, and I was still trying to figure out what was happening. She called Oran by name, and Oran introduced me. "Squat," she said, "I'd like you to meet Ruth Smelkinson." Which is when I figured she was Jewish. "Nice to meet you, Ruth." Ruth showed us into the living room where this old guy was sitting in a chair with a book of heavy yellow pages in his lap. He was wearing glasses as thick as the bottom of a Coke bottle. This was Ruth's father, Hyman Smelkinson, and he talked like old-time Jewish guys talk and he told me to call him Hymie. "My pleasure, Hymie." He told me he was reading the *Encyclopedia of Baseball* in Braille. He'd read the whole thing three times through, he said, from cover to cover, and did I know that Sandy Koufax came from this neighborhood? "Sure," I told him. "He lived in the 608 housing project around the Belt Parkway." As soon as those words fell out of my mouth I thought I saw something very strange—a slight resemblance between Koufax and Ruth—not to put Ruth down, not at all, but she had those dark eyes and that dark complexion and that thin face—and I asked her whether she was related to Sandy. "In spirit," the old man told me, "only in spirit," he said, "but deeply in spirit."

"Ruth is a pitcher," Oran announced.

Oh no, I said to myself. To the ladies I said, "That's nice."

"Not just a pitcher," said Hymie, "but a good pitcher, a reliable pitcher. I raised this girl myself. Her mother, may she rest in peace, died just after Ruthie was born, and it fell upon me to bring up my baby as best as I could. She's a good girl, Mr. Squat, and she can pitch. I tell you that as a baseball man and a businessman, because I know you work for a very shrewd businessman. I, too, had my own business for many years—I repaired radiators—until I lost my sight, but by then it didn't make much difference because I had saved my money, Mr. Squat, and my Ruthie already knew how to throw the ball. I say it because I saw it in those years when I could see. I say it because—and I hope you don't think I'm being immodest, Mr. Squat—I instructed her myself. Baseball I always understood. I saw at an early age that she was strong, not just for a girl, but for a person. She could take a bow and arrow and shoot it right in the middle of the target, Mr. Squat, and she could knock down cans, any can you told her to knock down, from the other side of the yard using only a—"

"Dad, please. Mr. Malone doesn't need to hear a history of my childhood," she interrupted Hymie. She wasn't mean to him, she was just embarrassed. She was blushing.

"You see how modest my daughter is, Mr. Squat. Well, that's the problem. She's so modest she doesn't want anyone to know about her gift. She won't play on the boys' baseball teams, she's refused her whole life, because she doesn't like to embarrass boys by striking them out. Can you imagine that?" He was talking with his hands, and all the time he was speaking he was smiling and turning his head in my direction.

"I've seen her pitch," Oran said to me. "Now I want you to see her pitch."

"Where was she pitching?" I asked.

"Around the campus at Brooklyn College. It was just a pickup game," Oran explained. "I happened to be walking around, looking for the athletic department. I was researching a story. By chance I looked over and saw this woman pitching hardball to a bunch of tough-looking guys. They were betting each other who could hit her, and they all lost. Every one of them."

Pictures of me and Bobby as kids flashed through my brain, but then I thought—good, Oran, great. Just what I need. A girl pitcher who can fool a couple of college boys with a curveball. What was I doing there with this blind guy and his dark-haired daughter, who, I had to admit, was sorta foxy in her own way. There's something about a dame who sits real quiet and doesn't say much. Makes you think there's more than meets the eye. Makes you sorta curious, especially her wearing this sweatsuit and everything.

"I myself was never much of a baseball player, Mr. Squat," Hymie was telling me. "Where I came from, baseball—who knew from baseball? But when I came to this country I appreciated the game, Mr. Squat, and I became a student of it. I watched the pitchers. I saw that they were the most important pieces on the chessboard. I studied their styles. All the great ones. Dazzy Vance was my favorite. I remember when in 1924 he won twenty-eight games. I was young then, but I was too old to learn to pitch myself. Then so many years later Ruthie came along and grew up and loved to play baseball with me in the park every day when I picked her up from school, and I immediately knew she wasn't just a pitcher, she was a miracle, Mr. Squat. I want you to remember that when you see her pitch, because I know at first you won't believe your eyes. My eyes are gone now, but I know what my Ruthie can do, not just one style or one pitch, but many styles and many pitches, which you will notice because you are a baseball man. It is no accident that your friend Miss Ellis came along when she did, and it is no accident that we are talking now. Because when I heard on my television set this business about your Mr. Hanes building Ebbets Field again I knew that God had heard my prayers for my daughter, and that He was working through your Mr. Hanes and through your Miss Ellis and, yes, through you, Mr. Squat."

"Dad, please, I'm not sure Mr. Malone has time to listen to all—"

"My sweet daughter, let the man speak for himself." Mr. Smelkinson stopped, he jutted his chin into the air, turned his ear toward my mouth, waiting for me to say something.

"You know," I said, "I used to be a catcher."

"So much the better! You will be able to see her genius immediately. So much the better!"

We went over to Dyker Beach Park. Ruth drove us in her Volkswagen van. It was getting a little chilly, and Ruth saw that I wasn't dressed warm enough, so she got me a hooded sweatshirt out of the back, which was loaded with mitts and balls and bats and old copies of *Sporting News*. We walked through the park— she walked ahead of me and Oran—and I noticed that she swaggered a little—not too much, just a little. I wouldn't exactly call it manly, but I wouldn't call it feminine either. Somewhere in between. She was probably a tomboy.

The park was pretty clean, and I was remembering how Bobby and me had played on this very same field and she was throwing the ball to me and I saw that she could throw. She had a strong arm and she could throw. Not like a girl, because you know that most girls throw like girls. But Ruth, she threw regular, like a guy. She was throwing lefthanded, though she told me she was born a righty, which was just like Sandy. She wasn't throwing fast yet, but she was throwing straight. Real straight. And I swear, when I looked down at her for a minute I thought she was Koufax's sister, 'cause she was so dark and thin and everything. Then she was throwing with a little more stuff and I saw she was pacing herself. I saw that her curveball was very sharp and that it dropped—just like Sandy's curveball used to drop. And then I saw her picking up speed, and her fastball was nothing to sneeze at. It started hopping and rising, it always seemed to rise—just like Sandy's. Both these pitches were very exact, and she delivered 'em both from the top, a high overhand delivery, just like Sandy's. I wasn't saying nothing, nothing at all, but the ball was definitely moving in there and her kick was real pro and her follow-through real smooth. She was throwing strikes. She was throwing harder and harder, and my palm was starting to burn, and she saw that and began throwing junk. She was shaving the corners and floating the ball, but getting it where she wanted it. And her junk reminded me of Maglie, reminded me a lot of the Barber, and I was trying to remember whether her old man mentioned Sal Maglie or not. I saw she had a lot of different styles, and there was something of Oisk's curve—Oisk had an overhand curve, too—and I was wondering what in the hell I was really seeing 'cause I couldn't crouch—this fake leg wouldn't let me crouch—and there wasn't no batter there, and even though she was throwing strikes and showing good stuff she was a dame and this was make-believe and what about during a real live game?

Afterwards she told me that she wasn't even on the flunky Brooklyn College team. She said she didn't see any point in it. So what good was she? Maybe she could be a third-string reliever for the new expansion team out in L.A. that was replacing us. Maybe I could call Schmidt and give him a tip, but if she didn't like to compete she wasn't no good for no one. Except that she was throwing even better now, she was throwing fire, and I wasn't so sure now 'cause I liked the way she didn't mess around out there. I liked the way she took it and wound up and kept throwing rockets at me. But she was a girl, and girls . . .

"That's no way for a girl to talk," I was saying to Oran when we were alone later that afternoon.

"Let me repeat myself," she said, even louder this time. "*Hanes is going to shit a brick!*"

FIVE

I STILL WASN'T sure. I wasn't all that happy about the situation. I didn't like the idea of Oran sticking her nose in my recruiting business. I felt like I was being used. I knew she was using me to get to Bobby.

Besides, it was the dead of winter, and there's nothing happening in baseball in the dead of winter. Bobby had gone off to see about some fabulous deal in China and left me with instructions to keep interviewing managers. I hadn't said a word to him about Ruth. She was there in the back of my mind, along with Bo Solomon and Sonny Muse, who kept calling me all the time now 'cause they knew it was for real. They saw what was happening over in Flatbush.

Brooklyn was thinking baseball again, and every morning after I got up and made a few calls I'd go down to Thirteenth Avenue and see some of the young kids who wore black hats and had sideburns and were being raised up in the religion of the old guys, and I'd wonder whether there were any baseball players among them. Sometimes I'd go crazy wondering whether people I saw —a delivery boy or a kid putting a fresh batch of charlotte russes into the window of the bakery shop—whether they were sluggers, whether they could steal bases or pull a perfect squeeze play. I knew I was being stupid, and I had to stop dreaming and start thinking straight, but it was hard when every day I went over to the weird square formed by Montgomery and Bedford and Sullivan and McKeever, the site of Ebbets Field.

I had to go there every day. I couldn't miss a day. Every morning I had to prove to myself that the army of bulldozers and trucks and cement mixers were there, the hundreds of construction workers, the cranes and the crews and the crowds who came to watch—no matter how cold—they came each morning. I'd try to see some progress, I'd notice that the old apartments were almost all cleared away, that a new foundation was being dug. I'd talk to the supervisor, who told me that Bobby personally promised him a lifetime pass if the stadium was ready for the '88 season, and I'd talk to one of the guys running a crane, who told me the same thing. And I'd wonder whether there was gonna be any paying customers. I'd wander up toward Eastern Parkway and see all the work being done on Crown and Carroll and President and Union, the old stuff coming down and the new parking garages going up. It was tough—real tough—to go way over to the townhouse on Willow and sit in my office and look across the river at the skyscrapers and keep my head calm and my mind on work.

I had to find a manager. Cobb was gone and Jacobs hadn't worked out; Bobby had canned him, too. Now who was gonna manage a team in a city the club was deserting—who could I get who was any good? I had already talked to all the guys in the know; I had put out the feelers and spoken to my scouts. So far nothing. And in a couple of weeks there was this big trading meeting in Montreal and here, on my desk, was this memo from Bobby saying how we weren't gonna spend any money or mess with free agents or trades which ain't sure things. "Our money," he wrote, "is going into our facilities, back into the borough of Brooklyn. Whatever happens to this club in the way of talent is going to be unorthodox and unpredictable."

I looked over all these pages of facts and predictions about income and expenses for this year and next. I read down the lists of the costs—team salaries and spring training and scouting and promotions and group sales and souvenirs and merchandising and bonuses—and I looked down the list of revenues—season gate and exhibition gate and TV and radio and concessions and program sales. I read the accountant's notes and the financial analyst's analysis, and it was all Greek to me. My head was swimming, and I felt a little dumb sitting there, like the Great Pretender again. I started wishing for the cold weather to stop and the spring to start so we could play a little ball and see what's what. "Unorthodox and unpredictable"—I read Bobby's words again, which is when I picked up the phone and called her. 'Cause I'd been itching to all morning even though I didn't wanna admit it.

The old man answered. "Hi, Hymie," says me.

"Mr. Squat, it's a pleasure to hear your voice, but my daughter isn't home. She teaches over at Erasmus Hall High School on Wednesdays. She helps kids who have reading problems. It's part of the special-education degree she's getting from Brooklyn College, which makes me very proud, except that I know—just as you know, Mr. Squat—that this girl's talents lie elsewhere. Tell me, what did you think of her pitching?"

"Great, just great, Hymie, but we'll talk some other time. I'm kinda busy this morning."

"If you want to see my daughter, you'll find her at Erasmus Hall. Would you like me to tell you where that is, Mr. Squat?"

"No, that's all right. I wouldn't want to bother her."

Erasmus Hall High School always looked like a little college campus to me. It's real old and pretty and sits over there between Flatbush and Bedford around Snyder and there's this weird Dutch Reformed church and the Flatbush Town Hall next to it, which proves something many ignorant people don't know— Brooklyn's got history. I was wandering around the joint, looking for the office where I could ask about Ruth Smelkinson. I was in the Erasmus Hall Museum Courtyard, which was also real famous and historical, and suddenly there she was, coming toward me, wearing a sweater and a skirt, bouncing along real chipper. I was wondering about this manly business, 'cause she walked something like a jock and I stopped her and she was surprised and started blushing.

"Mr. Malone," she said.

"Squat," I corrected her.

"Are you here on business?" she asked.

"I'm here because of you," and I almost said "honey," but I didn't.

"I don't understand," she told me.

"Me either."

"How did you know I was here?"

"Hymie."

She smiled. "Let's get a cup of coffee," I said. She nodded.

There was a sandwich shop across the street, right where that famous cafeteria Garfield's used to be. Garfield's was from the old days, and I was thinking about when I was in high school 'cause of all the high school kids in this joint and I wondered if Ruth thought I was an old man.

"You like teaching?" I asked her after I went to the counter to get me some java and Ruth some tea.

"I've just begun." She didn't say much—I saw that right away. And when she talked she looked down, not at me.

"You always liked baseball?" I wanted to know.

"Not like," she said. "*Love.*"

I was glad to hear that. "Your old man is quite a guy."

"He talks too much about me."

"He's proud of you."

"I'm all he has."

"Was he the one who really taught you all that stuff?"

"For years and years. Ever since I can remember. My earliest memories are of my father teaching me to pitch."

"And you didn't mind?"

"I didn't even try—that's the strange part. It came naturally. My arms have always had a great deal of strength. I'm not sure where that comes from."

"Want a cheese Danish?" I asked her.

"No, thanks."

Now I felt like a high school kid myself. I didn't know what to say to this dame. "You think you're good enough to play for the Dodgers?" I blurted out.

She blushed again and whispered an answer. I couldn't even understand, so I asked her to say it again. This time her voice was louder. "I know I can."

She didn't even say it with any bragging in her voice.

"*How* do you know that?"

"Because I've been watching major-league baseball my whole life, and I understand what's involved. I don't say it to boast, just to be honest."

"You *think* you understand major-league ball, but you don't. It looks easy, but it ain't."

"I didn't say it was easy"—she was still speaking so soft and low, and her eyes were so brown and pretty—"I just said I could do it."

"Then why ain't you done it?"

"I'm not sure. But I think primarily because I've never been interested in making a spectacle of myself. I hope that doesn't sound peculiar to you."

"No, no, not at all." I could see that this kid was sincere, and smart, and so shy and quiet, and yet she was sitting here telling me she could play big-league ball. "What about the guys?" I asked her. "You worried about what would happen in the locker room with you around? You worried about keeping up with them—training and getting hurt and all that?"

"It's never seemed as though baseball players are in especially good shape," she said. "So that part wouldn't bother me. I'm physically very fit. I'm a runner, and I usually enter a couple of marathons a year—not for the competition, just to see if I'll finish. I always have. As far as the social aspect of baseball is concerned, I'm not sure. I'm pretty much a loner. I can relate to people, though, when I have to. But I'm not interested in humiliating them. That's the part of the game I find distasteful."

What did she mean by humiliation? That's just winning, ain't it?

"Can I see you home?" I asked her, pushing those questions out of my mind.

"That'd be nice of you. I came by bus."

"Me, too. I like the buses."

She smiled at me with her brown eyes. A real quiet smile.

The bus was crowded with more high school kids wiseguying around and there weren't any seats and there weren't no gentlemen giving up their seats for the ladies, so we stood in the back, real close to each other, as the bus jerked its way through Flatbush. Sometimes, when the bus stopped short, we fell against each other, and I could feel that she was real soft and I asked her why, if she wasn't interested in humiliating major leaguers, had she hustled Oran? She said that she hadn't, that Oran had hustled her and that she had only wanted to please her dad by finally pitching for a big-league scout like me. When she talked I noticed how dark her eyebrows were and her black hair was very shiny and smelled so clean and I was wondering—I gotta admit it—whether she liked dames. I couldn't help but wonder that by the way she pitched and walked and everything, but maybe she was a switch-hitter. When we got off the bus in Bensonhurst and walked over to her house, walking real slow and just saying little things here and there, I felt like a kid again carrying home his girl's books. She asked me up, and I went, and Hymie was taking a nap in his bedroom. She showed me a picture of her mother, who had those same beautiful wet eyes, and some pictures of her father playing catch with her when she was eight and ten and twelve and fifteen years old. And then she told me that she knew about me.

"What are you talking about?" I asked her.

"I looked up your New Utrecht High record. It was quite extraordinary. You must be very proud."

"You took the trouble to do that?" My heart was beating fast.

"I also went through the archives of the Brooklyn *Eagle*. It's amazing how often your picture was in the paper."

I couldn't stop smiling.

"And from what I read of your rookie year in Montreal," she went on, "you were a shoe-in to take Campy's place."

I was looking at this girl who was maybe twenty years younger than me, and I was thinking that she was strange, but maybe not so strange 'cause she did look a little like Koufax. She wasn't beautiful, but what's beautiful? The way she was smiling at me now was beautiful, and if I reached over and took her hand, oh, if I told her that I thought she was real pretty and nice, if I said that I was glad I ran into her today, if I said it was swell the way she took care of her dad and the way she threw a curveball, if I sat down on the couch next to her, would she move away? Would she mind if I kissed her? Would she get scared and send me away? She wouldn't. I knew she wouldn't. I could feel she was a little nervous, and so was I, but I couldn't stop looking in her eyes and getting lost in her eyes and I felt myself moving toward her and I wasn't about to stop 'cause it felt so good and so warm, here in her arms, kissing her like this. She was all smiles and sweetness, but I backed off 'cause we needed some room to breathe and Hymie was in the bedroom, so I told her thanks, and I left her place and saw that the snow was coming down and the flakes were wet when they hit my eyes.

I was nervous that night. I wanted to call her again. I wanted to ask her over here. I was prancing around my apartment and dancing a little crippled man's jig. I was trying to get Bobby in China—I had nothing to say to him, I just needed to talk—but China wasn't answering my calls and at about ten o'clock there was a knock at my door and I answered it and there was Oran, her hat full of snow and her cheeks flushed. She smelled like high-powered lilacs and she was snappy as a new dollar bill and she grabbed me and hugged me and kissed me and produced a bottle of French champagne and started dancing around the apartment and singing at the top of her lungs. "I've made it! I've made it!" she kept telling me. "I'm network now! I'm going to the network!"

We drank the bottle, and I was really happy for her, and happy to get Ruthie out of my head and just be with Oran, because Oran had hit paydirt and she was celebrating with me. The thing with Ruthie was too mixed up in my mind. Oran was my pal, maybe my very best pal next to Bobby, who she couldn't stop talking about—drunk or sober, she was always talking about Bobby. She wanted to know what Bobby was gonna say about Ruth, and I told her I wasn't even sure I was gonna tell him. She said she was doing a story on Ruth, and I told her not to 'cause that could foul up the works, and she agreed. She listened to me.

"You can do anything you want, Squat, and so can I"—this is what she was saying—"because together we are absolute dynamite, and if it weren't for you and the Brooklyn story I would not have made it, never in a million years." I told her that was bull, she made it happen herself. And she was giggling and wanted to call Bobby in China, just like I had wanted to call him before, but we were too drunk to figure out the telephone. She was crying she was so happy, telling me that she'd do anything in the world for me because I was so true and blue and here she was a sports reporter for a national network. All I gotta do is name it, she said, and I got it 'cause she's never been as close to anyone as she is to me. I liked what she was saying, and I knew she felt safe enough around me to let herself go a little nuts, and there were all these high-class guys she could have been with—like Bobby—and here she was letting down her hair with me, offering me one of the sweetest things a gal can offer a man, which was funny, 'cause tonight I didn't wanna do nothing except think about Ruth and forget about Ruth and close my eyes and go to sleep. Which is exactly what I did.

SIX

WHEN I LEFT New York in March, it was tough to tell what was happening over at Ebbets Field. They were still digging and groveling around. The big bulldozers were picking up dirt and throwing it around, but nothing was taking shape. Were they on schedule? I'd always ask, and the foreman would tell me yes—

"The guys building this place," he'd say, "all come from here, all Brooklyn born and bred, and they're as anxious as you and me and everyone else to see what it's going to look like." And then I'd go away shaking my head as usual, noticing that the crowds watching the construction were growing larger as I went through this routine every day without fail.

Meantime, Bobby was still trying to pull off this big deal with a Chinese tractor firm, and he was in Peking half the time. When he was in town, he'd run over to McKeever and Sullivan with me, give the construction crew a pep talk, and that'd be it. When I'd ask him about buying and trading players, he'd say it was all up to me. He had to get back to China. But I still had practically no budget. I'd say something, but what good would it do? I knew Bobby, and I saw that he was in one of his floating frames of mind.

Basically I was the one who had to set up spring training, and I was getting the most help from, of all people, Luis. Luis had already started to prove himself as something of a baseball man. When he first came over with El Tigre, Bobby figured he'd need a long time to get settled and familiarize himself with the country before we went to Florida. But no. Just a few weeks after he arrived, he came to Bobby with this public-relations campaign aimed at the Spanish-speaking population of Brooklyn, ways to get those people interested in the Dodgers—interviews with the players in the Spanish papers, broadcasts on Spanish TV and radio. Of course it was a great idea, since it seemed like there were as many people around the borough speaking Spanish as English, maybe more. Bobby saw that Luis was a real pro and gave him all the authority he wanted. Luis was good at handling Bobby, which was no easy task, except that he had had so much practice with Fidel. They were two crazy bosses—Castro and Hanes—interested in pushing baseball. But aside from worrying about getting people in the ballpark, Luis also knew the game. He talked strategy with me and he was great at organizing stuff. He was a guy who got the job done, and, while he never said it, he was so happy to be fooling around with a big-league American team that he just couldn't do enough to help.

Meanwhile, I had hired a manager, Don Gumsy. He had won three straight minor-league championships in Scranton, and I thought he was real solid, plain-spoken and down-to-earth. He was originally from Bay Ridge in Brooklyn. Bobby met him and liked him 'cause he was quiet. Bobby gave him his usual pitch about how he didn't believe in interfering in the game itself—that was the manager's area—and I nearly choked but didn't say nothing. Bobby wouldn't think of giving him anything but a one-year contract—that was the sacred Dodger tradition—and Gumsy said he'd work doubly hard this last year in L.A. 'cause he wanted to be the first manager in the new Ebbets Field. Like everyone else was saying these days, the Dodgers back in Brooklyn was his dream come true.

The main thing I wanted to do in spring training was test this new talent—to bring in El Tigre, Sonny, Bo and Ruthie. Yes, Ruthie, which was still a real sensitive issue, because she wasn't all that convinced that she wanted to come to the camp, and neither was I. The people who did the convincing were Oran and Hymie.

"Are you interested in winning the pennant in Brooklyn?" Oran asked me a week before we left for Florida.

"You don't have to ask me that."

"Then you'll stop indulging yourself with prejudice and doubt. You'll do what's right for the team. You'll bring her down and see what happens."

"She'll cause problems, big problems. Bobby'll—"

"There you go, Squat, confusing the issues. If you're afraid of the boss, say so. If you think the woman has no talent, say so. If you're unable to control the behavior of the players, say so."

"You're just looking to get Bobby's goat. You're trying to prove something that's got nothing to do with nothing."

"Jesus, Squat! Can't you see that I'm just trying to help you? If anything, Ruth represents a way to pay you back for all the favors you've done for me. I'll gladly say nothing to Hanes. You present her as your discovery. Just let me have the exclusive on the story when you sign her up, and I'll be happy."

She'd be happy, but would I? Would I ever be happy with this Ruth around? The dame made me feel like a teenager. I'd call her and ask her out, and we'd go to the movies and stuff like that without jumping in the sack right away, 'cause I was convinced that I didn't wanna get involved with her because I wasn't sure what she meant or exactly who she was. She hardly said anything, but when she did it was usually straight-ahead and sincere. We'd go out to Dyker Beach Park or maybe take a ride over to Highland Park above Jamaica Avenue and we'd take our gloves and throw the ball around and then suddenly I'd be convinced all over again that she had a major-league arm. I was sure, but I wasn't sure. I knew I liked being with her 'cause she seemed to take me the way I was. She wasn't looking down at me and maybe was looking up a little bit, which I certainly didn't mind. Also, she was pretty. Also, she liked to do simple stuff like walking and talking and listening to music.

But I thought about Ruth too much, and I didn't really tell Oran how much I saw her or how much I liked her because . . . well, because it wasn't anyone's business. And it didn't mean all that much, because I had to go off to spring training, and Ruthie agreed that she'd better not go, and I agreed, too. And she wouldn't have gone if Oran hadn't screamed so much and if Hymie hadn't told her he'd throw her out of the house if she didn't give it a shot.

What could I do? Me and Ruthie talked about it one night while we were pigging out on cheesecake at Junior's and we decided it'd be worth a try. She'd stay with Hymie in a motel and we'd play the thing by ear.

"I'm playing it by ear," I told Bobby the first morning he showed up on the practice field at Vero Beach.

"What does that mean?" he wanted to know.

"Means I don't know what I got here. There's some new talent, but I ain't too sure about it. I want your opinion."

"What does Gumsy think?"

"He wants to know what you think."

"Sounds like a good man," said Bobby, who looked especially tan.

"Alvarado and Binder both look strong. They been staying in shape. But I ain't sure about Weller. He hurt his thumb."

"What about Ellis?"

"What about her?"

"She down here?"

"She's around," I said. "If you're interested, I'll arrange an interview."

"I was amused to see she made the network. I've been meaning to call and congratulate her, but I haven't had time. Who, by the way, are those guys over there?" he asked, pointing to Bo Solomon and Sonny Muse, who I had pulled out of school for a couple of weeks.

"Just a couple of kids from Brooklyn."

"Any good?"

"Hang around and see for yourself."

I had 'em put on a show—batting and fielding. Bo demonstrated his peg down to second base, and Sonny did his magic out there on the infield. I watched Bobby watching them, and it didn't take long to see that he saw what I had seen back there in the playground.

"I want to see them hit," he ordered.

"Right away, boss."

They smacked the ball hard. They swung smoothly and they swung with grace. They knew this was the Big Test, and they were passing it with flying colors. Finally, though, I knew it was their batting stances which would get to Bobby.

"Ah, Squat," he said. "What a sense of dramatics you have! To have tutored them in these stances, to bring back the batting postures of Campanella and Robinson, is definitely the year's most marvelous inside joke."

"It ain't no joke, kid. This is how they were hitting when I found them. And I found them where you told me to look. At the old playground at P.S. 105."

Bobby moved closer to them. He looked hard for a very long time, trying to see if the resemblances were real. He came and asked me, "Are you sure you didn't get these guys from Central Casting?"

He watched them play a while. He interviewed them. He saw that Bo was soft and strong and secure as the earth beneath him —just like Campy. He saw that Sonny was hot and edgy as a stainless-steel razor—just like Jackie. And as he spoke with them, he kept turning back toward me, looking to see if I saw what he saw, looking to make sure this was real.

"Why didn't you tell me about them? Why the hell have you been keeping them a secret?"

"What good would talk have done? You had to see 'em."

"Are they signed?"

"I been waiting."

"This afternoon. This morning. Now. This very minute. What are we waiting for?"

"Ain't any hurry. They got their last year of high school. They're on loan from New Utrecht."

"You're kidding."

"I'm giving it to you straight, kid. You thought El Tigre was something, but these guys are something else."

Which is when, for the first time, El Tigre trotted out on the field. Luis was with him, doing the translations, although El Tigre could say some things in English by now. We shook hands all around, and Bobby told Luis how he appreciated the bang-up job he was doing in the Spanish-speaking communities of Brooklyn promoting the team. "You have given me my own empire," Luis told Bobby, "which, I must warn you, I intend to expand." Bobby put his arm around Luis and told him what he and I had decided last night: Luis had learned so much about American baseball management—and knew so much already—had been studying so hard and was so good at it—we were making him general manager of the team, and it didn't matter to us whether he was a Cuban citizen. Bobby had already talked with Fidel, who was flattered that Bobby thought Luis was such a great baseball man. Castro gave Bobby the go-ahead and approved the appointment, though naturally he reserved the right to pull his boys back to Havana anytime he wanted to.

"The story will be on the air tonight," said Oran, who had come from nowhere to catch Bobby's announcement. She was wearing shorts and looking awfully leggy, and standing next to her was Ruthie in a sweatsuit.

"I see the network has given you an assistant, Ellis," said Bobby. "Someone to make sure you get the facts straight."

" 'Fraid not, Hanes," she bit back. "This woman does not work for me. She's just a friend. And she happens to be a pitcher."

Why was Oran doing this? She'd promised me she would butt out. But she couldn't resist. She had to create this little scene to get her jollies.

"Precisely what I've been looking for, Ellis," Bobby told her. "A female firearm. A damsel to befuddle our opponents. Does she throw over- or underhanded?"

"I suggest you save the jokes, Hanes," snapped Oran, "until after you've seen her pitch."

I didn't like this, didn't like this at all. First, I saw that Ruthie was nervous. I hadn't even had a chance to mention her to Bobby, and this wasn't the time.

"Why don't we have your little heroine throw a few past El Tigre?" Bobby suggested. Inside, I was dying. I was worrying that he was gonna smack one right back at her, that he'd tear her little head off. But I kept quiet, 'cause it was too late and Ruthie was going out to the mound and El Tigre was going to the plate.

We stood behind the batting cage—me, Oran, Bobby and Luis. Moon Weller moved in to catch her. She warmed up slowly. I could see her trying to concentrate, but I knew she was shaky. I also watched Bobby checking out her style; he saw she was no slouch, just by her form. No one was saying nothing, and after five or ten minutes, she was ready to go.

El Tigre stepped in. Cocked his bat. Stared out at the mound. Didn't seem to care if it was a man, woman or beast out there. He was a born killer. Waiting for the pitch, he snarled.

Ruthie looked in for her sign. My stomach was screaming. I didn't wanna look. She wound up, she kicked, she delivered. He reached for it, he connected, connected hard, got it right in front of the plate, belted it out out out, sailed it over the seven seas past Cuba to the Persian Gulf. Bobby was smiling. Oran was ticked off. Luis was interested. Next pitch, an overhand fastball, but without the stuff I knew she had. El Tigre drilled it against the left-field fence. Third pitch. A sizzler down the third-base line. Fourth pitch. Another rocket to Venus. I closed my eyes. I told Bobby that was enough. Oran was screaming that he needed to see her work against someone else. Tears were streaming down Ruthie's cheeks, Bobby was telling someone to get her a hanky. I wanted to slug Bobby, I wanted to slug Oran. I saw Hymie sitting alone in the stands, staring ahead, trying to figure out what was happening. I wish someone could have told me.

"You didn't give her a chance!"

"What does she mean to you? Why are you so passionately interested in her? If I didn't have some first-hand knowledge of your sexual preference, Ellis, I'd guess that—"

"Why are you always so threatened by the smallest signs of a woman's strength?"

They were sitting out on the veranda of Bobby's new Vero Beach home. The moon was full and the palm trees were swinging.

"Where did you find her?" he wanted to know.

"Brooklyn."

"Where in Brooklyn?"

"She's from Koufax's territory. Bensonhurst. She even looks a bit like Koufax. She has his style."

"You're seeing things, Ellis."

"Squat admired her style. He saw the Koufax in her."

"What does Squat have to do with this?"

"He's caught her. He's seen her several times. He suggested she come down here."

"You've been whispering in his ear, Ellis, and you shouldn't do that. You're far too pretty for any man to resist."

"Squat knows pitchers. Squat believes in her."

"He didn't say a word to me." Bobby lit a joint, took a drag, blew the smoke into the cool night air, offered some to Oran. Oran declined.

"Not while I'm working," she said.

"You're always working. On national television two or three times a week, and still starved for attention."

"I want you to pay attention to Ruth Smelkinson. I want you to see what she can do."

"I want you to stay out of my business. You're to report the facts, and the facts are that there is no female in this country—or, for that matter, any country—qualified to play major-league baseball, especially as a pitcher. You may quote me."

"You may regret this more than any mistake of your life."

Bobby laughed. He got up from his chair and went to Oran. He bent down and kissed her ear, her neck. He whispered, "It's flattering to see how far-out an excuse you will invent to invite yourself here."

She took the iced tea that he had given her and threw it in his face.

"I want you to fire Gumsy."

"Bobby, it's two A.M. I'm fast asleep here."

"Sorry, Squat, but I've been pondering this question and he has to go. I can't live with that man. He's too soft, too—"

"What the hell can you know about him? He hasn't even managed his first exhibition game."

"I spoke with him late this afternoon. I didn't like his approach. He's not going to train the boys hard enough. He's not going to insist on—"

"The guy'll do whatever you say."

"That's the problem. You've gotten me a yes man."

"And if I got you a no man, you'd never say yes."

"No! I require strength in a manager! I require character! I want someone who—"

221

"You're ripped."

"I'm ready to make some changes."

"Lemme go back to sleep."

"You're managing this ball team. That's clear as the spring air in Florida. That's always been clear. You're my man, Squat. Why have we fought the idea? It has to be you."

"I'm quitting."

"Do I have to speak to you, of all people, about destiny? You who preach to me about Divine Intervention on the baseball diamond. You who have been touched for this task by an authority much greater than my own. Yes, you who are led by the very hand of God to sacred discoveries such as Solomon and Muse. You are the one. You possess the magic. It is clearly manifest that you and only you, my dear Squat, are the single human being qualified to manage this team."

"You ain't thinking straight."

"I'm not thinking at all. I'm feeling. I'm feeling what I felt two hundred years ago when we met in our earliest incarnation, when together we hustled on the streets of eighteenth-century London, when we caught the fancy of country wenches and wreaked havoc at splendid costume balls."

"You're wrecked, all right."

"You're taking over. There can be no doubt."

"Tomorrow, kid. We'll talk about this tomorrow."

"And what about the girl?"

"What about her?"

"Can she pitch?"

"Forget her."

"Oran said you were behind her. Is that true?"

"I don't know what's true anymore."

"Don't get yourself upset. There's nothing to worry about. Just trust me, Squat. I'm here to help us both."

I hung up, but a minute later the phone was ringing again.

"Did I wake you, Squat?"

"No, I was just catching batting practice."

"Your phone's been busy," said Oran.

"Talking to my mom, seeing if she wants to do some relief pitching this summer."

"I owe you an apology. I realize I was a little hasty in introducing Ruth to Bobby this afternoon. It was just a question of—"

"I understand."

"You do?"

"Sure."

"He's incredibly pig-headed."

"He's right on this one," I told her.

"I don't believe you mean that. Surely you have more faith than that. Back in Brooklyn you saw exactly what I saw, and you couldn't possibly have changed your mind so quickly."

"My mind is closed down for the night."

"What did he say to you on the phone? He must have been talking to you just now."

"Nothing."

"I can't believe that."

"Quit pushing."

"I'm working, Squat, and I smell a story."

"Go away."

"He's pushing you around again. He's telling you a woman will never play on his team. He has you scared."

"Bull! He wants me to manage the damn club!"

"I knew it! I knew it was something big! He wants to fire Gumsy on his first day! Wonderful! Bobby Hanes is wonderful!"

"Don't use the story."

"You're mad. I'll be on the air tomorrow morning. It's perfect. It's just what I need—and just what you need, Squat. There are three dozen reporters crawling around camp, and only one is going to break with a major story. The first major story of the season. And as far as you're concerned, it's perfect. It's exactly what he should do. For once he's right. You're the only one with enough balls to tell him to buzz off."

"I am?"

"Of course you are. You're incredible, you're fabulous."

I put down the phone and rolled over toward Ruthie. She felt real warm against me. She was still blushing, and I could see her looking at the replay inside her head of every beautiful thing we had done together that night.

"Do you have any idea of what's going on out there?" I asked her.

"No, except that everyone wants you."

"I'm wondering why."

"You honestly don't know?" she asked in her sweet, shy way.

"No. Tell me."

"Because," she said as she looked at me with her soft brown

eyes, "you're the man who's bringing the Dodgers back to Brooklyn."

SEVEN

THE SEASON IN L.A. was a seesaw ride. I was on one end and on the other end was either Oran or Bobby or Ruthie or Luis or El Tigre or any of my players or coaches or scouts. Up and down, down and up. We were booed and hissed in L.A.—they hated us for leaving—and it was hell trying to concentrate on the team, 'cause the team was falling apart at the seams, which was quite an accomplishment, since they had already fallen apart the year before.

Before the season started, Oran did some stories on me being manager. She was excited, and she wanted to be nice, and she puffed me up plenty, and there I was on the TV set. The players said they were all real happy to have me in the dugout. *In the dugout.* Oh man, was that a change! I was watching the game from the dugout and I was actually wearing a Dodger uniform—can you imagine how it felt to wear that uniform?—and I was calling the shots, though my style was to mainly leave the boys alone and let 'em know I had confidence in them, which in this case was plenty tough, 'cause I didn't. There was also El Tigre with all the media mice following him around and making such a big deal about his being Fidel's favorite ballplayer. All the talk was getting to him, and El Tigre wasn't too happy, especially when he slid into a long, long slump. Bobby, he'd buzz in and out to tell me what I was doing right but mainly what I was doing wrong. Mostly, though, I missed Ruthie; I missed her something awful.

Who could figure out anything on the plane between Houston and Miami and Miami and Philly and Philly and St. Louis and back to San Diego and up to Frisco? I was missing Ruthie so bad. The only time everything was okay during the season was when we played the Mets in New York. That's when I could think. That's when I could stand still for a few seconds, but not too many seconds, because I'd be over there, at McKeever and Sullivan. Now the girders were up and there were beams. There was this skeleton of a ballpark, which, each new time I saw it during the summer, looked like it had a little more meat on the bones. I'd go over there with Ruthie and Hymie, and Ruthie would describe everything she saw to her father. "It isn't all there yet, Dad, but you can see the shape, and you can feel how the life is being formed." And then we'd take Hymie back home and maybe we'd go for a walk, just Ruthie and me, a really long walk. We'd just walk and talk and maybe we'd be together that night or maybe we wouldn't, because no one knew about us, which is the way I wanted it—I ain't exactly sure why, but I knew it was better for her and better for me. I'd been broadcasting enough of my business to Oran and to Bobby, and this thing with Ruth was real special. Besides, Bobby and Oran had their own thing going. They were doing this strange little dance and I didn't really wanna watch. Sometimes they'd be waltzing but mostly they'd be fighting. Who knew what was really happening?

Me and Ruthie were working out our thing alone. She was doing fine, she was getting her Special Ed degree so she could teach blind and retarded kids, and she was throwing better than she ever had 'cause we'd always go out with the mitts and the ball just like she used to do with Hymie, only maybe I was a little tougher on her because I knew what she'd have to do in the majors—not that it would ever come to that. Still, I was more and more sure about her strength. I could see it, feel it. And the more I knew her, the more I was convinced that it wasn't her arm holding her back, it was her head. Her attitude was bad, she was too nice; she just wasn't a competitor. Sometimes, when Hymie was snoring in his room and we'd be on the couch like a couple of kids, I'd ask her if it didn't kill her not to use her God-given talent.

"Yes, it does hurt me. I know I have this potential, but . . ." And her voice would trail off.

"But what?" I'd put her back on track.

"But I suppose I'm a fatalist. If I was meant to pitch, I will."

"There's certain stuff you gotta make yourself do. Don't you see that, baby?"

"All I want to do is love you, Squat. Loving you is no effort," she said, kissing me in a way that made all this talk sound so silly.

But the next morning I had to slip back to my team of big-league babies who were crying for me. Crying and beefing and, come August, threatening to break last year's record for losing games. It was so bad that even my best pals were beginning to wonder whether I could really manage. And I was wondering, too, but I had to figure that my strategy—just to keep looking and learning this year—would pay off next year, because if there was one thing I had my heart set on it was to bring back to Brooklyn a team of halfway respectable Bums.

I was trying to figure out why teams win and lose games, and naturally I knew all along—decent fielding, good hitting, great pitching. We were weak in all three departments. Weak in body, I thought, but not weak in heart, because on the final day of the season when we lost our last contest and finished 50½ games behind the division champs—the Giants, of all people—I saw that we had 53 wins and 109 losses. It was the gloomiest afternoon of my life, until Bobby arrived in the clubhouse with 53 magnums of champagne and invited in the press and carried on—pouring the stuff over my head and getting everyone drunk—screaming that this was the end and this was the beginning. Screaming like a maniac.

The playoffs were brutal. The Giants beat the Phils. The Yankees—back, just as everyone knew they'd be back, just as they always come back—took the Series four straight. Bobby said the Yankees won because of money. And then he'd explain for another half hour why he'd never enter the free-agent market, why we'd win with magic, not moola.

That was October. November in Brooklyn was especially cold and had me shivering. Sometimes I thought about L.A. and its sunny skies. But there was nothing left of L.A. Schmidt and his L.A. Stars were moving in. The Tucson Sunbelters were being born. Everything was changing.

Sometimes during the winter I'd be a little scared 'cause I'd see myself on TV or I'd get the *Daily News* and my mug would be on the back page, saying this or that. On the streets people would actually stop and ask for my autograph, and I'd sign their grocery bags and maybe bull with 'em for a couple of minutes about baseball, because everyone was talking baseball again. Even during the freezingest days of winter, everyone in Brooklyn was talking baseball.

Every afternoon and every night there'd be huge traffic jams blocks away from Ebbets Field—even below Caton, even above Eastern Parkway—'cause everyone was coming now, everyone was so curious and happy and proud. No one wanted to wait, and on Crown Street between Nostrand and New York Avenue they were already selling tickets to go on the roofs of certain houses so people could take pictures of the ballpark. Helicopters whirled around it every night, 'cause one TV station had day-to-day progress reports. Things were starting to feel very different in the old borough; the whole world was looking at what we were doing. I gotta admit that Bobby made the most of it: He went around like a politician delivering guest sermons in churches and synagogues, going to concerts at the Brooklyn Academy of Music, art shows at the Brooklyn Museum, getting the people in Gravesend to start an Italian street festival like the kind they had over in the city. Bobby had a million ideas to get Brooklyn going again, and he was working the borough like it was one big cocktail party.

"They're using antiqued bricks," Ruthie explained to Hymie. "Bricks which already look old."

"So there are brick walls," he asked, "just the way there used to be?"

"Brick walls and the old-styled arched windows," she said as the three of us stood there among the crowds. "They've just begun to put up the outside walls."

"And the awning in front?" Hymie wanted to know. "Will the awning be the same?"

"You can bet on it," I guaranteed. "We're going with the original plan. We're putting Humpty Dumpty back together again."

We walked around the ballpark, and I examined the beginnings of the three huge sides—on Sullivan, McKeever and Montgomery, where the grandstands would be—and the wall on Bedford which would house the scoreboard and the screen and the ads. There had been talk of putting seats there, putting up another group of grandstands in right field, but Bobby said no because that would ruin the design. The decision was rough, because more seats meant more money. "What would I do with more money?" he asked. "Just be tempted to play the free-agent market, a temptation I fervently intend to resist."

On some days I'd have to go over there three or four or even five times to see it, to walk around it, to watch the walls go up, to see the smiles on the guys on the scaffolds who were working harder than construction workers have ever worked 'cause they were determined to get it built by opening day in April. They wanted to make that deadline, because for so long everyone said it was impossible—Brooklyn could never do it, Ebbets couldn't be rebuilt in under a year and a half.

In the mornings at the construction site you'd see people—just ordinary people from the streets, old men and black boys and brown girls and shopping-bag ladies—giving the workers coffee and donuts and rolls, and in the afternoon they'd bring the guys lunch, offer them cigarettes, or joints, anything to keep them happy, to keep them going. When Bobby would arrive—mostly driven by Ralph in the limo—everyone would cheer, and once he was carried from his car. That's how delirious everyone was, loving it more and more with every passing day, paying no attention to hail or sleet, but coming back there, to stand and mark the progress, brick by brick, because no one could believe it. No one had seen a real honest-to-God miracle before.

At the end of February and the beginning of March, I didn't wanna think about spring training. I didn't wanna leave Brooklyn and head for Vero Beach. Ruth was practically living with me and I didn't wanna leave her and I didn't wanna take her, but there was so much else happening so fast. Bo and Sonny were signed. Their agent was tough, but so was Bobby. He came to speak to the January graduating class of New Utrecht High and spent most of the time talking about me and those two guys. He offered their fathers jobs with his companies; he called their mothers "Mom." He presented them with their uniforms on local TV, speaking of Campy and Jackie and predicting they would tie for Rookie of the Year honors. Everyone was talking baseball, baseball, baseball—on Atlantic Avenue, on Metropolitan Avenue, in Ridgewood and in South Brooklyn along the wharfs, the old Dodger pennants were being flown again, and naturally Bobby owned the rights for the new ones—the caps and the T-shirts and the shorts and the sweatsuits—but no one was complaining, everyone knew he deserved it. He was taking the hated "L.A." off the front of the cap and putting back the beautiful "B." The single "B." That's what this whole thing was about, and in the first week of March, when the weather got a little milder, everyone was wearing blue—officeworkers and busdrivers and nurses and pimps—wearing a Brooklyn Dodger insignia somewhere on their clothes, just the way people used to wear American flags.

Things were getting crazy and wonderful again in Brooklyn. People were talking to each other the way we used to, 'cause we were happy and 'cause we were nervous waiting for the season to start. We had waited out the winter, watching this ballpark go up, and now the frost was melting and the afternoons were nicer and every once in a while the sun would shine. And I think people who maybe didn't believe in God before started to believe in Him again, because how else could all this happen?

I'd go to church every Sunday now, 'cause I figured I could use all the help I could get. And on Friday nights or Saturday mornings sometimes I'd go to synagogue with Ruth and Hymie and Hymie would explain the prayers to me, and I'd pray there, too. I was praying as hard as I'd ever prayed before. I would hold Ruthie's hand and shut my eyes and pray to the Good Lord in Heaven Above for the greatest gift of all: a decent baseball team that could take a run at the pennant. Because if I didn't have that, I knew I was gonna be run out of this town on a rail.

...to Brooklyn!

ONE

BOBBY AND I flew back from Vero Beach in his Lear. Ralph met us. We got in the limo and drove through Queens to Brooklyn. I rolled down the windows. It smelled like it had been raining. My heart was beating fast. Beating harder and harder. My hands were shaking and my head was throbbing. I could feel my pulse. I worried that I might drop dead of a heart attack. I couldn't remember being this excited—for anything, even making love with Ruthie. Bobby was on the limo phone, still making business calls. That was his way of handling his nervousness.

We were close. Going up Bedford Avenue past Erasmus Hall High. Ruthie. I hadn't seen Ruthie in weeks. Past Linden. We were real close. At Empire. Waiting for the red light. One more block. I could see it. I could see it in the night, against the clouds. We were there. We jumped out of the limo. We stood. We stared.

People were there, a lot of people, and here it was way past midnight. People were there the way they tell me there's always people around the Colosseum in Rome, no matter what hour. I saw the old awning and, way above it on the very top, letters, in white: EBBETS FIELD. And the windows, the arches over the windows, the walls, the old bricks, the old feeling.

Now I gotta say something strange about the feeling. The feeling wasn't magic. The feeling wasn't high and mighty and thunder and lightning. The feeling was—*of course*. The feeling was

233

—*that's right*. It was seeing an old friend who hasn't changed. After all these years and all this work, after all this commotion, here you are, looking the same as you always did. Which was so wonderful, so perfect. "How does it feel?" Bobby asked me.

And I said to him, "You know something, kid? It feels the same."

"The same?"

"The same."

"Oh God, Squat, that's it! You're right! *It feels the same!*"

And he hugged me and his face was soaked with tears. We walked through the front gate, arm in arm. The marble rotunda was there, just the way it was when we were kids, and the way it was the day we almost caught the Phils in 1950. The spiderweb of walkways going up and the girders and everything were identical. We walked up a ramp—just the way you used to see people walking up the ramps at the start of the Dodger games when they were shown on TV—and we came out into the grandstands and someone turned on the lights and there it was: The right-field wall was bent the way the old wall had been bent. The black scoreboard was the same, except it was advertising SHOTKIN·BEER, which was the brand Bobby made a deal with, and the H in SHOTKIN was outlined in neon and lit up for "hit" and the first E in BEER lit up for "error" and underneath the scoreboard where it used to say HIT SIGN WIN SUIT ABE STARK, now it said HIT SIGN WIN SUIT FERNANDO PIZZARO. The billboards were for black hair products, and some were in Spanish, and there was a mesh wire fence —just the way there used to be—above the billboards going as high as the top of the scoreboard. The dimensions were the same —348 in left, 395 in center, 297 to right—and the grandstands looked the same except for the luxury boxes hanging down. It was cozy and small—this ballpark still couldn't hold many more than 32,000 fans. The seats were wood, not plastic, just the way they used to be. And it was the same, it was the same, Ebbets Field was the same, and even though it was cleaner and brighter than I remembered it last, that didn't change nothing, 'cause I could see that this was its oldest form, older than when I knew it. This was the way it must have been when it was built back in 1913, except now it had these sleek new lights and it was the same, the same.

I started to scream, and Bobby started to scream, we were screaming over and over again, *It's the same! It's the same!* when suddenly we noticed a minicam was on us and there was a mike over our heads and there was Oran smiling two rows down. She was holding a notepad and she was heading our way. She asked Bobby the first question, telling him that we were on the air live with this exclusive report on the first reaction of the man who rebuilt Ebbets Field, and her question was, "How do you feel?" and he looked at her and took her in his arms and surprised her with this big kiss on the mouth. She was stunned, she fought him off, and he kissed her again and picked her up and put her on his shoulders—she was wearing a skirt—and he started jumping up and down the aisles with her and she was beating him over his head with her notepad and by that time I figured we were off the air.

TWO

WE WENT IN on six police choppers, which the city got for us. We didn't have any choice; we wouldn't have made it any other way. From Jamaica Bay to the East River, Brooklyn was jammed up solid. This was Opening Day.

Me and Bobby and Luis and a bunch of newspeople, which included Oran and her crew, were riding in our chopper. The rest of the team were in the others. We took off from a platform in the old Navy Yard around Wallabout Channel and Bobby had the pilot circle the borough so we could see what was happening.

It was still three hours away from game time and the sun was shining. Not a cloud in sight. I saw the traffic going down Bushwick Avenue with Dodger pennants tied to the antennas of cars. Everyone was flying Dodger pennants—on flagpoles and from the roofs of factories—and when we flew over the Cemetery of the Evergreens I saw that some joker had stuck a bunch of pennants on the graves. Today everyone was rooting for the Dodgers. I spotted a parade down Rockaway Parkway with majorettes and huge banners with the Dodgers, the Dodgers, the Dodgers written everywhere. I saw Utica Avenue and later I spotted Dyker Beach Park and I thought of all these past weeks when

Ruthie was pitching to me—hour after hour. I tried to find her house but I couldn't 'cause we were moving too fast now, moving up to Bay Ridge, and a few minutes later I was looking down on Flatbush Avenue, people and cars, people everywhere, people pouring outside to feel the energy and taste the joy of this day. When we started flying lower I stretched my neck and saw that just a little way ahead it was coming into view: the strange shape, the flags waving on top, the real grass in the middle, the red dirt of the infield, the perfect diamond, the perfect field, and all the new parking garages behind it, the new restaurants and the little pocket parks and the walkways. And now I saw the white letters high above the awning, EBBETS FIELD, the letters that curve around in front of the ballpark. Now we were going down, and no one was saying nothing—Bobby wasn't even wisecracking with Oran now—because we saw that the stands were already filled and the fans were on their feet when we landed in the outfield. We got out, and as the roar of the chopper blades went down, the roar of the crowd went up, giving me goose bumps. The place was packed to the rafters—hours before the game was supposed to start—Ebbets Field was really here and I was really wearing the old Brooklyn Dodger uniform, which was when, just for a couple of seconds, I had to close my eyes and thank You, Lord, for helping us pull it off.

I tried to concentrate on batting practice. I tried to study my lineup, but it was rough. I couldn't stop looking around. I kept pinching myself and taking off my cap and seeing that "B" and, when no one was looking, kissing it. And just when I thought I had settled down, I saw these guys in rumpled tuxes with beat-up instruments marching across the field and I knew that Bobby had the Dodger Sym-phony playing. Someone over the P.A. system was singing:

Let's keep the Dodgers in Brooklyn,
A house is not a home without some love,
Don't let them leave our premises, L.A. would be our nemesis,
'Cause Brooklyn fits the Dodgers like a glove.

I tried to concentrate some more on my players—on Ben Little, who was starting; on Bo and Sonny, who were playing their first major-league game; on the Giants, who murdered us last year and were here to challenge us on the first day; on Ruthie and my relatives who were up there. . . .

But it wasn't any use. I couldn't get my heart to beat any softer and I couldn't get my stomach to stop churning, 'cause it was almost time for the game to start. Bobby came out to the mound, and the fans were on their feet. He introduced himself—and there was a huge roar—and he introduced me—and I don't think the roar got any softer. I felt my face turn red. I stepped from the dugout, I tipped my hat, I went back inside. Then Bobby introduced the Borough President, the Mayor, the Governor, and lo and behold, there was the President. They were all out there on the mound. I saw W.W. Percano back in the box above the Dodger dugout and I knew he was ticked off something awful not to be out there with them. Next Bobby acknowledged all the former tenants of the Ebbets Field Apartments, who were sitting there in their private boxes, and they waved and hollered. I looked around at the grandstands. Blue was everywhere, a sea of blue Dodger pennants and banners. Then the team was introduced one by one. El Tigre got a huge hand, with people screaming stuff to him in Spanish.

After the National Anthem was played, we trotted back to the dugout and Bobby, who looked like a prince in his royal-blue suit, announced that it was time to throw out the first ball. Suddenly thousands and thousands of balls—rubber balls, softballs, handballs—came flying onto the field, because Bobby had said that everyone would be throwing out the first ball, everyone in Brooklyn, 'cause this was our team. It took twenty minutes to clear the balls, and still no one had stopped shouting. There were signs all over, especially out in the bleachers, signs that said THE BUMS ARE BACK! Everyone was screaming so loud that they had to be hoarse already, even before the game began, as if to show the national TV cameras that we were the first and the craziest baseball fans in America and we were back and they'd never get rid of us again.

Back to the game, I had to get back to the game. I looked over my lineup card while Ben Little, a southpaw who'd won ten games last year to lead the club, took his warmup throws. I had Sonny leading off; I was taking a chance on the rookie, but he was a sparkplug and could get on base and steal the rug from under you. Davey Muntz, at shortstop, up second. Fair fielder, .278 hitter last year. Bo up third. Another chance, but with his Campy cool I had to take a shot. El Tigre, in right, hitting cleanup. We had built a mockup bent wall in Vero Beach for him to practice defense; he even studied old films of Furillo. Then third baseman Al Gleason, then Mark Hogie at first, then Ted Fromp and Carey Soster, the two other outfielders who should have been better hitters than they were. But what could I do? Harvey Binder, who'd hit .269 last year, had a lousy spring and a bad back to boot.

The pitching staff was weak: Alvarado and Fassbinder were my right-hand starters. Between them last year they didn't win twenty. Then there was Fredericks and Gern and Little to complete the rotation. Of the relievers, only Ted Stout, Neil Nash and Bingo Flash showed anything at all. You gotta remember: This was the same basic team that lost over two hundred games in the last two seasons.

But that was yesterday. Today was now. Today was the brightest day in the history of Brooklyn, and this was the team that was gonna get the party rolling. And it didn't bother me that much that Little was touched for three singles in the first inning, 'cause I was still so excited about playing in Ebbets Field. The Giants got a run, but we'd get it back. This was our magic territory, this was our Oz. I kept up the chatter, kept encouraging the boys, didn't lose heart when our first twelve batters couldn't hit the ball out of the infield. I had to put in Flash for Little in the fifth when the Giants scored their fifth run, but that was all right. Opening Day jitters. New ballpark. I winced when El Tigre struck out for the third time, when Bo and Sonny went after bad pitches. I kept my cool, I knew this was just the beginning. No need to lose heart. But in the seventh when the Giants walloped back-to-back homers and were whipping us 8–zip, it didn't overjoy me to hear those boos. It didn't take the fans long—less than ninety minutes —to fall from heaven to hell and take me with 'em: "Ya stink, Squat!" they were yelling at me, thinking I was taking too long in switching pitchers. "Ya got ya head up ya ass! Ya don't know shit from snot!" And then I remembered a whole side of Ebbets Field that I had forgotten, and the boos got louder and a couple of ripe tomatoes exploded in front of the dugout. Even when we managed a run in the eighth it didn't matter, 'cause the Giants had an even dozen. I saw that my little grace period was over; the fans hated to see this kind of lousy, sloppy playing—we committed three errors—and they were right, 'cause we gave 'em nothing to cheer about.

After the game was over and I was making my way to the locker room, I kept thinking about my job—my job was to get this team together just the way it had been Bobby's job to get this ballpark built. He hadn't let me down and there was no way I could let him down. And when Oran grabbed me and had the cameras ready for an exclusive post-game interview, I heard myself saying, "I don't care nothing about nothing. I'm just telling you right now that we're winning the pennant this year."

THREE

"*I LOVE YOU*, Squat, but I don't think you're going to win the pennant. I hate to say it, but the Dodgers may not even finish in the first division." Ruthie was holding me in her arms while she was talking, and I was in no mood to argue.

"Why mention that at a time like this?"

"Because I don't want to see you hurt. And besides, the triumph has already been realized."

"Bobby's triumph."

"And yours."

"Mine has to do with those guys on the field."

"It will take a while."

"Season's only got six months left."

"Not this season, sweetheart." She was speaking so quietly I could barely hear.

"You're wishing me bad luck."

"I'm wishing you nothing but success. I just want you to be realistic."

"You sound like Oran on the tube. You been talking to Oran?"

She kissed me and whispered, "The only person I talk to other than you is Hymie."

"And what does he say?"

"He says pitch."

"You should."

"I do."

"Not to me—but for real."

"We tried."

"Once," I told her. "But that was messed up."

"You saw what happened, honey. I'm afraid that will always happen."

"Maybe you're right, Ruthie. Most of the time I think you're right. But then I get to wondering what if—"

The phone rang from somewhere on the floor. I reached over the bed and answered it.

"Am I disturbing you?" It was Bobby.

"Yup."

"What are you doing?"

"Making love to a beautiful woman."

"Do I know her?"

"Maybe you seen one of her movies."

Bobby laughed. "What about the lineup for tomorrow?"

"Ain't done yet."

"When can we discuss it?"

"Call me later."

"Do you think you're making a mistake by using Solomon and Muse this soon?"

"Call me later."

"I might remind you that this is business, Squat."

"This is pleasure, kid. Call me later."

I hung up. Seconds later, the phone rang again.

"Do you know where Bobby is?" asked Oran.

"Bugging people on the phone."

"Where is he calling from?"

"What do you care?"

"I need an interview for the weekend news. I have a new angle I'm going to hit him with."

"Try the townhouse."

"I was just there. The lights are off. The limo's gone."

"You gotta get him right now?"

"Yes, I'm working against a deadline."

"Here's a number." I gave her a private number.

"Thanks a million, Squat, and if there's anything I can do for you, let me know."

"Tell me how to win the pennant."

"Get Ruthie out of bed and onto the mound."

I jumped a little. "How do you know about me and Ruthie?"

"I'm in the business. Remember?"

I hung up. I was mad. I stared complaining to Ruthie how I had no privacy, how everyone knew my business, how I was tired of all the meddling. Ruthie said she understood, she started massaging my back, and, oh man, she was real good at it, she could just ease all my pain and put my troubles to rest, she could . . .

But the phone wouldn't stop. Bobby calling back with a deal on a pitcher in Canada who had the best sinker in North America. Him and Luis were flying to Montreal tomorrow. Then he wanted to know why did I sic Oran on him? Didn't I know he wasn't about to give her any interview? He didn't have time for reporters. Then Alvarado called because his arm was sore and he was worried and I had to find Jesse the trainer and Benny Stern the pitching coach said he had a hernia and Harvey Binder called to say his back was better and if he wasn't starting in left field he was quitting. Ted Fromp called with the same threat, and Mark Hogie, the team representative to the player's union, said he had to talk with me immediately. Then Bobby was back on with new lineup ideas, which was when I took the phone off the hook and spent thirty beautiful carefree minutes with my Ruthie.

That night Bobby and Oran had dinner at a little Italian restaurant on Montague Street. I know 'cause they both told me about it. I was their father confessor.

They both were a little nervous. They couldn't figure out who had invited who, but anyway, they were there.

"You wore me out," he said to her. "Your pursuit of me is one of the great acts of tenacity since Lou Gehrig played in twenty-one hundred consecutive games."

"The number is twenty-one hundred and thirty," she had to correct him.

"I've never been too concerned with keeping tabs on the Yankees. The point is that you finally have me cornered." They were sitting in a corner table.

"If I remember correctly, you were the one who suggested dinner."

"Only after a greal deal of . . . oh, what the hell, Oran, we've been playing this game long enough." He took her hand and looked her in the eye. "I want to tell you, that . . . that . . ."

"I know we toy with our emotions," she helped him out, "and I know that we go too far. We cover up. We're simply afraid of getting involved."

"It's better not to get involved." He was speaking sincerely. "Better for both of us."

"As long as you're making news and I'm covering it, a personal relationship is neither feasible nor prudent."

"I couldn't agree with you more. Besides, neither of us has time."

"Or is willing to make the commitment."

"I don't want to interfere with your career," he said to her. "We're both adults, and we're perfectly capable of restraining ourselves."

"I'm glad you're talking this way, Bobby," replied Oran, surprised at hearing herself use his first name, "because I feel exactly the same."

"I hate to bring up business now," she said to him two hours later as she pulled up the sheets to cover their bodies, "but there's something I just can't get out of my mind."

"Go ahead. Say it. You can talk me into anything right now. What is it?"

"Ruth Smelkinson."

"Ruth who?" Bobby wanted to know.

"The woman you saw at Vero Beach, the pitcher."

Bobby started howling, then reached over and tickled her and said, "You never stop, do you?"

"It's not for me, it's for you," she giggled.

"It's for the network news, a scoop on the first female in big-league ball." He stopped the tickling.

"It's for the Dodgers, Bobby," she said, regaining her composure. "I promise. You have to trust me on this one. I don't want to see Squat's season go down the drain."

Bobby looked at her. He wasn't sure. So he snuggled next to her, and he kissed her and she kissed him, both of them trying to forget their minds and concentrate on the sweet taste of their mouths.

FOUR

IT WAS THE middle of the night in the middle of the country, thirty thousand feet in the air in the Dodger jet with Bobby sitting next to me jabbering away while I was trying to doze off and forget our first home stand in Brooklyn and our first series with the Phils and the fact that we hadn't won one game. Not one. And you can only go so far with losing streaks early in the season before you're knocked out of contention. I knew it, and Bobby knew it, which is probably why he was ripped.

"The pitching is definitely inferior," Bobby was saying to me. "The pitching will never hold up."

"If you had been willing to spend a little money I might have gotten a decent pitcher."

"Oran says you've got a pitcher." Now Bobby was smiling. I didn't say nothing, just the way I didn't say nothing when my folks asked me about this woman I was spending so much time with. "Oran says she's a phenomenon," Bobby went on, "and that I just happened to have seen her on a bad day."

"Oran's crazy," says me.

"She won't stop badgering me about your lady pitcher. She actually thinks the broad can throw." Now he started laughing, and I didn't like that.

"She *can* throw, kid. I seen it. I can't explain it exactly, but it's like the first time I seen Bo and Sonny. There's something about her that's strange and strong."

"Perhaps you're referring to her body odor."

"That ain't funny."

"And neither is the fact that Solomon and Muse haven't connected for a half-dozen hits between them."

"The boys need time, just the way Ruthie needs time."

"*Ruthie!* You're on such intimate terms with this female pitching fantasy that you call her Ruthie?"

"Quit it, kid. Ruthie ain't no fantasy. She's for real."

"A minute ago you were saying that Oran had overestimated her talent."

"I said that Oran was crazy. Ruthie shouldn't be pitching in the big leagues. She'd get creamed."

"Ruthie has you confused, dear Squat. That much is evident."

"What do I need with Ruthie," I said, "when I got El Tigre to worry about, and Gleason and Hogie and Fromp and the rest of these bums who ain't doing diddly squat?"

"You need to motivate them."

"Thanks for the tip, chief. I'll have it done by eight A.M. tomorrow morning."

The jet hit an air pocket. My stomach hit the floor.

"These guys are adults," I told Bobby. "You can't treat 'em like kids."

"They're infants who require strict supervision. In fact, they crave supervision. Without communicating your own notion of personal and professional behavior to them, they'll continue to wander through the labyrinth of . . ." Which was when Bobby stopped and started to sniff real hard. "I smell a most familiar odor," he said. "Either the plane is on fire or someone back there is smoking an illegal substance."

I closed my eyes and started to snooze. Next thing I knew, Bobby had jumped up and was standing in the aisle. "Do you intend to sit there and do nothing?" he asked me.

"This ain't the time."

And before I knew it, Bobby was heading to the back of the plane, toward the lit joint. I knew who was smoking—Alvarado was the pothead among the pitchers. The reason I didn't say nothing about it was 'cause I seen he pitched better stoned. But before I could drag myself back there I heard a bunch of yelling. Everyone was up now and the lights were on and Bobby began slapping fines around and when I got there he started off on me. The guys were all amazed when I told him that he was full of more crap than the Brooklyn sewer system. And that next night, in Pittsburgh, when Alvarado went the distance and we won our first game, I told Bobby to take a slow boat to China and meet us back in New York when this road trip was over, 'cause if he hung around I was gonna wind up hanging him. And he listened to me. He left. So far he was still listening to me.

That first win was a big deal. I seen something that night. Maybe it had to do with Bobby going nuts on the plane, maybe not. But the boys were stirred up, specially Tom. He threw real hard and he worked the corners real well. Also El Tigre hit one out very far and Bo caught a beautiful game and Sonny made one unbelievable stop and stole two bases. I didn't wanna make too much out of one game, but when I called Ruthie that night she told me she felt something, too, that deep down there might be hope. That's just what I needed to hear before we were on our way out to play the Giants again, the Giants who'd swept us in the opening series at Ebbets, only this time we were going to be playing back in California, at Candlestick.

"Wanna fly out for the weekend?" I asked Ruthie, and she said no. She had to stay with her dad, and besides, I needed to keep my mind on the game. "You ain't going out with anyone else?" I had to ask. "No," she said, real calmly and sweetly. She told me she was playing in some amateur hardball league she had found out about. She told me she'd be pitching, and she'd be thinking about me, and not to worry. But I worried anyway.

I was sitting in the dugout. I hardly ever stood or paced. I didn't chew tobacco, and I didn't like to yell or cuss at the umps. I knew it was important to watch real close and think real straight. Anything else takes you away from the game.

The game was tight. Candlestick was freezing. The wind was blowing off the bay and the ball was sailing all kinds of crazy ways. El Tigre had thrown out a runner at the plate in the third inning, and Fred Gern, our toothpick tall pitcher, was still hanging in there. It was the eighth inning now, and we were tied at 3–all, and I hadn't ever seen Gern this strong. He struck out the side.

In the ninth, Sonny led off with a solid single to center. Muntz sacrificed him to second. Then Bo, swinging the bat like Campy, walloped two terrific blows deep to left field—both foul—and wound up striking out. El Tigre was the man up there now. He looked ferocious, and I knew he was gonna blast one to Oakland, but the first pitch hit him in the thigh and he went to first. He wasn't hurt. Gleason walked. Bases loaded. Two down. Mark Hogie, not exactly the greatest hitter in the world, was up.

I saw Sonny bobbing off third, letting his long arms swing between his legs, teasing and squeezing the pitcher. I knew what he wanted to do. He wanted to steal home. Just the way Jackie loved to steal home. The gutsiest steal of 'em all. What do I do? Hogie wasn't hot. Hogie was fighting off a slump. I gave Wad Wilcox, my third-base coach, the sign: Let the boy go.

Sonny went. He waited for the second pitch and then—already halfway to the plate, his arms dangling down, his feet dancing— he took off like a bullet, kicking up dust, swiveling his hips and sliding right into the catcher's ankles, knocking him down, jarring loose the ball, touching the plate—clean as a whistle. "*Safe!*" The ump was right there and we got the run, and it didn't matter that Hogie grounded out. We were going into the bottom of the ninth with a 4–3 lead and I knew we had this game in the bag.

"What the hell is happening?" Bobby was on the phone from Rio. I was back in the clubhouse. The last thing I remembered before leaving the field was this sign that some fan held up: YOU BUMS ARE REALLY BUMS! GO BACK TO BROOKLYN!

"Nothing's happening," I told Bobby. "We got beat. That's all. Gern gave out in the ninth. Two-run homer beat us five to four."

"You should have never allowed him to go the distance."

"It's easy for you to say that when you ain't here, Bobby. You can't see what I'm seeing. Gern was strong. Sonny stole home in the top of the ninth. We played a heck of a game. We had it won."

"More reason for replacing him."

"The Giants are tough. Specially in the hitting department."

"I want to see immediate improvement. I'm flying back to L.A. tonight. I intend to be there for that series."

"I'd stay away, kid. They might murder you down there."

"I don't want it said that we're incapable of beating an expansion team. It's important to me that we beat Schmidt's Stars."

"It's important to me that we beat someone."

"And soon, Squat. Very, very soon. This season is not starting off well. My patience has limits."

"You're telling me."

It's a good thing Bobby stayed away. They had to have cops protecting us in L.A. Dodger Stadium—now Stars Stadium—was jam-packed with people yelling for our blood, holding up signs saying things like DEATH TO THE DESERTERS. We had managed to win one of three in Frisco, so I wasn't completely down. I had my hope back up, but when I saw the crowd, I began to worry. There were more fans—or enemies—in the joint than had showed up for the final twenty-five games we had played here last season.

Ducking beer cans and balloons filled with water—one had ink in it—we lost that first night, though I put the game under protest, (which never gets you anywhere). We also lost the second night, though the game was closer. But when we lost the third night by nine runs, when the stadium was rocking with people jumping and jeering "Brooklyn stinks! Brooklyn sucks! Brooklyn stinks! Brooklyn sucks!" my head felt like it was splitting in half and all my ideas about baseball strategy seemed dumb and doomed to failure now and forever more.

San Diego was a little bit better—we split the series, 2–2—and during the long plane ride back to New York I was sitting next to Luis. He said in Cuba there were managers who were always giving pep talks and didn't I need to do something like that? Or maybe I needed to chew the guys out. Or threaten them. But I told Luis that wasn't my style, because I knew too much about baseball and I saw the team for what it was—a bunch of okay players, and not much more.

Back in Brooklyn we had a day off. Bobby wanted to talk line-ups and my parents wanted to see me. I wanted to see Ruthie.

Earlier that day Ruth had called to say that she was playing in that league she had told me about. She was pitching today. Did I wanna watch? Sure, I'd be there. The game was at the Fort Hamilton Athletic Field over in Bay Ridge, and I kept my distance 'cause I didn't want to be recognized. I saw her pick apart this team of rough-looking Brooklyn guys of all sizes, shapes and colors. I mean, they didn't get a hit off her, and I was dying inside 'cause she looked so good out there throwing the ball. But the game was just bull, I told myself, and all her speed and control was okay on the sandlots but mainly I wanted to hold her and kiss her and tell her how I had missed her and she didn't need to get mixed up in my baseball life 'cause that was already a mess.

"You need her. Believe me, Mr. Squat, I know how much you need her," Hymie was telling me while Ruthie was in the kitchen fixing dinner. I didn't know exactly how he meant that, 'cause I didn't know what he really knew about me and her. So I asked:

"How do you mean?"

"You can answer that question better than I can."

I didn't say nothing.

"It's a miracle," Hymie was whispering now. He was afraid Ruthie would hear. He motioned for me to come closer to his easy chair. I did, and he sat up straight and talked with his hands. "A genuine miracle," he whispered even lower, "and you're ignoring it. You're hurting my daughter, and you're hurting yourself."

"What can I do, Hymie? The last thing in the world I wanna do is hurt Ruthie. I just don't know how we can make it work."

"Your heart is genuine, my son, but your brain is getting in the way."

"I tried once. You were there. And you know that only hurt her more."

"Listen, Mr. Squat. I'm not a father all these years for nothing. I know my daughter, I love her, and for me to say what I am about to say to you hurts me even more than it will hurt you. It hurts me because it will hurt my Ruth—but it is a hurt that is necessary. I think, and I believe in the deepest part of my heart, that you must leave my daughter alone. You must ignore her. You must get out of Ruthie's life right now, and you must stay out."

Was the old man cracked? What was he trying to say? I asked him and, still whispering, he told me:

"She needs to be independent of you for a while. It's important for her to follow her own heart. She's begun to pitch again, and that's good, but let's see where that leads—without you. Let us see, my friend, how she does when you tell her that you are too busy for amateurs, that you are a professional baseball man. You will see that in her own way she'll understand what it is she must do. I know it sounds cruel to cut her off just like this. But I also know my own daughter. How well I remember that first time she pitched against boys. She was twelve, maybe thirteen. She had always refused to get into a real game, no matter how hard I begged. Finally, I stopped having her pitch to me altogether. I refused. For weeks, we no longer played ball. She said nothing to me, I said nothing to her, and then one day when I was coming home from work I saw her down there in Bensonhurst Park pitching to boys much older and bigger than her. Oh, was I proud! But I didn't stop to watch. I knew that would embarrass her. You see, she had something to prove to herself. It was true then, and it is true now. You may think you're hurting her, Mr. Squat, but you'll be helping her later. Yes, stay away from her, leave her alone. For your sake and for hers, let her do for herself."

Just then Ruthie came back in the room with this gorgeous roasted turkey and a pile of fresh string beans, and it was only the next day—in the bottom of the seventh when El Tigre sent a towering shot over the fence into Bedford Avenue to put us ahead of the Cubbies—that I really saw Hymie's point: I had to cut it off with Ruth. She was driving me too crazy. Was she for real or wasn't she? Could she pitch or couldn't she? Did I want her to pitch for me or didn't I? She'd have to find her own answer. The old man was right—let her decide for herself. I couldn't give her any more time. I had a ball club to manage. I had my work cut out for me without some daffy dame messing with my head.

FIVE

OH, MAY WAS so bad. Some days I'd be sitting in the dugout in Ebbets saying why worry, why beat up on myself? We were here. We were back in Brooklyn and the joint was packed. The guys were playing pinochle in the bleachers and there was a bunch of ladies ringing cowbells, calling themselves the Hilda Chester Lives Forever Dodger Fan Club, and a local TV station had brought back the Knothole Gang. The dream had come true, except that the booing wouldn't go away 'cause the losing wasn't going away. Common sense said it would take three, maybe five, years to build this team. But Bobby was driving me nuts, calling night and day and working the lineup with me and wanting to trade everyone while I was telling him to blow off 'cause the season was young, but it was getting older every day.

El Tigre was keeping us half alive with his raw power, and Sonny was just starting to hit good and steady. Bo's catching was strong and Alvarado and Gern and Little hadn't fallen apart, but we were still at the back of the pack, tied with the expansion teams, and that was humiliating any way you looked at it. Sometimes I thought it would have been better not to come back at all than to come back like this, except there were all those years in the '20s and '30s when the Dodgers were mopping up the cellar, but they weren't my years. My years were the proud years, when the Dodgers were winners. And then I'd see Oran staring at me on the tube saying, "The Dodgers left Brooklyn winners, but it is becoming painfully clear that they have returned as losers, and one can only wonder how long the borough will continue to support a team which may be more suited for minor- rather than major-league play." And then I'd wanna smash the set or chuck my job, because I knew Bobby was right—Oran was as negative as they come—but I also knew Oran was right, 'cause she was at the games and saw for herself.

"I hate to report these things, I don't like hurting you," she said to me one day in my little broom-closet office after the Cards got

249

through acing us. "It's not fun to hurt anyone, especially a friend. Sometimes, though, it's necessary."

"I understand you, Oran. I really do." And I did, but I was tired of hearing this stuff about hurting and being hurt, because when you lose, everyone gets hurt. The players are mean to their kids and probably start beating up their wives and their wives are mean to their mothers and their mothers are chewing out the guys at the beauty salons and everyone's swearing. Everyone's getting hurt, especially Bobby, who told me losing like this hurts him worse than he thought it ever would, and maybe we should think about getting some players now. But it's too late; the deadlines have passed; there ain't gonna be no trading and there ain't gonna be no buying, and all I needed to do was stick to my guns and not call Ruthie, not talk to her. It had been a week and that wasn't enough time. I needed more time and patience, but meanwhile everyone was getting hurt and I was doing the hurting. I was hurting Brooklyn and I was hurting Ruthie and I was hurting myself the worst, 'cause late at night I was aching inside and having those dreams again when my leg comes back with blood racing through it and I'm up at the plate hitting 'em out to Canarsie.

Don't call her tonight, I told myself, 'cause tomorrow we're leaving on a road trip and we'll be back in two weeks. Just don't call. But the phone rang and it was her calling me, and what could I tell her when she asked, "What's wrong? Why are you avoiding me?"

"I don't got time for nothing 'cept the Dodgers," was all I could tell her, "and you were getting me confused, and I don't wanna think about you 'cause I got you and baseball all mixed up and that ain't right 'cause I can't afford to be distracted from the team now."

"By why have you changed? You had time for me before."

"We're losing more often. We're sinking fast, and I gotta figure out a way to bail us out."

"Can I help?"

I thought about saying yes, but I couldn't. I remembered what Hymie had said. She'd have to decide for herself. "That's up to you," I said.

"Can we talk about it, Squat? Can I see you tonight?"

Oh man, I was tempted, but I said, "No. There's nothing to say. I just don't want to see you now."

"I can't understand," and now she was crying, and I was about to start crying, so I had to hang up—oh God, she sounded so sweet on the phone—and I thought about calling her back, thought about running over there, about having her meet me in Philly, moving in with her and being happy for the rest of my life and forgetting about the pressure from Bobby and Brooklyn and El Tigre, who'd told me the other day that he had fallen in love with the president of his fan club who was from East New York and would I meet her—her name was Rosa—and could she come along on the team jet? No. I didn't need this aggravation. I didn't need to play the nice guy and try to keep the boys in line while I was breaking Ruthie's heart and Carey Soster was crying 'cause he'd lost four thousand smackers in pool games last week and needed an advance.

Back on the plane. Fly down to Houston. Close my eyes and don't think about the lineup, don't think about Ben Little's sore arm or Howie Fassbinder's sagging sinker. I could only think about Ruthie, and when I got to the Astrodoodle Hotel, or whatever it was called, the phone in my room was ringing and it was her, still wanting to know what was wrong. I wanted to tell her how I loved her, but I didn't. "Leave me alone," I said. Which was what I told Bobby, who was calling from Chicago, which was what I told Oran, who wanted to do another little profile of me —two months later—'cause now it was the end of May and now it was the middle of June and there wasn't much happening except the Giants were winning big and everyone else, including us, was losing big. We were back there with the stragglers, twelve games out. We were either ready to fold or to fly, and I told that to the boys before the series with Houston, where we took the first two games and lost the other two. El Tigre was still coming on—he had fifteen homers now—and the boys—Bo and Sonny —were hanging in. Sonny was hitting, and Bo was steady with all my five starters. In the bullpen only Bingo Flash was doing much of anything.

The longer the season lasted, the quieter I became. I told the boys I was behind them. They were my team. They knew I was fighting Bobby, who wanted to import Japanese wrestlers and Chinese Ping-Pong players to take their place. They knew I was fighting the press and the unhappy fans in Brooklyn. So I saved my breath and I sat in the dugout and watched and thought and made as few moves as possible, because really there ain't that much a manager can do. I hate to confess it, but it's true. Take out a pitcher; put in a pitcher. Juggle the lineup. Call for the steal. Call for the sacrifice. Most games have a rhythm all their own, a life of their own, and if you're quiet and relaxed, you'll learn more than if you're yelling and kicking. So mainly I kept my mouth shut, though inside I was screaming bloody murder.

Back in Ebbets at the end of June. The days were hot and the nights were muggy and the crowds were still big and booing. Bobby was getting rattled, Bobby was calling the president of the network to complain about Oran's reports, Bobby was telling me that I had to get tough with the team and show the boys who was boss.

"Who's pitching tonight?" he'd want to know while I was trying to nap at my place in Borough Park.

"Fredericks is up," says me, knowing I needed a southpaw against the Reds.

"I'd drop him from the rotation."

"The other guys need the rest."

"I don't want Fredericks pitching tonight."

"Then you go out there and you pitch the goddam game!"

I slammed down the phone. I didn't know how much longer I could take Bobby—or he could take me. He might do something, and I wouldn't blame him. Maybe I was trying to get sacked. Maybe this whole thing was a big fat death wish. But now I had to feed Pee Wee and try to get a little rest before I went over to the ballpark. Now I had to . . .

Listen to the knock. Recognize the knock. Know who's there. Know it's her. Remember it's been . . . what? Four weeks, six weeks. Listen to my heart thump. Walk to the door. Listen to the knock again. Think about not answering it. Stand there thinking. Reach for the doorknob. Turn it. Open it. Look. See. Smell her sweetness.

She was in this blue jogging suit, terry cloth like a towel. Her hair had grown a little longer.

"I was just passing through the neighborhood and I thought I'd drop by." She smiled at me. "Are you going to invite me in?"

What could I do? I couldn't leave her out in the hall. I couldn't look at her. She was too pretty. Her jogging suit was too cute. Go away. Go away. For God's sake, go away. "Come in," I told her.

She didn't look at me and I didn't look at her. She sat at my little kitchen table and I asked her if she wanted something. She said maybe a cup of tea. I went in and boiled water. I thought about how I wanted to take her and kiss her and hold her all day and all night and skip the game, just stay with her, stay with Ruthie, who had come here to see me even after the way I had been treating her—Ruthie, Ruthie, stay with Ruthie and never get out of bed, not for a day or a week or a month.

"Thanks," she said, sipping the tea.

I didn't say anything. We still weren't looking at each other.

"How have you been?" she asked.

"Oh, okay I guess."

She sipped her tea some more. I studied the floor. Minutes passed. Pee Wee jumped on her lap. She petted him. Out of the corner of my eye I saw Pee Wee licking her fingertips. Pee Wee was cuddled against her crotch. She kept stroking him.

"I hope you don't mind my stopping by," she said.

"No, it's just that . . ."

"Just what? I wish you'd say something to me, Squat."

"What's to say?"

"Her name. At least you could tell me her name."

"Oh God."

"I understand, Squat, I honestly do. It happens all the time, but I just wish you'd be honest about it. Is it Oran? It must be Oran."

"Listen, Ruthie, there ain't nobody but you."

"I wish I could believe that."

"There's the team, but that's something else."

"And there's Bobby."

"He's the team, he's baseball."

"And what about me, Squat? Where do I fit in? Or have you just blocked me out as though I never existed?"

"I've tried, I've wanted to . . ."

"Blocking out love, Squat—do you think it's right to block out something as precious as love?"

"It ain't love. It ain't nothing like love."

"You were the one who first used the word. You told me—"

"I don't care what I told you. I can't handle any of this right now, and I can't think, 'cause I don't wanna think about you, I only wanna think about my job and me."

"I've always thought you were the most giving man I've met. I've never known you to be selfish."

"*I'm* being selfish? How can you sit there and say *I'm* being selfish when you're the one who wouldn't do nothing for me even if you had to?"

"What are you talking about, Squat?"

"Pitching." The word just came out.

"I tried. I'm still trying. I've been playing in the hardball league. You saw how I was pitching. I wasn't bad, but I still don't like the idea of humiliating grown men who—"

"I don't wanna hear about it, Ruth, I've heard your line before. I don't care what you do and what you think as long as you leave me alone, 'cause I don't need your help and I don't need you scrambling up my brain."

"You keep saying that, and all I want to do is be with you and love—"

"You don't got what it takes." Now I was mad, mad at me, mad at her, now I was really raving. "I thought you had it, I was sure you did, you acted like you did and you said that you did, but when it came time to deliver, you folded, and I hated that, I really did. And I don't care anymore, 'cause I don't need you, I don't need any part of you, and I'm a jerk for thinking I ever did!"

That did it. She got up crying and Pee Wee flew off her lap screeching and she ran out the door. I had never talked like that to her before—never talked like that to any woman. What the hell was wrong with me? What was I doing, what was I becoming? I sat there and I couldn't stand it, so I got up and ran downstairs as fast as I could. I looked for her van and didn't see it and ran down to Thirteenth Avenue to look for her. But she wasn't anywhere to be found, and I limped back to my place and my fake leg was giving me fits—I pulled something in my butt when I was trying to run—and I picked up the phone and called and Hymie answered and I told him what had happened and he said, "I know it hurts. Believe me, I feel for you, my son. But you did the right thing. Everyone is doing what they have to do, and God will take care of the rest."

SIX

EBBETS FIELD WAS empty except for a few maintenance men. When Bobby arrived, Oran was waiting for him. Neither one smiled. She simply turned and walked down to the playing field. He followed her.

El Tigre was standing in the batter's box. Bo was crouched behind the plate. Ruth, dressed in a plain gray sweatsuit, was on the mound.

"I've seen all this before," Bobby snapped. He was angry. It was the All-Star break and he wanted to relax; he didn't want to be bothered with Oran's old scheme. Besides, seeing El Tigre in Brooklyn only annoyed him; El Tigre should have been voted on the All-Star team.

"You'll see it again," Oran snapped back. "Throw the ball," she demanded of Ruth.

Bobby could see that there was something different about Ruth this time, something almost fierce in her eyes. "Throw it," Oran repeated, "And remember—it's us against them, baby, so show 'em what we got."

El Tigre smiled. He was amused. He dug in at the plate and looked out at the mound and watched as she wound up. She served a sizzling fastball which he never saw, only felt. He swung —but the swing was late and confused. This got him mad. This also got Bobby mad, who watched her second pitch very closely. Another blazing fastball. Another swing and another miss. Bo beat his fist in his mitt and yelled encouragement to Ruth, threw the ball back to her, crouched, waited for the third pitch. It was a drifter, a wobbler, a change-of-pace, the kind of pitch El Tigre usually sends sailing into outer space. But when he reached for it, it moved away, it dropped, and El Tigre was tied up in knots.

Now he was real mad. Now he was ready for Ruth to serve up another scorcher. Now the fun was over and it was time to set the record straight. But an over-the-top inside curve got him. And what looked like a slider fooled him. And another fast ball destroyed his timing. And a juicy letup had him swinging too fast. Now he was almost frantic. He fouled off a few, he popped up a few, but mostly he missed. For five minutes, for ten minutes, for fifteen minutes, he couldn't get to Ruth. He couldn't hit her. After twenty minutes, she had turned the ferocious El Tigre into a harmless kitten.

"Convinced?" Oran asked Bobby.

"No."

"Do you see the similarity with Koufax?"

"No."

"What will it take to convince you?"

"This is an obvious setup. You've solicited the help of El Tigre, who has proven to be a most superb actor."

"It's no joke, Mr. Hanes," said Bo, who was still shaking his head with wonder. "That lady is for real."

Oran smiled. Ruth walked in from the mound. Luis, who had been watching, joined the group. Everyone was assembled around home plate.

"It's absurd." Bobby was boiling over. "It's positively and unequivocably absurd. The last thing this team needs is a woman pitcher. It's out of the question. I won't consider it for a single second, and I don't want to hear another word about it. It would break this ball club and be viewed as a vulgar publicity stunt. It will never work."

"Ruth was born to play on this team," Oran said, "in this very season, for you and for Squat and for the Dodgers."

"You sound like a cheerleader."

"I don't want to fight with you, I really don't."

The two of them walked away from the others. Bobby leaned against the railing along the third-base side of the field. He rubbed his eyes with his fingers, trying to find his composure.

"I don't understand you, Oran, I really don't." He was speaking more softly now. "You get on television and you kick me in the ass, you criticize my team and characterize us as a bunch of clowns, and then you drag me over to the ballpark, telling me that a woman pitcher is going to solve all our problems. What am I supposed to think of you? What am I supposed to believe?"

"You can believe that it's as unpleasant for me to do those reports as it is for you to hear them. It's just that I have no choice, Bobby. I've made a professional commitment, and I'm bound by the standards that I've set for myself. There's no going back at this point. Millions of viewers from coast to coast depend upon my judgment, and I must be fair. I have to report what I see. Do you think it doesn't hurt me to see myself hurting you? I won't tell you the number of sleepless nights I've spent agonizing over the things I've had to say about your club. Oh, Bobby, can't you see that Ruth Smelkinson is my way of trying to help?"

"I will confess that she did seem to have more stuff this time."

"That's because this time she came to me, I didn't go to her. She's undergone some sort of change. For the first time I sense in her the need to prove something to somebody—perhaps herself, perhaps Squat, I'm not sure. But I do know that she's ready."

"I'm not sure I am."

"Because of me? Because I'm the one who's pushing her? Because you can't admit that this one time I may just be right? Bobby, can't you see the ridiculous situation I'm in? I've worked for ten straight years, sometimes twenty hours a day, to get where I am. I've finally arrived. The broadcasting bureaucracy finally believes in me. And part of the reason I've gotten here is you, and the fact that I've stuck with your story—I was the one who broke the story. I understand you, I see what makes you tick, I respect your courage and your drive, I love your energy, I love so many things about you, Bobby, that . . ." And she stopped talking, realizing what she was saying, embarrassed. He took her hand and said:

"I know what you're going through. We have different jobs to do, and it's strange, so goddamn strange, Oran, how our jobs depend on each other. You need news and I need to make news. Our jobs are what keep us together and our jobs are what keep us apart." Now he leaned over and kissed her quickly on the cheek. "Do you see what I mean?" he asked.

She smiled and patted his hand and answered, "Yes, of course. And neither one of us is about to shortchange our jobs."

"We can't. We've poured too much of ourselves into getting here. No matter how deeply we feel about each other . . ."

"How deeply is that?" she asked, half-smiling.

"You can answer that question for yourself."

"I'd rather not think about it. It upsets me."

"I never told you this, but I do think you've got a lot of guts," he said, and then added, "for a woman."

She looked at him in a funny half-loving half-angry way. She was going to answer back, but she didn't. She had to be at the studio in an hour to do a piece for the evening news.

"It's a pleasant night and I thought you'd enjoy a walk. Besides, we haven't had a good talk in months."

I didn't trust the sound of Bobby's voice. I knew he was up to something. "Where you wanna talk?"

"I'll pick you up and we'll go to Coney. Just for old times' sake."

An hour later we were strolling down the boardwalk, passing Puerto Rican teenagers and Jewish grandmothers. The moon was full and the night breeze was cool. I loved the sound of the steady surf. We passed by the pizza stands, the ring-toss booths and the penny arcades. The smell of salt and fish and corn on the cob was everywhere, and I was starting to feel better, because I could feel that Bobby was happy. For the first time in months, he was in a good mood, and I didn't know why, so I asked.

"You," said he. "You make me happy."

And right away I was on my guard, 'cause I knew when Bobby was bulling.

"How do I make you happy, kid, when this team ain't going nowhere fast?"

"Your spirit makes me happy, Squat, because your spirit has always been the spirit of Brooklyn. Raw and real and never-say-die. At the lowest point of our lives you were here—always here—rooted in the most wonderful reality I have ever known. You taught me that reality. Were it not for you, dear Squat, I might be squandering away my talents in some stuffy Wall Street law firm."

"I doubt it."

"I don't. You have a way of picking me up and putting me on the right path. And that's as true now as it's always been."

We stopped for a frank and an orange, and the fat man smearing on the mustard asked us what was wrong with the team. He was sorta nasty, but Bobby was cool and charming and the guy backed off. We took our franks and sat on a bench facing the ocean. Some bonfires had been lit on the beach. Looked like young lovers running around down there, having a ball. I could smell marshmallows toasting.

"I know we're far behind the Giants," Bobby said in between bites. "But I know it could be far, far worse. I know we're within striking distance."

"I wouldn't call it that."

"Perhaps not yet. But soon, Squat. Oh so soon."

When Bobby talked like this, it was tough to resist. You could feel his power, you remembered that Ebbets was back up and the Dodgers were home, and you wondered why you couldn't just reach out and grab that old silver moon.

"It'll take some doing, kid," says me, "but maybe we can win a few more games."

"More than a few. Many. Most. We are in contention. I am certain of that. Just as certain as I believe in the miracle of discovery, in the miracle, Squat, of your ability to discover talent."

"Sonny's almost there, and Bo's about to start hitting. He ain't as distracted at the plate as—"

"They have brilliant games before them, to be sure. But after this All-Star break there will be something else. A new addition, an addition which could only be an invention of yours, dear Squat."

"You've lost me, kid."

"You found her, Squat."

"Who?"

"Miss Smelkinson. Miss Sandy Smelkinson."

"Ruthie? What does Ruthie have to do with this?"

"She revealed herself to me."

"How?"

"With perfect grace, poise and style, with Sandy Koufax's over-the-top delivery."

"What are you talking about?" I jumped up from the bench and stood right in front of him. He was leaning back and smiling through his big blond beard.

"This afternoon in Ebbets Field she revealed herself. She had El Tigre eating out of her hand. I have never seen such pitching. Never seen such fire. Ask Luis. Ask your man Bo Solomon. They were there. They saw. They, like myself, were weeping tears of joy. I was mistaken, and I am proud to announce my mistake to the world."

"Hey, Bobby, this is crazy. I don't wanna have nothing to do with that broad. She's gonna mess up the works. I don't care what happened today, 'cause El Tigre probably took it easy on her."

"He swore on a stack of Fidel photos that it was no fix. I'm telling you, Squat, that she was real. She's always been real. She's your girl."

"She ain't nothing of the kind. You just can't sign up some

dame who ain't even played minor-league ball. She'll get blasted and she won't last a week. It'll be a disaster."

"Now it's you who's turning against the miracle. You, the man who spoke of Solomon and Muse in mystical terms. You, who believed, when no one else believed, that this team and this move was possible. Are you not the man who sold Herr Schmidt—the world's must cunning corporate wolf—not once, but twice? Come come, Squat. Shrink not from your visionary soul. Embrace your own genius. Follow your heart! Lead us on to victory!"

"She ain't playing for this team. She doesn't even wanna play. It was Oran, I bet, who was twisting her arm—"

"You're wrong. She tried out again today because *she* wanted to. It was her idea this time, not Oran's."

"I don't believe that, and I don't believe that the guys on the team are gonna like it and she ain't gonna like it and I'm gonna hate it. She'll be murdered, those sluggers will bloody her head. How the hell can a woman play in the National League? Especially her, 'cause she's too soft, you don't know how soft this Ruthie is, you don't wanna know, and neither does anyone else, and that's it, that's the end of the story."

But by the time I got home it was on the news. Oran had the exclusive. Bobby had made room for her. Bobby had bumped a player and was about to sign her, and Ruthie was talking to the camera and saying that she had always dreamed of pitching for the Brooklyn Dodgers and Oran was beaming. Oran had gotten the biggest scoop since the Dodgers moved back to Brooklyn. Oran had gotten a broad on a big-league baseball team.

SEVEN

WAS IT ORAN or was it me or was it Bobby? Or was it in the Brooklyn air, 'cause that summer kept getting crazier and crazier. Crazier because the story was everywhere—Ruthie's picture was in the papers more than Bobby's—and crazy because a hot spell had hit. It was ninety-five in the afternoons. Inside I was sizzling, and I made Oran and Bobby promise to say nothing about her being my girl and I got Bobby to pay her more than I thought he would. I wouldn't talk about her with any of the press, not even Oran, and the first time I saw her after all this happened was in my office at Ebbets Field.

I was nervous and she was nervous and we just stood there for a long time and I didn't know whether to hold her or kiss her, I didn't know what to do, so I said, "This is gonna be a royal pain in the ass." And I meant it.

"You're still mad," said she.

"I ain't real thrilled about this thing."

"I had to do it, Squat. And I think you realize it's also what you wanted me to do."

"I don't realize nothing except that I got the world on my back wanting to know what's happening and the team's all upset and where the heck are you going to get dressed?" She was in her sweatsuit and I had this uniform for her to wear. "Where the heck you gonna shower? And what's gonna happen when you get out there and face the bullies in this league who want nothing more than to blast some broad off the mound into an early grave?"

"You still don't believe. Now Bobby does, but you don't."

"Bobby sees the publicity and the dough. Bobby's like Oran. He smells the ink the papers are gonna spill on you. Can't you see how these people are using you?"

"There's a difference between use and need."

"I ain't arguing no more. I just want you to go into this thing with your eyes wide open. And that means you and I can't have nothing to do with each other off the field. You took care of that the day you decided to try out again."

"You had made up your mind before that."

"I said then that this thing is too mixed up, and I say it again. I don't like it and it scares me real bad."

"You're protecting me, Squat, and you don't have to."

"I'm treating you just like any other player. Just like one of the boys. And if they start fooling with you in the locker room, you're on your own. And if the hitters start pounding you in the early innings, I'm yanking you out. The minute you start crying, I'm sending you back to Hymie."

"I do *not* intend to fold in the early innings." She said that with so much force I almost fell down.

"I'm wishing you luck, but I'm warning you—it's real out there, it ain't no neighborhood game. These guys play for money and they don't mind drawing a little blood."

"You're trying to scare me, Squat, but no matter what you say, I'm not frightened. Not now."

"Because you don't know what the hell you're doing."

"Stop saying that! Do you want to help me or destroy me?"

"I just want you to stay away from me. I don't want you calling me at the hotels and I don't want you sitting next to me on the plane and if any of the guys make a play for you, I'm telling you again that's your headache 'cause I don't have time for it. So take my office and make it your dressing room and use my shower and I'll get dressed with the boys and we'll figure something out on the road. And if you got any problems talk to Stern, the pitching coach, and leave me alone 'cause I gotta concentrate on managing this team."

And I threw her uniform on her chair and left so she could get dressed, and when she came out—looking too pretty for her own good—the boys were standing around. I introduced her and told them if I caught anyone putting a move on her I'd personally break his neck.

For the next hour I sat in my office and thought about her. Why was I being mean? I wasn't sure. Part of it was honest. I was worried about having her around, having her parading through my brain and stomping on my heart day after day. How would I ever be able to think about my business? But she was my business, I knew the gal was a great pitcher, and I knew that she wanted to prove something to herself, but also to me. And I was scared that if she had me, if I started playing Big Brother or Daddy again, it wouldn't work. She needed something to work for. Hymie understood that. She didn't need me patting her on the head and telling her she was a sweetheart. She needed me to treat her like just another jock, and that's just what I was gonna do.

First game after the All-Star break. Ebbets Field. Big series with the Giants. If we didn't sweep them, we might as well not even think about catching them. We were eighteen games out.

We played in the afternoon. We played lots of afternoon games. Bobby always remembered how, in the old days, everyone would take off work and sit in the sun at the ballpark and guzzle beer and fan themselves with scorecards and scream till they were hoarse. But today it was so hot I was wishing the game could be played after sundown. It was boiling, and the crowd had been coming in since early morning, 'cause everyone had read about Ruthie and seen her on TV. Everyone knew she was gonna start today and everyone was wondering about her, everyone wanted to be there. They wanted to tell their grandkids that they had seen the first girl in the big leagues.

I walked around the field during batting practice and I tried not to look out in the bullpen, 'cause I knew she was warming up. I wandered around the field and I looked up and saw that the place was already packed and there seemed like there were more women than usual and some of them were holding up signs saying KILL 'EM, RUTH! and MOW 'EM DOWN, BABY! The men didn't look as happy. I spotted Hymie a couple of rows above the dugout, just sitting there and staring ahead, and I wanted to go say something to him, but I didn't 'cause I didn't know what to say. Not now.

I spotted Bobby and Oran, and I saw that the Commissioner had come over from the city along with a bunch of other big shots. I wanted to go out there and see her throwing in the bullpen, but I stayed where I was, I tried to watch batting practice, and I went back to the dugout and I sat down and told myself to take it easy, told my stomach to stop churning, my heart to stop hammering. I didn't even hear "The Star Spangled Banner." I was just watching her out there on the mound in her Dodger uniform and her Brooklyn cap, and now I felt rotten that I hadn't said anything to her before the game started. Maybe I should have, maybe I should go out there right now. What am I gonna feel like when I have to yank her out? Oh man, this was just what I didn't want. But the crowd was yelling for her, the crowd was all hers the minute they announced her name, 'cause Oran had been playing up the Koufax connection just like she'd been comparing Bo and Sonny to Campy and Jackie. The papers had also been telling everyone that she was from here, from Bensonhurst, and I was still sure this whole thing was going to blow up in my face.

How could I watch? How could I look at Freddy Lipps, who had a twenty-five-game hitting streak going, eagerly march up to the plate and face her? How could I listen to the Giants back in their dugout screaming at her? "Hey, doll," they were screaming, "better make sure your bra's strapped on tight." "Ya didn't forget to stick in your Tampax, did you, honey?" Animals, that's what

263

they were, but I knew that, and I wasn't about to do nothing 'cause I'd promised myself to stay calm, even though I knew she was hearing every word. Yet she looked calm, she looked cool, she looked like Sandy out there. She played with the rosin bag and fooled with her cap and took a plain white handkerchief from her back pocket and wiped her brow. I gotta say that she looked real pro out there—not exactly like a man and not exactly like a woman, but like a pitcher. Her hair coming down over her cap didn't seem much longer than the guys' hair, and I remembered the first time I kissed her and the first time she slept in my bed and how she looked in the morning when the sun came through the window and . . .

Lipps stepped in. He was wiry and strong, the smartest hitter since Rod Carew. He hit anything. His instincts were sharp as a tack. He settled in his easy stance. He looked out at Ruthie. She looked over at me. I looked away. She looked down at Bo, got her sign, nodded her head. I was sweating. It was too hot to play baseball. The place was dead silent. She went into her windup, she reared back, she came over the top, let loose a blistering fastball. He let it go by. The ump yelled, "Stee-rike!" The joint went nuts. Everyone on their feet like we had won the pennant.

She looked for another sign. She got it. She came in with another fastball. He was waiting for this one. He had smelled it out. He went for it. He came up with air. Ebbets Field was a madhouse. On two pitches.

She went back to the rosin bag. I could feel her settling herself down. I remembered when she had fixed me eggs and told me that I was the sweetest man she had ever met. I could feel her concentrating on Lipps. She looked down at Bo. She didn't like the sign, shrugged it off, got another one, took it. Leaned in. Wound up. Kicked. Delivered a wobbler, a floater, a freaky change of pace that Lipps chased like a Keystone Kop chasing a clown. He missed and tripped himself up and fell to the ground and fans started pouring out of the stands and rushing onto the field—women by the dozens—to do a little dance—they couldn't control themselves. The umps had to stop the game, and even my pitchers—Fassbinder and Alvarado and Fredericks and Little —who had been giving me such a hard time about her were jumping up and down. The Giants weren't saying anything. It took ten minutes to clear the field.

She got the next two batters to ground out. When she came

back to the dugout I couldn't help it, I had to walk over to where she was sitting.

"The fastball ain't looking bad," says me, "but keep it down."

She looked at me with those sweet brown eyes of hers. "Thanks," she said, "I will."

"How does the arm feel?"

"Fine."

"Don't strain it in the early innings. Remember to pace yourself."

"I'll remember."

"And . . ." I couldn't say anything else, 'cause if I'd stayed around and kept looking at her I'd wind up telling her how I loved her with all my heart, and I couldn't do that 'cause of the guys right there.

When she came to bat in the fourth inning and flied out deep to left field I nearly had a heart attack. The crowd thought she had hit one out—and so did I—and even when the ball was caught they yelled like we had won World War II all over again. Hymie had also taught her to hit. When she gave up her first hit in the fifth inning, I was half relieved. I didn't know if I could live through a no-hitter. But by the seventh inning I saw they weren't gonna get to her. By the eighth, I saw she had gotten even stronger—the fans had made her stronger, she had made herself stronger. Oh man, she was really burning 'em in like Sandy.

Sonny had whacked one out and Bo had a triple and a double and El Tigre was three-for-four. She was doing something to these guys, she was doing something to everyone—and I was excited and jealous and getting crazier by the minute, but I just sat there and acted cool, 'cause we were winning the game 9–0. She was shutting 'em out, and here it was the top of the ninth with two out and the last batter she had to face was Big Bull Mison, their 250-pound cleanup man. He came up there with his shirt sleeves rolled up so his muscles showed—the way Kluszewski used to do. I could see he wanted to hit her. He wanted to ruin her shutout. His eyes were red and mean. He wanted to murder her, and I wanted to murder him for even thinking such thoughts. But Ruth was on a different plane. Ruth was sailing ahead. Ruth hit her stride. The first pitch was a sizzler. He got a piece of it and fouled it back. Then her curveball just barely missed the corner. She came back with the fastball and he connected, sending it high high high to left field—no one breathing, everyone watching as it curved slightly foul. Thank the Lord in heaven. She took the first sign from Bo on the next pitch. She didn't waste no time. She was ready to head home. She used that big motion, came roaring over the top and got him swinging with a sinking fastball to his knees.

Suddenly the stands emptied out and I was scared that she might be mobbed to death. But the players got to her first, and they put her on their shoulders, and everyone was crying what I already knew—a miracle! it was a miracle!—and they carried her into the locker room. I was worried that they might be getting fresh, but the feeling was too good for that, there was another miracle in Brooklyn, which was what the papers said the next day and what Oran said on TV and what I felt in my heart—except that once upon a time she was my own little miracle, mine and mine alone, and now she belonged to everyone, and I still couldn't start up with her again; I knew that I still had to leave her alone.

We swept the Giants, and in her second outing, against the Phils, she scattered four hits and we won the game 6–1. Bo was really starting to cook at the plate, and Sonny was stealing bases like they were apples. El Tigre was hitting the hide off the ball. The team was on Cloud Nine and I still avoided her. I still didn't go near her.

By the beginning of August, we had won a dozen games in a row—she had won three of them for us—and the National League hitters still hadn't figured out how to see past the Smelkinson smoke. Ruthie was the biggest story in the country. She was filling ballparks from Miami to Montreal. But finally, at Candlestick, she got slapped around for the first time. I had to pull her in the third inning after she gave up six straight hits, and when I went out to the mound I didn't look at her and she handed over the ball without looking at me. The crowd was booing and yelling both—they were mixed up 'cause they wanted to see her win and they wanted to see her lose. After the game, I wanted to go see her. I wanted to say something. But I couldn't 'cause the hurt was too deep and I couldn't take a chance on breaking down and crying with her, because this was a baseball team and this was a pennant race. I knew we were coming on, El Tigre was on fire—he had hit eight round-trippers in the last seven games— and everyone knew we had a shot, and I wasn't about to blow it by cuddling and cooing.

I wasn't gonna do nothing but ride on the bus with the team and not think about her riding in the back there. I was just gonna head for my room in the motel by the bay and rest my eyes and talk to Bobby back in Brooklyn, who wanted to know whether she was falling apart or not. "How do I know?" says me. "Ask her." A few minutes later I told Oran the same thing, told her I didn't wanna talk 'cause there was nothing to talk about. No, I was gonna lay in bed and not think about all those marriage invitations the newspapers said were being sent to Ruthie every day. I wasn't gonna think about what she was doing right now in her room. She needed to be left alone. If she was crying, she had to cry alone, and she could always call Hymie, whose nephew was taking care of him back in Brooklyn. She could do whatever she wanted to do, but I didn't wanna see her, didn't wanna have nothing to do with her. The pennant. We were chasing after the pennant now and we had to keep this thing straight, because dames can gum up the works with all their feelings and sobbings and carrying on. . . .

Knock at the door. Her knock.

Didn't wanna answer.

Stumbled over there. Opened it. She wasn't crying. She was just looking at me. She stepped in my room. She closed the door. She kept looking at me. It'd been so long—I was thinking—so long, and suddenly she was in my arms. Oh, she smelled so good and felt so good and kept kissing me and we didn't know what we were doing, moaning and sighing and crying, but we were together, we were together now and we were gonna be together till . . . .

"This was the worst mistake I've ever made," I told her. It was over. Okay. We had made love because we had to or because we wanted to, but now it was over and now I was ticked off all over again and I didn't want her here 'cause we had been weak and I was sending her away. What if any of the boys knew? What if word got around? What would they say in the papers? READ ALL ABOUT IT! HOT LOVE AFFAIR BETWEEN MANAGER AND PITCHER! This was the one time that Oran was sitting on the story—she knew what it would do to us—but no one else would be so kind. Oh man, this had been a big mistake—me and her getting together like this—and it was hurting all over again, but I couldn't help it, I had to kick her out of my room, just like she was some half-hour whore or something. She looked at me with more hurt on her face than I had ever seen. "Sorry," I said, dying inside, "but this is the big leagues, and we're going for all the gold."

Next time she went out, against the Padres, she struck out twelve. She pitched with a vengeance. And when the game was over she walked by me in the dugout and slammed the ball in the palm of my hand, real hard, so it stung.

On September 1, we were in second place, seven games behind the Giants. No one could put out our fire. El Tigre had passed Big Bull in the home-run and rbi departments. Bo and Sonny were hitting right at .300. And on the plane back to Brooklyn, Tom Alvarado—who'd been pitching his butt off—got stoned and started fooling with Ruthie, started squeezing her or something, and Sonny flattened him in the aisle and I flattened Sonny for flattening Tom and the pilot started yelling over the PA system and Bo calmed us all down, just the way Campy used to calm down Jackie, Furillo, Oisk and the rest of the boys.

EIGHT

"*THIS SEASON REMINDS* me of 1951," Bobby was saying to Oran on national TV.

"But don't you have the facts turned around, Mr. Hanes? In 1951, it was the Giants chasing the Dodgers, the Giants who were thirteen and a half games behind Brooklyn on August 11 of that year."

"Certainly, though I thought it obvious that in my analogy the teams have switched places. But if not, let me point out that it is now the Dodgers who are in the midst of a most incredible comeback drive. It is we who have another fourteen-game winning streak. It is we who, under the brilliant management of Daniel Squat Malone, have generated more electricity than a summer storm over Gravesend Bay. It is we who have given life back to the National League, while, over in the junior circuit, the Yankees continue their tedious and colorless sleepwalk to still another division win."

"In 1951, the Giants had a new player from Minneapolis who joined the team in late May whose name was—"

"Willie Mays."

"And Mays was the—"

"Spark which ignited the flame. Certainly. And the comparison you were about to make is most apparent. Yes, Bo Solomon and Sonny Muse have provided that spark, but so has the ferocious El Tigre, and—"

"You would not discount the contribution of Ruth Smelkinson's pitching, would you?"

"As a team, Miss Ellis, we are destiny's children. And at this point it is clear to everyone that Ruth Smelkinson is destiny's daughter."

"What do you gauge your chances of catching the Giants and winning the division title at this point?"

"As good as the chances of my taking you out to dinner tonight," said Bobby right there on TV as Oran turned scarlet.

Two hours later they were sitting at Gage & Tollner in downtown Brooklyn. She had gotten over her anger. They drank and ate and fought and teased each other. They spent the night at the townhouse and the next morning he took her to have breakfast at a dive up in Ridgewood, on Myrtle Avenue, where a crowd formed around them, women and kids and men on their way to work and play, getting her autograph and slapping him on the back and kissing him on the cheek and telling him that no one could stop the Bums, the Bums were going to catch the Giants.

Catch the Giants. Still four games out in the middle of September. The Giants weren't folding. We weren't folding. Ruth was still pitching, still winning—eight outta ten games—and no one could believe it. Brooklyn belonged to Ruth. Even Davey Muntz was making spectacular plays at short and Gleason was steady at third and Fromp and Soster were hitting again, but the real stars were Sonny, who was burning up the bases, and Bo, who was steady as a rock, and El Tigre, who had his girlfriend, Rosa, traveling with us and half the Spanish-speaking people in North America coming out for him wherever we'd go. He was the biggest thing since Pele. Back in Brooklyn there were huge paintings of all these people—of Ruth and Sonny and Bo and El Tigre— like they had pictures of Mao or Fidel in China and Cuba, big drawings in color that were hanging everywhere—from schools and churches and synagogues and candy stores and delis—and there were smaller versions that kids stuck on their lunch boxes and shopkeepers put in their windows. I even saw a big picture of Bobby hanging outside a joint called the Smoke House of Schmulka Steinberg "Where Kashruth is King and the Dodgers are God." It was a crazy time.

It was crazy because it kept on getting hotter and everyone was sleeping on the fire escapes and everyone knew that life was different because the Dodgers were making it different. The cops even said crime had gone down ever since our fortunes had gone up 'cause everyone was too happy to steal or mug. Everyone was too busy listening to the radio or watching us on the tube. And no one talked about nothing 'cept the Bums, which is the way it was in the old days, only this time it was even better 'cause we weren't folding the way we did in '51. This time we were after their asses.

October 1. Two games left. The Giants were one game ahead. If they won both their remaining games against Houston, no matter what we'd do, we'd lose, and they'd nab the division title. Meanwhile, we were playing the Phils twice in Ebbets Field. It had come down to this.

Oran on the national news wearing a black suit and a white silk blouse: "Going into the last day of the regular season, the Brooklyn Dodgers are still a full game behind the league-leading Giants. The Dodgers beat the Phils today behind the strong pitching of Tom Alvarado, two to one, while the Giants edged by the Astros, five to four, on a two-run seventh-inning blast by Big Bull Mison."

I spent the morning at Ebbets Field, alone, pacing, looking around at the empty seats. Thinking how much I loved this ballpark, how much it meant to me. This was our home, and we weren't about to lose here. We weren't about to lose today. The problem, though, was that we couldn't do it alone. The Astros had to beat the Giants for us down in Houston.

Gern was up in the rotation. This was gonna have to be Gern's day. It was another scorcher, felt like the thermometer hit a hundred by noon. Fred looked like a skeleton out there, sweating through his warmup pitches. I kept my eye on him. I was praying that he had it today. But as I was watching him, I was also thinking about another final game of the season—the one so long ago —when was it? 1950, that time Robin Roberts and Big Don Newcombe went after each other, the time the Phils whipped us in the tenth. Pushed that thought out of my mind; went back to today, the game, the last game of the season.

The heat was unbearable, but it was somehow working for the pitchers. Gern and the Phils' Joey Sinreich were both murder on the hitters. They were mowing 'em down like grass. First five innings no score. Everyone had one eye on the game and one eye on the big Shotkin Beer scoreboard in right field to see what was happening in the Giant contest, which had begun an hour later than ours.

Sixth inning. The Phils scored on a double and a slow single up the middle. My heart stopped. We were gonna have to get it back—and get it back soon. Bottom of the sixth. Muntz struck out. Bo lined out to left field. Time for El Tigre. "Come on, baby, come on, El Tigre, do it for your honey, do it for your fans, do it for Fidel!" First pitch—he missed wildly. Crowd groaned. They knew he was going for the fences. Second pitch was over his head. Third pitch, high. Then a curveball just missed the outside corner. Count was 3–1. Sinreich might be coming in with the next one. He did, got his fastball up a little high, El Tigre caught it on the seams, sent it sailing halfway round the world, kissed that baby bye-bye! Ebbets exploded! We'd tied the score! And then on the scoreboard another explosion—the Astros came up with six runs in the fourth inning, the Astros were creaming the Giants!

Back to work. The pitchers bore down again. No score in the seventh, nothing in the eighth. Going to the top of the ninth, score still tied. Gern was hanging tough, Gern put 'em down in order. The scoreboard showed that Houston had scored two more in the fifth. The Giants couldn't catch 'em today. All we had to do was beat the Phils, beat the Phils.

Bottom of the ninth. Just like 1950, I was thinking. All we gotta do is push across one run. Sinreich walked Hogie. The place went nuts. Winning run on base, no outs. I told Fromp to lay down a bunt, and he did, and the sacrifice worked! Man in scoring position, only one out. Soster up. Soster popped it up—goddammit!—and suddenly two were down. I had to go with a pinch hitter, had to use Harvey Binder. But remembering 1950—I couldn't get that game out of my mind—remembering Cal

Abrams's wide turn around third and the way Richie Asburn nailed him at home, I called time and went out to talk to Hogie. "For God's sake," I said to him, "if we wave you in, cut the corner close. Don't make no wide turn."

Sinreich bore down. Binder went after the slider and missed. Went after the curve and missed. 0 and 2. I didn't even wanna look. My stomach was a disaster zone, my head was throbbing. Sinreich came back with a fastball, and whack! Binder blasted it to left field, but Burrow, the left fielder, got it on one hop and holy smoke here came Hogie hustling round third and yes, yes, we were waving him in—we had to, we had to go for it—and he cut that corner—oh yes, he did!—and Burrow was up with the ball and fired it in and look at that collision at the plate, look at the smoke, listen to the crowd, on its feet, roaring, and watch the ump, watch his hands, watch which way he's gonna motion— "*Safe!*" SAFE! SAFE! SAFE! We did it! We ran the bases right this time and we did it! Beat the Phils on the last day! Caught the Giants! Tied for the division title!

Oran on the national news wearing a white suit and a black silk blouse: "It's happened again. The Dodgers and Giants have ended the season in a deadlock, and on Monday the division title will be decided in Candlestick Park in a playoff game that has all the earmarks of a contest held thirty-seven years ago, a contest in which the Giants came from behind in the ninth while trailing four to one. That was the game in which Bobby Thomson hit his 'shot heard around the world,' giving the Giants an unprecedented comeback victory which, to this day, haunts the memories of Brooklyn fans like an endless nightmare."

Sunday. Traveling out to the coast. Too nervous to think straight. Too nervous to talk to Bobby, who was sitting next to me. Too nervous to mess with the lineup or read *Sporting News* or do anything.

The plane ride was long and the sky was choppy and I wanted to go back and sit with Ruthie, because Ruthie was gonna be pitching tomorrow. It was perfect, because she was up in the rotation, which is the way God planned it, the way He planned this whole thing, so why was I nervous? She was sitting and talking to one of the boys—real quietly, the way she always talks —or maybe her eyes were shut and she was sleeping or maybe she was reading one of those good books she always reads, but I wasn't going back. I wasn't going near her, because now she knew we had to stay away from each other. We couldn't mix up the personal stuff no more. But it was tough not to think of the personal stuff, specially going into San Francisco, which was where we got so personal last time, and oh, that had been beautiful, but it had been too personal for our own good, and the team's good. Since then we had hardly been speaking to each other—only when necessary—and she'd been pitching stronger than ever and was set on doing what she had to do and I wasn't about to get in her way. Not now. Maybe not ever. I knew it hurt, but it was the kind of hurt you gotta have to keep your head straight. Ain't that right, Hymie? I kept asking him in my mind, 'cause Hymie had known what to do all along, Hymie understood what she needed and I wasn't gonna think about her, I wasn't gonna take any chances and go back there and—

"Something's wrong with Ruthie," Bo Solomon was telling me. He was standing in the aisle next to me and Bobby.

I jumped up. "What?" I almost screamed. "What's wrong?"

"She's been in the toilet for the last hour. I knock on the door but she's not coming out. Something's wrong."

Bobby and I charged back there, just as she opened the door and came out of the john. She was pale. Everyone was looking at her. Jesse, the trainer, started asking her questions. Bobby started asking her questions. I told everyone to get away. I took Ruthie to the last row of the plane, where we could sit down and be alone. I looked at her and saw that she was green as a bad apple. Her face was all drawn. Her hands were shaking.

"What is it, baby?" I whispered. "What's wrong?"

She was dizzy and spacy. She was talking crazy. "I can't let you down," she was saying. "I won't let you down. I'm going to prove to you that—"

"How long have you been feeling lousy?"

"Just for the past few days."

"You look like you've been throwing your guts up."

"Just in the mornings—" She tried to stop herself when she realized what she had said, but it was too late. *In the mornings.*

I looked at her again. She looked at me. I knew it.

I took her hand. "Are you sure?" I asked her.

"No. It's not what you're thinking. It's nothing, it's—" But she stopped herself again. She saw it was no use.

I couldn't say anything. I couldn't let go of her hand. I felt
. . . I felt . . . I felt everything: I was happy, I was furious, I was
grateful, I was scared, I was angry at her and angry at me, angry
at Hymie and Oran and baseball, and I was, I was . . . I didn't
know what to do. I just didn't know what to do.

I let go of her hand. I looked her in the eye. I told her, "You
can't pitch. That's one thing I know. I can't let you pitch."

"I have to pitch."

"You won't."

"It may be nothing, Squat."

"We can't take that chance. I *won't* take that chance."

"It's the division title. That's what we've been aiming for, that's
why we met. Can't you see that? That's why you told me I could
do it. And then you showed me I'd have to prove it, and I will, I
know I will."

"Listen, Ruthie, there are certain things more important than
baseball and pennants and I ain't letting you pitch and I don't
wanna hear nothing more about it."

And I went back to my seat and everyone wanted to know what
was happening and I said nothing, she wasn't feeling good. I
wasn't going to spill the beans about her not pitching until the
next morning 'cause I didn't want a lot of questions asked. I
wasn't saying nothing to Bobby or to no one. Before we got off
the plane I just whispered to Hart Fredericks to get himself ready
for tomorrow because he was probably starting.

I snuck into her room that night. I had to. I couldn't leave her
alone. I tried to make her feel better and I told her how I was
through hurting her. But she said I was hurting her even more
and I had to let her pitch, I just had to, because she had the
Giants' number and she had to prove something. You're hurting
me worse than ever, she kept saying. I couldn't sleep and she
hardly slept and I was just about to think she was right when,
about six in the morning, she went to the bathroom and vomited
for nearly an hour. I cleaned her mouth and held a cold towel to
her head and kissed her cheeks and knew there was no way I
could let her pitch.

The announcement was a shock, and everyone came running
over to me—Bobby included—but by then Fredericks was warming up in the bullpen and I just said that she was too sick to pitch

and that was it. Bobby said he was firing me, but I paid no attention to nothing. I sat in the dugout and looked out at the cloudy sky and the banners saying, THE BUMS ARE BORN AGAIN ONLY TO DIE AGAIN! and KILL BROOKLYN! I saw lots of faces from L.A., 'cause people from down there were still mad about what Bobby had done and they were looking for us to get murdered here, the way it happened in '51. Everyone was thinking about '51, though I knew that was then and this was now—at least that's what I told myself. Fredericks had been good the last half of the season. Like everyone else, he had been inspired by Ruthie, and I had confidence in the kid and he knew it. He was a farmboy and he was the calm type, real good under pressure. The kid would pitch his heart out today.

And he did. He kept 'em to one run, and El Tigre and Bo each hit bases-empty homers and Sonny drove in two more. We were sailing, we were about to win the division. It was God who had kept Ruthie from pitching today, because this was Frederick's day. Everyone, Bobby included, was seeing that I had done the right thing. Until the bottom of the ninth.

My palms were wet. My mouth was dry. My knees were weak. I was trying not to think, trying not to remember, but everyone was thinking and remembering the same thing. In 1951, going into the bottom of the ninth, the Giants were behind 4–1, just like they were today. That was when Thomson hit his home run. That was when the Bums blew it. But that was then and this was now.

Except that Fredericks was thinking about it. Fredericks was looking nervous. Fredericks was thinking too much.

He walked the first batter, and I yelled out to the mound, "Stop thinking and just pitch your game. Relax." He relaxed so much he walked the next batter, too. So I trotted out there and told him to stop messing around and strike out this next clown. He did. Two on, one out. I was sticking with Fredericks. I was feeling better. We got the second out on a pop-up and we had one out to go and we'd have the title. Just one lousy out. But Fredericks looked real shaky now—I saw it in his eyes—and, oh God, he walked another man and now the bases were loaded, the bases were full with two outs and up comes the winning run—the championship winning run—in the person of Big Bull Mison. I had to take Fredericks out. I just had to, 'cause he was too scared and he had lost it. I had to make this move.

I looked out to the bullpen and I saw that someone else was warming up next to Bingo Flash. I wasn't sure who it was, and then I saw: It was Ruthie. She wasn't coming in—no way. I gave the signal for Bingo. Which was when something very weird happened.

Bingo didn't move. She did. Against my orders. She started coming in. And I looked up behind the dugout and saw that Bobby was sweating and smiling at the same time and I could imagine what Oran was telling the country—the network had her broadcasting all these games—and I was about to send Ruthie back to the bullpen, but I didn't. I don't know why I didn't. I can't explain it. But when she got to the mound, I just gave her the ball, and before I walked away, after Bo had gone back behind the plate, I whispered in her ear, "I love you, but if you give this bum anything good, I'll break your neck."

Bobby Thomson. Everyone was thinking Bobby Thomson, and I was thinking about Ruthie and her condition and why was I letting this happen, except it was happening. Everything was out of my control, and if Big Bull hits a home run, then he hits a home run, because it was meant to be and I ain't gonna pass out, I ain't gonna throw up or have no convulsion. I was just gonna sit there and watch her take her sign, watch her stretch and set and throw the ball—oh Jesus—right in his wheelhouse, right where he wants it, and he connected and it went up up up, it went far far far, it went down down down the left-field line—just like Thomson, just like Bobby Thomson—except at the last second it curved foul and I breathed again and she had one strike on the Bull. God help me. My heart had flown out of my mouth. I could feel all the planets in the universe sighing in relief.

She was gutsy. Oh man. She was bearing down. She didn't look scared. She just leaned in there and fed him another fastball, only this one was tighter inside and he couldn't get it, he swung too late, and now she was ahead of him 0–2. She was way ahead of him.

Do I pray now? Do I ask God to help her get Mison? Do I promise something in return for a win?

I saw her out there. Ruthie. My lady, my pitcher who shouldn't have been pitching, who should have been back in her room resting or knitting booties instead of serving Big Bull this change-up which wasn't floating right, which wasn't fooling him, which he smacked—holy shit!—whacked a straight shot to her gut. My

276

worst nightmare was coming true—her world and my world was over—except she coolly lowered her glove and protected her tummy and caught the line drive in the webbing of her mitt and we won the game! We won the division! We changed history and paid back the Giants for giving us thirty-seven years of misery!

NINE

THE DOCTOR SAID she was pregnant. He said that to me and to Ruthie in his office. No one was there except us, and I kept on looking down the hall expecting to find Oran so she could break the story, but she wasn't there. No one knew but us, and that's the way it had to be. Ruthie was pregnant and we were going to have a baby and that was the most beautiful thing that had ever happened to me, even as beautiful as beating the Giants, except that the playoffs were starting tomorrow against the Expos, who were not to be underrated, not by a long shot.

But she was pregnant and there was nothing to do about it except that Doc Longley, who I had known ever since I was a kid and who I trusted with my life, said she could pitch.

I didn't believe him. "You're a Dodger fan, Doc. You're letting that get in your way. You're toying with this girl's life."

"Listen, Squat. Women do far more strenuous things than pitch baseball games in the first few months of pregnancy. Ruth is a remarkably strong and courageous lady. She's also fit as a fiddle and knows how to take care of herself, and she will. When she hits, she should be careful. She doesn't have to be a Sonny Muse if she gets on base. She doesn't have to slide and carry on. But she knows what to do far better than us. She understands her own capabilities."

Had Ruthie paid him off to say this? Had Bobby? But Bobby didn't know and Ruthie had never seen this doctor before— Longley was my mom's doc—and the guy was being straight.

It didn't surprise me, it didn't surprise Bobby or Oran or anybody, that we beat Montreal three straight, just like the Yanks beat Texas three straight. It was like we couldn't wait to get at each other in the Series. It was like we knew this was gonna happen, so why waste time? Why mess around? Let's just get it on.

A subway series. There ain't nothing more beautiful in the world. The Bronx against Brooklyn. The battle of the boroughs, and a chance—thank you, God in Heaven—to show up the Yankees for being the assholes of the century. A chance to pay 'em back.

"There is no team," Bobby was telling Oran over national TV, "that is more dependent upon the insidious free-agent system than the Yankees. They are a bought team. They're convinced that victory can be purchased for a price, but they will be shown once and for all that the Dodgers have returned to Brooklyn if for no other purpose than to humiliate the Yankees and reveal them to be the Fascists that they are now, that they always have been, and that they always will be."

"Don't you think it's a bit silly, Mr. Hanes, to view baseball as a moral allegory? After all, the Yankees are—"

"Despicable. Enemies to the death. The Yankees are dirt, just as one fine day even you, my dear Oran, will see that the Dodgers are divine."

She started to argue with him, but something stopped her. Suddenly she lost that professional tone and said, right there on the air, for everyone to hear, "I just have to say I've been following your team for three years now and I love them, I really do, and I hope they knock the Yankees on their rears!"

Was I hearing right? Was it a joke? Oran had really come out and said it, and she was laughing. She'd probably get canned, but this Series had made everyone nuts—even the network bosses. No one was acting normal, 'cause it was the Yankees and the Dodgers again fighting it out for the World Championship.

The air between the two boroughs was polluted with bad feelings, but the streets of Brooklyn were alive with people running around and slapping each other on the back and carrying pictures of all the Dodgers. Everywhere I went in the neighborhood fans chased after me and wound up lifting me on their shoulders, so I couldn't go out. I hid in Bensonhurst with Ruthie and Hymie and no one knew where I was. I told Bobby I was hiding out to plan the strategy, and he wanted to know how Ruth was and I said fine. I had the feeling that he knew, but he didn't say nothing, because we were all scared of fooling with fate, except that he knew she was gonna pitch, we all knew she was gonna pitch the first game of the Series against the Yanks.

"She can't pitch the first game," Hymie was saying to me from his easy chair.

"But Hymie," I started to explain, "the doctor says—"

"I know all about the doctor, and I bless him for his advice, and I bless you, and I bless her. But it has nothing to do with that. Believe me."

I looked over at Ruthie, who was sitting on the couch and not looking back at me. She was staring at the floor.

"What's he talking about?" I was practically screaming.

"Yom Kippur," she said softly. "The Jewish High Holy Day of Yom Kippur. The first game falls on Yom Kippur. You understand, Squat, I know you do."

I told Bobby and two hours later Oran was on the air. She had the scoop. I was over at the townhouse on Willow Street, looking at his TV set:

"In a move which will remind all Dodger fans of the year in 1965 when Sandy Koufax refused to pitch the opening game against Minnesota in deference to the religious holiday of Yom Kippur, it was announced today that Ruth Smelkinson will not . . ."

Bobby turned off the sound. "Just remember, Squat," he said, "that Sandy came back to pitch the second, fifth and seventh game, the one that won the Series for us. It's a good omen, Squat, I promise you it is."

I kept quiet. I couldn't argue—not with Bobby, not with Ruthie or Hymie. I couldn't go against God. I thought of the word Doc Longley had used to describe Ruthie. "Courageous." We all had to be courageous now. We were going up against the Fascists.

I hate Yankee Stadium. It's too big and noisy and impersonal and cold. But there I was, and there were all the flags and the bunting and the big shots and the Yankee fans. The sky was gray and overcast. I had to go with Alvarado, and they were going with their ace, Brian Londis. Londis was throwing fire, and for the first three innings we were hitless. But in the fourth El Tigre smacked one out—I kissed him when he got back to the dugout —and I thought the one-run lead might last a while, 'cause Tom was steady. Until the Yank half of the fourth. They bombed him for six hits and four runs and I had to pull him. My long reliefer, Neil Nash, put out the fire, and then in the seventh, with Sonny on first, Bo unloaded and blasted one to kingdom come. We were within a run. Nash held them, and when we came to bat at the top of of the ninth we still needed that run.

I kept Nash in,' cause he was a fine hitter and baserunner, and he paid me back by singling up the middle. Then Sonny sacrificed him over. Tying run in scoring position. I had a feeling we were going to tie the game; I had a feeling we were going to win it. Davey Muntz was up. Davey Muntz had developed into a very crafty hitter. All Davey Muntz needed was a single. He got good wood on one of Londis's curves and at the crack of the bat I thought—hit hit hit—but the line drive went right to Warga at second base, who doubled off Nash and that was it. We lost the first game.

Ruthie came back in the second game, naturally the first game she'd ever pitched at Yankee Stadium. They yelled for her—even the Fascist fans had to respect her—and oh man, she was murder that day. She pitched as though her life depended on it. She was beautiful. That big overhand delivery was something to see. Her fastball was burning and her curve was churning; she was playing with the corners like she owned the plate. But for some reason —don't ask me why, I don't really understand these things—our bats were cold as ice, and we couldn't get no runs. Stan Ryebow, another Yankee ace, was smokin'. In the bottom of the seventh, the Fascists got to Ruth a little, just a little—two singles and a double got 'em a run, but that was all. They left two men stranded. We didn't do nothing in the eighth, and when we came up to hit in the ninth, we were still losing 1–0. Sonny beat out a surprise bunt down the third-base line. And when Muntz tried to move him over with a sacrifice, his bunt kept hugging the line— just like Sonny's—and there wasn't even a throw to first. Now Ryebow looked a little shook. He strung out the count to Bo, 3– 2, and walked him with a high fastball. Bases loaded, nobody out. El Tigre lumbered up to the plate. El Tigre cleaned off his cleats with the small end of his bat. El Tigre took his time. El Tigre stood in there, staring down at Ryebow. El Tigre let the first pitch go by. Strike one. El Tigre swung and missed the next pitch. He swung so hard I could feel the breeze in the dugout. El Tigre walked out of the batter's box, hitched up his pants, scratched himself, rubbed his hands together. El Tigre went back to face Ryebow and sent the next pitch, a slider, into orbit. El Tigre hit a grand-slam home run and Spanish-speaking fans all over the world went nuts! I cried myself hoarse. And in the Yankees' half of the ninth, Ruthie pitched like I had seen her pitch in the sandlots—so relaxed and sure of herself. Three infield grounders, three easy plays, and we had tied the Series.

The people of Brooklyn were up all that night, hooting and hollering and kissing and hugging, 'cause they knew we were coming home. The Series was skipping over the bridge and the flags were flying at Ebbets for the third game. A World Series game was about to be played in Brooklyn for the first time since 1956, when the Yankees . . . well, no one wanted to think about it.

There were nineteen million balloons and parades all day and choppers flying above and people dancing in Prospect Park, dancing over in Williamsburg and on the porches of those pretty houses in Crown Heights and Park Slope. We were back in Brooklyn and bringing the Series with us, and when Bobby walked into his box above the dugout he had Fidel with him—he had flown in from Cuba, he couldn't stay away—Fidel was hugging and kissing Luis and El Tigre and Bobby. Fidel had to see us whip the Yankees, Fidel hated the Fascists as much as us and he knew peace-loving people all over the planet had a stake in this thing. Bobby let him throw out the first ball, which he overdid and nearly knocked down Bo.

So what happened? It was El Tigre. El Tigre in the first inning —sending one into Bedford Avenue. El Tigre in the fifth inning —hammering one into the upper decks in left field. El Tigre in the ninth—tying Reggie Jackson's record and hitting his third round-tripper of the day, this one deep into center field, making the score 7–1 and sending Fidel and Bobby into a swoon of ecstasy, into a dance of delight around the field with everyone else in Brooklyn, 'cause we were leading the Series 2–1 and what could go wrong? What could possibly go wrong now?

Fourth game. Ebbets Field. Top of the ninth. We were winning 4–3. Fassbinder had pitched a solid game for us, and the little guys like Muntz had come through again in the clutch. Now the bases were empty and the Yankees had two out and were down to their last man—Newt Cane, Bobby's old pal from spring-training days. I wasn't worried, 'cause Fassbinder still had his sizzle and it was only later that someone told me what Oran was telling America up in the broadcast booth:

"This situation reminds me of the 1941 World Series, when, playing in Ebbets Field against the Yankees, the Dodgers blew the fourth game in the top of the ninth inning. With two outs and two strikes on the batter, Dodger catcher Mickey Owen dropped Hugh Casey's spitter and Tommy Henrich, who had already swung and missed for the third strike, reached first base. You know the rest. The Yankees went on to rally and win the game and the Series."

Seconds after she said it, Fassbinder got Cane on three straight strikes. Bullets. Beauts. But the third strike was too blinding, because Bo—who was just as good as Mickey or even Campy—dropped it, lost it, desperately scrambled after it, with me yelling "Get it! Get it! Get it!"—and I never yell like that—except that Cane was safe on first and Fassbinder folded and so did Bingo Flash and Neil Nash. The Yankees scored four times and we went down in order in the bottom of the ninth and instead of being 3–1 for us, the Series was suddenly tied at two apiece.

The rain was driving me nuts. I went over to see Bobby, because I had to see someone and I couldn't see Ruthie 'cause Hymie said she wasn't feeling real good and I should let her rest, which made me think God was raining us out today because Ruthie couldn't have pitched today and by tomorrow she'd be fine to go back and pitch our last game in Ebbets. She'd pitch the fifth game, just like Koufax pitched the fifth game in '65. We needed to win so we could go back to face the Fascists in the Bronx one game up.

"Don't worry, Squat," Bobby said, understanding that I needed comforting. "We're going to win and Ruth will be fine and this will go down as the greatest Series in history. You've done the best job a human being can do, and I love you for it, I love you for every minute of this season."

I stood there, listening to Bobby's nice words and looking out the big plate-glass window of his townhouse, looking at the rain falling into the East River.

"You got guts, kid," I had to tell him. "If it wasn't for your guts we wouldn't be here."

And he put his arm around me and both of us knew what the other one was thinking: Mickey Owen dropping that third strike, Bo dropping that third strike.

"There are always forces greater than us," Bobby said. "You were the one who taught me that."

But I couldn't say nothing else, 'cause I wasn't thinking too straight. I had to pick up the phone and call Ruthie. Hymie answered and said she was still resting, and I went back to my apartment in Borough Park and got real scared when Pee Wee had a convulsion and threw this terrible fit. So the night before the fifth game of the Series I had to take him to the vet around the corner from Thirteenth Avenue. Doc Morrissey got out of bed to look at Pee Wee and gave him some medicine and told me there was nothing to worry about.

I went over to Ruthie's place in Bensonhurst real early the next morning. I had Pee Wee with me. Ruthie was in the bathroom. She was sick. Another doctor was there, a woman doctor. She said it wasn't anything abnormal for a pregnant woman, but Ruthie had been sick to her stomach all night and she had a touch of the flu and had lost her strength and she was going to have to stay in bed for a few days or else risk some injury that no one wanted to think about. When Ruthie came out of the bathroom she was crying, and she said that she loved me—right there in front of Hymie and the doctor—and that she'd watch the game on TV, 'cause she was too weak to go to the ballpark. And for Ruth to say that, I knew she had to be hurting.

"You know that I ain't used to making speeches like this," I told the boys in the clubhouse before the game, "and I don't like 'em 'cause I don't think they do anything for anyone. But there's something I gotta say today. Today's the last day we're gonna be playing this year in Ebbets Field. If we win today, all we gotta do is win one outta two in Yankee Stadium and we can wrap up this season for good. There's lots of reasons to win, and everyone wants the money and the glory and I ain't got nothing against that. But I also have to tell you that Ruth won't be playing—she's got a temperature and won't be able to get out of bed until the Series is over—and I'm thinking about her today and I know you guys are thinking about her and I know this is gonna sound real corny but I wanna win this thing for her, I really do." And everyone let out a big tremendous yell, and I felt like a million bucks. Before I went to the field I called her and told her I loved her.

In the first inning the sun broke through the clouds and when Roger Arrowsmith led off for the Yanks against Tom Alvarado with a screaming scorcher down the third-base line, our man Gleason threw himself at the ball and twisted himself around and made this backbreaking incredible stop—and don't tell me about no Brooks Robinson or no Graig Nettles; this was a stop worthy of Billy Cox—and he picked himself up and he fired to first and nabbed him, and the first Yank was out by a hair and we were really clicking. The clouds were all gone now, and Tom got the next two men on easy flies. In the bottom of the first, Sonny, leading off, socked one into the lower left-field seats, and Ebbets, which looked so clean and red and white and blue today, exploded with love. We were beating 'em 1–0. Newt Cane tripled in the third inning and a long fly to right got him home, but that's all Tom was giving up—for a while.

In the sixth, Sonny walked, stole second, moved to third on a grounder deep in the hole between first and second. Bo was batting, and Sonny had the itch. I knew he had the itch. He was far off the bag at third, waltzing halfway down the line, daring and darting back and forth, and finally, on Brian Londis's third pitch, he took off, streaking like a starship, the fans screaming their lungs out and him flying home feet first, the ump holding his hands out to the side; Sonny had slid under the tag; Sonny had stolen home in the World Series and, even though the Yanks beefed for ten minutes, we were now beating 'em 2–1.

Looked like the lead might hold. Looked like we might get away with it. Tom's curve was breaking beautifully, and the game stayed steady with our one-run lead till the top of the ninth. Then something very strange happened—maybe the strangest and most beautiful moment in the Series. Robbie London, the first Yankee up, went down swinging. Phil Rodriguez looped a Texas Leaguer into center field, which set the scene for Newt Cane. I thought about going out to the mound to talk to Tom, but what the hell; there was nothing I could tell him. He looked like he still had some fire left, and I wasn't about to pull him. But Cane met the first pitch and pulled it to right field—deep to right field—

and El Tigre went back back back against that crazy curved wall, and at a certain point he stopped running and turned around and let his arms fall to his side as though he were watching the ball sail out over the fence. And naturally me and everyone else thought it was a homer, and naturally the baserunners slowed to a trot. But then, outta nowhere, El Tigre played the ball on one hop off the wall—it hadn't been high enough to go out; El Tigre had been faking it—and he spun and threw an incredibly vicious strike to Bo, who nailed Rodriguez at the plate and then, without a second's hesitation, whipped the ball to Gleason at third to nail the dumbfounded Cane. Double play! Oh, so beautiful! And even more beautiful, 'cause I knew it had come out of Furillo's bag of tricks—I remembered the Shotgun making that same play—and it was beautiful how El Tigre had studied those old films, beautiful how we won the game and were going back to Yankee Stadium with a 3–2 lead.

I can't tell you how much I hate Yankee Stadium. It gives me the creeps. It makes me feel small. They should be putting on operas in there, not playing baseball. Game 6 drove me up the wall. Game 6 had me eating my fingernails. Game 6 had everyone saying that this was one of the best-pitched Series in years. In Game 6 the hitters' dry spell got even drier. No one did nothing in Game 6 except Ben Little and Stan Ryebow. They pitched like princes, and the game zipped along lickety-split. Before I knew it, we were up in the top of the ninth and our only hits were singles by El Tigre and Fromp. There was no score, and Ryebow, who hadn't walked a single man, struck out the side to hang out his ninth goose egg of the day. Ben had been almost just as stingy; the Yankees had four hits. But the bottom of the ninth saw them just as frustrated at the plate as us, and the bottom of the tenth, and the eleventh, and in the twelfth, when we didn't score, I put in Bingo, 'cause I saw Ben's arm was about to fall out. Maybe that was a mistake. Or maybe it would have happened anyway. But Bingo was a little wild. He walked the first two batters. And then Rodriguez got hold of an inside fastball and blasted it down the alley, which in Yankee Stadium goes all the way to Yonkers, and that was it—goodbye Game 6, hello Game 7.

I couldn't sleep that night. I had gone over to see Ruth, who tried to soothe me, but I wasn't about to be soothed. Ruth was much better—no more temperature—but the doc wasn't letting her play, and neither would I. We could win this thing without her. We would win this thing for her. Except I was wishing something awful that the last game wasn't in Yankee Stadium, wishing that maybe there'd be a tornado in the Bronx or maybe someone would blow up the Stadium and we'd have to go back to our ballpark. I spent a lot of time talking to Pee Wee about this stuff, and he purred and cuddled next to me but I still couldn't sleep. And when I got to the stadium the next day the sky was dark, the clouds were hanging heavy, but it wasn't raining. It just looked nasty.

Funny, but everyone was saying that this was gonna be the greatest game in the history of sports. The seventh, the last. This would be the contest to end all contests. The world was watching. This was the moment.

But you know what? The game stunk. It stunk to high heaven. It might have been the lousiest game of the whole goddamn year —you'll pardon my French. The Yankees went through our whole pitching staff, the Yankees went through us like melted butter, beat us 12–3 with one hand tied behind their backs, made it look easy. It wasn't close, it wasn't fun, it wasn't even respectable. No spectacular plays, no nothing. They whipped us. And maybe it was 'cause they were supposed to or maybe 'cause we didn't have Ruthie—I don't know, but the Yankees were the World Champs for the seventeen millionth time, and I was exhausted from all these games; my head was hanging low and my heart was as heavy as a lead balloon and I remembered a feeling I hadn't had since 1956—they dumped on us that year, too—and I couldn't help but cry my eyes out when I was alone in the clubhouse, 'cause I felt like I had let everyone down, everyone I loved. And I would have cried for hours if Bobby hadn't come in and told me that Ebbets Field was all sold out for tomorrow— 32,000 fans would be there, the press and the Mayor and maybe the President, maybe even the Pope. Tomorrow, he said, was the big day at Ebbets Field.

TEN

SHE TOLD ME that they had this bet. She told me that he had agreed to do it if the Yankees won the Series—that's how sure Oran was that the Yankees would win. He hated her for saying that, for predicting that. He would have bet her anything. And he did. And now he'd lost. And now she was finally getting what she wanted, because, in her own way, Oran was courageous, too.

And now the Dodgers were lined up against the first-base line and against the third-base line. All the boys were there. They were smiling and they were wearing their uniforms and they were each holding a red rose. The sun was shining and the breeze was blowing in from Bedford Avenue. Ebbets Field smelled of mustard and beer and looked the way it always looks—the same, always the same. So small you could see everyone. There was Hymie and my mom and dad and my brothers and all the big-wig politicians. The joint was packed, just like Bobby said it would be packed. There wasn't an empty seat and there wasn't a dry eye in the house when me and Ruthie, in our uniforms, and Oran and Bobby, in their fancy duds—both of 'em in gorgeous white suits —slowly walked out to the mound, where the minister and my priest and Ruthie's rabbi were waiting for us. We walked out there to the sounds of "Here Comes the Bride," and the organ reminded me of when Gladys Gooding used to play it in the old days when me and Bobby were kids.

I turned to my bride, to my little Ruthie, and I told her I would take her for my wife, and that's what Bobby said to Oran, and then the ladies took us to be their hubbies, and the gentlemen of the cloth blessed us every which way, and the gentle people of Brooklyn, my people of Brooklyn, my mom and dad and brothers and Hymie, stood up and cheered and clapped and screamed their heads off, screamed and stomped and shouted that they loved us and that they loved their Bums. And when I looked up into the blue October Brooklyn sky I saw that Bobby must have hired this airplane which was flying low over our beautiful Ebbets Field, skywriting, in billows of soft white smoke, WAIT TILL NEXT YEAR!